Dedication

To the extraordinary women with whom I've had intimate relationships, you'll see the romantic in me is still here. You'll recognize facets of me within these pages.

You'll recognize facets of you, the strong impression you made on me, the ways you shaped and refined how and why I deeply cared.

If you're no one's loved one, consider writing. You can create him or her, your perfect love, as I've done here. Best, you can access that love, always. *Olivia's Meadow* does that for me.

Prologue

I strenuously resisted the suggestion to write a romance. "Not my deal. Not my genre. I know as much about that as I do about space ships," and expletives followed.

The trouble was, I'd written a book I chosen not to publish about my heartbreaking and only marriage and its calamitous end only 7 months in. I'd proven I could write romance but sopping my shirt with tears while writing my own story made me avoid what could be emotional quicksand. I was spent.

Four nights later, I made myself a liar by getting out of bed at 2:45am and sitting down at the laptop. That's when Olivia was born and the next thing I knew, it was mid-morning or day and I was 12,000 words into Olivia's life. Her story was flowing, coming to me as fast as my fingers could fly over the keyboard. For six months, the story kept evolving and tugging at me to write every day for six months.

Other Works Available
at Amazon.com

"Cupcakes in Love and War" – A WWII romance story about a young sailor, shared for the first time by his then girlfriend. Poignant and heartwarming of an 80-something woman and a college student.

"On the Rim of a Dream" – Two people form a unique friendship that transforms the life of a 30-something woman enchanted by her new American friend in his 60s. She's in Scotland. His dangerous work assignment takes him from Washington, D.C. to Thurso, Scotland, UK. The evolution of the friendship is dynamic and will you leave you feeling uplifted and wonderful.

Olivia's Meadow

Dwight Peattie

Copyright 2022 - All Rights Reserved
ISBN: 978-1-953531-15-5
EvocativeReads

"To every thing, there is a season,
And a time to every purpose
under the heavens;
A time to be born, and a time to die;
a time to plant, and a time to pluck up
that which is planted;
A time to kill, and a time to heal;
a time to break down,
and a time to build up;
A time to weep, and a time to laugh.
A time to mourn, and a time to dance."

--Ecclesiastes 3:1-4, KJV

Change Now or Never

Love is a bully that bangs on doors it shouldn't and, when a particular door doesn't open, love will liquefy itself to flow underneath.

Love gets hot enough to melt through defenses and existing relationships. It intervenes, interferes with committed relationships and does anything it can to kick someone out, usually hurting someone, to get through to the person Love has targeted for its own desires and consumption.

Love hates and ignores rules such as workplace relationships. Its consequences can be harsh when it churns, rapidly winding itself up between a nurse and a patient. When that happens, an education, a job and a career are jeopardized. And as you just learned, maybe already knew, love hates rules and ignores them.

If love is doubted or it isn't felt, if it's entirely missing, it can be demoralizing and debilitating. At its absolute worst, love can bolster false courage whose perils may hurt you or deprive you of your very life.

There's got to be a middle ground where love is contained without self-sacrifice at destructive levels but I can't say I've found it.

Yes. Love *is* a selfish and persistent bastard until it gets what it wants, persistent even if sent away by time and circumstance. But once inside, it can be transforming.

My turn *has* to come. Other people find love all kinds of ways. Maybe I'm one of those who isn't the finder but the 'find-ee.'

I'm a hypocrite.

I've told the world—between my ears, anyway—all about love and have none. Maybe it's because I'm complacent in the quiet way I live life. I like flying kites at the beach, going to the museum when the exhibits change, reading book reviews and adding a book to my shelves, long rides up Highway 1 along the Mendocino coast and beyond.

I grew up being afraid to venture out probably because I was that unadopted orphan who got bounced around. Nothing seemed steady. My inner self told me to seek safety.

I bought the motorcycle to break some of those chains of constraint. I know it's working. I feel it. But that need to be needed is still hollow. Sitting in my apartment wallowing in self-pity isn't solving anything. I'm the problem and I know it.

My apartment is adequate but tiny. Its best features are the fringe benefits I have with a terrific landlord who loves classical music.

That got me a nice discount and Mrs. Lentini let me slide on half of the security deposit. She didn't cave-in because I was good looking or Catholic or nice. She gave in because of something that glared at her from my application. "Employer: KACM Radio. Job: Announcer." She could listen to me on the radio and brag to all her cronies that an announcer from her favorite radio station lived in her little mother-in-law flat around the back of her nice house in the Sunset district.

I probably gained three listeners, one being Mrs. Lentini's cat, "Phoebe," who gets an occasional treat from me. I buy sardines exclusively for Phoebe because she keeps dead mice lined up at Mrs. Lentini's door. Sometimes, when I'm sitting on the stoop reading, Phoebe is against my thigh with her head moving to follow anything that moves above or on the street or sidewalk. She'll occasionally meow and look up at me, for which she'll get some physical attention from me until I hear her purring.

I was born with a big deep voice, 'long pipes' as they say in the industry. I used my voice to get into the most sought-after university program in the country, at San Francisco State. My advisor and the department's job placement landed me an immediate job using that voice to earn a living in one of the most expensive cities in the country relative to the cost of living. I'm barely getting by on what's considered huge money in cities the same size as San Francisco.

My motorcycle's not good in iffy weather but it's only six months old with a small payment and effects huge savings, getting 70 miles per gallon. I work some overtime and do extra voice work for commercials to have walking around money.

I gotta bust myself out of the doldrums.

The last time I spoke to my mentor and college advisor, Norm, he hinted there was something in the wind. That was two days ago and he said he'd call. I need a big change. I know I need to do it in the next 6 months or I'll be at risk for accepting life as 'ho-hum.' If he doesn't call today, I'm going to pull his chain.

I needed thinking time. 'Play a long selection that won't hit the break, David,' I tell myself. Vivaldi. Perfect. I'm searching for the CD in the library. The private line rings.

Here's the call, maybe my future. Norman Lydell is connected to everybody who's anybody in commercial radio all over the U.S. We liked each other the minute I introduced myself to him as he was coming out of a classroom when I was a freshman. I wouldn't settle for anyone else but this guy

air as I shaved and brushed my teeth. I reached into my 'ditty bas my advisor. This call could change everything.

"David, Norman."

"Dr. Lydell! Are you listening and critiquing or is this just a social call?" I loved the guy. Couldn't help it.

"I'm worried about you, David. You're one of the most talented and promising on-air talents to come through here in a long time and you're burrowed into a little complacent hole at a classical music station. I guess I want to know how come."

"Doc, it's easy money. In this ADI (Area of Dominant Influence)? Our percentage of the listening audience during the day is staggering. I'm at $55 an hour and it's easier than watching weeds grow...and I gotta remind you. Do you remember one of the jobs you threw my way when I was a senior was for a Disney station in Duck Droppings, Oregon, where I would be making $450 a week with nothing to do with my time and chicken-scratch money? 200 miles from nowhere? Remember?" I genuinely laughed so he would know that I had no hard feelings about it.

My mouth was saying one thing and the logical part of my mind was telling it to shut up. *'Why am I defending my status quo with my insides screaming for a change? He's probably going to pull some strings or call-in a favor to put you on the next level, David.'*

"Like I told you David, your next step from there would have been a 500% increase into a major market slot."

"Duck poop is foul, pun intended, Doc."

"Touché. But here's news, David. You're a pet peeve of mine. When I became your advisor in your freshman year, you needed all your basic prerequisites for graduation... English, math, humanities. What I remember most? You couldn't pick your electives without help. One of the brightest and most promising guys I know and no sense of self-determination or direction."

"That's harsh. Where's this going?"

"If someone points, you go. Great...if you're a robot or infantry man. Someone has an idea that needs work? You'll pick up a toolbox. Jesus, you have a creative mind, David. Why aren't you using that and your toolbox to go leading-edge??"

"Hold on. I have a station ID."

"K-A-C-M, San Francisco. All Classical Music, twenty-four seven. I'm your host, David Tyler. 56° in the city at 2:31, looking for a little rain later. Here' a treat for an

*overcast afternoon: Vivaldi's The Four Seasons, in its
entirety."*

"Okay Norman, I'm back."

"David, I'm going to lay something at your feet. The
price? You're going to pay it forward and lay it at
someone else's feet. That's gonna take a little
discernment, judgment and risk so it won't be
squandered. I'm wondering if you can or even *will* do it."

"I didn't know the prize in my cereal box this morning
was an ass-chewing and psychoanalysis from Norman
Lydell."

"Nice attempt at diversion and deflecting the issue,
but no good."

"So, what's my life challenge to pay forward? Where's
my post-graduate lesson in creating my own destiny?"

"I don't know. I <u>do</u> know of an opportunity you
should seize, because, when the window closes on it,
you'll long regret it. I made a couple calls and sent off a
couple of your air checks."

"Wow, who does *that*! You sent air checks without me
knowing? Pulled from where?"

"I pulled them, myself. You were born in Kentucky,
David, so maybe you'll see it if I explain it a different way:
You are *not* going to be my apathetic, potential Kentucky
derby winner who's content to pull a plow over seed corn
for bourbon. Stand up and run this to the finish line for
the win I know you can get, David."

"You've beaten me into submission, Norman. What
gig inspired you to send out my air checks and aim me in
a direction that I don't know I'm going?"

"I'm putting you in front of the general manager at
KFCG, Sandy Tuttle. He heard your tapes, let a couple
department heads hear them, and called me wondering
why I haven't set up a meeting with you two before now."

"I'm listening."

"Quellen Media Entertainment Group. Heard of
them?"

"Who *hasn't* heard of Q-MEG [*cue-meg*] as in megabucks. Some of the top talent pay in the country and growing."

"They're even a little darling on Wall Street, David. They hold fourteen licenses. Ten, David, ten of them are format-top-ten's in the U.S. Their properties include 2 rockers, 3 classic rockers, 2 country-western, and 3 news/talk stations. Three of their stations are _overall_ #1 in market."

"Where's this going, Norm?"

"You mean, where are *you* going? How about the number one station in its state. I know you're a music guy at heart, rock-jock wannabe, but this is great money just for doing news.... News at a country station that ranks *Top 10 Country Format* in the U.S. You have the pipes for it and they pump money into their news because they can afford to."

"That's more interesting than the anesthesia of classical music. I'd get to write and deliver...maybe report? I could probably get into that, Norman."

"The GM wants talent who can keep listeners from switching stations at the breaks and I convinced him you are the talent that can do that."

"Right up front, I'm not moving to Wyoming to work at a ten thousand watt 'boot-scooter,' Norman, even if I *can* fool locals with my highly energized delivery of 'Hot diggity, this just happened,' or 'Yee-Haw! The Chickens beat the Pigs three to nothing in extra innings.'"

"It's not hicks-in-the-sticks, David. I'm putting your ass on a plane to *Phoenix*. It's the 11th largest listening market in the nation. Like I said, Q-MEG's KFCG is nationally ranked in the Top 10 of _all_ country-western stations. Let that sink in."

"Can I afford this, I mean, I don't want to lay a pile of money down for a trip if they blow me out the door in 10-seconds. I know they go after who they want, but you put me in there. Q-MEG didn't come after me."

"Oh yes they did. They're going to fly you in as soon as I call Sandy Tuttle back and tell him when you're willing and available to spend two days there. On my recommendation and your air checks, you're a lead-pipe cinch. Done deal. I told you his reaction to your air checks. It's an overnighter, two days, hotel paid, and it's your gig as long as you show up sober and not stoned."

"Phoenix, huh?"

"A hundred and forty to start, Phoenix. A buck-forty's great money on that economy. It's their morning drive news slot, 4am –1:30pm. Plus, and this is big, there's relocation in the package Sandy's willing to provide, thanks to me. That's *huge* in Arizona, David. You'll be out of a rental flat and into a gorgeous house before you can blink."

He had me. Q-MEG was a career-maker if they pursued you. They ignored all others.

I laughed aloud. "THAT much money for rip/rewrite and read the news? I'll wear a pink bikini and high tops to do that for that kind of dough, Norman."

"Bad visual, David. Thanks." We laughed.

"Just curious, where are their three news-talk properties? If things really clicked, it could be one hell of a ride, professionally and financially."

"Is this a picture of you discovering ambition?" and Norman's sarcasm landed on my funny bone.

"Lemme see," Norm said, trying to recall, "I know San Antonio is one of them, Denver, and don't hold me to the third one but I want to say…Albuquerque-Santa Fe?"

"Cool. I'm good to go, Norman. Everything to gain and nothing to lose, right?"

"I'll call Sandy Tuttle and have him get back to you, himself. Keep me in the loop."

"*Yee haw*, Norman!"

"You're off tomorrow, right David?"

"You knew it because you always do your homework Doc, don't you," and we both laughed.

"On second thought, let's do this instead. I'm going to call Sandy to set up a conference call with you and me. Make yourself available, tomorrow. Don't jump on your bike and ride to Cleveland or anything. I'll call you and let you know what time the conference call is going to happen."

I was stunned. Radio news was pretty easy money but there wasn't much money in it. You were sometimes stuck doing traffic and weather as well. Listeners loved it and it was critically important but it wasn't anywhere near the big money that large-market on-air jocks were making. I almost choked when I heard $140,000 for radio news at a non-news/talk format station.

Q-MEG dominated the ratings and put their money in talent who could reach and maintain market leadership. If Norman was right about the locations.... If I stayed in news and made the jump into news-talk in the Q-MEG group, my career would be in Albuquerque-Santa Fe, San Antonio, and Denver. Big Q-MEG money would make me happy and more than comfortable in any of those cities.

I got off work and was floating on air. On a whim, I headed for my favorite clothier's, a thrift store just outside the city limit in Daly City.

I saw what I was looking for. On the shelf calling my name was an old soiled cowboy hat. It was made out of yellowish straw and well-worn, complete with a finger-sized hole in the side. It fit like it was custom made. Yee haw. I would wear it for the conference call with Sandy Tuttle, KFCG's general manager.

After a nap and a quick bite, I knew what I needed: some fresh air in my helmet, running across the Golden Gate with the skyline lit up. It was light drizzle but no fog, two-wheeled therapy for sorting things out. I could see my new life in front of me but not what was coming.

The Angel of St. Dominic's

"MISTER CALLAN! DAVID!"

My dream is echoing.

"MISTER CALLAN!! Squeeze my hand!"

Hand. Squeeze. Squeeze both.

"DAVID, YOU'RE IN THE HOSPITAL! DAVID, CAN YOU HEAR ME?"

Light. Bright.

"OW! OWWWWWW!"

"NO, NO, NO! DAVID, LIE DOWN!"

Burning pain seared my waist and leg. It made me scream as my eyes focused on six or eight masked faces over and around me.

"There you are, David. I'm Dr. Sessman. You had a motorcycle accident but you're going to be okay! You're in the emergency room at Saint Dominic's Pacific Heights Hospital.... Give him fifty more of Demerol, please."

"Fifty more of Demerol going in, sir."

"David, we're managing your pain and making sure you are stable, right now. It will help if you can talk to me. Will you try?"

"Water," I croak-whispered. "Water."

"Squeeze my finger, David.... Good. Now with the other hand? ...and good, good again. Glycerin swabs for his mouth, please," and I tasted gooey, wet citrus and sucked at swabs dripping with the stuff. It was nectar.

"Talk to me, David."

I could barely get words out, "What happened?"

"A witness told the police you ran a stop sign. A car hit your motorcycle's front wheel. The bike spun violently, hurling you through the air about 25 feet or so and you landed on some very unforgiving concrete on the sidewalk. Ten more feet and you would have been part of a store's window display."

"How bad? How....?"

I could tell the Doc grinned despite the mask.

"You're better off than your motorcycle, David. They might be able to make pizza pans out of what's left," and I heard muffled laughs and rolled my eyes to see about ten or so pairs of young ladies' eyes over the tops of their surgical masks off to my right.

"You broke some ribs. Your neck x-ray is clear and we removed a brace we had on you just in case. Your worst injuries are to your right hip and leg. Broken, but will heal. But to heal with 100% chance of full use, an orthopedic surgeon needs to get in there and install some hardware. That's why we're focusing on your pain and getting you stable. The surgeon and an operating room are ready and waiting for you. As soon as I think you're stable enough to go, the surgeon can start fixing everything that's wrong in your hip and leg."

"Pain. Just help the pain."

"We're laying it on thick, David. Top shelf stuff, the best we've got and lots of it for you. We've got to be cautious because you're going to be under general anesthesia once you're in the O.R. You're understandably breathing shallow because of the broken ribs. We took that in consideration and the shot we just gave you should be delivering you to la-la land pretty soon." 'La-la land' made the masked girls giggle, again.

"David?"

I must have fallen asleep.

"DAVID! Surgery's ready for you! Just "X" this authorization to give us permissions, and, do you have a next-of-kin? Relative or something?"

"No, I'm an orphan. Norm Lydell, San Francisco State faculty. Call him? Landlord's number is in my wallet, Mrs. Lentini."

"But I need an *emergency* contact, David. Who would I call if things went south?"

"Dr. Lydell's fine. He'll always do right by me, Doc."

"We found your insurance card in your wallet. You're not going to pay a penny for any of this, David, not even therapy afterward. So don't worry about anything financial."

"Hurts too much to think about that – but thanks. It would have hit me later."

I looked up at the clock as they rolled me toward surgery. 8:10pm. My brand-new bike. Goddamn. Brand new.

"Mr. Callan, you're awake! I'm Libby. I'll be taking care of you while you're in surgical recovery. I need to take your vital signs, David. First, I want you to blow into these bottles as hard as you can for as long as you can. We need to get that anesthesia out of your lungs and replace it with some good, wholesome air."

"Busted ribs."

"I know. Just do your best. The painkillers will dull the pain a little. Just try for me?"

If that pain was dulled, I don't know if I could have withstood or survived the heavy breaths without painkillers.

I felt myself drift out as soon as the blood pressure cuff eased-up.

I woke up in a regular hospital room with my leg elevated slightly. It was in a sling supporting a giant half-cast. It felt like my hip had taken ten shots from a 20-pound sledgehammer and there was weird bandaging and padding all around it. I tried to look around but was very drowsy. I saw a small bottle with a fluorescent orange label intersecting my I.V. line and tried to read the label but my eyelids kept closing, putting me out.

A blood pressure cuff woke me up, again.

"Vitals looking good, sir," and she smiled. "I'm your nurse, Mrs. Wei. You went through a lot but you are doing remarkably well!"

"Thanks. Any water?"

"Sure."

She reached to my left. A full, iced pitcher was nearly touching my elbow. She held the pitcher's straw to my lips. I drained half of it.

Mrs. Wei took the pitcher back, "You *were* thirsty! You have a pee-pee tube, so if you get the urge, go ahead." And I nodded. "You'll get vitals again at 6am followed by grand rounds and then breakfast, okay? I worked a double, today but will see you on my regular shift. Your call button's pinned to your pillow. Any questions, David?"

"Um...yeah. Did they reach Dr. Lydell or Mrs. Lentini, my landlord?"

"I'll find out and be right back."

She slipped through the curtain and was back inside of two minutes.

"Yes, both were contacted. They know you're at St. Dominic's Pacific Heights Hospital. We gave them your room number, phone number and visiting hours. If I'm not mistaken, there's an older gentleman in the visitors' lounge who may be here for you. Your Dr. Lydell, maybe?"

"Grey short hair, walking cane? Probably a blue-striped suit?"

"You're good! Fits him to a T!"

"That's Dr. Lydell."

"If he's awake, I'll allow him to come in if you'd like to see him."

"God yes! Please!"

Mrs. Wei made her best attempt to smile.

"Thank you,' and she turned and left.

I saw Norman's form fill the doorway coming closer.

"Oh God, David, you okay??"

"I hurt like hell."

"Looks like it. You look like hell."

"You do too, Norman, but I'll trade you places."

A pause.

"Okay, Norman, I'll say it. In the blink of an eye, my job's gone, my future job's gone, and I'm making motorcycle payments on something in the junkyard. Close?"

"No. Not anywhere near close, David. Your motorcycle did relocate to 'Honda Heaven.' After you flew off of it, a city water truck ran over it to make sure it won't be going anywhere soon."

I tried to laugh, "OW! Don't be funny, Norman! My ribs are broken! Actually, you're not funny but you *are* sadistic. Only you could fail a whole class on an exam and sleep at night."

He smiled and shook his head. Then his expression changed.

"David, your classical job's still there if you want it. As far as Phoenix goes, here's the back-story. Sanderson 'Sandy' Tuttle and I go back, forever. I put him onto some *big* job leads and he landed them without too much direct help. He did well. And then I threw another golden deal his way. He landed that and did well. He doesn't owe me just one, David, he owes me several."

"Meaning?"

"Meaning he'll take you anytime you're ready. He'll move people and things to take you, David. He'll do that because he feels he owes me. In exchange, he lands you, who will make Norman look like a genius."

"I'm that important to you, Norman. To call-in this guy's markers for me." It wasn't a question.

"I didn't invent the way that the back-alley business of broadcasting is conducted. I observed it and have done very well at it. Past tense, because I'm done."

Norm continued, "David, I'm ready to move to Belize and catch minnows for the rest of my life. I want out. Before I *go* out? I want one more big, huge thing for someone I think is deserving. Maybe my star-maker ego thing, and you have that very real potential: orphan kid who stayed outta trouble, did well in school, comes to us on fire to excel and blows everyone away, students <u>and</u> faculty and gets national exposure and recognition while a full-time student. And you're not an egocentric goof which our crazy business is filled with. You're my legacy project because, in twenty years, you'll pass this on or as the kids say nowadays, you'll 'pay it forward' and you'll do it for me."

I was floored, feeling suddenly unworthy and confessed.

"I've been suffering from complacency. It hurt, hit home when you called me out on it...hassled me about pissing my life away. I've had nothing to do in here but think. So, I'm ready. I want the Phoenix job and I'll accept passing on your baton, Norman."

"I hate the accident happened, but you're seeing the light, David. You made my day. Now, I gotta get outta here. I'm in need of a good meal and my comfortable bed."

"Norman?"

"What?"

"Will you come to Phoenix to see me, sometime?"

It was his turn to serve-up a sarcasm ace. He reached for the handle on the door, looked back at me and said, "And waste my time to visit a rip-'n-read newsie? Hell no. But I do have a buddy named Sandy Tuttle who works there," and he pulled his scarf up around his neck and left wearing his wry grin.

My head was swimming. My body was killing me but the career aspirations swimming in my head were nice diversions. I was feeling pretty good between my ears.

I don't remember being awakened through the night for vitals or anything else. The room was bright from outdoor light.

"Mr. Callan?"

Jesus, there were a dozen or more people traipsing into my room.

Pick of the Litter

The parade of medical uniforms arranged themselves around me. The obvious guy in charge, MD-looking, approached.

"Good morning. I'm Dr. Kerstein, one of the senior physicians here at St. Dominic's. We call this 'grand rounds' where I discuss your case with these nurses, interns and students. They learn about your injuries in hopes of you receiving better care because of what they'll learn about our overall plan for your recovery."

"M-kay."

"You feeling okay this morning?"

"Not particularly. I'm assuming I got creamed on my new motorcycle but my memory's hazy."

"That's exactly what happened, but you saved your own leg from being amputated by lifting it just in time to avoid it getting destroyed by the car that rammed you. Your helmet and leather gear saved your melon and skin, Mr. Callan."

Dr. Kerstein continued, "I know your multiple fractures hurt like hell. I glanced at your x-rays and it looks like your surgical team did a great job."

He half-turned to the onlookers he brought. "David Francis Bernard Callan, 27 years old. He'll also answer to 'David Tyler' because he works in radio. Arrived by ambulance last evening," and I started going drowsy as he continued describing my injuries.

I opened my eyes again, someone touching me, and there was only one person in the room. The soft hand against my shoulder was that of a chiseled, mature nurse looking at me.

"I'm Janice Delacroix, Mr. Callan. I'm the chief nurse here at St. Dominic's. May I call you David?"

"Sure."

"David, among my responsibilities, I supervise nursing students from the University of San Francisco's School of Nursing and other area programs. Upon graduation and passing the RNs national exam, they'll become registered nurses."

"Okay."

"I have nine seniors who are finishing their program, soon. They'll graduate, take their test and get their RN pin that we all work so hard to achieve."

Her expression brightened, "I have a young woman interested in orthopedics. I approved her to finish her clinicals on this ward although, for all intents and purposes, she's completed everything but the time requirement. I'm going to assign her to your case because I understand she was around when you came in last night."

"Fine with me."

"Her name is Olivia Macias. Your regular RN is named Kathleen Wei whom, I see from your record, you've met. Mrs. Wei will directly oversee and guide Olivia's handling of all your nursing needs while you're here. To do that, I need a signature that you're okay with that."

"I'm okay with it if she can sneak-in cookies and stuff!" and that made the nurse in her 60s laugh.

"If your prescribed diet allows it, cookies may be okay, but I'm not so sure you'll convince Olivia to break or even bend any rules anytime soon. She's remarkable, one of the best candidates USF has sent us in the last few years."

"Where do I sign?"

"I'll send Olivia around to do vitals with Mrs. Wei. You can sign the authorization, then. Off the record? Olivia's at the top of her USF class of 63 graduating RNs. I'm giving you my best."

"Thank you—appreciate it."

"I'll throw you a bone for conversation starters. Your real name's David Francis Bernard Callan? Olivia has four names, too. Maybe she'll share them. If not, I think you're the kind of guy who could get her to tell!"

"I do like a challenge."

"Don't be surprised if I look in on you, David, because I'll be glancing at your chart every now and again."

"Oatmeal raisin."

"Pardon me?"

"My favorite cookie… if you're so inclined."

"I don't bake for myself or anyone, Mr. Callan, but noted. I'll have Ms. Macias put that in your chart," and she patted my good arm before she left.

The Chief Nurse didn't pull the curtain, leaving it open so I could see the passing foot-traffic in the hall. The room directly across from mine had its door open, too, and that room had a bay view. I lay there watching passers-by, staring at the bay, thinking of nothing.

Masks were required in my room to control infection because rods and screws in my leg and hip were considered open wounds, even bandaged. I'm thinking that door shouldn't have been left open. God, I'm glad was.

In walked a masked nurse, dark brown hair pulled back into a bun. Nurse hat but scrubs different than Janice's or Kathleen's. Sheerest of white hosiery, nice legs. 'Bout 5'7-ish, medium build in a more sinewy, muscular, not fleshy way. Wei was more petite, maybe 5'5 and didn't seem to be much older than this apparently-student nurse who was painfully attractive. The nurse I'd met, Mrs. Wei was right behind.

"Mr. Callan, good morning! I'm Olivia Macias. I was in your grand rounds this morning and the Chief Nurse assigned me to take care of you as long as you're here."

"Hi, Olivia. I mean, it's alright to call you Olivia?"

"Just fine, and Mrs. Wei, here, is my overseer—immediate supervisor."

"You can expect excellent care, Mr. Callan, because we provide it without compromise," said Kathleen Wei.

All business, no giggles and grins with that one. Maybe because she had an underling right beside her.

Wei was pleasant without seeming forced but it stopped
there.

"Could you please drop the 'Mister' and call me David
or Callan or Tyler, please…. You allowed to do that?"

"Sure," Olivia replied, "I need to get your vitals."

Wei put her arm on Olivia's and said, "I'm going to
catch the vitals on my other patients, Olivia. You've got
this," and Olivia nodded.

Her spiral notebook landed on my little table and she
used her stethoscope and the blood pressure cuff that
was already a fixture on my good arm. Olivia explained
she trusted the old-school method, comparing it to the
electric blood pressure gizmo.

Since I came to, my vision had been hazy beyond
about three feet. It was only when she bent over was I
really able to see Olivia in focus.

Olivia Macias had what looked like a European olive
complexion with a bit of a suntan on it. I'd only seen skin
tone that color on high fashion models.

The angle of her body was such that, taking my B.P.,
I couldn't look anywhere but straight down the V-neck of
her scrubs shirt. White lace brassiere, kind of sheer, and
revealing enough to know her breasts were full and a
little darker in their centers. This girl's guy was one
lucky dude.

She straightened, removing the stethoscope and
pocketing it. "Looks good, David!" and she reached for
my wrist, taking my pulse intent on her watch.

"Fine, too. With that done, I need a signature to
continue being your assigned caregiver, acknowledging
that I'm a student nurse. I'm sure they'll task me to do
your dressing changes, give you meds and other
advanced care."

"Well, I'm impressed so far, but I kind of have a
preference with caregivers."

She grinned, suspecting I was going to tease or mess
with her.

"I have four names. I think I might relate better to someone who has four names."

"I understand all too well, David. *What* I understand is that somebody tipped you off, maybe?" and she cocked her head and grinned at me.

"In my own defense, I am actually a fiver: David Frances Bernard Callan with a necessary work pseudonym, 'Tyler,' thrown in for sport."

"I can continue to be on your care team if you find *Olivia Maria Christina Macias* acceptable."

"I find her better than acceptable. It really-really works for me, Olivia."

She giggled, rolling her eyes to the ceiling, "And that's because...?"

"Between you and me, we have six of the Catholic Saints covered in just two people's names."

Olivia shook her head and laughed, "I don't even think that would help us at the parish bingo, David."

"Okay, I'm laughing and it hurts, but I'm glad to meet you. Honestly."

She was receptive and already using my first name.

"Oatmeal raisin."

"What??"

"My favorite cookie is oatmeal raisin. The Chief Nurse said she or you would put that in my chart but I might play Hell trying to get you to bake me some cookies even if it was within the rules."

"Fat chance. I'm in a dorm room the size of a broom closet. Bringing you cookies from the cafeteria? Cookies are, at best, negotiable but not on the table just yet. Time will tell. That might be a privilege I make you earn, David. What I will promise is to help to make you well. We need to make sure you can poop before we can talk about anything like that."

"Well aren't *you* a buzz-kill, taking me from fantasizing about eating homemade oatmeal raisin cookies to *poop*??? Thanks."

She laughed, "Reality's part of my job. Deal with it. You're a mess and I'm going to un-mess you, David. I have rounds and need to catch up with Kathleen. I'll come back later with your meds."

"Nice to meet you, Olivia Maria Christina Macias."

Her eyebrows raised as she cocked her head and asked, "How did you do that?"

"Do what?"

"I mentioned my name once and you recalled it perfectly."

"You're pretty. That makes it easy. Or, I can stretch the truth and say I remembered your name for religious reasons, your roster of saints names and all that."

There was no denying her smile was flirtatious, 'You're a mess, an impressive mess, Mr. Callan, but a mess."

It was four hours later when I saw her again.

"Hiya!"

"You're a busy girl!"

"We're loaded up, today. Four more people got admitted and we're hustling. Can I shut the door?"

"Sure."

As soon as she shut the door, she leaned her butt against it, looked up at the ceiling and exhaled loudly. I couldn't tell if it was a sigh or frustration.

"I just needed a minute."

"I'm glad you took that minute in my room, Olivia," and I smiled.

"You require a lot of care with your dressing changes and stuff, so I don't need excuses to be here. I have plenty of work to do."

She walked over, lifted the covers and looked at my bandages and dressing. "They need attention."

She was back within a half hour, leaving the door open as she entered. Olivia went right to work on me, changing my hip dressing and making notes in my chart.

"I have a request."

"Denied. No cookies."

"Not that. Please tell me about Olivia Maria Christina Macias."

"Why?"

"Because I said 'please' and I'm kind of needy wanting someone to talk to and you are pretty and you are nice and you're the only person I want to talk to, it seems."

"All that, huh?"

"No, there's more. You stick around longer than everybody swooshing in and scurrying right back out. So yeah, all that. PLEEEEZ?"

"Sit up, and I know it's gonna hurt," and she started to fluff my pillows and wedge them again between my back and the mattress as she went to work.

"O-kay. I was born in the middle of nowhere and grew up on a small ranch working on a bigger ranch."

"Define 'nowhere.'"

As soon as she said "Abiquiu," the words 'New Mexico' came out of both of our mouths in unison. She stood there frozen and just stared at me.

"How did you know Abiquiu was in New Mexico?"

"Been there. I know where Abiquiu is, not far from Taos and even closer to Chimayo."

"Jesus, David, are you for reals? How do you know about Chimayo?"

"Truth? When I was a senior in college, my senior project was writing and producing a sixty-minute, broadcast quality radio documentary, an in-depth look at something. I read about Chimayo and was fascinated. I did a lot more digging and reading. I got in touch with the *Santuario* and they said they'd throw their doors open to me if I came down. I went. Beyond the radio gig, Olivia? That place—the whole area spoke to my heart and soul. I spent the remainder of my grant money sticking around there."

She looked like she was in shock but I had all of her attention.

"My senior advisor - whom you'll meet because he's my only visitor here - anyway, I had presented my proposal and he pre-approved my 60-minute radio documentary on the *Santuario de Chimayo*; why people have been trekking to it since the early 1800s, why local pilgrims arrive on bloody knees, why the hole with the dirt and its healing properties is so special. Not only that, some of the radical pilgrim groups who choose a member to have his hands nailed to a cross and dragged on a crucifix for the last 100 yards of their pilgrimage walk during Easter week."

"David. This...this is crazy. Nobody but us locals know all of that stuff."

"I've probably driven right by your birthplace, right through Abiquiu, Olivia."

It overwhelmed her. She pulled the chair up next to my bed, sat and took my hand.

"You ready for the next part, Olivia? Other than the fact I fell in love with the entire area, I was and am convinced it's a truly Spiritual place. God hangs out there. I feel Him."

She laughed nervously, "I don't know if I can *take* any more, David. This...it's not just a small world. We have, like a population of eight or nine thousand in Abiquiu and really spread out. I almost fell over when you *pronounced* it right."

"I'm a professional pronouncer," and I winked at her and she giggled.

"Ask me about the documentary, Olivia. Please."

"Tell me about it."

"National Public Radio aired it and gave me what I thought was a ton of money at the time."

"Really?? It was on NPR??"

"Yep, the CD has their label on it and the date that it aired."

"I would love to hear that!"

"Chuckster, our station engineer, can burn a copy of the CD and bring it by or send it with somebody who comes by to visit. It was my first claim to fame."

She grinned, "I would love that! I still can't believe you know Abiquiu and say it right."

I mocked a bad radio voice, "Pronouncing is my business, from Abiquiu to Española!" and she laughed, "*Dios mio!*"

"I still can't believe you grew up on a ranch. You could easily pass for a city girl. Maybe not a hippie, a phony San Francisco-type but a normal city girl. So, do you ride and rope and stuff?"

"I barrel raced when I was young but gave it up when I was 12 because of work. My dad is a general foreman on a big ranch owned by a rich white guy. My mom's the chief cook for all the hired help and even the owner when he and his family's in town."

"My parents did well enough we had our own house. My dad had it built. I used to tease him that he was the only commuter in Abiquiu. Since my dad loves horses, we have some. I guess that qualifies for him to call our place a *ranchito,* a little ranch. I think, legally, for raising and selling the horses, the legal name is Macias Family Ranch."

"And why not!" I said with a smile, "So, you're a pretty good cook, I take it?"

"Yeah, like the best! I learned from my mom who has to please the tummies of very hungry cowboys!"

"Okay, well here's my list. My favorite breakfast is *chilaquiles con pollo.*"

"And?"

"And warm tortillas, of course, *masa harina* with real butter."

"And?"

"And I have Hatch chilis in a jar at home. Gotta have those."

"And?"

"And I eat jalapenos like they're pickles."

"And?"

"And I can make the world's best enchiladas and taquitos from recipes in my head."

"And?"

"And, I love menudo but only if it's homemade and I mean I love it whether I have a hangover or not which it's usually not because I'm really not much of a drinker at all."

"And?"

"And why the _hell_ do you keep asking me 'and?'," I said laughing. "Are you testing my patience, because I think I'm out of it!"

"David? I'm asking because you're scoring so well," and she gave me a movie-star smile that nearly caused my blood pressure to spike.

"You're keeping score on me?"

In a confident tone, she scrunched her eyebrows down and said, "I'm a woman. Of course I'm scoring you. You're already in the bonus round," and she emitted a pretty laugh because she was enjoying taunting me, maybe enjoying it a little too much.

"What's my prize for top score?"

"Depends."

"I'm not wearing depends for you or anybody!" It caught her by surprise and she doubled over laughing.

"If the doctor orders them you will! It depends on when the dietitian will give you an unrestricted diet so I can bring you a special something-something to eat," and her cheeks suddenly got a little pink in them.

"You would do that for me??"

"I would do it but I would deny it. I'm not going to get in trouble right before I graduate, silly man."

Olivia left and walked in two minutes later.

"You have a new doctor's order. I have to walk you and it's important that you give it your all. The good news? I'm going to wheel you out on the patio so you can get some warmth in those painful bones of yours."

It took a few minutes to load me into a wheelchair that could accommodate the I.V. bottles and raise my leg. I was looking forward to this as much as having a healthy tooth yanked out with pliers and without a shot to numb me up.

Olivia shaded her eyes from the sun so she could look into mine. "I'll help you up, and then use the chair to hold onto. I've got your back."

I looked over and there were huge windows with tinted glass but I could make out 8 or 10 stationary bicycles and every one of them had a rider. All of the riders seemed to be laughing, some waved and one was pointing at me as she pedaled. I was pissed.

"That's not cool at all. Nice, they're laughing at me because I'm limping and hurting," and I held up my middle finger toward the tinted glass concealing the stationary bikers' identities.

"David? The back of your gown came open and I guess I was kind of pointing at your buns to show the employee gym crowd that you have a cute ass."

I didn't know whether to laugh or be pissed. Olivia had me in the palm of her hand and she knew it and I loved it. Pissed? I couldn't be pissed.

"Well...just how cute do you *find* my ass, Olivia?"

"I think we should probably start heading back. Here, let me tie the back of your gown."

"Non-answer noted."

"It's not that I hadn't noticed but you have to remember that I've stuck a lot of needles in your adorable ass and regard it purely from a medical standpoint."

"Is that 'medically adorable,' Olivia?"

She whispered, "Hot, and I'll deny saying that."

She moved me around to the front of the chair, helped me sit, and she looked at me a long moment and then burst out laughing.

I wanted in on it and looked to Olivia to let me in on it.

"I think that's the first time anyone's buns have drawn applause out here, David. You should be proud."

"You do this regularly?"

"I didn't know the gym was watching and was more worried about you falling than your gown being open. When they gestured? I pointed. Once."

Olivia got me tucked safely back into my bed and made sure my leg was elevated and my hip padded. While she was charting notes, one of the attendants stuck her head in from the hallway and said, "Olivia I need to talk to you a minute, please."

"I'll be done in a sec, Janelle," and Olivia promptly stepped out the door to her waiting colleague.

Olivia walked back in blushing. "Do you know what that was about, David?"

"My ass in the quadrangle?"

"Ever since you got admitted, that girl has been telling people that she knows you from somewhere but couldn't place it. It's your voice, David; she recognized you from the station. Now, she's telling everyone that you're famous."

Olivia was going to razz me and love doing it: "Wait! You ARE famous, aren't you! I love dancing to Rimsky-Korsakov and Rachmaninoff and those guys!" She jumped up and down, applauding and quietly saying "Yee haw" like the cowgirl she truly was.

"You have that poor girl's heart. She thinks she is the hottest thing going because she knows your real name."

"FYI, Olivia, I use 'David Tyler' on the air because my grandparents live on Tyler Park Circle, back East."

"I'm sorry I didn't recognize your voice, David. In rounds, Kerstein said you worked in radio and I knew your job and employer from your chart. I'm a country girl, not a classical fan when it comes to radio."

"Sorry? I do it for the money. I'd be in rock 'n roll or alternative if I had that kind of sick ego."

Accelerated Courtship

Hospital time crawled like no other. Every time Olivia's back was to me as she was leaving, it was almost unbearable. She was just leaving and I didn't want her to go. I turned my head away from the door.

There was something tapping.

"Excuse me. I'm looking for David Tyler but the sign outside the door says you're David Callan. I'm sure I have the right room number."

"I do local radio and use a fake name. It gives me a personal life!"

"So you're Tyler on the radio."

"Yes. KACM-FM. David Tyler."

The guy turned his body 90 degrees and positioned a huge cart to roll into my room. "Some guy from your radio station, I'm guessing, dropped these at our loading dock and we didn't know what to do with them. They ended up in the mail room. Sorry."

It had to be over a hundred pounds of mail in the sacks he lifted off the cart and dropped on the floor next to the chair.

"Folks must be missin' you and wishing you well, Mr. Tyler... er, Callan."

My bedside phone quietly rang.

"Hello?"

"Hi. It's Olivia."

"Hey, nice surprise! Wanna help me open a thousand greeting cards from radio fans?"

"My schedule just went very weird, but that's kind of a good thing."

"Weird?"

"There's a patient that needs to be 'specialled,' have a nurse sit at his side 24/7. They were having trouble finding somebody. I volunteered with another girl from my class. We'll take turns sitting two or three hours and when I'm not his bedside, I thought I could catch some winks in the chair at yours!"

"I'll wear my best evening gown, low cut, backless."

She laughed. "We start at midnight. I'm going home to get some sleep and pack a small bag."

"Does this mean we're spending the night, together, Olivia."

"Shut *UP*, David," came her voice through a restrained giggle. "This means I work all night with a few hours off every so often. It also means.... Never mind.

"Olivia, this is a picture of me remembering you just said, 'Shut UP, David.'

"I'm outta here. Seeya later, cowboy."

I picked up the phone, immediately.

"Chuckster!"

"Sup, David!"

"You keeping the new talent out of trouble?"

"She's okay. Passable, but not you. She's temporary. Your slot's still yours."

"Thanks, and thanks for 10,000 greeting cards I've just now seen for the first time."

"I got sick of looking at them. The GM's best thinking was to keep them here until you returned but right in the middle of the staff meeting, someone-as in yours truly-said, 'And so how is he going to be doing his air shift and opening all these, boss?' He didn't like that and barked at me to get my ass out of the meeting and get the bags over to St. Dominic's," and Chuckster was cracking up.

"You've always known how to work him, Chuck. Listen, I need big-time favor."

"Name it, I'll claim it."

"The Safeway in the Marina has buckets and buckets of fresh flowers. Can you get by there and pick up forty bucks worth and have them here before midnight? Please say 'yes,' Chuck."

"They close at midnight. I'll be there at 11:15 and then head over to you."

"OH, and burn a copy of my NPR show, too, will you?"

"You are so gonna owe me, Callan."

"If you come through, name it and I'll claim it just like you said!"

"See you with the buds and CD 'bout 1145-ish."

"Out."

"Out."

I didn't see Olivia until about 3am. By then, my room smelled like a funeral parlor. I lied and told the night nurse the flowers were from listeners at the station. She told me the door had to stay shut so no one would sneeze their ass off. When she said that, a very loud "Ha-ha-ha-ha!" came out of me because it never occurred to me how many flowers two twenties can buy at a grocery store and that some poor schmoe in the hospital might have serious allergies. The laugh brought pain but laughing is supposedly beneficial to healing.

Olivia waltzed into my dimly lit room, looking frazzled.

"Holy God, David! If your light wasn't on I'd think you had died! Look at all this!"

I honestly didn't know whether she was remarking about the flowers, the mail bags, or all of it.

"People like my show, I guess. Now you know why I need a 5th name, 'Tyler.' Classical chicks dig me except they're between 70 and 110 years old."

She didn't react and looked beat. She pulled the chair over and propped up her feet onto the lower part of my bedrail.

"I'm worn out, David, and I don't know how somebody can get worn out just monitoring a patient who's going straight downhill."

"Emotional stress, Olivia. It's subconscious but probably sucking away at your energy and spirits."

"You're probably right. You feeling okay, David?"

"Yes, believe it or not, no complaints."

"Oh, hey, there's a bunch of white daisies among the flower forest. Could you grab them for me?"

She groaned, "You're asking me to get up?"

"Yes and I'm sorry but I'll reward you handsomely!"

She pulled herself up, grabbed the wet newspaper wrapped around the bunch of daisies and started to hand them to me.

"What's that?"

"What's what, David?"

I pointed to a flower that had a little folded note with 'Olivia' on it as neatly as I could print. She looked at me and the note as she eased herself back into the chair and unfolded the note from me:

"O—

Not a flower in this room came for me.
I got every blossom for you because
our tomorrows aren't real clear.
I want our now to last and
to keep getting better.
xox, David"

She started to get up. "Olivia, don't get up."

"Not even to thank you??"

"It can wait. I can be patient. Hey, can you grab that lotion and toss it to me, please?"

She grabbed the pump bottle of hospital-quality skin conditioner and leaned close to hand it to me.

I pulled off one of her shoes and an anklet in a single motion and I patted my good thigh. "Put that nurse-tootsie right here!"

"You're kidding."

"Not. I'm a giver. You're getting a foot rub."

"Are you trying to seduce me?"

"Under any other circumstances? Yes. If this could do it, that would be a resounding YES! Seeing as that may have lots of downsides to it in my condition and in your workplace, I think I just want to make you feel good, give you a little relief."

She kicked off her other white athletic-looking nurse shoe and removed her anklet sock. There was a small ankle bracelet, 14kt gold, that she left on.

"You know what they say about women with beautiful feet, Olivia? Because I sure don't. But, damn! You have beautiful feet!" The nails were perfectly pedicured and she had an iridescent blue polish on them.

I went to work.

She started emitting little moans. "Oh...David. Oh... I...I might have to keep you around, David, at least in reach."

I smiled at her. Her eyes closed and I could tell I was applying just the right amount of pressure as I rubbed the moisturizer into her aching feet. I slowed to a stop, that brought her eyes open with a sleepy but sexy grin. She pantomimed, 'Thank you.'

I supported her calf with one hand, her ankle with the other. Looking right into her eyes, I slowly raised her foot toward my face. I craned my neck a little to plant a sensuous kiss, just a little pressure, on her instep. And then ever so gently, I kissed the pad of each of her toes. Then, I did the same with the other foot.

As I cradled her feet in my warm hands, my fingers wrapped around them, still rubbing them, I lay very still. Her eyes were closed. We both must have drifted off. The alarm on her watch chimed and our eyes came open.

"I have to go relieve Tracy," and she pulled on her anklets and got into her shoes.

"I know. See you in a few hours, maybe?"

"After making me all... after all that? If there's a better alternative than that, than you, David Callan, don't tell me or I'll be gone!"

She bent over, me, "Here's your thank you I didn't get to give you."

Her quick kiss wasn't quick at all. I don't know what got into me. Guilty: I slipped my hand into her scrub top and my fingers found the edge of her bra. I freed her breast, finding her nipple, and her response was intensity in the kiss.

She broke away from the kiss with my hand still caressing her.

"David, you're so bad but oh so very good," and she kissed me again. I've got to get."

She neared the door and pointed at me. "If Tracy gets near this door, I'm throwing things at her, I swear. If she comes *in here??* I'm throwing things at *you*, David!"

What wasn't to love about Olivia. Answering my own question, there was everything to love about Olivia.

The next time she came in, I was sound asleep. I awoke with her chair scooched up right next to the bed and the bedrail was completely down. Her head was on the mattress. Her hand was under my PJ top over my belly button. She was sound asleep. I'd swear she was smiling. I knew I was. I kissed the top of her head softly, even though it hurt like hell to make that happen. She reacted by rubbing my tummy with two or three gentle strokes. I fell back asleep and she was gone when I awoke again. There was something under my PJ top. A note.

"I'm going home. The gentleman passed away on Tracy's watch. I'm off tomorrow. Enjoy your physical therapy. Yes, you're going to start walking around, David. And you can start ordering your food from the dietitian. Thank you for my special treats – flowers and feet among them ☺ xo O."

I awoke to the hospital's morning bustle, folks in and out of the room. Lab, vitals, breakfast that was tasty and then a physical therapist named Ted who put me through some simple movements just short of torture.

"Nobody but nobody with a hip repair like yours has ever come in here and done as well as you did today, Mr. Callan! Awesome job!"

"I was willing to try, Ted. When do you come back?"

"Another roving therapist is going to come by your room later and do some bedside exercises with you. Tomorrow, you'll start twice-a-days with me."

"Thanks, Ted. You rock."

I've had crushes on girls and women. Nothing new. Olivia? This was withdrawal. It was starting to hurt, I swear.

The next morning, I had an incredibly good breakfast of my own choosing! OJ, milk, cinnamon toast and two over-easy eggs. Lasagna was going to be coming for lunch and I was like a kid expecting his first popsicle. I got something better.

Olivia breezed in. "I have nothing but good reports about you, Mr. Callan!"

"Thank you, Almost-Nurse Macias!"

She was in a yellow scrub top with beautiful flowers all over it. My room was still a funeral parlor in blossom and some of the flowers' heads were beginning to droop.

"Olivia? Think you'd like to share your flowers?"

"I can get someone to get them out of here but I can't take them home. I *did* take the daisies home," she said with a blushed grin.

"I figured a volunteer might freshen them up and send them around to people who could use a little cheering-up."

"Good call."

She went to the phone, called the volunteer coordinator and explained. Olivia gave me a smile and an okay with her free hand.

"Maybe I can get one of the volunteer folks to help you tackle all these get-well cards from your fans."

She got a thumbs-up. And off she went to her other patients. She bustled in later in the afternoon and we brightened just seeing each other. She got right to work, got my vitals taken care of and repositioned me.

"Thanks, that feels a lot better."

She pulled the curtain around me. She said, "David, do you know what day it is?"

"Not fair. I've been in here a while now."

"You know what month it is, don't you?"

"I got this, Olivia, YES! It's February."

"Excellent. I'm going to give you a hint about what day it is. Hold out your hand," and I did. She reached into her scrubs-top pocket and pulled out a box. I couldn't see what it was, but I knew it had to be candy, and she shook three little red cinnamon hearts into my palm.

"*Wait!*" and she picked one up and put it under her tongue.

"What's this?"

"It's your only clue."

I didn't get it.

"It's Valentine's Day, David!" and she leaned over and gave me a kiss on the forehead and then brushed my lips with her hers. "Happy Valentine's Day, David," she whispered.

I got tears in my eyes and she could see them. "Olivia, I don't... I mean... I don't know what to say. You know I don't have anyone and then you come in here and you do this after being so sweet and nice to me all the time? And I know you're not supposed to because you're my nurse?"

"Well, nobody's supposed to come in here and kiss you, especially me, but after my feet thing right behind the flowers?? Technically? I'm not your nurse. I'm a student here. I'm not an employee and I'm not an RN. I have been caring for you. You're my school project," and she cocked her head at me, smiled and pushed my bangs out of my eyes that were still drying from the tears.

. "I'm supposed to follow the rules and I just broke a big one. Several. A lot. But something tells me you won't tell."

"Why are you so sure?"

She leaned over closely and whispered, "Because I'm going to buy you off, buy your silence."

Olivia kissed me like I hadn't been kissed in a long time. I could taste a hint of the cinnamon heart. We were nose to nose. "You're rocking my world, David. I won't deny I'm loving it, your kindness... affection and attention," and she pushed my bangs away, again. It felt my world changed in that moment.

She threw the curtain back she said "Mr. Four Names, I have patients I need to attend-to today. I'll be back in 2 hours for your vitals."

"Thank you, Ms. Macias... Oh, and Happy Valentine's Day. Did you know it was Valentine's Day??"

"For a few moments? I was more convinced than ever, Mr. Callan." She kissed her finger, blew the kiss to me, and darted out the door and down the hall.

My little bedside table had a hidden drawer with the mirror, the kind that when you pulled out the drawer the mirror pops up. I could still taste some sweet saltiness from her lips. The mirror didn't show any lipstick had transferred to my mouth.

Olivia decided to stop-in, again.

"David. P.T. at 11am. They are going to stand you up and get you moving around, again!"

"Olivia why are you smiling, because you know what's going to hurt like hell?"

"No, I'm smiling because the better they get you walking the more I'll be responsible to really put some intense pain into your recovery," and I got her sexy smile.

"Sometimes I think you enjoy your work a little much, Olivia."

"Oh, I assure you I do enjoy my work," and there was the sexy smile, again.

We were both momentarily startled by a male voice with some authority entering the room.

"I'll testify to that. This young lady works her butt off around here and shows great promise in orthopedics."

Olivia said, "Thank you, sir."

He turned to me. "I'm Dr. Drew, David, your orthopedic surgeon. You've made remarkable progress and I mean truly remarkable. No infection, great range of motion, and the reports from physical therapy are glowing.

Here's what I want you to do: I want you to walk, David. Walk your ass off, excuse the expression. I need you to push a wheelchair or use a walker and I'm going to require you have an escort. You need the muscles to build back up and the increased blood flow will help that. How about it? You up for it? Will you try?"

"Yes, I'm all over it, sir. I've had enough of this room confinement thing. Way enough."

He patted my leg. "Terrific. I'm thinking you're going home in a week or so. Get busy, David."

I was still thanking God, above, when the tray delivery lady popped her head in the door. But without a tray. "Mr. Callan?"

"Yes?"

"They cancelled your lunch tray, said you're getting outside food, today."

I whined, "NO LASAGNA??" For extra drama, I hid my eyes behind my palm, grieving. Lasagna privation. Even hospital lasagna. Not nice.

"Could I at least have some iced tea or something in the meantime, please?"

"Sure. Got that right on my cart for you," and she returned with iced tea and an orange juice.

"Thank you!!" The OJ was gone in a flash. I was slowly sipping the iced tea. I don't like lemon in my tea but she had left two lemon wedges on the side of the small tray with the drinks. I ate them. Sour, but yummy. My mouth felt alive again. I leaned over to pitch the rinds and heard her voice.

"Hungry, there, Cowboy?"

"Yes ma'am, I was just fixing to eat my horse!" and she laughed as a diaper bag-sized, insulated zippered thing swung off of her shoulder. She kicked the door shut, putting a 'Do Not Disturb - Procedure in Progress' sign out.

She kicked off her shoes, cleared my little rolling table, and used the counter to lay out six snap-top containers. Out came two small plates and the silverware.

She came to the little table with two heaping plates of homemade Mexican food. Taquitos, tamale pie, and a cup of real green chili—just green chilis, seasoning and pork. New Mexico-style chili.

I must have looked stupid staring at the plates. She opened a little thingy, picked up a taquito, dunked it in the thingy which had guacamole, and put it up to my mouth. I gently grabbed her forearm to guide the food, and bit the taquito in half, pulling her the rest of way into me for an open-mouthed kiss, taquito and all.

She put her hand to her mouth to cover and chew, both of us laughing.

"I wanted to share. I LIED. I wanted to eat and I wanted to kiss you and I tried to do both at the same time."

She said, 'Drinks!" and she grabbed two Mexican sodas out of the cold side of her bag. Ice cold, and she opened them. I extended my soda to toast her, "Here's to your mom's cooking lessons, to this, and to us!"

"I can drink to that, David!" and the bottles clinked.

"And?"

"Very funny."

"And?"

She set the bottle down on the little table.

"And would you kiss me. Pretty please?"

Stepping All Over the Lines

I swung my legs around, pushed the wheeled table off
at an angle and rose. I extended my hand and she took
it. I helped her up in a fluid motion, pulling her to me. I
put my arms around her, approached her very slowly as
our eyes closed and our lips met. The shudders
exchanged by both bodies had to have been real. I was
getting aroused. I knew she could feel it and she used my
PJ waistband to pull me even more tightly against her. A
little moan confirmed she was getting aroused too....

She broke away, pulling me toward the bathroom,
locked the door behind us, and backed up to the sink.
She undid my PJ's drawstring and pulled down my
shorts as I pulled her scrub pants and panties to her
ankles. I raised her arms to pull her scrub top and bra
off in a lover's frenzy.

She was sopping wet as I glided slowly into her. We
were kissing and caressing, sweating, both of us cooing
and moaning. My hips were killing me, but I
couldn't...wouldn't stop.

She sensed how much I hurt.

"Easy, David. Let me...I'll get us there, David, let me,"
and her hips undulated as I concentrated on simply
keeping myself steady. My hands were tugging at and
pinching and pulling her nipples. My hands were
running up and down her back. It wasn't long before I
thought she'd explode and was right.

I let myself go at the same time. "Oh God, Oh God,
Oh God," she frantically whimpered as she shuddered
again and again in a full-blown orgasm. She was kissing
me voraciously, using both hands to rake through my
hair. I was kissing her all over as we panted, our lungs
heaving, pleading for air.

We instantly froze in place when two forceful raps on
the door sounded loud enough to crack it. Thank God
neither of us made a sound.

"MR. CALLAN, IT'S KATHLEEN, YOUR RN. ARE YOU OKAY IN THERE?"

"I'M ON THE THRONE. NO WORRIES."

"OKAY. JUST CHECKING ON YOU. JUST PULL THAT RED CORD IF YOU NEED HELP?

"OKAY!"

Olivia was so scared her head was crushing my collarbone. She eased-up as we waited ten long seconds to make sure Kathleen Wei wasn't going to override the lock and barge into the bathroom.

I was deep in Olivia, clutching her tightly. Her breasts were wet with perspiration against my throbbing ribcage. I reached up to the sides of her head, framing her face with my hands, "I'm falling, Olivia, completely falling for you," and I moved gently from side to side to let her sense I was still very much inside of her.

She kissed me and then pulled back just enough to devour my eyes with her own. She whispered, "Let me clean-up a little. Gimme a minute."

I collected and organized myself. In case Wei was nearby, I hit the flush handle. I slipped out and I heard water run briefly and she was out of the bathroom a minute or two later.

"We almost got busted because of that sign I put on the door."

"Almost. It didn't happen. We're fine."

"I'm not. My heart's racing and I need to deal with this," and she looked into my eyes, "and I will. We'll figure this out." She kissed me.

She got me situated in bed and I reached over to the little rolling table and grabbed the remains of a taquito.

"Open wide," and she bent down to let me feed her the taquito remains of what started all of this.

We recovered enough to have just a couple more bites of a very quiet and intimate meal. I hadn't eaten much but everything she made was authentically New Mexico-style cooking.

"How'd you pull off an amazing meal in a dorm room?"

"I found a coed with access to the kitchen in the Home Economics department. In exchange for some of this food, I got all the kitchen time I needed. That girl can put it away, I'm telling you, and I was generous with a purpose, you know, for a next time?" and she giggled devilishly.

I grinned at her, "Mmm, bring it."

Olivia hastily organized everything. She stacked all the containers and pulled open the door of an undercounter refrigerator I hadn't noticed was there, put the containers inside and shut the door. She washed the utensils and wrapped them in paper towels before she secreted them away in one of the drawers.

"I need to get to work. I'll tell Kathleen I left the floor a minute for the vending machines. I'll grab a candy bar from there now, so I have an empty wrapper."

"I need to pinch myself." I kissed her chest at the 'V' of her shirt and then, after she stooped down, her mouth.

"Best meal ever, Olivia."

"You knew I could cook."

"I meant you. I want seconds. 50ths."

"Day's not over, cowboy" she teased, and was gone.

Later, someone else took my vitals. I was understandably freaked out that Kathleen might have somehow busted Olivia, and it was all I could do to sound calm.

"Olivia gone home?"

"No, she got called downstairs to the E.R. She may have a new patient coming up."

"Thanks."

Olivia walked in at the end of her shift.

"What a day."

"Me, too," and I felt myself blush. "I had a great lunch date and a better dessert."

She broke into a wry smile. She was in a different pair of scrubs and I wasn't going to let it go.

"New scrubs?"

"Yep. A patient got the other ones wet. Very, *very* wet," and she came to me as the door was shutting. My leg was over the edge of the bed and I moved my knee so she could get in close. She did. I put my arms around her waist.

"I have food if you've got the munchies."

"*Oh my God.* Leftovers! I could eat a horse, cowboy!"

She spun around and stepped over to the counter, flinging open the refrigerator door and spreading the containers on the counter so she could hold them all at once to put them on my little rolling table. She grabbed the utensils out of the drawer and sat on the chair beside me, feeding me and herself.

"Wait, Olivia, you're getting me fat. You eat—I had a tray I didn't really touch, except for the applesauce and coffee. You're eating like a starved child!" and she tried to laugh with a mouthful of cold green chili.

Afterward, she stacked all the containers in her carrier to take them home and rejoined me, bedside. I held her hand.

"Dr. Drew told me you're out of here in about a week."

"I can't wait. We'll be free. We can be us!" I was so happy to hear myself say that. Her smile said she was happy to hear it, too

"In two weeks, my mom and dad are flying me to Denver for a four-day seminar. Three days are in the classroom prepping for the written RN exam. The last day, they give you a mock-test using questions from previous exams. People who take this course, and it's not cheap, have a 99% success rate passing the test the first time."

"Denver?"

"Yes. The test package includes a hotel near the classroom site. I think it's in South Denver, the Denver Tech Center area."

"That's like, what, March 18th you start?"

"The 19th."

"I can call—we can email and text, right?"

"You just better, cowboy. You wouldn't break this girl's heart so early... so quickly, could you?"

I kissed her, "I'd be breaking my own, Olivia."

She said "early." Breaking her heart 'early?' I interpreted that to mean she considered this as a start of something lasting or bigger or both. God how I hoped so.

"You've got enough things broken right now, David," she teased. "We don't need to add your heart—or mine—to the list, deal?"

I purred at her.

In-Home Care

Dr. Drew didn't bat an eyelash when I asked him to discharge me on Tuesday. Olivia was off.

The 'handicapable' van got me loaded and buckled up and I dialed Olivia, "Woo-hoo. Goin' home!"

"Yay! If you give me directions, I'll meet you there."

"Special request. On your way over, pick up a couple cans of sardines packed in water, please. The brand doesn't matter. My other girl, Phoebe, is Mrs. Lentini's cat. She's probably pissed that I just upped and disappeared."

"Yeah, you can't do that to us girls and get away with it.... Sardines packed in water. Check! On the list."

"I'll text you the address and cross-streets. It's one house off the corner."

"Eek, I'm excited, David!"

"Me, too!"

She made a kissing sound on the phone, "On my way, cowboy."

"Can't wait."

I called the station and was put through to the program director.

"Jerry Voss."

"Hey, this is David Callan! I'm out of the hospital and they cleared me to work if I'm in a wheelchair and can occasionally prop-up my leg!"

"Great news, David! Get in here day after tomorrow and be ready to go. We've been slammed with listeners wondering about where you are."

"I know. I have a hundred pounds of cards to open!"

"Just one fly in the ointment, Jerry—I need a quick up-and-back to Denver for personal reasons."

"When?"

"18th and 19th."

"I'm not thrilled.... But we'll manage, David," he said, sounding more miffed than he was letting on. "I really need you in here doing your magic."

"Not to worry, Jerry. I'm 100% ready."

"Day after tomorrow, David.".

"Gotcha. Thanks, Jerr," and I heard the call disconnect.

There was a hottie on my doorstep when the van pulled up. A doll in a white unzipped U. San Francisco hoodie with green lettering and gold trim. Underneath, she had a green and white-striped top unbuttoned to the top of her cleavage with no sign of a bra. She was in nice jeans and some really nice boots. Very nice, very expensive-looking hand-tooled leather boots. She was stroking Mrs. Lentini's cat, my porch pal, Phoebe. I think I was purring with Phoebe.

"Ah, my two favorite girls conspiring about sardines," I said, coming into view from the side of the van as Olivia rose and came over.

"No, we were just gossiping about you, David. Girl talk."

She grabbed the armrests of my chair to steady herself as she leaned down to kiss me.

"Welcome home, cowboy. The last time I saw you with street clothes on, I was watching someone cut them off of you."

"Now you can just ask. No scissors required. It's your 'Naked, now!" card you can play whenever you want, Olivia," and I grinned at her. She blushed, removing the small plastic bag-PJs, hospital shaving kit and disposable slippers-from my lap and tossing it into the corner of the couch once we negotiated the door lock and entryway. The van driver lugged-in the mail bag and set it in the corner of my small living room.

"I met your friend Chuckster and his girlfriend, Jenny, just as they were leaving. I told 'em I was a friend who was gonna get you settled in and they let me in. They were bummed they couldn't stay but Jenny said she hadda be somewhere. They said they cleaned the place and it looks like it. Chuck told me you need two new houseplants and a new goldfish. I told him I'd buy you a used one," and we laughed.

"Yeah, sad about my goldfish. My track record's not very good keeping them alive, anyway. I think I'll be kinder to their population and not own anymore."

"Could you live anyplace *smaller* than this, David!!"

I put my hands on my hips and with a slight smile, said, "Yes. Your place."

"Women's dorm at a private Catholic university, David. Really? Overnights and wild sex are frowned upon, cowboy, and not worth getting kicked out of my program right at the finish line."

"Thank God overnights and wild sex aren't against the rules here, Olivia."

She smiled seductively, "All in the name of my in-home care for you, David. Heightened emotional therapy with twists and turns."

I rolled my chair into the bedroom and dropped my little bag inside the closet. She sat on the bed next to me.

"Give a cowgirl a hand, pardner?"

"Sure. Whatcha got?"

"Grab a boot toe and heel and tug like crazy until you see my foot fly out."

"Got it," and the other boot came off as well. I took a liberty. With both boots off, I removed her socks and gently rubbed one of her feet.

"I may not be responsible for what happens next if you keep that up. You got me wet at the hospital doing this."

I put the brakes on the chair and one-stepped to the bed to sit beside her. I reached for and pulled her hoodie over her head. We were already kissing before our heads made contact with the bed. I stroked her hair.

"Out to eat? Order in?"

"Let' do delivery. I saw a Chinese take-out menu under a refrigerator magnet. Wanna do that?"

"Sure. I can impress you with my ninja chopsticks routine."

She bounced up from the bed, "I'll get the menu." I laid back.

She flopped onto the bed on her knees, tucked them under, holding the menu so we could both read it.

Before she could speak, she had to know, "Anything's fine, but I have to have their hot 'n sour soup. After that? Anything, Olivia."

"General Tsao Chicken, egg rolls, lo mein instead of rice and almond duck, okay?"

"And my soup, please." She leaned over and grabbed the land line phone and grimaced.

"Dead. No dial tone, David."

"Shit. Mr. Fin, my goldfish couldn't even call for help."

"Corny."

"Sad. I'm in mourning."

She grabbed her cell, dialed and ordered. She played that 'naked now' card and we made love. Sweet, tender, unhurried and private love.

Olivia answered the door in a bedsheet with two 20-dollar bills in her hand. "Over there, please," she said, directing the food to the table. "Thank you. Keep the change. Bye, now," she said.

She let the sheet fall and came to me, naked.

"I'm your main course, cowboy, and I'll stay hot. The food won't. Soup first, then me. And me, again. And me for dessert, *claro*?"

"Clear."

She rattled around in my kitchenette a second and brought the soup, lo mein and the duck back to bed. She loved the soup. I loved her. We both loved the duck.

The dessert was magnificent, interrupted only to clear the Chinese containers and put away the spicy chicken's container. She came back to bed.

She lay on her side, a hand supporting her head, looking at me.

"You've been sweet not to ask. I'm going to tell you. Yes. There was someone else. Was, not is, four years ago when I was 19. We just started dating, sparks were flying and he got orders to go to Afghanistan. He was killed his 2nd day there. Their helicopter crashed, some sort of accident."

She went on, "I promised myself I wouldn't get involved for a while and I haven't. I've focused on my classes, labs and clinicals. I needed to get over myself, mostly, because I realized I had nothing to feel guilty about in that situation. I wasn't good company, David, and didn't want to be."

I slid my arm under her torso, pulled her to my chest, held her closely.

She was soul-baring and I dared not interrupt.

"I haven't been out, not even asked out since all of that went down. I feel shitty because I feel like I should pine for him, like, miss him all the time but I don't. He got close to me and got killed. Boom. Gone."

"Then, you appeared. You knew Abiquiu and had been there. I wondered if it was some sort of sign and then tried to dismiss that. I couldn't take my eyes *or* my mind off of you because you emitted this...this just... different vibe. Not a player. Not all that and a bag of chips. An earnest, nice guy who wants to be great at what he does and nothing, *nothing* is forced. What someone sees is what they get, without pretense."

"You pegged me, Olivia, about who you perceive I really am. I don't know how people miss that. You didn't but most people miss by a country mile because they try to read-into stuff that's not there, presumptions."

"Well not this country girl from Abiquiu, cowboy."

I brushed her hair back, kissed her eyebrows, then eyelids.

"Careful callin' me 'Cowboy.' I may have to lasso you and keep you as breeding stock." We laughed until I blurted out, "Did I just say *that*??" and she giggled.

"I heard it. I'll swear I heard it."

Her hand slid down and stroked me gently as I began to get aroused. She kissed me, and still holding onto me, whispered, "Take a cowgirl for a wild ride, cowboy?" and she got onto all fours looking back at me.

I woke up and she was staring at me, grinning. "I'm wondering, David, if you aren't a little *too* good at this!"

"Your assessment's different than mine. It's not that I'm any good at all, Olivia. It's you. I'm responding to you, what you do to me and how you make me feel. I've never reached this altitude so quickly with a woman before and confess I'm normally a little scared of heights."

"Right answer, David."

"True answer, cowgirl."

"And?"

"And if *you're* taking requests, will you kiss me now, cowgirl?"

It was bliss. I was working. Olivia was working and the reality was that she was living with me. I asked Olivia to stay and told her to take as much drawer and closet space as she wished for her clothes.

The Denver trip was on top of us.

I heard the door, "Groceries! Come 'n get it, cowboy." I used a cane and walked out from folding clothes in my bedroom. Over dinner, she gave me the 4-1-1.

"I'm staying at the Sheraton DTC and will call you with my room number when I get checked in."

"I'm still taking you to SFO, right?"

"Change of plan. I'm going to take a shuttle, David."

"Shuttle?"

"I don't want to be a crying mess at the airport anticipating being without you. I need to pull up my big girl jeans and go this one alone. If you're good with me leaving the Accord here, I'll give you the keys, or I can grab the shuttle from USF student parking."

Mrs. Lentini had the luxury of two off-street spaces and let me use one. She was fine with the Accord and seemed to approve of Olivia being an add-on tenant. She would have let me know, otherwise. It was probably because I had been so banged up. And what landlord didn't love a guy who romanced her cat with sardines?

"Then I'm driving you to the airport, Olivia. It's an automatic, and my chair will fit in the back seat."

That thought registered and put nothing but happiness across her face.

"I'd love that."

Olivia and I went to bed early, made love and spooned. We slept restfully until her alarm went off and we scrambled out of there, arriving at the 'Departures Curb' in plenty of time for her 7:25 check-in time. I'd be back here in long-term parking with the Honda in just a few hours.

My phone recon to the exam prep training company yielded good results. They told me the students had to sign-in by 12:30pm for 1pm orientation. Ah, so that's why she needed the early 'redeye' flight to Denver. Just in case. It went like clockwork.

Unexpected Pleasure

I got to the Sheraton about 1:30, checked-in and ran my bag to my room. I hit the grocery store for some flowers and a bottle of wine. By the time I got back, I'd been sitting in the lobby for less than an hour when a very weary looking Olivia walked in, an Olivia I'd never seen.

Tight, grey woolen skirt, low matching heels, navy cashmere sweater with grey windowpane striping. There was a thick, sterling silver rope around her neck. From it, dangled a native American, turquoise squash blossom-type silver pendant the size of a baseball. Her blue clutch looked expensive with its long strap, like a Coach bag. Her hair was coiffed to look tousled which seemed somehow more beautiful than her exquisite norm.

My pulse quickened and I'm sure my cheeks flushed. They were warm. I stood and retrieved the bunch of flowers from the coffee table next to me. She never saw it coming. Or me.

"Excuse me. You look like you could use a glass of wine and maybe a little dinner company." I startled her. Major shift from a busy-brained travel day to joy. In nanoseconds, I raised the white Gerber daisies I'd been hiding behind my thigh. Her look of love oozed all over me.

"I thought they might make your room smell nice."

Her clutch hit the floor with a *thunk* and she threw her arms around me more tightly than I expected. Her eyes were moist. Not a word or even a whisper, just a look and a kiss that said it all.

"I've got a room, Olivia, but I don't want to screw up what you're here to do. My boss gave me two days off, not happily, but he okayed it."

It was hard to get that out because she was all over me and I wasn't complaining.

"Here's my spare key. The room number on the envelope's correct. Call or come by when you unwind or want to unwind," and I felt myself grinning.

"I'm gonna get out of these clothes and freshen up, put on something more comfortable," and looked into my eyes. "I love you for you, and this is you, David."

"You've taken such care of me, I'm reciprocating."

She kissed me again and I took her hand and we walked over to the elevator.

"Go on up, I have to grab something from the rental car," and I used the time wisely, walking to the counter.

"Hi. I just checked in?"

"Yes, sir, is everything all right?"

"Better than you know. Hey, I need to find the best Western-style steak house in South Denver for tonight...kind of a special occasion." Winner! A name and the general directions came right off the tip of her tongue.

"Thank you."

Back at the room, I shaved for the 2nd time that day, splashed on some Lagerfeld cologne, and put on a nicely pressed dress shirt and slacks from my hanging bag. I flipped on the TV looking for the news. I answered the ringing, blinking phone.

"Hi." I grinned.

"I'm probably about 10 minutes from being in the lobby. Okay for you?" "On my way. How's the room smell."

"Almost as yummy as you. We need to discuss your cologne, cowboy."

"I think you mean I scored, so thank you."

"See you in ten."

"Roger dodger," and I went down to the lobby.

I heard the elevator door a few minutes later and looked over. Again, 'Oh my Jesus.'

A transformed Olivia, another one I'd never seen, glided into the lobby to meet me wearing pressed turquoise slacks, white heels, and a shimmering silk blouse. I held out both hands and she came to them as I admired her. I took her delicate hands into each of mine. I was putty. Done. I drew her to me, almost nose to nose. We were close enough for sexy whispers.

"My God, you smell good, Mister!"

"Lagerfeld. It's the only cologne I wear and I'm selfish because I like the way it smells on me," and I chuckled.

"Works for me. It'll probably get you lucky, cowboy."

Her perfume was delicate and subtle. Sensory overload. I tilted my head to kiss her and she accommodated my lips meeting hers. I didn't want to smear her freshly applied lipstick. But I kept my lips in contact with hers. I took another liberty, giving her a slow, sensuous 'Eskimo kiss,' gently rubbing the tip of my nose against hers. I felt her small shudder. "Let's get that wine I promised you," I whispered.

The dinner crowd had come and gone, the steak house bar had low lighting and we had the perfect corner booth, perfect for lovers. It was clear the server knew this was romance happening and she was terrific, being present without being intrusive at all.

Our wine arrived. Olivia put her hand on my leg just above the knee and our shoulders were resting against one another. I prodded her about her day to give her the chance to let any nervousness dissipate.

"Tell me all about your day," and she opened up. It didn't take long before the stressors of her day were gone. The wine and I triumphed.

Throughout dinner, she'd look over and smile, shaking her head like, 'Okay, you got me on this one.' Her eyes were sparkling brown diamonds, dazzling even in low light. We didn't want to leave but it looked like the place was starting to close.

As we walked into the hotel lobby, she looked over at me with pleading eyes, "It's okay. You can come up and we can hang out for a while. It's just a training thing and it's not that late...but I know you had a long day, too."

The flowers' presence filled the room. She had repurposed the ice bucket as a vase. Big room. Only then did I notice we were in the sitting area of a suite.

Olivia One-Upped

The wine relaxed us both. It was time to tell David I missed my period and tested positive two different times. He surprised me. It was my turn. My heart said his reaction would be negative or big. He'd could fly home and have a few days to process it. We could talk and text, all day and night long for that matter.

I had twinges of morning sickness, emotions jumping up and down, sore boobs, and frequent peeing—all those joys of early pregnancy.

However he reacted, I was going to be the mother of his child. David would get to choose his level of participation from this next moment until eternity. He felt like my natural mate. I wanted him with me for every step along the way and my innate sense said he'd be there.

When I joined him on the couch, he was preoccupied. I was certain even though I hadn't seen distant or pensive or uncertainty in him before. That couldn't be present for what I had to tell him. I needed him to let it out or dismiss whatever it was before I told him.

I moved toward the couch and she came to me, curling her legs under her as she joined me, leaning over to whisper, "Dinner was beautiful, thank you, David."

"I had help. The desk highly recommended the place."

"Olivia, I know you're here for something big.... But I want you to realize something big's going on with me, too. It's life-changing and I'm bursting at the seams to tell you about it because there' s no down-side."

"Sounds wonderful! Tell me, tell me!"

"There's a broadcast media ownership group that's the hottest thing in all of radio-land right now. They're known as Q-MEG, Quellen Media Entertainment Group. In fact, QMEG is their trading symbol on the New York Stock Exchange, and it's over 200 a share and growing."

"Bottom line, they want me. Big money. Once-in-a-lifetime chance like being hand-picked to land on the moon, Olivia."

"In the Bay area?"

"Arizona. Eleventh biggest radio market in the U.S. and they have the top country-western station there. They're going to give me a huge package, including stock and retirement, and crazy money. I have to do it."

"I'm *thrilled*, David! You have to go for it!"

"Norman says I'm a shoe-in, he's already got me the job. But...but Olivia, this is a too-good-to-be true thing. If anything—and I mean anything—caused me to blow this thing I think I'd be the next stat high-diving off the Golden Gate Bridge."

Olivia threw her arms around my neck, and I felt her tears on me. She was happy for me, us.

"I'm proud of you, cowboy! I'm certainly not gonna stand in your way, and I'd hog-tie anybody who did," she said, looking in my eyes, still with tears falling. I could taste the saltiness of her tears in the tender kiss.

"I think we have a future to talk about, Olivia, a bright one," and I felt the day and the wine and the excitement overtaking me.

I guess I dozed off a minute because the next thing I knew, she was turning off the lamps and walked toward me. I figured...hoped she would cover me, but she didn't have anything in her hands. I was gathering the energy to get up, until Olivia put her hands flat onto the arms of the huge chair and rotated as she lowered herself down into my lap and curled up as if my lap had been custom molded to fit her body, alone.

She rested her head against my collarbone and we were one. She undid a couple buttons on my shirt and gently rubbed my chest. Pure tenderness, not sexual. Sensual. Caring. Serene. Zen-centered. All, wordlessly.

I had no concept if we were that way for 5 minutes or 40 because time itself had vaporized. I felt her head move against my chest. Her hand came to the side of my head, raking her fingers gently through my hair.

She moved to look in my eyes and whispered, "Take me to bed?" With her hand in mine, I angled through the darkened room toward the bedroom's open door, and the clock radio on an end table gave me just enough of a landing light to align myself and her for touchdown. She stooped and grabbed the bedcovers and pulled them back as she crawled onto it on all-fours. She reached for my hand as she repositioned herself to make room for me. Fully clothed, we gravitated into each other's arms.

Our love story was gracefully moving along. Nothing forced or rushed. I looked over at her on the bed beside me. With her looking in my eyes and stroking my hair, this was very, *very* different than anything I had ever felt with a woman. New ground, unfamiliar territory.

My alarm went off at 3:45 and awakened us both. Curiously, our clothes were on the floor beside the bed. It hadn't been a euphoric dream. Our love-making was real, *was* other-worldly and had continued. It seemed a canopy of magical faerie was showering down on us.

I kissed her on the forehead and eye and other eye and nose. I slipped my arm under her bare back and turned my body, now ¾ to her, and gave her an Eskimo kiss during which she pulled herself up into me and kissed me with the kind of passion that reduces fireworks to the level of a cork coming out of a warm, leftover bottle of pinot noir.

This was gonna hurt, but I had to say it.

"This man's got to get to work. And getting into the Bay Area in the morning is 100 times harder than getting out."

She gave me her sad, puppy dog frowny face but her hand, with pressure behind it, pushed against my shoulder as she hungrily kissed me and I yielded to let Olivia who rolled onto her back and pulled me on top of her. Her body was on fire. Work could wait if I had to get another flight. She mattered. Work didn't.

I wanted more of it, of her, constantly her and it was the level of desire a person who's on fire feels for a cascading bucket of water. I needed to be quenched and quenched again. Olivia made my fires rage. I was consumed and, at present, a smoldering hot mess of willingness and renewable desire.

We stayed in bed and ordered room service at 5:30. Lots of room service. Love murmurs continued streaming between us. Recharged with some sleep, nourished and hydrated, we headed for the shower together only to return right back to the bed. I was laughing at what a complete wreck we made of the bed, so bad that we both had the same thought at the same time and reconstructed it to look like a bed. Just so we could destroy it again.

We took another shower, longer than the last, knowing it was for bodies on which clothing needed to go. With constantly moving hands and lips, we eventually got to the soaping and shampoo part. She was first out of the shower and did the towel turban thing with her hair. I dried every inch of her with one of the suite's plush towels.

At the basin next to me, she worked the towel and then a rake-type brush through her hag' I'd from my room before she woke up, and pulled out my Lagerfeld.

She put her hand on mine, stopping the cologne from being uncapped. "You sure you want to put that on when I'm standing next to you, naked?"

"If bottled anything can keep you naked anytime I spray it, I'll buy cases of it and maybe even have a little fun with that" and I thought she was gonna pop me with the towel. Instead, she took the cologne and uncapped it, splashed some into her palms and rubbed it under my jaw bones and down onto my chest.

"There. Now you can kiss me."

It was the instant I fell unrecoverably in love with her.

We couldn't even take our eyes off of each other while we were dressing. For the record? I can put on a necktie with a perfect knot and length in a pitch-black cave. It had been in the back pocket of my slacks in case I felt I needed to be spiffier to complement her dinner outfit and the restaurant. But she came up to me, adjusted the knot near the top button, and buttoned-up my collar. Only then did she make sure the knot's pattern was perfectly aligned.

I pretended there was something wrong with her face. "Hold still. You have an eyelash about to go into your eye." I leaned down and stared at her eye and surprised her with a dramatic, big kiss.

"You said I could."

She smiled and let out a big sigh. "How am I going to deal with you, Mister Callan?"

"You're a quick study but I'm hoping you'll give it a lifetime…. I have to grab my bag out of my room."

"I'll come down with you."

I slipped the key into my door and opened the unused, now-refreshed Sheraton room. I pointed, "*Look*! There's a bed! We could have used this one instead of rebuilding yours!" and her laugh came from deep-down. I pretended to look at the bed, my watch, the bed…. "Ain't happenin'. I gotta jet, Nanette!"

I kissed her in the parking lot and the cab whisked me away.

I knew I could live in a tree and eat leaves as long as the tree was her most cherished and the one she visited most in *my* Olivia's Forest.

Alone and Walking

I was waving until David's cab was out of sight. I started crying which escalated into full sobs. I felt a little woozy and wobbled myself to the trunk of a big luxury sedan. I crossed my arms on the trunk lid to cushion my forehead. I realized I was in view of half of the hi-rise hotel's windows and righted myself to walk back inside. I only made it two steps before I had to turn abruptly and put my hand on the sedan's trunk and my other hand on the car next to it. I threw-up most of what I'd eaten from the room service trays.

On the short walk back to the hotel entrance, what I had to do was as crystalline as the Denver sky.

I looked-up and dialed a number.

"University of San Francisco, how may I direct your call?"

"Student housing, please."

"I'll connect you."

"Student Housing, Mrs. Wahler."

"Mrs. Wahler, I'm Olivia Macias in 314D."

"Let me get you pulled up, here. Verify your last four and birthdate for me?" and I did.

"How can I help you?"

"I finished my program and am taking my Registered Nurse exam on Wednesday. I'll be completely finished. I'd like to move out early, please."

"That's not a problem, Ms. Macias. We can't refund anything except the cleaning deposit, of course. But you can certainly do that."

"When can I meet with you to fill out any forms you need."

"Honey, you verified your I.D. with me, I'll put the contract termination in right now if you like. What date would you like?"

"I'm going to pack Friday and be out before midnight. So that's my last occupancy day."

"I've got you down. Good luck with your RN test and career, Ms. Macias."

"Thank you, you've been very helpful."

I used the ladies' room off the hotel lobby to rinse-out my mouth. Instead of going back to the suite, which would be full of David's presence and aura, I opted for an overstuffed chair in the lobby.

My physical strength was sapped. It just wasn't there and my phone felt like it weighed ten pounds.

"Daddy?" He heard me fighting-back the tears.

"Daddy, I need help."

My phone showed an incoming call from David but I was still on with my dad. As soon as we hung up, I called David back, which was almost twenty minutes later. My talk with dad was involved.

"Hey, cowboy, miss me already?"

"Like crazy! You don't sound like yourself. You okay?"

"Uh, yeah, I'm sorry. I was on with my dad and something upsetting happened back home."

"Want me to call back, later?"

"Oh, no. No. Please, let's talk."

"Don't make any plans for after the test on Wednesday, okay?"

"I never thought about it, David." A lie.

"We're gonna celebrate in style, Olivia."

"I won't have my score back. What if..."

"What if you only get a 98 instead of a 99 or 100 on the test? There's not a written test you can't ace, anywhere, Olivia. We're partying Wednesday night. Pinky promise?"

"Pinky promise!" Another lie.

"They're boarding. Gotta go, baby! See you home, soon. I love you, Olivia."

"Me, too."

Me, too. That was a lousy thing to say. I couldn't even say 'I love you to him' because I would have burst out crying and made things worse.

Impossibly Hard

Ever-dependable David, grinning from ear to ear, met me as soon as I cleared security. We hugged and kissed.

"I don't know about your flight, but mine was like driving across lunar craters without shock absorbers, David."

"I thought you looked a little green."

"Let me hit the ladies' room really quick," and it was close-by.

We got my bag and took the parking shuttle to the car and got home pretty quickly. I threw my stuff into the washer, had David help me get my boots off. He sat on the bed beside me and put his arms around me.

"It's going to be a big week for us! So here's my thought. I'll be as present or absent to you as you want and need, give you space or whatever you need to keep your head right before you write the exam."

"Let's just roll with it. I'm okay. I feel ready. Do we have anything to eat in the fridge?"

"Matter of fact, I picked up a rotisserie chicken from the store, some fresh veggies and fruit and stuff, and some yogurt."

"Ooh, the yogurt sounds good. What kinda fruit did you get?"

"A bag of apples, a grapefruit, and the peaches looked good so I got four of them."

"Your girl's hungry," and I got up and headed for the tiny kitchenette area for some yogurt and peach slices. I shared, feeding him. I loved feeding him and he was always appreciative.

"Chuckster wants me to go up to the transmitter and tower site on Friday after work. It might be 3:30 or 4 before I get home."

"That's actually fine because my housing contract's expiring and I have to go on-campus and deal with all of that."

I could only pull this off if I was intentionally aloof to the point of pretending to study the foot-high stack of spiral notebooks I had beside me, along with the prep course materials, right up until Tuesday night. David had been loving and fulfilled his promise to give me space.

I had to be checked-in and ready to test by 7:15 Wednesday morning or I would be denied admission to the room. No purses or cellphones were allowed, and we candidates were advised there were strolling proctors.

I asked David to get me up with him and he did. It had been a few days since we enjoyed a shower together but I didn't let it lead to anything. I couldn't let it.

We dressed and I walked him out and down to the stop for his commute. He wished me luck and kissed me, tenderly. I brushed his bangs away, "Seeya, cowboy!" and managed a meager smile. Phoebe was on the stoop meowing at me. I let her in with me for my awful chore at hand.

I didn't have to leave for the test site for another 2+ hours, and I'd be back at the apartment, if I needed to be, for a couple hours before David walked into an empty place.

I used huge garbage bags for my clothing and shoes, and hand-carried my boots and hats out to the car, arranging all of it in the Honda's trunk. I took nothing of David's, only my own clothing and toiletries and the few trinkets I'd brought.

I sat at the tiny table alone with Phoebe at my feet. She was meowing and I was crying. I gave her some milk and a couple cans of her sardines. One of us was happier. I had just erased myself from David's apartment.

I double-checked the bathroom. His cologne was right there. I picked it up and smelled its enticing fragrance from the cap. With a twinge of guilt and heap of longing for him, already, I slowly unscrewed the cap and put a drop of his cologne on the inside of each of my wrists. I replaced the cap and bottle as they were.

I picked up my phone and brought up his number. I was in a crying jag as soon as I confirmed, "BLOCK THIS NUMBER?" with a "Yes."

I rinsed-out the sardine cans and dish, and Phoebe's milk bowl.

I picked up Phoebe and, on the way out, locked the door and put my key in the mail slot. I drove to a stacked parking lot near the test site, locked the car, and walked down to the nearest espresso place for a sugarless decaf hazelnut latte and a plain croissant.

We were allotted six hours for the exam but I was finished in four hours and five minutes. I didn't breeze though the test. It just seemed easier than I thought it would be and I was back at the car at five minutes to noon, knowing I'd done very well and blowing off steam by walking around a little.

As soon as I started the car, I hit the radio button. *"David Tyler, KFCG For Country Girls, Everywhere, and especially mine!"* It was a punch to the gut. I guess I deserved it and looked to the sky. "Really, God? Really?"

I headed to the dorm and approached the main desk.

"I remember you! The nurse moving out!"

I saw her name tag, "Yes, Ms. Wahler, I'm aiming at being gone before Friday. If anyone, and I mean *anyone* asks about me, I've already left. Can you do that for me?"

"Sure. Give me your name, again, honey. No need to verify, I remember you."

"M-A-C-I-A-S. Olivia Macias."

"All taken care-of. I'll notify security as well."

Student parking was controlled with an electric pass-gate and I could park behind the building. I knew David would walk in and look. I also knew he wouldn't look in front of the humanities building next door.

The dorm room was minimalist at best. I paid extra for a 1-person room and there was a single bed, small hanging closet, very small lighted desk, and that was it.

Making three trips with a laundry cart I hijacked from our laundry room, I was out of there in short order.

I looked at my watch. David would just be walking into the apartment, and I would be on Interstate 5 in a little while, headed for the junction of Interstate 10 and a reunion with my dad after a quick overnight in Palm Springs.

Tell Me, Phoebe

I was approaching the apartment from the bus stop when I saw and heard Mrs. Lentini calling me over to her.

"David, I saw your lady friend crying and throwing things into her trunk and back seat. I asked her, 'Are you okay, honey?' She said, 'No, not really. I have to go.' Breakups are hard, David. I feel badly for you."

I couldn't respond. I could only rush to my door with Phoebe right behind me. The cat followed me in and I bolted around the apartment. Every sign of her was gone. There wasn't a note on the bed, nightstand, dresser, nor was there a note on the refrigerator.

I dialed her phone. "The subscriber you are trying to reach is not available." I made my way to the overstuffed chair. As soon as I sat, Phoebe hopped into my lap and turned over on her back. I was in shock as I stroked her.

"Up, get up, Phoebe," I said as I stood. I looked under the sink and grabbed the tequila, three-fourths full, and returned to the chair, already in tears. Phoebe curled herself up in my lap.

Meows woke me up in total darkness. My stomach was churning and my head was exploding. My phone displayed "9:23PM." I hurried to the sink, heaving as the stream from both faucet knobs swirled everything that was coming up. I tried to text her. 'Unable to send."

"The love of your life just doesn't disappear," I heard myself mutter, "but mine did." I broke into sobs. When my crying jag got over, I put on some soothing music and opened the door for Phoebe to go home. "Go on. You don't want to see this." As the cat scampered out, I pleaded, "Tell me, Phoebe. Tell me where she's gone."

I don't know when I dozed off.

Deserted and Disheveled

An ambulance brought me here, originally, and it made me feel good my return visit was on my feet, coming in under my own power. I needed answers and I knew they were in here.

I walked into the St. Dominic's elevator and pushed "5." As soon as the doors opened, I spotted Kathleen Wei and called out, "Ms. Wei!" She was the overseer, the RN assigned to mentor Olivia in her final clinical phase. "MS. WEI!!" The nurse stopped and stared at me. Her expression was neither kind or welcoming.

"You're awfully brave to show up, here. The chief nurse thought you'd probably come around. I guess I owe her a cup of coffee."

"Excuse me?? I barely know you and you're being petty with me. Olivia was doing *your* work while you were getting paid for it, and for whatever reason, you're treating me like shit, today?? You've got some nerve, lady."

To twist the knife, she emphasized her sigh and put her hand on her hip. "Mr. Callan, lose the attitude. The nursing care and *strictly* the nursing care that she gave you was at my direction and supervision. Anything else that may have occurred between you and Olivia Macias was <u>not</u>."

She knew or had figured out we were involved. How involved didn't matter. Whether a nurse or nursing student, there were consequences, none of them pleasant, for involvement with a patient.

"You need to speak to Janice. In fact, you have a very *compelling* reason to talk to her. Janice put it out to the whole staff that she wanted to be notified if you were seen on the premises."

This was stupid and I was tired of it, "Be on the lookout, huh?" Wei ignored it.

"I'm going to call her from that nurse's station," she said, pointing ten feet from where we stood. "You should speak with her." The Sino-American nurse picked up a phone at the nurse's station and, with a grim expression and rolling eyes said, "I'm paging her."

The phone rang immediately

"Kathleen Wei, 5 North. …Guess who is standing in front of me? Mr. David Callan." She covered the phone mouthpiece with one hand and said, "Mr. Callan, do you have time to see Janice right now? Again, I'm going to tell you it's in your best interest to do so."

"Absolutely. Olivia's missing and I've got to find her. I need help and I came here to get it."

That drew an odd look from Wei.

"Yes, he said he can meet, now. We're on our way down."

We used the stairwell to the 4th floor and turned down a non-descript hallway full of closed doors. One of them had a room number and an engraved plastic plate that read "Chief Nurse." Kathleen Wei knocked twice, loudly, and we heard Janice say 'Come in.'

There wasn't a smile on Chief Nurse Janice Delacroix's face awaiting me. Anything but. It was an acidic scowl hardened by time that greeted me and roughed-up by her countenance.

"I would invite you to sit down but you're not going to be here very long, so don't bother, Mr. Callan," Delacroix snapped.

"Olivia vanished. She's missing, underground…I dunno, just gone. I came here to for help. Instead, you and Mrs. Wei are throwing spiked attitude at me." I turned to face Wei, "And you, Kathleen, just told _me_ 'Lose the attitude?' What's your deal!"

Wei was fuming but she deferred replying in her boss' presence. The Chief Nurse gave her a slight nod, as if giving her permission.

"My 'deal' as you call it is your shenanigans with a student nurse. You jeopardized her career as an RN, caused us to question whether she should become licensed in our profession. If an RN attaches emotions to

this job, he or she is done. We nip it in the bud if and
when we see it in students. Didn't seem to faze you, Mr.
Callan. You had nothing to lose."

Then Janice Delacroix took over, "Olivia almost lost it
all because we were onto you and her, Mr. Callan. We
knew that she was involved with you. Our paperwork
was in-process to call a formal fitness inquiry that may
have ended with the possibility that she *would not*
become a registered nurse for quite some time, *if ever.*
But she left of her own volition with no urging from the
St Dominic's side, maybe at your urging perhaps?
Because there was no request or action at all from
human resources *or* me pressuring her to go. Not yet,
anyway."

I'd had enough tirade and shot back, "This is
bullshit. She's disappeared and I'm looking for her!"

"Hear me out!"

"By strictest definition, Olivia completed her final
clinical and we were <u>forced</u> to sign-off on her completion
of clinicals as 'Successfully Completed.' Forced, Mr.
Callan, because she got away with a professional
indiscretion that costs good nurses their careers for such
an indiscretion. In our business Mr. Callan? Bad
judgment kills people. So if your feelings are hurt that
Mrs. Wei and I aren't all starry-eyed and nice to you
today, grow the hell up!"

I was stunned, numb, back on my heels. My worst
foster parents never ripped me apart like that. No one
had.

Janice opened the top, right hand-drawer on her
desk and began shuffling things around.

"Even I have a conscience, though." She was holding
up a blue envelope she had fished from the drawer.

"I'm going to give this to you despite the fact that my
first instinct was to throw it in the trash when it was
turned-in to me. She was a good kid with a good heart
and a promising future, Mr. Callan, and you put all of
that at risk at no cost or consequence to yourself."

She paused, the blue envelope moving back and forth as the Chief Nurse moved her hand.

"This was in Olivia's locker and it's addressed to you."

It was a baby blue envelope the size of a greeting card, addressed, "David." There was a sticky note on the envelope:

"*Janice, this is for David Callan. I'm sure he'll come flying in here wanting to see you. Thanks for all you've done for me, including this. You've never let me or anybody down.... Olivia*"

I know Janice could see my hand trembling and there was no way in the world I was going to open this in front of these two women. I needed to find my voice and now, plea to have not wasted my time.

"She's missing and I'm not asking, I'm pleading, I'm begging you, do you know where she is?"

If the temperature in the room had dropped 50°, it couldn't have been any colder than Janice's voice. It was quiet and viciously venomous.

"If I did, I wouldn't tell you. It's a personnel matter I won't compromise because of the legalities. If you want my personal opinion, you have to ask for it."

I snarled, "Okay Janice, <u>now</u> who's playing games. GIVE me your personal opinion. I can't wait."

Janice reached up and undid the bobby pins holding her 'old school' nursing hat to her hair. She removed the hat slowly and it made a noise as she set it on the desk because the cloth was permeated with so much starch it was brittle.

"If she really cared about you, wouldn't you *know* where she is? The envelope I gave you is sealed but I don't think whatever's in there is going to help you in the *least*. She used the term that you'd probably come 'flying in' here. To me, the smart money says she figured you out, wrote you a 'Dear John letter,' and she's gone. You've probably destroyed a nice young lady's promising career if not destroying her personally as well."

"I couldn't have been more wrong about you, Janice. I thought you might help me, care enough about Olivia to give a crap about her as a human being. I misjudged you, mistook you for having compassion."

"We're done here. You can see yourself out or I can have security help you find your way. Get out of my office, Mis-ter Callan."

I took the stairs one floor down and found a lounge for visitors. It was empty. I sat in the corner and muted the TV just above my head. I peeled away the sticky note, and carefully opened the envelope and pulled out the card.

Spring wildflowers. I wasn't sure I might survive what it said because finding every trace of her gone from the apartment almost did me in.

Janice may have nailed it and that hurt as much as it sickened me. There was only one way to know. In her beautiful hand, she wrote:

David,
Right now, this is for the best and it's not for good.
Hold onto hope because our trails will cross, cowboy.
I'm convinced that you know I love you, and I will love
you into those tomorrows you mentioned in the note
with my daisies. You are my heart. My everything.
– Olivia

My hand clutching the card went to my thigh and I laid my head back with the crown of my hair resting on the wall. The air handler in the room made my face cold from evaporating my tears. My head was running nonstop with every kind of thought crashing in. I killed her career, or nearly, and she bolted to keep me from ruining everything she'd dreamt of since she was 12 years old. Her life was shit because of me.

While I was still sitting there, I did an internet search on my phone for 'RN License Exam' and eventually got to the link I was looking for: "National RN Licensure Exam Results." I put her last name in the 'Search' window.

Macias, O.M.C.

Status: Passed

*Score: 98.9%**

**Top 1% Among Test Group*

Desert Heat

Angel of the Desert brought me on-board under their "Top Graduate Employment Contingency." I'd go to work as and RN and, when qualified, would start with the next class of candidates for the orthopedics nurse practitioner certification. I needed 2,200 full-time hours of paid RN experience. As far as I knew, it was one of the few programs of its kind and its graduates were rated much higher than nurses practitioners from the other programs.

My dad was looking at property in the Phoenix Metro area, mindful of my distance to work and commute time.

He found a lease/purchase option and I moved into a beautiful condo in a gated country club community. The lease/purchase option allowed me to move in immediately. I was settled in just a couple days after three rooms of rental furniture arrived. Dad exercised the purchase option and did so in my name. Outright purchase paperwork processing would have delayed my move.

The condo was secure, prestigious, luxurious and almost 1,800 square feet.

According to my pre-hire physical, I was in excellent health and my 'baby bump' suggested I was on track to bring a little boy into the world in late December or early January.

My dad didn't waste any time addressing the 500-pound gorilla in the room and he lit into me. He was frustrated, pacing and gesturing as he spoke, with tantrum indicators pegging in the red. I'd only witnessed this level of anger when his crew had deserved a big ass-chewing and got way more than they wanted.

It was loud and the veins on his forehead were bulging out, "You asked me to help you, but you *knew* that David is here, that he's on the radio *every damn day*. Olivia, what the *hell* kind of a woman gets pregnant and won't even tell the father of the baby while she's *claiming* she's *madly* in love with him? And the father is *right* down the _road,_ working nearby? It's crazy, I mean it's nuts, Olivia. That's not you, not the daughter I raised! Those aren't your values!"

I couldn't stop the tears. In fact they were coming faster and I was beginning to sob. He was making his point, scoring lots of hits. Daddy grabbed a box of tissues off an occasional table.

"Here!" and the box hit the table in front of me hard enough to bounce.

I think it was the first time I ever saw him glare angrily at me. That realization jolted me enough to return my composure and fortify me to take him on for the first time in my life.

"I will _tell_ you who, what kind of woman does that, Daddy!! A woman who's *so in love* that she's willing to put herself _second_ to David getting the biggest break of his life, one that will set him up for a giant career. A once-in-a-lifetime shot! The daughter you raised!? That's ME! And I couldn't and _wouldn't_ walk in and fuck that up for him!!"

He was boiling hot, "_Watch your language_! I'm still your father!"

I got madder but eased-off on my tone.

"Let's say it's Mama pregnant with _me_! Crazy hormones making her think irrationally sometimes, and she shows up out on the rodeo circuit and tugs at you to come home and take care of a child, your child, to do your fatherly responsibilities. But here _you_ are in your first and biggest earnings year of your rodeo career, the most fame, the most glory. You've got a pregnant woman yanking on your sleeve, taking your eye off the prize, saying, 'Hey, look at _me_! Hey, help _me_!!' Would my mom...would Ofelia do that to you? _AW HELL NO!_" and I stomped off to my bedroom and slammed the door.

A few minutes later, I broke down so completely that I almost didn't hear my dad knocking gently the door.

"Olivia?"

I opened it and he threw his arms around me and pulled me to him. I sobbed against my father's chest, trying to...willing myself to stop crying.

As soon as I could speak I told him, "I wasn't going to keep our child from him, forever. You didn't raise a cold-hearted bitch and I'm sorry to use that word Daddy but there's not another one that fits."

"Sit on the bed with me, honey. Olivia, do you love him enough to marry him if he asks you to do so?

"Yes, Daddy, I do."

"Olivia, I'm going to ask you a different version of the same question. If you were _not_ pregnant, are you 99% sure he would continue the relationship and love you enough to want to put a ring on your finger, to propose?"

"I'd bet my life on it. In a heartbeat."

"Just a minute," and he disappeared down the hall only to return with a folder in his hand. "I'm going to show you and tell you something that's going to hurt. You need to know this and I'll help you through it. He is seeing someone and she is mighty good looking. I had a private detective get photos of them together but you don't have to look at them."

"I'M NOT GOING TO LOOK AT THEM! Either put that folder BACK you're your briefcase or throw it in the fireplace and turn on the gas!"

Daddy dropped the folder onto the floor. "I'm sorry," he said, in a conciliatory tone.

"Daddy, do you know what his being with someone should tell you? Lots of things! That he's not a loser, that he's desirable... And do you really know if he gives a crap about her no matter _how_ heavy or serious it looks on the surface? You ever heard of a hurt guy being on the rebound? _And,_ he's in media and women _throw_ themselves at media guys all the time! It's an occupational hazard."

I had to hand it to him. He was paying attention and his anger had left.

I was on a roll, now. "If you're a girlfriend or wife of on-air talent and you *don't* accept that down to the very level of your soul? You will <u>never</u> trust him and your relationship won't be worth shit!"

I caught a breath and gestured, extending my arms with both palms skyward.

"No, I might not be happy if she's a bed warmer, but he's *not dead.* My David's going to be a father and he's going to know it. He's going to have a say in our child's life.'"

My dad took my hand and was rubbing the back of it, "I have to accept this and *you do, too,* Daddy: I AM THE ONE who split. I ran. I was sitting on his porch talking to his landlady's cat, saying '*Girls don't do that; girls don't just run off*' and that's <u>exactly</u> what I freaking did to him. I ran off carrying his child. I could be a single mom but I could never forgive myself or fix David's professional life if I wrecked it."

"So the man will get to know he's a father, see his child, Olivia? Because I'm a failure as a father if my own flesh and blood handles this any other way."

"We're going to have that 'come-to-Jesus talk.' He's going to meet me and see that I'm carrying his child. I can make all the decisions I want in the world but he has to decide. I can't make his decisions for him. He is his own man, just like you, a different wrapper on the outside maybe, but just as resolute and honorable as you are Daddy."

"I don't know him and can't possibly judge him. You're my concern, my *only* concern here, here and now and always, Olivia. I'll never be okay seeing you in pain."

"I want and need you on my side. You've never faltered or failed at that."

I felt a smile rising and spreading. "Look at you, you're here now!" I leaned my head against him. My heartbeat was returning to normal.

I looked up to him, "You always told me: '*Family gets through things and gets things through.*' We are getting through this and we *will* get things through. The timing couldn't have been worse for each of us. Regardless, I have David's and my child inside of me; they're my family. David gets to choose whether he's a willing participant or not, Daddy."

We were at peace.

With his mission complete, my dad flew back to New Mexico before the Memorial Day weekend.

I worked through the end of the year. In my last trimester, my folks knew I couldn't travel so they came to the condo and spent Christmas with me. Christmas was very quiet with the gifting a hundred percent about the arrival of the baby. I was going to give birth at any minute and it felt like it.

Tyler David Macias Callan was born at 2:58am on December the 28th, just one day after David's birthday. I didn't need postpartum depression. The proximity of their two birthdays was enough. I struggled and fought to get myself in shape to go back to work as soon as I could, hiring daycare for my son.

I prayed, daily. Went to Mass, weekly.

Commencement

I called USF.

"School of Nursing, this is Dawn. How may I direct your call."

"I'd need information about your graduation ceremony."

"I think I can help you, sir. It's 2pm on March 27th and each graduate gets 8 tickets for admission. The venue isn't large so admission is by ticket, only."

"Thanks for your help."

"Happy to help, goodbye."

My next call was to the station. I begged for and got my boss to make me a press pass that was a cinch for getting into Olivia's graduation.

When the day came, I was handed a program and walked in. I paused to scan through the program and spotted her name.

"With regret, our valedictorian, Olivia Macias could not be here. Our salutatorian, Stan Greene will address you."

I crushed the program in my hand and dropped it on the floor. I left and boarded a bus toward little joint on Clement Street. I don't remember getting home.

The QMEG Visit

One of the station's cars picked me up from the airport on the Arrivals curb. I greeted the driver and threw my overnighter on the back seat. As soon as I got buckled up, I heard the station I.D.: *"Kountry For Country Girls. We've got your girl <u>and</u> your music, 24/7. KFCG, PHOENIX-TEMPE-SCOTTSDALE."*

I was in the General Manager's office. Sandy Tuttle had Norman on the speakerphone.

"We're really impressed with you David. Norman doesn't usually brag on people. He tells it like it is and I've known him for over 20 years. We think we know what you can bring to the table but what do *you* think you can bring to the table?"

"Listeners, Mr. Tuttle. I'll make your listeners cringe at the thought of changing stations at our breaks."

"That's strong, David. How?"

'Twists' I'll hook listeners with strange news stories, ones with an angle, a twist. I'll key-in on traffic's reports from the traffic reporter. For example, when stations report someone dead on the commute, you hear alternate routes and backups and delays. I'll add the human element, like, *"Hey, my KFCG family. Nobody got up and planned to get killed on their commute, today. Be safe, watch out, cuz we have some great things ahead for you. And now the headlines...."*

"Jesus, David. I've never heard that empathy angle."

"You won't. It's been my pet peeve as a listener for years. People, listeners are getting killed and we exclude that human element, negating loss of a human life. Not on my shift. I can bring, and *keep*, listeners."

Tuttle said, "Norman, he's certainly smooth with the right answers."

Norman replied immediately. "One of kind and he just proved I wasn't kidding, Sandy. People are going to clamor to get David's take on their news from KFCG."

The GM turned back to me. "What's it going to take to have you here?"

"How do you mean that, sir?"

"What do you think you're moving costs are going to be, David?"

"All I need is a rental truck, some per diem and gas money."

"I'll tell you what: if you do that, I will give you 3 grand to get yourself established in an apartment right away."

The station reeked of money because they were making it hand over fist. They were one of the most profitable in the Q-MEG group and certainly the media company's country-western flagship. Instead of a folding chair and table to prepare my newscasts I had a full-on cubicle, semi- enclosed with tinted glass, a computer and dedicated printer, my own telephone and private line, and even police scanners.

All that was missing was Olivia. She vanished. I drank my way through it. Toyed with driving to Abiquiu but figured I'd get greeted by guns.

I had to let go. I had screwed up her life and she had to bail to try and resurrect what was left of it. It would have hurt less if I cut off all of my fingers to let go of her. She disappeared before she even saw the love poem I wrote to her.

I found it when I unpacked and sat on the bed to read it. Tears crawled slowly down my cheek as I vividly recalled her tenderness. Her love. Her touch.

"For My Olivia, Strings of Kites"

Around me, you're sparkles and aglow.
I'm alive'r by your woman-ness,
healed and strengthened by your nurse care,
bordering trouble with your profession
should our love collide with it.

Take my hand to common ground
to that in-between niche where
deepest friendships flourish and
lovers may have stolen away
to languish in their first kiss;
arriving, where we can play, exhilarated....

Laughing, watching tangling strings of kites,
kites that bob and bump
in their wind dance, overhead;
a hand to warm, sunset to watch,
anticipating swirls and circles
just before a poem on the sand, and then
to see reflections in each other's eyes
of another day to play.

We can. There's promise.
Trust enough to take my hand and feel,
know by your soul informing you
nothing's been surrendered,
that it's safe and healthy
as my own soul's wings wish to soar,
thirsting for a dance on earthly legs,
my tattletale soul whispering
there's but one partner
my soul will embrace and she is you.
Come to me.
Come to me and dance, for,
I sense you are my now
and my tomorrows.

Please come.... David

Extra Effort

I had to try. I located a couple phone listings for "Macias" in the Abiquiu area. One thing's for sure, they don't want, like or trust anyone poking around in that part of New Mexico. If the intrusive acts are by phone, they're easier to quell and there aren't any bodies to bury.

I called commercial ranches until I struck gold or thought so. A 'Roberto Macias' was the General Foreman of a multimillion-dollar cattle ranch named *Abiquiu Toro de Oro Inc.*—translated, Abiquiu Golden Bull. Its most profitable sideline business was selling sperm from proven championship rodeo bulls and to inseminate cows for beef-cattle ranchers.

The call didn't go as I expected.

'Toro de Oro, may I help you?"

"I'm from an Arizona radio station, trying to reach Mr. Macias, please."

"From Arizona, you said?"

"Yes, David Tyler. I work for KFCG, the #1 country-western radio station in the state."

"And you want to speak to Mr. Macias, huh?"

"Yes."

"About?

"I'm not at liberty to say. That's for my conversation with him."

"Give me your number."

"555-XXX-XXXX."

"Thanks. Here's our policy so's you know. We're like the Boston Red Sox or New York Yankees of the cattle breeding industry."

The unidentified ranch employee continued, "If you call those baseball teams and ask for the GM? We have the same answer they do: Go fuck yourself, mister. You don't just call-in and get put through. And if you are who you say you are, a news man, you ought to know that."

"Have a good day and have a Toro de Oro steak for dinner," and the line went dead.

I was sick of dead ends:

USF Records: sealed

USF Student Clubs & Activities: nothing.

Nursing registries: nothing.

Vital statistics: nothing

Obituaries: nothing.

Wedding announcements: nothing.

Could I spend thousands of dollars on a private investigator? I could. Would I? With a guaranteed live-locate and guarantee to speak to or meet with her? Yes. Would that be likely to produce results? No.

I needed her, had to find her but was damned if I was going to get soaked by hucksters in the process.

I looked out the window at the tallest peak I could see....

"Olivia: My prayer is simple. I pray you're okay. I pray you know I love you. I pray that you're safe and healthy and that one day, someday, you'll forgive me for the damage I did. Be my answered prayer, Olivia. My heart is breaking again and again."

Drinking while depressed is underrated.

New Guy Fitting-In

The morning air talent was so highly paid they had superstar attitudes and generally distanced themselves from everyone because they were better than everyone. They'd proven it by building giant followings in the increasingly larger markets in which they worked. It sounds harsh. But KFCG's guys were some of the highest paid people in the radio industry because they were worth it and this was one of the hottest country markets in the country. These people were at the absolute best in their game. To get your head around it, I was the bat boy on a baseball team full of future Hall of Famers who are courteous at best and I'm lucky to get a 'Hello' when I'm standing next to one at the sink in the men's room.

They called their gig 'The Backwoods Brothers' and on their way up the ladder of fame and fortune in other markets, their 'M.O." was to always bring in a local woman, usually being their 'traffic girl' to bounce their schtick off-of and using her to transition into the news and long commercial breaks paying for all of it.

Stephanie was the traffic reporter in-place and perfect for the talent each making well into six figures on the morning drive shift from 5:00 to 9:00 a.m. According to ratings numbers, Stephanie had been measurably expanding the station's ladies' listenership market because she was insanely funny at the razor's edge of the censors' nerves as well as the legal department's. She got away with it because she never crossed the line. Ever.

Stephanie was on her way to a six figures gig as a rock 'n roll jock. Everyone knew it and feared the day she got the chance, an offer and enough money to take the risk of epic fail or instant stardom.

Even her jet-black hair that looked like a weed-eater had gotten hold of it fit her persona. She was cute as hell and knew I thought so. She flirted with me whenever she walked by, exaggerating batting her mascara-caked eyelashes at me and giving her butt an accentuated wiggle. She was nutzoid enough to goose me as we passed in the hall one day, cackling after she did.

I was in my condo-cubie one morning and she rolled up and said, "Hey, new guy! Can I bother you?"

Two could play this.

"Again?"

She got it and laughed immediately. I thought it was probably work-related but Stephanie had a rep that kept the whole building on its collective toes.

"I don't know what your private life deal is, David, but I know you're new *here.* If you're interested in meeting someone, I have a girlfriend that's finally getting her head straight enough after coming out of an abusive relationship. I think she's ready to go on a date. And you seem to have enough wuss in you to be harmless to her but cute enough for her to look at. Interested? And if you say no, then that guy who said you liked boys will win our bet."

"First, you win the bet. I like women. Interested in meeting a girl outside of work? Yes. A girl you recommend? Scarier, but yes. But not a date, something casual like happy hour or whatever, some evening. I'm awkward on dates. Not first ones, all of 'em."

"Yeah, I think I could put that together. I think you'd like her, David. She's brainy. A high school teacher who teaches French to my 17-year-old sister at the Catholic high school in Scottsdale. My little sister dragged me to a school thing and introduced me to her and we liked each other instantly. So we hang out, do girl things. Her name's Vanessa."

"I might like that, yeah." The ink was barely wet on my new business cards and I grabbed one from the holder and flipped it over to write down my phone number. "Here you go. By the way, Stephanie? I appreciate it. I was thinking I was going to have to start doing paint by numbers to kill the boredom."

"I had you for being an ogler at the gym. But I'll give Vanessa a call."

Stephanie got off and out of work about the same time I did every day. I worked Monday to Friday with weekends off and, because I started so early, I could be walking into my apartment by 2:00 in the afternoon. My phone was ringing as soon as I walked in.

"Hey, it's Stephanie."

"Hi."

"I called Vanessa, that French teacher I told you about? I lied and told her you were hot. How about you meet us for happy hour out by her school?"

"Sure, when?"

"Um...like 4:30, unless you can't leave your paint-by numbers or are in your unitard getting ready to ogle at the gym, Dave," and she roared.

"Touché."

Half of me thought 'What's wrong with this girl, Vanessa?' because it seemed like it was quite a hurry-up but the other half of me was grateful that I had something to do. I agreed. Going out to be with someone or staying home with no one. Easy call.

"It's called 'The 5 Sisters Cantina,' corner of Lincoln Drive and Leaning Tree Lane."

"Cool, I'll see you then. I'll wear my green unitard."

"Because you *are* a tard."

"I like attention and I'll get it. One guy sitting with two hotties at happy hour. See ya."

I didn't need directions. I'd been listening intently to Steph's traffic and looking at road maps learning the streets for a living. And quite a living it was.

I had a big 1-bedroom apartment with a view of the mountains and a covered motorcycle parking place for my baby; a thousand CCs, white with custom painted pinstriping and customized with chrome to the tune of $9,000. It was so shiny that blind people shaded their eyes thinking it was the second coming. Not nice or 'PC.' 'Never say that aloud, David.'

Duality of Hypocrisy

Stephanie's hair was kind of dark reddish. Auburn, I guess, except for the blondish tips of the parts sticking up and pointing everywhere. It couldn't have been more different than Vanessa's hair which was long and honey blonde with cascading curls.

She had an angel face and a slender, very tan body. I guess I was surprised she taught French but didn't have a French accent. I was comfortable around both of them and we just had drinks and small talk getting to know each other a little bit. Vanessa would glance over and shoot me a smile and I'd return it. She was catching a lot of attention from guys all over the bar.

After our third margarita, and they were strong, Stephanie blurted out, "Raise your hand if you own a blender!" and both of the girls raised a hand. I didn't raise my hand.

Stephanie looked at me, "Seriously? You *don't* have a blender!? How the hell do you make a margarita without a blender?"

I told her.

"We don't drink margaritas in San Francisco cuz it's too fucking cold. We do warm things," and the girls laughed, "like drink Irish coffee to keep from shivering."

"That's it, Vanessa. You stop and get a blender and I'll pop for some tequila and margarita mix. We'll converge on *Studley Dudley's* place bearing housewarming gifts. Okay with you, *Studley Dudley*? Cuz we're coming, anyway. What's your address!?"

As I was writing the address, I looked up and flirted with Vanessa, "You'll have to excuse my place. I do paint by numbers and I have a few originals drying. It may smell a little weird," and Stephanie, who had put an entire lime wedge into her mouth, spit it at me, hitting my chest, faking like she nearly choked on it.

I was a little tipsy but, hell, it was Friday and none of us had to work tomorrow.

"Nessa?" Stephanie said, "if *Van Gone*, here, has wet paintings at the crash pad? We're tying him up and painting his entire body." While Vanessa was giggling I was trying to believe that Stephanie was kidding.

I didn't have to straighten up, the apartment looked fine. I knew the girls would snoop through the place so I did tighten-up the bed covers and wipe down the kitchen counter even though they were fine the way they were. I made sure the toilet seats were down, no hair in the sink.

My doorbell rang and I opened the door to see Stephanie holding two grocery bags. Vanessa was behind with a big box. Stephanie pushed her way in saying "Wow! this is really, really nice!"

Vanessa quietly said, 'Hi' and made eyes at me as she headed toward the kitchen right behind Stephanie.

I shut the door and joined them in the kitchen as Vanessa was raiding the freezer for ice cubes.

It was the first time I ever had a refrigerator with an ice maker and it was furnished by the apartment building. So was the washer and dryer. It would make Mrs. Lentini, my S.F. landlord faint. Hell, it even had a built-in vac system. Plug the hose into wall outlets and sweep!

Unexpectedly, Stephanie was looking around and turned to Vanessa and said "I'm sorry, Jesus God, I'm sorry. I didn't know he was gay!"

I protested, "Where did <u>that</u> come from?"

"Look at your apartment, David. Perfect art, perfect furniture, perfect every little thing right down to scented candles. I mean, come on, only gay dudes do that. You can 'out' with us," and Stephanie was trying to see if she'd made me squirm. I thought I caught Vanessa shooting me a look that this was typical Stephanie, no worries.

"That's a bad assumption, Stephanie. Truth is, I moved here with exactly nothing and went to those places that will furnish an entire apartment. I didn't even get to pick out the colors of stuff. The only thing they let me pick out was the artwork on the walls. Everything here is rented," and the girls just cracked up because I must have sounded like I was pleading and whining.

"Wow that really got your goat, didn't it," teased Stephanie.

"Not really, it just seemed like a long leap from having a nice place to being gay."

"Okay, Vanessa, he's fair game. Jump his bones or just make him miserable taking you out to expensive dinners, or both." and that made both Vanessa and I blush.

Vanessa drank so much she told me she needed a cab and I called one for her. Stephanie was still going strong and not even thinking about going home, at least she wasn't making any kind of move to do so.

I walked Vanessa outside toward a huge fountain in the middle of the lot where the cab would probably arrive. "It was nice to meet you Vanessa despite that crazy thing I work with!"

"I'm used to her. She's fun and admit I probably live a little bit vicariously through her. We're very different."

"Noticeably and thank God, 'Nessa. Oh, sorry. *Van*essa. It's the tequila."

"You're fine. I'm comfortable with you calling me that," and it was she who gave me a little kiss that brushed my lips and then one on each cheek before climbing into the cab.

I shut the door, smiled and said, "Bye."

I got back to the apartment and Stephanie was out like a light. Passed out in the chair. I folded-out the couch which had bedding already in it and lifted Stephanie onto the blanket, putting a pillow under her head and shutting off the light.

The next thing I knew Stephanie was naked in my bed and all over me. She was hot and I was willing and it was incredible. *Housewarming*, my ass. This was a barn burner.

She curled up next to me for a while and stayed longer than I thought she would. I did have enough food to make her a small cheese omelet for breakfast before she gave me a sister kiss and said, "Don't expect that ever again. I'm kind of impulsive and I was very hornym" and she reached down between my legs to give me a little tweak.

"You're cute and I like you but I've got to work with you, David."

I no sooner got rid of Stephanie, thanking her for the party and blender, when my phone rang. There was no caller-ID on the land line. I hoped it was Olivia despite what had just happened with Stephanie.

"Hey, sunshine! Good morning, David." Sounded like Vanessa and I was right.

"Hi there."

"It's Nessa. I have to come get my car this morning."

"Oh, crap, I completely forgot you left it here. I'll tell you what, how about if I pick you up for lunch and, after lunch, I'll bring you back and you can get your car?"

"Really?"

I was giving her an out, "Sure, unless you don't want to see me. I understand."

"I want to see you."

"Hold on, let me get a pen," and I scrambled to the junk drawer in the kitchen and picked up the wall phone, ready to write on my hand.

"I live close to the school and to The Five Sisters Cantina. So, if you can remember how to get there, my address is 13119 Cholla Blossom Ln. It's a tiny little house and you won't miss it because it's bright yellow."

I repeated the address, "Noon or 2:00 or what's good for you as far as lunch?"

"Later is probably better. My stomach's been a little cantankerous this morning."

"Mine, too. I'll be there 2 on the button and of course you get to pick where we're going to eat cuz I know absolutely nothing about anywhere."

I don't know how to say this but Vanessa's house was nothing but cute, small and attractively painted, with a little desert garden that was well tended.

As I pulled up on the bike, her door opened and she said "Wow. A motorcycle. Okay."

"Yeah, I stopped and got a helmet for you on the way even though there's no helmet law here. Are you okay with the bike? I'm sorry I didn't mention it. I'll pay for a cab."

"No, I'm fine, it's fine."

She was in jeans and a polka dot halter that reminded me of Minnie Mouse: red background white polka dots and it looked sizzling hot on her. She had her pulled back hair and tied with a white ribbon. I hadn't done badly in guessing her helmet size. It was a little too large which was always better than a little too tight and the lunch place wasn't far.

She got on the bike, got her feet on the pegs, and wrapped her arms around me. She smelled really nice.

I hit the starter and, over the engine noise, turned and said, "Where to?"

She said "Let's do 5 Sisters, they have great food."

"Hair of the dog, Vanessa?" I teased. I felt her lean forward, close to my ear, "Tequila cooties? No way, David."

She wasn't kidding, it was about 5 blocks to the Cantina. I chose the bar for seating because it was quieter, a better place to talk. There was a college football game on but I kept my attention on Vanessa, sneaking peeks at the game. We ordered a pitcher of iced tea.

Vanessa took a long sip, toying with her straw afterwards.

"Stephanie called me this morning and I know she stayed all night. She said she jumped you in your sleep and had her way with you."

It hit like a sucker-punch.

I looked Vanessa dead in her gorgeous eyes, "I wasn't as squeamish from the margaritas as I was knowing I had to tell you, Vanessa. I was pissed. We work together and she wanted me to meet you. Then she jumps my bones? I have to see her every day and, as they say, I don't 'dip my pen in company ink.'"

Vanessa chuckled, "I've never heard that expression. Look, she's as wild as she looks and, no offense, I'm sure it didn't mean much to her, David."

"And she said as much. She better live up to it."

"David? It doesn't affect me and you...that is, if you want to see me again. She's impulsive as hell and you got ambushed."

She was forgiving me? I was getting a pass? Un-real.

"I'm sorry if I stammer. This is awkward. Yes, I'd absolutely like to see you again, but like this. No Stephanie," and Vanessa reacted much more outwardly than I expected. She put the palm of her hand behind my head, drew me close to her and said, "The normal-acting Stephanie you never get to see told me everything she knew about you. I was the instigator. I asked her if she'd introduce us. I was glad. Still am," and Nessa kissed me for the first time.

Her kiss was warm and delicious and it was obvious we were connecting on this first kiss. I knew I was flushed.

My little taco plate arrived. The server set down her huevos rancheros for which The 5 Sisters was famous. It was on the menu all day even though it was a messy egg dish.

"Stephanie told me that you had a rough break up and had just been focusing on work for about the last 6 months."

Vanessa replied, "That's accurate. I'm not...haven't been looking for anyone or anything, David. Steph said the yack around your office is that you were in love with someone who just POOF! Disappeared."

"She did. I walk into walls in the middle of the night thinking about her, Vanessa. You need to know that."

"My relationship was violent, like bloody beatings violent, David, and you need to know that."

"Then how 'bout we hang out and see if we can define some comfort zones?"

"I like that. The here-and-now feels awfully good, David. Besides, I'm already into you for a motorcycle helmet!" and she snickered.

That made me grin, "Vanessa, I don't even have a friend here, yet, and yes: you *are* already into me for a motorcycle helmet. I'd say that's a committed relationship, committed to a safe start, wouldn't you?"

When she grinned and grabbed my hand, the pressure was off, all of it.

"Well, David, maybe committed to ride with you again but beyond that I'm not so sure. That's your play," and she turned on the hot sexy smile at me.

Goddamn, she was a livin' doll and it wasn't like I hadn't noticed yesterday but today? All of her attention on me? And I'm sober? I was feeling like I wanted this to go horizontal. I couldn't wallow in constant misery.

"Look I don't mean to rush you, Vanessa, but I'm doing something tomorrow and wonder if you want to tag along?"

"I'm not doing anything—what's doing?"

"I was watching the TV movie the other night at 10:30 and saw a bunch of commercials for this place called 'Miracle Rides,' a used car place that says if it's a decent car it's a miracle. So, I think I'm going to go get myself a miracle ride so I don't have to rely on the motorcycle all the time. You feel like going car shopping with me?"

She took a sip of her tea and smiled.

"Well, that's an interesting first date."

"I thought this was our first date?"

"No, you were just giving a girl a ride, remember?"

"Well, I've got the lunch tab so that makes it a date."

She held out her hand and I shook it and said "Deal!"

When we got back to the apartment, the helmets were coming off and she said, "David, I've got to run up and use your bathroom. I'm sorry. Must be all the iced tea."

I hope she was impressed that my apartment was completely clean and free from any visible damage from last night, including new bed linens. She came out of the bathroom and grinned at me.

"In case you're interested? I didn't think you were gay when I saw your apartment, David, I just thought you were a neat-nick."

"Well, I'm a little of that. My place in San Francisco was smaller than your little house so there wasn't room for me to be messy or cluttery. In fact, with all this space, we could make 5 dates out of all the shopping I have to do. The rental thing is not cheap and month to month."

I gestured around the apartment, "It's not furniture I like or want to keep. I'd rather own stuff in colors and styles I like."

Vanessa got right up in my grill and looked me in my eyes and she said, "Well I'm not month to month. I'm day to day and I'm not cheap, either," and she gave me a little kiss that turned into a nicer and more promising kiss.

"Vanessa, something tells me I wouldn't mind the upkeep with you."

"You don't have to ask this girl twice if she wants to go out and spend lots and lots of your money on furnishing your place."

"First things first Vanessa. I need a truck so I can keep you dry when we go somewhere."

"I have a car and besides, this is the desert; by definition, no rain, David."

"How about I need something to drive that's got air conditioning and won't crush that beautiful hair of yours underneath a helmet."

She conceded and smiled, "Okay, works for me," and we shook again.

"I've got to get going. I have to do stuff for school, teacher-y things like grade papers and all that kind of jazz."

"You know what's funny Vanessa? You teach French and I guess I expected to hear an accent. More impressive? You didn't say one thing in French since we've met. I love that and love that I noticed."

She was going to tease me. I could tell from her devilishly sexy grin.

"David? If I taught welding, would you expect that I would weld something for you on our first date?"

"You just served an ace, Vanessa." It was sassy enough and funny enough to make me like her all the more. "All right then I'm going to grovel, beg and ask you, Vanessa. Now that we know each other a little better, I think it will be sexy. Will you *please* say something to me in French?"

Her eyes twinkled. I don't know exactly what she said but it *was* sexy and she knew I thought it was seductive or sexy. I momentarily wondered if she would even tell me what it meant.

"Okay Nessa, I give up. Are you going to translate that for me or you going to keep me guessing?"

"You wanted 'sexy.' Are your sure you won't blush, because I'm going to whisper it, not say it," and she got close enough that I put my arms around her waist.

She kissed me just under my earlobe and said, "Your football game is on channel 10. I saw you peeking at the game in the Cantina."

Whoa. She punked me.

She started laughing, "You're beet red, David!"

"I'm aroused in a French, you just scored a T.D. kind of way."

"Well, I'm sorry I got you aroused right when I have to go," and she kissed me and was gone.

All I could do was flop down in the chair, grab the remote, turn on the football game and think about her the rest of the day and all night long.

I kicked my shoes off and put my bare feet on the coffee table and tried to concentrate on the game but Vanessa was just too much. Be still my heart. I wanted Olivia. I wanted Vanessa. I loved Olivia. Vanessa was here and was hot. Olivia intimated that we'd reunite and that small thread was the emotional lifeline that got me by, day after day.

Vanessa was a diversion and we agreed to find boundaries. I needed more diversions.

I was going to try another Catholic Church in the area and get some groceries the next day and then call her about car shopping when I got home. That plan changed about 5 minutes after the game was over. My phone rang.

"Hey it's Vanessa. How was your game?"

"It was hard to concentrate, but it was good, I guess."

"What about this David: After we do your shopping thing tomorrow for a car? Since I left you in a bad way? How 'bout you let me cook for you?"

"Funny you should say that because I was just reminding myself I need groceries tomorrow."

"No, I mean here. Let me cook in my little house for you!"

"I'd love that."

"Tell me five things you will absolutely not eat, David."

"I won't eat Brussel sprouts or Brussel sprouts. Brussel sprouts or Brussel sprouts." She was already laughing.

"That's only four, David. Don't mess with the teacher."

"Oh, and I won't touch Brussels sprouts."

Still laughing she said, "Okay, so you're telling me you will eat liver and onions?"

"Love it."

"Yuck! I hate it and I'm never making it for you. You're telling me you'll eat okra?"

"I love it but I've only had it in gumbo, Vanessa. I love green veggies."

"So, you'll eat lima beans?"

"I make the best ham and lima beans on the planet, Vanessa, in a slow cooker."

"David, anybody ever tell you that you're easy?"

"Only in the kitchen. Wait. Stephanie would tell you that I'm easy but that's really not true. She manhandled me."

And Vanessa laughed and said, "Stephanie would sleep with a fence post if she was lonely and horny enough!"

"Wow thanks. Now I'm a piece of slumber-lumber."

By this time Vanessa was howling, "Oh my God, no, David I'm sorry, really I'm sorry."

"It's okay, Nessa. That stung but I'm not wounded. Be forewarned: If you're going to attack me, I have to be awake and willing and semi-sober."

"I don't need a permission slip or note from a teacher? 'Cuz you know I got that."

"You're a teacher and I'm a willing learner."

"If we get done shopping early enough, David, I want to lay out before dinner."

"Huh?"

"Catch some rays, like chaise lounge lay out, and get a tan."

"If you want to do that, Vanessa, come over here and bring the ingredients for dinner. This place has a trillion-dollar pool that's pretty damn spiffy."

"Are you sure David?"

"No problem at all. It's nice, Vanessa."

"No, David, I mean are you sure you want me to come over there... because I can't take my top off over there without causing a stir and getting arrested. But I can, here."

"What time do you propose I start staring at your voluptuous chest, Vanessa?" and we both laughed.

"I think I caught you peeking at my halter. All will be revealed, tomorrow."

It took me a sec to recover, "You tease."

"David, if we go truck shopping in my car and you find something, you can drive it home or just on over here."

"Now I know why you're a teacher, Vanessa, because you're so smart and organized."

"David, I'm a teacher because most Arizona kids don't know how to speak French fluently or otherwise. And David?"

"And yes, Vanessa?"

"You're going to be topless too so I might just be staring at your chest, too."

Sleeping might have been difficult after that conversation, but I got enough.

It was only the second car lot we browsed around before I found a truck I wanted. It had just had a new engine put in, the paint was in decent shape and the air conditioning was ice cold. The owner was in the Air Force and had just come down on orders for Alaska and couldn't take the truck with him. At least that's the way the story went and I got a good deal. Could I afford a new one? Yep. Didn't need a new one. I needed a ride with some character.

When we pulled up to Vanessa's place she got out of her car and said, "Sure is a lot of blue smoke coming out of that thing. Is it riding rough?" Evil woman. She saw me start to pale and then leaned over and put her hands on her knees laughing.

"I'm kidding! I'm kidding David."

"Don't make me spank you, Vanessa."

"I might like that a lot."

"There's a new bed in the truck right behind us."

"112 degrees in the shade and your truck bed's steel. You get the bottom, David."

"Can we please talk about something else, it's hot enough out here."

"Sure. I've got some iced tea inside."

I began to follow her in and she shot me a look over her shoulder, "Chicken."

I went in and it wasn't much bigger than my San Francisco flat. As small as it was, it looked like she had used a decorator because it was so homey. Her dinette set was the smallest I had ever seen. It was a tiny table with two matching chairs and she had a chianti bottle in the center with a candle sticking up. Her whole place was cooled by a window air conditioner, the first one I had ever experienced that made exactly zero noise.

Vanessa grabbed two big tumblers, set them on the counter and filled them with cubes.

She was putting in the second sugar when she looked over at me and said "I remembered from the bar you take two sugars in your iced tea," and she smiled sexily at me.

"You noticed the channel of the football game I was pretending not to watch, too."

"David, teachers are like moms: we have to have eyes in the back of our heads or all hell breaks loose."

"I'm going to get my suit on," and she disappeared into the tiny bedroom and came out wearing a skimpy bikini.

"Crap, I forgot to tell you to bring something to sun in, like swim trunks."

"Underneath," I said, patting my jeans. "I put on trunks instead of boxers this morning so I'm good."

She picked up our iced tea glasses as I slipped out of my pants right in the kitchen and put my nicely folded Levi's onto one of the two little dinette chairs. She looked me over and smiled. "Nice."

"We don't wear bathing suits very often in San Francisco. I bought this pair in Mexico for cheap." It was Hawaiian floral print and, while it wasn't a form fitting, it was a little tight in all the right places.

Her patio was just big enough to handle a couple chaise lounges separated by a little plastic table and some beautiful potted cactus. The stifling heat had burned off and the day was just simmering down as we lay down on our respective chairs. She said "Turn over," and she grabbed a bottle of lotion, "unless you want to sun your chest, first."

"Front first, please." Nessa rubbed some stuff on my nose so it wouldn't burn and then gently rubbed the lotion all over my chest, arms and legs. God, it felt good, and I wasn't so sure it was just the lotion.

"How long do you want me to bake on this side, Vanessa?"

"Until I say you're done, David."

I laid back and closed my eyes.

"Oh no you don't, mister. What about me?"

I turned my head and opened one eye as she was starting to recline in her own chair reaching behind her to remove her top. She handed me the lotion.

"I thought you needed me for your flip-side."

"I do. But what fun would that be? I want you for my top-side," and she grinned.

"Okay but I'm not responsible for any involuntary physiological responses my body has while I'm doing this."

"That's a 2-way street. In fact," she put her chin on her chest, trying to look down, "my nipples are already reacting and you haven't touched me, yet."

It took all the concentration I had to handle the business of rubbing sunscreen on the naked upper torso of a hot girl who could speak French. I leaned down and kissed her, "That may have been hardest thing I've ever done as far as pure concentration goes."

She shielded her eyes from the sun to look at me, "My feelings would have been hurt if I didn't get at least a little rise out of you," and she closed her eyes and sighed heavily.

I blushed, "This heat may be hell but I know I'm not dead," and I got back in my own chair just 18 inches away, knowing I was now fully aroused and grateful her eyes were closed.

Before too very long she said, "Okay, let's go in." We hadn't exchanged another word while we were out there, just letting the sun exhume whatever toxins it could take from us.

"I want to get dinner started. Would you do me up?" and she held the tiny cups of her bikini top to her breasts and I reached back to get her top done up. I knew she could have done it on her own but I also knew why she asked.

As soon as we went in, out came the ingredients from the refrigerator and I could already tell it was going to be one hell of a spaghetti dinner with all the trimmings and a big salad.

It was delish right down to the wine.

"Only two glasses for you, David."

I looked up, surprised. "You don't need to be weaving in a truck with a temporary, paper tag." She was right again.

I helped with the dishes and she looked over and said "Spumoni?"

"No way, I'm stuffed."

Then we collected ourselves and Vanessa took me by the hand and walked me to my truck. I got in, turned it over and pulled-on the headlights.

Son of a bitch, one of the headlights was out.

She put her arms across my open window, "Don't I get a ride? I thought you bought this to keep me dry and cool?"

I answered with a smile.

She disappeared into her place and was back out in a few minutes with a backpack. I leaned over and opened the passenger door for her, and patted the seat, "All yours!"

Vanessa stepped up, kicking off her shoes as soon as she got inside the door.

"Can I turn on some music, David?"

"Go for it. Except country."

"You work country."

"The station's country. I'm news guy and I hate country music." I heard her laugh.

"Thank God, I don't like country music either and I was hoping you weren't a *'goat roper'*.

I laughed at the term 'goat roper' with stomach acid reminding me I was in love with a girl from a ranch. A missing girl with the enticing girl in front of me clouding my judgment, bringing pangs of guilt while accelerating my heartbeat and making me want to take her to bed.

"I've never heard that."

"It's a pejorative around here for 'shit kicker' or 'boot scooter.' My kids at school can say *goat roper* but they are not allowed to say *shit kicker*."

"Why don't you teach 'em how to say it in French so they don't get in trouble at school?"

"Because I love my job and want to keep it."

She found a classic rock station on my pride-and-joy stereo, one of the few things I had brought from San Francisco.

"Excuse me a minute, the swim trunks are not right in these jeans. I'm going to get out of this swimsuit." I was back in a minute, commando. I didn't put a shirt back on because I was pink and stinging.

She looked at my chest. "Oh, I'm sorry, David! I burned you!! You needed stronger sunscreen."

"It's okay, I'll be okay." I joined her on the couch and we sat there holding hands with our feet on the coffee table making small talk and kissing here and there. I finally looked at her, "Would you like to stay?"

She put her finger on my lips and said, "Yes, David, conditionally. What you may want to happen... hell, *what I* may want to happen just won't. Can't. I need to be in control and we can't just go wild, all the way in the traditional sense. I have to pace this thing."

Nessa gave me a somber look, "I was hurt a few times, worse than just a little pushed around and roughed up. I'm sorry, but for now, that's the way it's got to be. I can go if you're not okay with that."

I stood up from the couch and scooped her up in my arms and kissed her and carried her into the bedroom.

I laid her down in the bed and turned off the lamp as I noticed her unbuttoning her dungarees. I got them by the bottoms and slid them off of her as she was getting out of the bikini top, too.

She angled herself around to pull back the spread so we could feel the coolness of the top sheet. I was glad, because of somebody's stinging pink chest and I don't mean hers.

I stood next to the bed and couldn't take my eyes off of her. Her hands were slipping my pants down. I stepped out of them.

We were naked.

When she said "in control," she meant it.

She was busting every hot move she could on me. I expected and got some gentle pushbacks, straddling me, riding and grinding on me. This had to end her way and her way, only, within her comfort limits. If it didn't, it was our end.

Before long, her breathing and moans increased rapidly and she was nearing a climax, rocking and writhing and moaning with pleasure and encouraging me with every whimper, raking her fingernails on my back and up through my hair.

"Ahhhhh, GOD! GOD! Oh, GOD!" She climaxed the same time I did.

I was spent and had done everything except penetrate her. I used my tongue, my mouth and my fingers, grinding and grinding against her, bringing several orgasms.

I held and kissed and caressed her. It was quiet, just murmurs riding along on our soft breathing. We were both satisfied. Exhausted.

About 2:45 a.m. I was awake. Damn it, autopilot for work. She lay quietly curled in and around me. She smelled like the gardens of heaven, themselves, and I pulled her to me to take in even more of her before I snuck out of bed to the kitchen and got a tumbler with some water. As I got back into bed she stirred and I saw her eyes come open. Without a word or sound her expression and her gaze into my eyes said, 'I love you.'

I whispered "Water?" She nodded. Nessa went up on one elbow and kissed me. She took the glass and began to sip at the water without ever taking her eyes off of me. I didn't see the next thing coming. An apology.

"David, I don't know how long it's going to take me to get over this thing. I really wanted to make entire and complete love to you. I'm not complaining because you got me to and beyond the point of no return a few times over. I've got serious demons and if this doesn't…if this doesn't work for you, tell me. I feel like I'm being selfish taking what I want and not giving back enough."

I took a breath and started to say something but she cut me off.

"Shh, let me finish. We went as far as we did because you respected my guidelines. That makes you different, special. You're kind and compassionate and oh my God so passionate."

She smiled with a little guilt and pursed her lips just so. "Are you okay with all of this - I mean, are you okay with what happened?" she asked, "because, if you are, I'd like this to happen again."

I responded with my hands and my lips as she turned to set the glass on the nightstand behind her. And then she pulled me over on top of her. All I could do was run my hands over her, up and down her thighs, tracing her collarbone as I kissed her shoulder and stared into her eyes and dotted her supple body with semi-wet little kisses everywhere I could without losing eye contact with her.

She made me breakfast and brought it to me in bed. Then, we showered together and she used her brush and my blow dryer on her hair, flirting and teasing me as I tried to move around her naked body to get my own toiletries and morning thing done.

She laid-out a cute outfit from her backpack. It was a pullover top with half sleeves, blue and yellow horizontal stripes accentuating her nice chest, and the boat neck revealing her gorgeous tan. She slipped into white panties and white, drawstring dungarees and fancy flip-flops.

We headed out to the furniture store that had entire rooms-full of furniture on display. I stood back as Vanessa kept our poor sales guy writing, non-stop. At the end of 45 minutes, she looked at him and said, "Cash deal if you can have this off the truck and in our apartment by 6pm."

As soon as I got into work, a typical Monday was staring me in the face with a pile of weekend news to filter, select and rewrite. Stephanie popped her head into my cubie.

"We good?"

"The answer's yes and that's not happening again. What is happening again is Vanessa. We spent some quality time together and I owe you a thanks. She's amazing."

"She texted me. You blew her away, David. She's crazy-possessed about seeing you again."

"Count on it. I'm on in about 27 minutes and have no material. Scram."

"Your 27 is my 23. Later, Studley."

I spaced out, just sat there contemplating the naked woman I'd been grinding my mind and body against with guilt, missing the woman I loved. Olivia. Bottom line, I was using Vanessa and the realization made me feel shitty. She was a complete, look-good feel-good diversion. I was lying to her by being a phony. Or was I?

The other side of me thought I might have the patience and understanding to help a girl with a jumbled psyche from a physical attack. She needed respect, kindness, some tenderness and companionship, I rationalized, and I could give her plenty of that.

It was like taking arrows to the head when Olivia would dance into my thoughts. I was always caught unawares and uplifted. I wasn't suppressing her with Vanessa. I was surrendering to the present. This Vanessa-something was better than an Olivia-less nothing. I had trouble looking at myself in the mirror, sometimes. Ironically, it was my feeling Olivia would want me to have some joy and companionship, even sex, in my life over being lonely and incapable of social interaction.

My head snapped back into the moment with the plethora of stories I had to scan, rewrite and pull. Before we went on air, Stephanie pulled me aside and said, "I don't know what's up with you and Vanessa because she just texted me, like, a-<u>gain</u>. You must have released the love monkey on her full force."

"Steph, I have a lot on my plate. I can't even address Vanessa and me or anything else at the moment."

"Come on David, girls tell things to other girls and she's not telling very much at all which makes this weird with anyone else but Vanessa."

"Stephanie, are you trying to get me to gossip with you? Does it strike you as mean or weird I'm not going to report my life to you on a daily basis? Do you think I care that you gave her your opinion of me in bed?"

"I gave you a mediocre-plus, Studley."

I gave her the finger, "Well thank you for that, I guess. I'll use that as my lead story this morning, maybe submit it to network."

"I've got your lead, chumpster-in-the-dumpster," and she imitated a bad newscaster: FROM OUR NEWS

CENTER, DAVID CALLAN, RADIO NAME DAVID TYLER
IS IN LUST AND IN LOVE. MORE ABOUT THAT AFTER
THIS."

I popped her in the ass with a rubber band.

"Hey!! Isn't that sexual harassment!?"

"Nope," I said, spinning another one around my index
finger. "I used a rubber." We both laughed and went
about our nutzoid, crazy business.

When I got home, I walked in and realized Vanessa
had transformed my apartment as much as my
demeanor. It was suddenly beautiful in muted gray and
steel blue and black. There were soft greens in the living
area and orange and beige themes in the bedroom. It was
gorgeous right down to the lamp shades. Vanessa was
gorgeous in it. Was she window dressing? A fixture? Or
more?

It was late September and the early tourists were
starting to come in, the snowbirds coming to nest.
Feeling Fall coming, I think Vanessa was toying with the
idea of inviting me to her parents' house for
Thanksgiving in Minnesota but I was done with cold,
forever, even with Vanessa to keep me warm which
probably wouldn't happen in her parents' house. Meeting
her folks? No way, not now, not ever. What was I
thinking.

Olivia Rising from Within

Vanessa took off for nine days and after she left, something grabbed me, wouldn't let go. Olivia's presence descended on me like a mist from which there was no escape. Was it unfinished business of Olivia? Dammit. Olivia wasn't unfinished business. It was me, something in the deepest part of me, not an ethereal mist of Olivia that was my hungering for her, her eyes, her smile, her touch and presence. One last shot. I had to take one last shot.

"Sandy, I have some personal shit I'm going through and before it does affect my work, can we talk about this? I actually want to ask your advice on something. Thanks, David" I sent the note interoffice mail because I didn't want anybody to incidentally hear or overhear that I was losing it.

A couple hours after the interoffice envelope was taken from my cubicle, my phone rang. It was Sandy on the inside line.

"David, this is Sandy."

"Yes, sir."

"We really haven't had time to have lunch together. Feel like knocking back a few beers and watching some college football on Saturday?"

"Sure, sounds great Sandy."

"I'm looking forward to it and I know a great sports bar you might like. It's called Gretchen's, just off Shea Boulevard near 103rd or thereabouts. Noon good?"

"Works for me Sandy, thanks."

I could see why Norman and he were so close. Sandy was shrewd but he was also smart with a keen sense of applied finesse. He knew this was sensitive and the way he approached it showed the finesse that probably made him successful in his professional life. I was actually looking forward to just hanging out with him.

I rolled into Gretchen's Sports Bar but didn't see Sandy's car nor did I see him when I went in the good-sized sports bar that must have had 15 large screens. I grabbed a table just off the serving station at the bar and was immediately greeted by an attractive girl wearing a whistle, striped referee uniform, and tight black shorts.

"Hi, welcome to Gretchen's. Do you want to hear our drink specials or do you know what you want?"

"I'm going to hold off a minute because my buddy should be here any second now. When you see him, you can come back around if that's okay."

"Gotcha. I'll keep an eye peeled."

I stared of one of the screens with a college game with more disinterest than usual.

I'm sure Sandy would give me clear and concise direction on what to do and how to do it. Somebody who looked like Sandy walked in from the bright sunshine outside. The guy was wearing golf shorts, a golf polo and athletic shoes with a golf hat, sunglasses on top, and was tanned a dark shade of brown.

He waved at me and I heard his voice.

"David, there you are. Whew, I just got off of Desert Diamond after playing 18 holes with one of our advertisers and it was heating up out there. I can use a beer but my head's saying cocktail."

The waitress was at our elbow almost immediately.

"Would you guys like to hear our drink specials or do you know what you'd like?" Sandy deferred to me.

"I'd like a margarita, rocks please."

Sandy said, "Now you're talking," and told the server, "Make that two and I tell you what, why don't you give us the top shelf with Grand Marnier please."

"You got it. I'll be back in a minute with your drinks" and she put a bowl of popcorn on the table and spun away heading straight to the bar.

"Thanks for being discreet, Sandy. If anybody knows what direction I need to be pointed in, it's you."

He knew bits and pieces about Olivia and me and because of Stephanie's big mouth. He knew more than he should have about me being wrapped-up with Vanessa.

"Sandy, on the surface it might appear Vanessa and I are in love and a great big deal. Underneath that facade, she's a fixer, a basket case and told me that from the very start. We don't have a normal relationship. And from her side, I myself am a basket case because I'm still hugely in love with Olivia."

"Here you go guys, two margaritas Grand Marnier top shelf rocks. And I brought a couple menus for you to look over. "

"Thanks."

We sipped our drinks as we continued to talk.

Sandy nailed it, "So you're with a beautiful girl and that feels good and all the while you can't get your mind off of the one you love. So you feel like double-layered shit, twice."

"Yeah, thanks. Well stated, boss," and I smiled and held up a thumb.

"Sandy, I've searched high and low, at least everywhere I could think of but stopped short, hesitated to get a private investigator because I'm afraid of getting financially soaked without anything really being done. What do I do to find her?? I honestly don't think I can live without her. I've got it that bad for her and, frankly, I feel some kind of endgame coming head-on at my relationship with Vanessa. But I'm rational. I don't need a shrink or counseling, I need a finder, Sandy."

"David, this is easier than you think. I know you have some dough because you haven't been spending it lavishly. You're not in a big house or driving some flashy new ride so I'm figuring you're been investing or banking your money."

"Too much instability in the industry, Sandy. I know whole stations get wiped out and one bad ratings period can blow talent out the door, taking months, sometimes, for people to get a new gig. So, if I err, it's on the conservative side."

"The only private investigator I would trust with my money is one that works for a law firm. Here's what I'm going to do. I'm going to call the station's law firm and talk to one of the senior partners. We're going to get a referral from that guy and get you a real live investigator who actually earns his money instead of charging you thousands for a 30-second internet search."

"You make it sound easy, Sandy."

"It is easy. The difficulty is only and always the money: is there enough to go the distance? Most people don't have the cash to get something real going in that regard. If you have some money put away, dough you're willing to spend..." and I was nodding before he finished.

"Absolutely. Simple guy, simple needs. I have an apartment and I'm not flashy. I don't see a reason to spend the money on something I don't need. I need Olivia."

"Good. I bet you we have a name by Wednesday morning. I'll call you into my office and we'll get you going." Sandy and I had burgers and couple more drinks and left.

At the end of my shift, Tuesday, he buzzed my phone.

"Hey, Boss, what's going on?"

"David, can you come down to my office, please."

"On my way." I tapped at the door and heard Sandy say come in. When I did, he was with another gentleman, also standing.

"David Callan, I'd like you to meet Dan Giorino, an independent licensed private investigator contracted to the law firm the station uses. Dan, say hello to David Callan, our top news guy and one of the best in the country."

We shook hands.

"I'm going to excuse myself and let you gentlemen have my office as long as you like. Thank you for getting over here, Dan. It was great to meet you. I'll be in the sales department, David."

Giorino stood and offered a shake, "Good to meet you, too, Mr. Tuttle," and Dan took a seat and dove in.

"David here's what I already know. You had a motorcycle crash in San Francisco and got involved with the nursing student named Olivia Macias. Your boss confirmed that Olivia is the reason I'm here."

"That's correct."

"So, tell me the circumstances of her disappearance."

"After I was discharged from the hospital, I was going back for therapy three times a week and Olivia was living on campus at USF but would come to my apartment and spend a lot of time and sometimes spend the night. She moved in. She had this nursing boards preparation thing in Denver..."

"I already know some things about that David, that you met her there and returned."

"And then poof, no more Olivia. Disconnected cell phone. USF semester ended and the dorms were cleared. I tried the ranch her father manages and was told to go fuck myself because he is the big dog, there. I frankly don't know if her dad even knew me by name."

"You can bet he does," the investigator said. "I know you've done some extensive checking on your own but let me relieve a little pressure you may be feeling. Olivia is not dead, nothing evil occurred such as murder or kidnap or any capitol crime for that matter. Next, the reason you're having trouble locating her is that someone is actively covering her trail and doing a damn good job at it. Her dad's the runaway favorite in that suspicion. It's something we can overcome, though."

Dan produced a file I hadn't seen.

"David this is everything we *think* we know about her. If we've got any of it wrong, you have to tell us or it could send us off in the wrong direction costing us time and you money."

"When do you want me to get back to you Dan?"

"I don't. I want you to sit right here and examine every single page and use this red pen to circle anything that's questionable or wrong, okay? If you want me to leave you alone while you do this I will."

"You're fine Dan."

I learned things I never knew about Olivia like her mother's middle name, Antonia, and how much Olivia weighed at birth, what schools she went to, and that her dad was a bull rider when young, in the Hall of Fame Cowboys Association and Museum, inducted at just 21 years of age. It took me almost half an hour to go everything that the investigator had amassed.

"I didn't see you pick up the red pen, David."

"As far as I know, everything is correct."

"David, your prospect of finding her is slim and I'll tell you why. For somebody to be covering her this effectively means there's money behind it and being reasonably smart guys, you and I *know* that it's her dad. He's got enough money she could be anywhere using an assumed name or whatever. This should actually comfort you."

"Comfort me?? How the hell can you say comfort me! It's eating me alive because I love this girl like I've never loved anyone! Nothing happened or was wrong and *POOF*!, gone!"

"It should comfort you David because you know she is alive and probably safe and very well hidden. I know that's not much. But we're going to do some additional checking and I will get back to you with anything we learn."

"How do I pay you and when...and how much, Dan?"

"Our initial, up-front fee is $12,500 and you can see that we got a running start tracing her. Mr. Tuttle busted my balls until he negotiated the rate that the radio station would pay the law firm for our services. So, you will be billed at that cost which is-" Dan used the calculator on his phone-"$10,343.75."

"If you come down to my cubicle with me, I can give you a check right now, Dan."

The admin people had already left for today so there were few people left in the station. As we walked down the hallway toward my cubicle, Dan turned to me and said, " I don't know if you know it, but Tuttle thinks the world of you. He guaranteed payment...was going to pick it up for you if you couldn't or wouldn't. Plausible deniability, David: I will never admit I told you that, David."

"His best friend is my college professor and advisor who landed me this gig. They're apparently cut from the same bolt of cloth."

"Well, you are one lucky SOB to work for the guy."

"Here we go," and I sat in my cubicle as I wrote out the check and thanked him. He helped himself to one of my business cards.

"I'll call you with whatever we turn up next, all right?"

Dan Giorino lifted a weight from my chest. He suggested I may not find Olivia but at least I knew she was all right and going to stay all right; if that's all I could have, then all I could do was pray and wish that I could get over her and heal quickly. I wanted to believe she was always around the next corner or behind the next door ready to walk into my arms and life.

I stopped to get groceries after my shift. By the time I got home, Vanessa was in my apartment. I'd given her a key. It felt right. She could have a safe and secure place to go. I could smile just seeing her car in the lot and knowing she'd come to me with open arms and luscious lips.

Baking didn't seem to be a thing foster parents did. I never remembered anything but fish getting baked at home. Anything that we had in the form of bread or pastry came from a bakery or from a grocer's shelf but when I walked into the apartment, there was no mistake that something or somethings were in the oven. There was flour and other ingredients everywhere in the kitchen. I think every dish I had and every bowl was out with some type of ingredient in it.

Vanessa had the music on loud and didn't hear me and when I walked in and set a couple of bags of groceries on the counter. She turned around and startled. It was almost like a movie scene from a rom-com. She had a little bit of flour on her nose and had pulled out one of my polo shirts to use as an apron and there was flour and egg and who-knows-what smeared on it. She was as cute as beautiful in the moment and the aroma was intoxicating.

I was losing my mind. Olivia, the 100% resident in my heart and Vanessa the perfect place-keeper who walked over to give me a kiss and pointed down toward the window of the oven. On the left side of the rack was a pie and on the right was a bread pan.

"I don't know what possessed you to do this but I hope this possession happens again without making me fat."

She said, "Apple pie and zucchini bread."

"What's the occasion?"

"Because I want to do something nice for you? Because I'm not just another pretty face that's clueless in a kitchen?"

"You *are* a pretty face, the prettiest…and I like you whether you can bake or not! *Merci, boo-coo!*," and she laughed at my poor attempt at French. I wrapped her in a hug, "Thank you," and kissed her.

The phone rang and I happened to be right next to it. It was Stephanie who shouted, "Act like it's *not me* if you know what's good for you, David! I know Vanessa's there and it's her <u>birthday</u>! You better get your ass out of there and get her something."

I barked, "Wrong number! The people that <u>used</u> to have this number raised chihuahuas! I live in an apartment that'll evict me for a goldfish. Goodbye!" and I hung up.

"OH SHIT, Vanessa," I said looking around, I'm
missing a bag of groceries!"

I pecked Vanessa on her on the cheek grabbed my
keys, "I'll be right back."

On the opposite end of the strip mall where the
grocery store was, there was a little jewelry store. I ran in
there and as quickly as I could, got a saleslady to help
me find a gold chain and search for a charm. The chain
was too easy. She showed me tray after tray of 14kt gold
charms.

"That one." It was a stylized Aztecan sun about the
size of a half dollar. As much as a sun worshipper as
Vanessa was, it was just the thing.

"Could you put the charm on the chain for me,
maybe give me a little gift box?"

"Yes, no problem putting it on there for you. I'm
afraid there's a charge for gift boxes."

"That's fine," but I wasn't, impatiently tapping my
foot because I still had to walk in with a so-called
missing bag of groceries.

"All done. $195 for the chain, $67.50 for the Aztec
charm—that's actually lovely, together! $8.50 for the bow
and gift box... It's $271, with tax, $288.62, sir," and I
already had my card out. She gift-boxed the chain and
put the ribbon on it for me. As soon as I was out the
door, it was a dead run to the grocery store door.

I bought a pound of butter, a loaf of rye bread, head
of lettuce and a bottle of wine and skedaddled back to
the apartment. I walked in as if nothing happened with
the gift box hidden in the grocery bag.

"I got delayed, had to get gas on the way back,
sweetie." I kissed her and started putting the groceries
away also putting the small box up in the cupboard
where I kept the bread.

"You've been working hard, baking. Can I reward you
with dinner, out?" I hadn't seen anything that even
hinted dinner and I didn't want to celebrate her birthday
with a BLT and glass of iced tea.

"I've got dinner right here."

She took the butter from my hand to put it in the refrigerator along with the lettuce. "If you put out some plates, I'll get dinner on."

She brought out a beautiful platter of smoked salmon, some cucumbers and onions in a vinaigrette, some potato salad, tomato aspic, and assorted cheeses with crackers, carrot and celery sticks with dip.

"My parents sent the smoked salmon to me for Minnesota. They get it directly from a Canadian packing house. We love it."

"Me, too. How about some wine?"

"Please. That white wine you bought is fine!"

"I don't normally drink white wine but this is the only one I like. It's a chardonnay from California wine country and I saw it on sale." I grabbed a couple of wine stems out of the cabinet and stuck my hand into the next cabinet to put the small box in my pocket. She already had the cork out of the wine and was pouring as soon as the glasses were on the table.

We dug into the great meal. She stopped eating for a sec, sipped wine, and said, "Can we go away somewhere for like a long weekend or something, David? I'm thinking like Sedona or a cabin up near the Mogollon Rim lakes before it gets too cold?"

Harmless enough. We'd snuggle and have a nice time.

"You know, like, make a campfire and roast weenies and marshmallows, just hang out and drink wine and look at the stars and stuff?"

"Give me a little notice and I'll put in for a Friday and Monday off. We can make it a long weekend," and she lit up. She squealed and jumped out of her chair, jumping up and down finally landing in my lap.

"But on one condition." She froze, looked at me not quite sure if I was kidding or not. I handed her the tiny box and said, "You have to wear your birthday present." She was honestly taken by surprise.

She took the box, smiled at me, nodding, "Stephanie, huh."

I nodded. She was like a little girl, carefully sliding the bow off the box. Her tears were already in free-fall as she gently negotiated the packaging.

"Oh David, I love it!" She stroked my hair, "Put it on me, please?" Against her dark-tanned skin, the contrast was beautiful.

"You're so amazing. I didn't want to tell you it was my birthday because I didn't want you to feel pressured to get me anything. I just wanted to spend it with you. You were my secret present to myself." Her kiss was convincing validation, with what seemed like a little sexual hunger behind it.

"I'll be right back," and she headed, I thought, for the bathroom. I turned my gaze back to my wine glass. Pondering.

Vanessa's voice brought me back to reality.

"How does it look from a distance?" She was stark naked except for the pendant.

"How does what, look?" I said as I grabbed both wine glasses and shut the kitchen light off with my elbow, walking toward her saying, "Oh, the bling. I need a closer look... much closer."

"Then come and get it, David."

She took a wine glass from my hand and a big sip from it. Then she took the other glass and set them both on the nightstand.

Less than 10 minutes later she was moaning so loud I was sure the people in the next apartment would beat on the wall as she tugged at my hair calling my name with hastening urgency, "David...oh, David, my GOD David!!"

Her final hip thrust was so powerful it nearly threw me onto my side. She was completely spent. Her chest was heaving slowly and quietly. Her fingers were still in my hair and caressing my neck and shoulders as I moved to lie beside her left side.

I kissed her.

She answered with a small whimper. I kissed her on the forehead and rolled off my side of the bed and slipped into the bathroom. I grabbed a washcloth and ran some cool water over it and wrung it out tightly as I could. I slipped quietly back into bed into her outstretched arms. I applied the cool washcloth to her forehead.

She grinned and shook her head slowly from side to side, "Mmm, that feels so good, you don't know." I left compress in place and located the wine glass on the nightstand.

I sat on the side of the bed as I removed the compress and rolled it as tightly as I could. I dunked it, completely immersed the end of it in the wine glass, putting the glass on the nightstand. I put the wine-soaked washcloth against her lips. She spread her lips and begin to suck at the end of washcloth. I was sucking the other end of it. I was touching her nose with mine as softly as I could, rubbing from side to side. She put her palm up beside my cheek and with her other hand removed the washcloth.

"I never want this birthday to end, David." We lay there quietly caressing each other. She looked over at me, 'Shower?"

I slid out of bed and held my hand out to help her up and we made our way into the bathroom where she got the water going and adjusted the temperature.

I'm a guy, use plain old soap. But when we were picking out the stuff for my apartment, she bought a soap dispenser for the shower and filled it with gardenia-scented body gel, gardenia because it's my favorite flower.

There was also a loofah, this weird looking thing with holes that she started scrubbing my back with, slowly. It was like getting my back scratched which I love and getting it softly massaged with soap which felt really good. I stood there enjoying it with her nude, warm body against me. I looked at the loofah and reciprocated not quite knowing what to do but simply mimicked what she had done. Her hands were in my hair and I felt her sudsing-up of nice shampoo that matched the gardenia body gel.

Instead of grabbing the shampoo, I took the luxurious foam from my own hair with my hands and began to wash Vanessa's hair. As soon as our eyes met, I couldn't keep my hands moving the shampoo through her hair. I could only look at her and kiss her and lead her out of the shower toward the bed as she grabbed a towel with her trailing hand to do one of those hair turban things before she lay back down.

"I don't want to soak the pillow."

"I thought we burned 'em down and soaked 'em already." She chuckled softly and pinched my cheek.

She looked over at another of the pillows, pointed and said, "Nope! An escapee! I guess we have more work to do, David!" and she used both hands to forcefully push me down onto the bed, crawling on and atop me to straddle me as she leaned down and began kissing me.

Technically, we didn't make love as in full-on penetration, but if what we'd done wasn't making love it was a satisfying substitute. She could make every nerve in my body emit little charges that took me to euphoria's edge and then take me right over that edge.

Vanessa wasn't Olivia. Where Vanessa was a tender and good lover, Olivia was extraordinary.

As cold or sexist or harsh as I thought it may seem, I could only resolve that Vanessa was eye candy and arm candy and good company. Part of me hated myself for it. The empty, longing part of me was getting soothed. Not numbed, not healed but soothed which was better than the nonstop emotional beating I had been enduring.

A shaft of light from the living room window came into the bedroom and shone brightly on her face. My eyes opened a nanosecond before hers opened. I could swear she looked like an angel. I toyed with her bangs and kissed her on the forehead and lips softly and said "I'm going to get some breakfast started. I'm starved and I have to have pancakes."

"I want one! With apricot preserves!"

"Coming right up, birthday girl!" She sat up and from inside one of my t-shirts over her perfect body, used an index finger to hook and pulled out the chain I gave her.

"I love this, David," and she kissed me.

I reached up under the shirt, caressing her breasts, "Hold it a sec?" She stopped and looked at me. I faked a serious expression and pointed at one of her boobs. I moved my face under the t-shirt.

"WHAT! What, David!?"

I said, "Whoa, is that a <u>hickey</u>??" And I took her semi-erect nipple between my lips which hardened it immediately.

She emitted a little squeal and said, "If you're going to start, you're going to finish!" and she yanked down the t-shirt with purpose, smiling with an implied challenge.

I looked at her innocently and said "Of course I'm going to finish. Pancakes are my realm and I, their king, Princess Apricotta!" Even if she had wanted to, she couldn't suppress giggling, with me holding a spatula in the air like a scepter, looking regal.

Nessa got the coffee going as I was combining the ingredients and mixing the batter for the pancakes.

"I think there's bacon in the box. Can you grab it for me sweetie?" She did.

She used the pound package of bacon to point at me and said "How the hell did you get batter on your butt??" As I twisted my upper torso and pulled my shorts around to look, she wound up and slapped my ass with that bacon hard enough to bring a howl. So much for the hickey.

"And now you are a battered king, my liege!!" which she thought was the funniest thing she had ever said.

I turned my butt toward her, hooked my boxers with my thumb and slipped my shorts down exposing one cheek. "Well? are you going to kiss my owie??" and she slapped my ass again, but good. I sucked wind. It stung that bad.

"I think you left a mark, Vanessa. Do you know what that means? I have to report this on my first newscast, tomorrow." I mocked a bad broadcaster voice, 'Pancake king punked and porked, yesterday! Details after the break.'"

My phone rang, "Nessa, I have to take this," and I stepped onto the patio.

"David, Dan Giorino. One little break and probably our last. She's registered with the State RN Board here in Arizona but that doesn't mean she's practicing anywhere. She can't nurse under an assumed name but I'm betting she's working, somewhere—old folks home? I'm guessing she's at a small town's clinic or hospital because she's a country girl and used to that pace. It's a good bet she used her resources to find you and already knows where you are."

"She knew this job was a career-maker, Dan."

"Had you accepted it?"

"Not yet, Dan."

"David! Wake up, guy. You two were in California. There were 49 other states where this girl could have gone with her disappearing act. She picked the state you're in. Why?"

He was right.

"I think the mountain is going to come to Mohammad, David."

"But she hasn't, Dan. She hasn't. If you knew her you'd know that nothing in her is even remotely some weird kind of stalker. She grew up without pretense. WYSIWYG! What you see is what you get."

"Keep the faith. I'll let you know when we've got her pinpointed. See ya."

"Thanks, Dan."

"I'm sorry," I said, returning to the kitchen, "I forgot to return Norman Lydell's call and that's never good. He got me the job, here. Now, where was I?"

She grinned, "Hint. Eggs and bowl on counter."

I grinned back, put four uncracked eggs into a bowl and left them there and she looked at them kind of funny. "I'm going to fry those and put them on top of my pancakes."

"Four eggs David??"

"Yes, I'm going to make two for you but I'm going to scramble yours because I don't think you want apricot-goo-fried eggs."

"Sometimes you're a nice man, David."

"And sometimes I'm good in bed."

"*Those* eggs are off limits to you, buck-o."

"Got it."

We ended up feeding each other just because.

"I've got major stuff to do tomorrow, David. I gave the kids a writing assignment and I have to read and critique 26 papers which is going to take forever not to mention grading them. Plus, I've got a pile of laundry to do."

"Bring it here-use the laundry twins in the hallway and lay out by the pool reading your papers while the clothes dry."

"As nice as that is and sounds, David, we both know if I do that, I'm going to get exactly nothing done. You are *already* the biggest distraction in my little French-English mind and life. Don't take that as a complaint. It's not. There's a little laundromat around the corner and I'm going to knock it out there. I promise I'll call when I'm done and we can get together later. Deal?"

I didn't need to answer and she gave me a quick little smooch.... "You're welcome to be around chore-woman all day but you might feel neglected and get bored."

"How about I do some stuff around her and then come over and we can order pizza or have something else delivered for dinner?"

"Great plan, sexy man!"

I put off fixing the truck headlight. I didn't really drive it that often so it wasn't the foremost thing in my mind. But I started my day at the auto parts store getting the correct headlight and installing it right there; in case I had a problem, the guy from the store would bail me out. One less chore.

I had boots and athletic shoes and some really nice dress loafers. What I didn't have was sandals. Everybody in Arizona was wearing sandals and I owned exactly none. I found a couple of pairs of sandals I liked, online, looked at my watch, and ran over to the store and picked them up.

There was enough time to get home and start thinking about getting over to Nessa's and giving some attention and energy to what we might have for dinner. A ride after dinner might be nice, so I made for my bedroom to slip into my biker boots.

Forces of Intervention

Something on the radio caught my ear. A laundromat. Something happened at a laundromat, the one I knew to be right by Nessa's house. I had the presence of mind to pick up my press pass, grabbed my helmet and bike key and tore out of the apartment on a dead run toward the bike. I did a power skid all the way around the fountain leaving the complex.

The laundromat was blocked off with police "Crime Scene" tape and the doors of the laundromat were cordoned-off with investigators inside.

I knew. I knew and I was in shock. Still, I wandered up and saw blood everywhere. I'd seen an ambulance taking off and it was a good distance away.

I flashed my press pass at one of the cops in the parking lot and said, "Holy hell! What just happened in there—Somebody get killed?" and I was holding my breath for the answer.

"Some goon just beat some poor girl half to death and I don't know if she's going to make it. He did a job on her. It was bad." My heart stopped.

"Thanks to the guy in the liquor store hearing her screams, we've got the guy in custody and he's on his way downtown. We're going to charge him with attempted murder-one because of the premeditation of taking the blackjack with him."

"Her name is Vanessa Sorensen, isn't it." The cop looked at me weird. "How do you know that?"

"She's my girlfriend and said she was going to be here, today."

"Oh Jesus, buddy—I'm sorry."

My knees buckled and I bent over, put my hand on my knees and nearly threw up. The cop said, "You need to sit down," and he helped me over to the police car and grabbed some smelling salts, waving them under my nose.

"Let me up. I have to get over to the liquor store and make a call."

The cop said, "No need. I'll patch you through to a landline."

"Who do you wanna call?"

"KFCG radio, I work there. Vanessa's best friend works there and knows her parents."

The officer handed me the police car's microphone as I leaned against his car to steady myself.

"Engineering, Chuck."

"This is an emergency. It's David. Vanessa got attacked and is seriously hurt, fighting for her life!"

"Dude!"

"I need you to leave this line open while you go to another phone and call Stephanie and let her know that Vanessa is on her way to..." and I realized I didn't know the name of the hospital. I left the mic keyed as I asked, "Officer what hospital is she going to?"

"Angel of the Desert on Palo Verde Terrace," came the reply.

"Get that, Chuck?"

"Copy, David."

"Tell Steph I'll see her at the hospital. I'm on the bike, six minutes from there."

"Prayers, David—I'm sorry."

Tears fell for the first time. I handed the cop his microphone. The cop said, "I can give you a ride if you'd like."

"I need to shake this off. Just this once, please, could you just look the other way for about the next thirty seconds while I open up the throttle on my bike and get going??"

"You got it. Oh, and buddy? I'll pray for her, too." His saying that told me she was dead or nearly so. Cops didn't look the other way and they didn't say they'd pray. None I ever knew, did. This cop was okay.

I ran into the emergency room and spotted the admissions window, flashing my press pass at the clerk.

"David Tyler, KFCG News. I'm here about Vanessa Sorensen. I need to know about Vanessa Sorensen."

She was kind, slid her glasses down her nose, "I heard you, sir." She could see I was scared out of my mind and must have some personal angle.

"I can't release any information to you right now unless you can show me or prove to me that you're a relative."

I slapped the counter, looked at the ceiling and yelled "DAMMIT!" When I turned around, I heard Stephanie shriek as she came running to me and threw her arms around me, sobbing.

Still squeezing me tightly, she sobbed, "When Chuck called, I was already on with Nessa's parents who called me right after they got off the phone with the hospital. They're flying down from Minnesota; said they'll be here in about 6 hours."

"What did the hospital tell them, Steph?"

Stephanie's voice changed, it sounded like she was weeping, "Nothing good, David."

"Stephanie, what about her condition? What did they say about her condition?"

"Her parents were told that she has multiple skull fractures and is in a coma. She needs surgery but they can't take her in until she's stabilized."

"David?" I looked at her but didn't say anything. Stephanie said my name again.

"Yes?"

"She's in love with you, David. Crazy, madly, full-on wildly in love with you. I told her parents about you and how she feels about you. They authorized the hospital to give you information."

"They sure fuckin' didn't act that way five minutes ago, Stephanie!"

"IT'S BECAUSE YOUR PRESS PASS SAYS TYLER, not Callan, David."

All I could do was bury my face in my hands and weep.

"Honey," Stephanie said, "let me walk you up to the desk. Get out your driver's license and show it to the lady."

I proffered my license to the same clerk and said, "I'm sorry I barked at you. My real name's on my license."

She looked at my driver's license and then back at her computer. "Okay, I see you're authorized Mr. Callan, but I'm not permitted to discuss this case. I'll have an M.D. come out and speak with you."

"Thanks again, I'm sorry."

She nodded.

I looked over at Stephanie with dread and her head was down, chin on her chest and she was using her blouse to soak-up the tears. We helped each other back over to where we were sitting. It wasn't ten minutes later when a doctor came out in a white coat and was directed toward us. I stood up.

"David Callan?" and I nodded. "I'm Dr. Cleveland, a neurosurgeon and the lead doctor on Vanessa Sorensen's medical team. Have a seat and I'll join you."

We moved to a couch with a chair and small table.

"This is going to be very difficult and painful to hear. Vanessa is in extremely critical condition, bordering grave condition. Right now, I don't know if we can save her so it's going to take lots of love and prayers from you and the rest of your family. Her injuries left fragments of her skull penetrating her brain and may have compromised her spinal fluid. She's alive but needs a respirator to breathe. We don't know when or if she'll regain consciousness."

The surgeon put her hand on my arm. "David, Vanessa may *survive* but *never* regain consciousness. We need her to stabilize her before we can even think about surgery."

Stephanie and I were a mess. Dr. Cleveland said, "Any questions?" We could only shake our heads. As she rose, Dr. Cleveland said, "I'm so, so sorry," and she slowly walked back into the E.R.

"Stephanie, I'm going to run home and get a shower
and a change of clothes. I'll bring back lots of snacks for
us for the long haul. Will you be okay without me for an
hour or so?"

Stephanie looked up from her saturated tissue and
nodded. She put her arms around my neck and drew me
in for a hug.

I rode back to the laundromat, up to the same cop
who helped me out. "How is she?"

"Not good. Coma. Might not make it. She's hanging
on by a thread."

The cop slowly shook his head in empathy. "Can you
tell me about the guy you have under arrest?"

"One of the investigators filled me in-he's 33 years
old, a bouncer at a local nightclub and had been in a
previous relationship with the victim. She had filed a
peace bond against him and this was his second
violation of it. He's being held without bond for
attempted first degree murder. This guy's gonna go down
and hard."

"Thank you, officer." I pulled my helmet on and drove
off, this time, observing the traffic laws, thinking of the
few things I could pick up for us to munch on for the
indeterminate number of hours we'd be in waiting rooms
at the hospital, hoping and praying for Nessa.

I pulled in next to the truck and jogged into the
apartment, laid out some fresh clothes and grabbed a
medium sized backpack from the closet; plenty of room
for some snacks and stuff. It was probably the quickest
shower I'd ever taken. My hair was still wet when I pulled
on my helmet and strapped on the backpack to head for
the grocery.

My head was spinning, heartbroken, thinking of her.
I wondered. I had guilt and remorse and sorrow
sickening me. I spent my early life as an 'Is this my
punishment for what I did to Olivia?' orphan and my
adult life was shaping up to be spent alone. It was more
an observation than self-pity.

The bike roared to life and I took off.

I realized everything in my apartment had Vanessa written all over it, the comfort she created with furnishings and girly touches. I started bawling, flipped up my helmet shield and used my thumb to wipe my eyes clear so I could see and....

Stephanie was grief-stricken and curling up in her seat. There was a television blaring in the cavernous the E.R. waiting area of the hospital. Despite sixty people filling some of the 100-odd chairs, no one else was really paying attention.

It was the 5pm news.

"It's 5:00 p.m. Time for the news. I'm Janie Goodwin."

"...and I'm Scott Pruitt."

"Scott, this is a horrifying story involving one of our own. A motorcyclist is fighting for his life after losing control of his bike on the way to the hospital after learning his girlfriend, Vanessa Sorensen, was nearly beaten to death."

"This is what we know so far, Janie. The victim was at the Suds for Duds laundromat when attacked by Jean-Philippe LeBroussard, 37. The injured motorcyclist is a local broadcaster, David Tyler, from radio station, KFCG."

"LeBroussard stalked David Tyler's girlfriend in the past. He was a nightclub bouncer who checked Vanessa's driver's license for her address so many times that he had memorized it. He had threatened her until she decided to go out with him and get it over with. It's clear that she was sexually assaulted by him yet she never pressed charges. At some point, she filed a peace bond against him, one that he violated. Then he violated it a second time, before today's brutal attack with a blackjack just a day after her birthday. Ms. Sorensen was taken to Angel of the Desert hospital in North Scottsdale and arrived unconscious with multiple skull fractures and lacerations. At this time, she is reportedly in grave condition."

"Janie, Sorensen's boyfriend, KFCG's David Tyler, is being treated for head and spinal injuries. His condition is

Meant to Be

Sometimes decisions are taken out of human hands and never have to be made. My dad used to tell me that.

I was working the 3 to 11 swing shift on the orthopedics ward.

The intercom alert sounded for Trauma Team One to which I belonged. Protocol dictated I report immediately to the emergency room. The nurses on the ward knew to take over my current tasks.

Using my emergency elevator key, I arrived in under 90 seconds.

There were two patients. A woman in Trauma 1 had been severely beaten with a blunt object and was not expected to survive extensive brain injuries. She was in a coma.

There was another victim in Trauma 2, a motorcycle crash victim, multiple fractures suspected, and that was the one to which my team was directed. I had my surgical mask up as I rushed in with co-members of my team.

It was David.

I shrieked.

I was fighting for my breath and my vision was fluttering. I pulled on my mask, felt myself falling, losing consciousness. One of my colleagues grabbed me and got me seated and popped some smelling salts under my nose. I came around. They were all yammering "Olivia are you okay? What's wrong with Olivia?"

A wheelchair arrived and they strapped me into it. I was hustled me into a treatment room by myself. One of my favorite ER physicians, Maddie Hale, rushed in with a nurse I didn't know. The RN gave me some oxygen as Maddie started examining me.

"Olivia, you've got all my attention now, girlfriend! What's going on?"

I motioned for her to close the door. As soon as she turned back around I was sitting up. I got weepy.

"Maddie, the guy that's hurt in Trauma 2 is my David, the father of my baby... He doesn't know about the baby. He doesn't even know I'm in Arizona!!"

"I'm going to give you a mild sedative to calm you down, Olivia," and she turned to the nurse, "Bobbi, get me a syringe and 25mg injectable Demerol, please."

"Right away, Dr. Hale," and the nurse was back in a hurry.

Maddie Hale rolled me over, gave me the Demerol in my glute, then practically fell backward into the chair in the examining room, resting her elbows on her knees and staring at me.

"Okay, Olivia, there's only one way this thing's going to play out and that's the way that *you* want it to play out. Here's what I suggest." She looked at her watch, "Oh crap, let me make a call really quick."

"Eric, it's Maddie down in the ER. I'm glad I caught you before you went home. Can you please swing by here. I'm in Treatment A-2 with one of our top nurses for what I suspect is neurogenic shock."

She paused, "Thanks, Eric...."

"That was my boss, the assistant chief of staff, Eric Reilly. He's a good guy and I have an idea. You got to trust me on this one, Olivia."

"You know I trust you, Maddie, and I know Dr. Reilly."

"Well, your color's coming back," and she checked my pupils and took my pulse and blood pressure, again.

"The Demerol's helping."

The door opened and the Assistant Chief of Staff said "Olivia, I didn't know it was you!" He looked at Maddie and said, "Olivia and I worked on a couple of tough cases together and you're right. She is one of our stars around here. What's going on?"

Maddie said, "I'll let you explain, Olivia."

I did. When I was finished, Maddie said, "Eric if she signs a waiver to give absolutely no treatment to... I'm sorry Olivia what's his name?"

"David Callan."

"...to David Callan, can we give her unlimited visiting privileges? He doesn't even know he's the father of the child for Christ's sake!"

In a calming tone of voice, Eric said, "I don't have any problem with that at all," and Dr. Reilly patted my leg. "He's damn sure not going to find out from anyone who works here or it's their last day, Olivia."

"Thank you, Doc."

"Olivia, and I mean this, if anybody gives you gas for hanging out with Mr. Callan's in his room or anywhere else in this hospital? Tell them to look for my order in the records."

Maddie Hale looked down at me, "Now you see why I like my boss, Olivia?"

"I don't know what to say except thank you, Dr. Reilly."

"Okay. You two are all set and I have an appointment to go home and watch football with my teenaged boys."

"Thank you. Goodnight, Dr Riley."

"Goodnight Eric, and thank you for picking up my call so late."

Maddie let me sit up and dangle my legs, making sure I could stand and walk without being 'woozy.'

"Olivia, I sent a text to the charge nurse that I treated you and you're now off for 24-hours. So you can go be with David, but you're not on duty. *Capiche*?"

"Thanks, Maddie."

I wandered back over to see how David was doing. Then I checked Trauma 1 for the young lady just as they were pronouncing her, noting the time and pulling the sheet over her face to await her gurney ride to the morgue.

Seven hours later, at 20 minutes past midnight, David was in the surgical recovery unit in critical but stable condition with three cracked vertebrae, a compound fracture of his left arm, and a broken left leg and ankle which were in posterior splints that would be cast as soon as the swelling went down.

I was at David's bedside. My uniform was perfect other than the saturation of tears that kept coming. I curled my pinkie finger around his, my chair so close that it scraped the aluminum bedrails. I knew, from training and experience, even comatose patients could often hear and sometimes recall conversations.

Coming Around

Everything was a blur. Whoever it was, I couldn't make him or her out but knew it was a white-uniformed person, probably a nurse or attendant, maybe a tech. There was the rise and fall of a conversational tone, but nothing as distinct as words. It was that smell only hospitals have that told me where I was.

I was only catching a word here and there, sometimes a small phrase.

"David? David? My dad found you. He found you and found out you were hooked up with someone and he didn't want to tell me. I got it out of him because I'm his baby girl and will always be his baby girl. Daddy told me it hadn't been going on long. He told me to remember that I had suffered through the same thing. Remember, David? I told you about that guy I was with a short time and he got killed overseas? My dad explained it was the same thing."

"I understood but it didn't make it easier, David. It broke my heart and I cried my eyes out morning, noon and night. I'm doing it again but my tears are for you, my love—that you have to suffer what I did."

"I didn't stalk you. I came here because this is one of the best programs in the country for RNs to get practitioner certification in orthopedics. I was fortunate to get accepted. You'll know soon, David. And I hope you forgive me for why I vanished like I did."

My hearing was coming back. She couldn't stop crying and rested her forehead tenderly on my right forearm, "Oh, David, David, David. Please. Please forgive me."

My name. Her voice. Pain. Olivia's voice. Olivia.

My eyes were crusted shut and there was something warm on my arm. A hand, maybe. Now, it was rubbing my arm, definitely a hand.

"Wake up, my love. I'm here and never leaving."

It was Olivia's voice, her real voice, not a dream. One of my eyes opened and the most beautiful sight of my life began to come into focus: beautiful brown hair, Olivia's eyes, her smile. My Olivia.

"Oh my God David! David! David, you're awake!"

It was my turn to cry and alarms were sounding from the signals my telemetry unit was sending. A nurse came in, "Olivia!? Is… Is Mr. Callan, okay?"

I nodded and heard Olivia say, "He just woke up. I think he's a little overwhelmed that I'm here holding his hand, is all. He's okay," and the nurse reset the alarms.

"Olivia. I worried…looked everywhere. I love you."

Right in front of the other nurse, Olivia bent over me nose-to-nose, "It's me. I'm here, cowboy!" and she gave me a long slow kiss wetting my face with my tears, their saltiness a welcome sensation on my parched lips.

Nothing was making sense because Olivia was in a nursing uniform at a Scottsdale hospital. How could she be working in the same town and I didn't know it? The investigator didn't know it? How could the love of my life be right in front me but invisible? Why did it matter. Olivia was kissing me and my own tears were clearing the crustiness from my eyes, bringer her sharper and sharper into focus through the pain and meds.

"Did you get my note from Janice?"

"Yes…. Bitch."

If Olivia was surprised I called Janice a bitch it didn't register on her face.

"I knew our trails would cross, David. I planned on it, David, but my God, not like this."

"You got me through this once. You're my angel. You can do it again…Any ice?"

She reached into the pitcher and got a couple cubes in her fingers and slipped them into my mouth. I sucked at her fingers a second, and got that movie star smile of hers.

"I…uh…Vanessa."

"I know about Vanessa, David."

"Hurt badly, Olivia."

I felt both of Olivia's hands wrap around my good hand.

"She didn't make it, David. I was there, watched everyone try their hearts out to save her."

My neck was stiff. If I could have turned my head, I would have. In front of Olivia, I was crying for another woman.

The monitor alarms started screaming.

The charge nurse rushed in and gave my I.V. an injection after shutting off the alarms.

"My fault. I told David about Vanessa Sorensen not making it. They were very close."

I know Olivia saw me react like I'd been blindsided, because I had. Olivia wiped my face with a warm washcloth, followed by a cool one.

"You knew...us?"

"My dad found you and with Vanessa. He thought it might break my heart but I made him tell me, anyway. I wasn't going to break your heart again by interfering, David."

"David, I didn't come here to stalk you; I came to Arizona because this is the best program in the country for nurses to become orthopedics nurse practitioners. They accepted me and I jumped at the chance."

She was weeping, trying to prevent her choked-up throat from triggering sobs. "My life's been <u>hell</u> without you every single day, every single minute and every single hour. I've had sleepless work-nights longing for you, ached for you, cried for you and, my God! I have missed you."

Her hands were wrapped around my arm, rubbing and caressing it, caressing my cheeks.

"Remember that young man I told you about, the one who went overseas got killed right after our relationship going? Now it's happened to you, David. You've been put through the same fire which I was and I don't know why. At this point, I don't *care* why. I was scared and I ran off

scared that you'd toss me aside when I saw you again.
All I could care about and think about was your love.
That's the hope I've been holding onto, the prayer that
you're mine and will be, again."

"Oli... Olivia? Every time the phone rang I hoped.
Anyone who remotely resembled you? It hurt to see. Here
I am again, and again nearly dead. Maybe you're not
even real, just an angel taking pity on a loser who
wrecked a nurse's life."

"I'm *bursting* with love for you. There's no room for
pity. Here," and she took my good arm and gently lifted it
to rest on the rail, moved closer, took my hand and
slipped it into her shirt so deeply that my fingertips were
inside the edge of her brassiere as she gently placed my
hand on her heart.

"Feel that, David? You're my heart. It's beating for
you and hasn't stopped. It's not going to change...." and
the tears came back. "Go to sleep, my precious love. I
won't see you tomorrow, but I will see you soon."

I slept for I don't know how long. I knew it was 11
hours from when I had talked to Olivia or imagined I
had. I rolled my eyes to the other side of my bed, looked
over and saw Olivia sleeping in the chair. Someone had
covered her with a hospital blanket. I reached across my
body with my good hand and barely caught the edge of
the ice water pitcher. I took a big gulp and it made me
cough, which woke up Olivia who quickly moved to my
bedside and held my hand.

"Am I in heaven? Olivia? It's you and you're with
me...? Here?" and I managed a smile through the pain
that wouldn't leave me alone.

All her crying had left riverbeds of eye makeup down
the sides of her face. I was able to catch the edge of the
washcloth of Olivia used on me and handed it to her. She
knew she probably looked like she'd had a rough go, and
wiped her face clean.

"Do you remember we talked a while ago, David?"

"I know we talked."

"It's been 11 months since I've seen you, David. Nothing has changed and everything has changed. The nothing part is that I love you and adore you. The everything part is good and we'll get to that, too. Right now, I need you to heal and get stronger."

"As long as you're here, Olivia, I know I will."

"You know, you remember that I can't be your nurse. I work here. But because of our history, you and me? I've got special permission from the Chief of Staff and Chief Nurse to see you whenever I want."

"Really?"

"Yes, really, cowboy. I'll be here every minute I can. We've got catching up to do."

"If there's catching up on you loving me, Olivia, sign me up." She grinned and kissed me on the forehead.

"Just wait and see."

Olivia was there every day before and after her shift and sometimes she could pop in for lunch but she never did stay very long. I assumed it was the orthopedics program.

I didn't have all the hardware from surgery this time so I was up and around and getting therapy after just a week. I was in a back brace but the pain was managed with meds and the brace really helped. I had crutches, a walker, a cane and a wheelchair, none of which I needed all of the time. I used what I needed at the time.

Sometimes Olivia would wheel me outside and we would sit and hold hands, spending quiet time. While out there with her, I reflected that God gave me two second chances. One at life and the other with Olivia. Nothing short of dying would take God's love or hers away, ever again.

It never occurred to me why the hospital had given Olivia permission to spend time with me. I assumed she'd proven she was a student when we met. Whatever got her that permission was my world, she was my world, and God gave me access to my world by way of a broken body, just like the first time. I reasoned my body could die. My love and desire for Olivia would never leave me.

After two weeks of continued improvements in physical therapy, there was talk of me getting discharged.

Revelation and Jubilation

Olivia came by after my dinner tray had been taken and took me out in the garden and steered me to a different spot than where we usually talked. She rested her buns against of the rounded edge of a large, tiled birdbath.

"David, I want to take you home so that I can nurse you completely back to health."

"Home as in?"

"Home with me. I have a condo here in Scottsdale. I'm being selfish because I love you and want you in my life and present 100% of the time. I want to nurse you back to health because I love you and I can't live without you. It's a lot to throw at you. I'm begging you to be candid, I want and need to hear what you're thinking."

I had the biggest lump in my throat I had ever had. Olivia just verbalized everything I could ever want to hear from her mouth.

"Now or ever, you never have to beg me for anything, Olivia." I reached out to the back of her neck and pulled her to me and kissed her with all the love I had in me. Then, I rested my forehead against hers, feeling her warm breath, swelled with love. I pulled back just enough to lock my gaze onto hers.

"I will love you forever, Olivia, and can't possibly love you more than I do in this moment. Will you marry me?"

She broke down and cried and went to her knees, putting her head on my thighs. I could hear her saying "Yes, yes, yes!" through the tears as she looked up into my eyes.

"You will?

"Yes David. I'll be proud to be your wife, always," and she paused, "If you would rather, I can take you home to New Mexico, to the ranch and get you well, there. We don't have to worry about money. I have plenty and my dad's got an empty rental that's gorgeous. I can get some parttime hours at the hospital in Taos."

I couldn't get the words to sound out the way I wanted her to hear them. It was taking a minute.

"David, I want you whole and I want you happy and I want you healthy and I want you in my bed-oh how I want you in my bed."

I could do nothing but kiss her. I was helpless.

"Yes, Olivia, take me to the ranch and let's do life, there. I'm going to let you decide and I'm never going to regret it. Yes, you _are_ the love of my life."

Olivia held up two thumbs and all of a sudden, I heard cheering from all around the courtyard. All of her hospital colleagues had been looking on and quietly slid the hallway windows open. She tipped them off that _she_ was going to propose.

She started laughing and looked in my eyes and said, "Gotcha!"

People streamed into the courtyard hugging us both. I guess she had been sharing our story with colleagues.

"I want you to meet someone, David."

Then, as if Moses was parting the sea, the crowd split in half making a path toward the pair of sliding glass doors we had come through.

A woman walked out. I was at a really bad angle but could tell she was carrying something and Olivia stood up now, completely blocking my view of the woman, and walked toward her.

Olivia reached the woman and turned around. She had a baby in her arms. She was walking to me as slowly as a bride to a groom.

Olivia stopped about four feet from me, with the infant positioned to look right at me and said, "Tyler? Look! It's Daddy, _your_ daddy, Tyler. Say 'Hi' to your Papa!" There were cellphones out in everyone's hands, taking pictures and video.

I started crying uncontrollably. As she stooped to gently lay our son on my thighs, looking up at me, she said, "David this is our son, Tyler David Macias Callan." Everyone around us was crying.

The stars were suddenly brighter and twinkling a lot more rapidly. She caressed the baby's forehead and looked into my eyes and said with a grin, "You can't doubt this is your boy. He looks just like you, David."

"He's ours, all right, Olivia. He's got four names!" I said in my emotional overwhelm, "but he's too beautiful to look like me. He looks like you, Olivia, the most beautiful sight I've ever seen in my life."

Her eyes misted up, "Tyler was going to meet his dad. I was always going to come back to you, David. Always."

"OH! OH~ Uh-oh. He's wet."

"Yes, babies do that, Daddy. Let me take him."

She grinned at me, "It'll be a while until you do his potty training," and everyone who was still milling about chuckled. She got up and walked toward the nurse who had brought my son out to me. They exchanged a few words and the nurse took Tyler inside to change him. Olivia stood up and addressed the 20 or so people that were in the courtyard.

"I love you guys. Some of you know what this man and I have been through. Thank you for spending the most special moments of my life with David and me. I will never forget you or this night or this feeling."

She pushed my wheelchair through the crowd as people touched my shoulder and wished us congratulations. She got me to my room and helped me into bed just as the other nurse walked in with our son.

"Here's our son. I still can't believe that I'm getting to say, 'our son!'" She laid Tyler's little head on the pillow next to mine and reached into her purse for her cell phone.

"I'm going to take a picture of my boys for my mom and dad. Okay cowboys, smiles up for Grandpa and Grandma!" She showed me the photograph and my tears started up again. Olivia was glowing like the angel she was, never more beautiful and never more loving.

The regular medical routines happened the next morning as well as my going to physical therapy. Olivia passed me in the hallway with somebody's chart in her hands and said, 'Excuse me,' to the colleague she was walking with. She looked around in a comic kind of way and then bent over and laid a big kiss on me. "Hi there, cowboy. You feeling like coming home, soon?"

"As would be your wish my queen," and her colleague laughed, "Boy have you got him trained!" The mood was jovial. Olivia squatted down so she could look at me eye to eye and rest her hand on my wheelchair's armrest. "Admin just let me know my leave of absence is approved, that my last day is a week from Friday. We'll go home to the condo and just let you get used to family life a little bit and we can enjoy each other's company. How does that sound?"

"It sounds like I can't wait to get there."

"Do good in physical therapy! I need you big and strong, cowboy, and our little cowpoke needs you that way, too!"

I was all grins and Friday came. Olivia bought some clothes for me and had put them in my room. I was in a nice polo and some comfortable Chinos.

"They're going to do a little social thing for us before we leave, David. So, let's swing by the employee nursery and pick up Tyler and we'll get on our way!"

I leaned my head back in the wheelchair to look up at her and she bent down and kissed me. I felt like I was going to levitate right out of that chair.

We got to a door that said 'STAFF ONLY' and had a room number on it. Olivia inserted her card key and went in and there was a counter and several rooms with children of all different ages. There was a segregated area behind glass for babies and that's where Tyler was. The attendant met us halfway there, "Olivia I'm really going to miss you and Tyler."

"Paula. Let me introduce you to Tyler's Dad, who's exchanging wedding vows with me as soon as we can get it figured out. This is David Callan."

"Nice to meet you, Paula. You've known my son longer than I have! Regardless, thank you for taking care of him."

Paula squeezed my hand and said, "I think both of you guys are very lucky to have her," nodding her head toward Olivia.

Olivia handed Tyler to me and put his baby bag across the handles of the wheelchair.

"I can tell you this, I don't know if we deserve her but we're going to work every day to prove that we're worthy, aren't we, Ty," I said, looking into my son's eyes as he lay in my lap. He had Olivia's eyes.

Paula held the doors and we went down the hall into the executive wing near the conference rooms and entered a room full of people and presents and cake and streamers and signs. The place erupted. Ty, in my lap, started to cry and of course I looked helpless. I said, "Mommy, a li'l help here?"

She laughed and said "I've got this."

"And?"

"And so do you, my love."

Everybody went around the room and expressed why they would miss Olivia and regrets at not having gotten to know me very well. She opened all the gifts and kept all the gift cards so we could send thank you cards. There were some medical carts staged to get the gifts out to Olivia's Accord, the same Honda she had in California only this time there was a baby seat in the middle of the passenger seat. My wheelchair went into the back and I hopped into the back seat.

Home and Fathering

She took off toward what looked like open desert and then there was a lone road with a sign for a country club's turn-off. I noticed there were 40 or 50 condos terraced on a rise, where each of them had a view and every window was tinted. It was desert landscaping. There was even a guard gate which lifted and opened as Olivia drew the Accord nearby. We pulled up to a condo that had the number 122 next to the front door.

"How about I get you settled on the couch with Tyler and I can get this stuff inside in a hurry and get the car into the garage before it gets too hot."

"All good!"

I transferred myself from the couch into my wheelchair and put Tyler in my lap so I could cruise around and look at our house. In less than 10 minutes, I heard the garage door and Olivia came in through the kitchen.

The condo was stunningly beautiful as was its décor and furnishings. The couch and overstuffed chairs were beige leather and the oversized area rug's patterns were in pale greens matching cacti colors just outside the broad, floor-to-ceiling windows. There were potted ferns and plants everywhere. The kitchen was ultramodern with every imaginable convenience.

It felt like the condo was 1500 ft or so. I was way off; it was closer to 2,000 square feet. There were four bedrooms. One was an office Olivia had set up. Another was a cozy guest bedroom. The other was a nursery. The master was huge and must have been at least 12x18. I shook my head and looked at Olivia when I saw it.

It was a Western motif carried off very tastefully with a couple of charcoal sketches of weathered cowboys, one holding a saddle standing next to his bareback horse and another, a close-up of a chilly-looking cowboy, his collar turned up, clutching a steaming cup of coffee near a campfire.

By itself on a small table, under a recessed light's focus, was a bronze. It was a rodeo cowboy on a massive bull, his one hand lashed under a rope, the other high in the air with his body leaned way back fighting to keep his balance and stay on. It looked to be 24 inches tall or better and probably weighed twenty or thirty pounds

The furniture was hand-rubbed oak. On the dresser was a small vase with two fresh red roses. She must have gotten them that morning and they were exquisite. The master bedroom had a set of sliding glass doors and a patio with a trellis woven with blooming star jasmine through it to keep outsiders from seeing the elegantly tiled in-ground jacuzzi.

I looked at it and at her. "Therapy?"

"Yes, but clothing is not allowed in our private little pool. In fact, only my cowboys and me are allowed in our private little pool."

"Shouldn't it be bigger, Olivia?

"Bigger??" She looked perplexed.

I tried to look lascivious. "Yes. I may feel a need to breed, darlin', and we may need more room for more li'l cowboys! In fact, the mood I'm in right now. I might even be able to be talked into getting a little practice!"

Olivia grabbed a bottle from the baby bag and situated Tyler in the middle of the huge master's bed.

Her clothes fell away faster than I thought she could get them off. "In the water or in the bed, cowboy?"

"Ladies' choice." The tub filled quickly with the digital thermometer showing 102-degrees. She started the jets and got into the water and reached up to help me in. I no sooner got settled than her legs were around me, I was inside of her, and she was undulating slowly, kissing me as we rocked in unison adding gentle waves to the bubbling warm water. I held her as never before.

We held each other for a seeming eternity until Olivia said, "Let's check on Tyler."

"Let's go. We have an unattended little cowpoke asleep in our bed."

In her terry cloth robe, Olivia picked up Tyler and put him to her shoulder, cooing him.

"Do you want any tea or water or anything sweetheart?"

"I'm good David, thank you. I'm going to breastfeed Tyler and you're the only one welcome to watch the show. It's pretty intense. Come watch."

Olivia handed-off Tyler to me and hung her robe up in the bathroom. Once she was seated on the bed, she reached for and cradled him. She squeezed at her nipple repeatedly as it lay on Tyler's lips, and he took it into his mouth just as I saw the first drop of mother's milk appear. Olivia looked over at me, pouring more love my way than I could know.

"We're glad you're here, Daddy, aren't we, Tyler. We've missed you a long time," and I put my hand on Olivia's upper thigh, leaned, and kissed her as our son suckled at her breast. Being a dad was one thing. Being a new dad, part of this emotional and spiritual and physical combination of dad-ness watching my son, dependent on his mother whom I loved wholly and exclusively, gave me a feeling like I'd never known.

Olivia looked up from Tyler to me, "I promised God and my dad we'd find you, that we'd be together. That's why he's Tyler David and not named after my dad or named anything else." She smiled at me as she tenderly moved Ty over to her other breast.

"I think I want to be finished with traumatic injuries to get to you, Olivia."

"I was never, _ever_ going to keep our son from you, David. Spiritually, I wanted to grow to where I could withstand you rejecting me entirely for running off, but I resolved our son would know and have a relationship with you, with his dad."

Tyler was drifting off so I quieted my voice to a whisper.

"Tyler didn't come into this world alone. It took both of us, Olivia. And he wasn't born to a guy who got drunk and had a 1-nighter. We made love. Our *love* made Tyler. We're inseparable from Tyler. You worried about me forgiving you for disappearing? It dismantled my world and unraveled me. Deep down, I knew it wasn't to hurt me. Whatever it was, it wasn't hatred or retribution. So all I could do was find some inner peace and hope you'd seek me. Your note told me as much. I figured your family was a sanctuary that I wouldn't approach although I tried."

Olivia listened intently, gently rocking our baby gently as he slept. She rose and took Tyler into his bedroom and returned. She crawled onto the bed and I lay beside her, tracing asymmetrical patterns on her abdomen and lower chest.

"I can go on. Or shut up."

She turned her head toward me, "You're telling me why and how much you love me and I won't tire of hearing you say it, David."

I touched her lips with my index finger, then kissed them.

"Go on, because it seems like you need to, honey."

I never wanted her to have to wonder, and our frames of mind were in sync.

"Before Stephanie arranged for me to meet Vanessa, she told something big and serious had hurt Vanessa. She said life was just getting to where Vanessa could consider even being around a guy, that she was willing to go out socially, again, at least try."

"Vanessa was timid but braved being honest enough to tell me she couldn't and wouldn't have so-called 'regular' sex with me because she'd been hurt. It was clear she meant physically hurt, Olivia. The man you love, Olivia, the one you know to be sensitive enough, respectful enough not to run or mock or criticize someone like Vanessa for risking telling that to another soul? I respected that and when we did get physically involved, there were expressed limitations. Vanessa knew about you, that I was in love with you and there wasn't

going to be a future. She knew. I was the first few steps
of a new direction for her, Olivia."

Olivia pulled her body up into mine and we were as
close as could be.

"I left and, relatively quickly, got to a place where I
accepted that you might—probably would-hook-up with
someone, David."

"You're there for someone else until God took it out of
your hands. Yeah, it's a little bizarre that it took two
tragedies, her passing and your accident to bring us
together."

Olivia was collecting her thoughts and I didn't
interrupt that.

"Spiritually, I belong to you. Essentially, I belong to
you," and she took my hand and guided it up her shirt
over her heart. "I did this in the hospital, put your hand
on my heart. Do you remember?"
I nodded and whispered, "And you said I was your
heart."

She went on, "I see a life ahead, for us, you and Tyler
and I as a family, something you never had and another
calling I need to answer, as a mom and wife, your wife.
You didn't have a sense of family and took-on life with no
net under you, no escape chutes. Nothing."

"I didn't exactly have a say."

"But you have tools and developed more to negotiate
everything that comes along, unlike most of us. Not
rewarding emotionally, but survival's highly underrated.
I'm called to be a healer and I'm going to pursue
responding to that call. You've already answered your
call to be a husband and dad, and we're winning at life.
Already. Life is pretty promising for us, David."

"I don't feel that family father leader thing going on
inside me, how that's acquired. If I ever will get it I may
have to flip coins to make decisions, Olivia."

"Are you looking at some rule book, somewhere?
There isn't one. Together works for us and I'm fine with
it."

She went on, "A physically broken man drops into my lap, into my care even before I'm fully legal to be his RN caregiver. I'm a mechanic put on Earth to heal the Davids who recur, reappear? No, I won't short-change God. Loving you and making love to you seemed foolhardy and it was a big risk. I took it, accepted it with faith, David. I knew we could last, survive anything beyond that and we have....

She paused, "David?"

"Yes?"

"Were you made for me?"

"I honest-to-God believe that and before you ask me, 'And,' you were made for me, Olivia. I agree with you 100%, that we can overcome things that would destroy others—not lessors, but others. How? Why? I don't know or have to know. I know I won't quit, throw-in the towel on us, Olivia."

"I love you, David."

"I love you, Olivia, with love that's been fire-tested and is bullet-proof. I will never stop loving you. Now, will you marry me, dammit??" and she grinned.

"Yes, cowboy."

Phone.

"This is David." And I covered the mouthpiece, mouthed 'your mom.'

"We're fine, Ofelia. Just went for a swim, put Tyler down after he ate."

"Yes, much better. Pain's still around, but Olivia can see it's easier for me to move around.... I've heard a lot about you, too, and can't wait to meet you, either!!"

I laughed, "So you think that's the magical cure, Ofelia?? I'm not one to argue with THAT! I'm going to love every bite.... Yes...yes, she's right here."

"Hi Mama! Yes, he's as great as he sounds and his daddy lessons are going great, too," and she laughed.

"Oh, okay. Tell him we love him, and that I'll keep trying to get Tyler to say, 'Grandpa.... Okay, Mama – thanks. I'll look for it.... Bye."

"I bet you've never had a freshly butchered steak directly from a ranch before, David."

"I'm sure I haven't."

"She's going to pack and send a box of steaks, roasts, ground beef and prime rib. I'll make as much room as I can in the freezer."

"That sounds yummy!"

Tyler screamed. We threw on some clothes and I went into his room. "Hey, Tyler! Daddy to the rescue!" and I lifted him out of the crib and took him into the kitchen. "I'm gonna warm up a bottle for him, David, and fix us some sandwiches, okay?"

"Sounds good."

They weren't just sandwiches, they were club sandwiches as good as I'd eaten, anywhere. It took some directions to find the filters and coffee but I made a pot.

"Did you like lunch, honey?"

"Loved it! Love you!"

"Oh yeah, for how long, Cowboy?

"It's a process. Ask me in 150 years," and I patted her fanny as she rinsed the dishes because I could and because of the grin and blush it drew when I did it. Then I bent over and made a big smooch sound against her butt cheek as I kissed it, just because I could. I kissed her on the neck as she was putting away the last utensil.

Olivia scooped up Tyler and started down the hall with him in one hand and a bottle for him in another. I trailed with my coffee mug. She put Tyler down in his crib and we stepped around the corner into the master bedroom.

Olivia helped me undress. She approached the bureau and pulled open some drawers to show the rest of the clothes she had gotten me, including undershirts and shorts, boxers and socks. The closet looked like I won a men's wardrobe on a TV game show and everything was the right size. There were even shoes and flip flops. On the back of the door in the master bath, there was an oversized terry cloth robe. It matched hers.

When I turned around, she was naked, leading me with just a look.

Olivia pulled back the bed linens and patted the mattress next to her. "This is your spot, cowboy. Come and claim it."

"I think I'm going to claim the beautiful naked lady right next to my spot if it's okay with you, ma'am," and I crawled onto the bed and put my arms around her and kissed her in our own bed, under our own roof, in our very first house, with our son just a few steps away in his room. Through the baby monitor on Olivia's nightstand, we could hear Tyler working on his bottle.

We made love and cuddled a little while before dressing and heading into the kitchen.

Olivia put together a nice salad complemented by lean, sauteed chicken fillets with spicy green beans. I noticed there was a bottle of Hatch jalapenos in the refrigerator, unopened, and all I could do was smile.

I heard Tyler and scampered down to get him, bringing a dry diaper with me.

I was holding the baby until she got dinner on the table and lifted him from my arms, "Okay Tyler, first some dry pants and then chow time." As she stepped over to the couch to change him, over on the couch, she looked up, "This is easy."

"Let me. Show me how?" and she was right. Very easy. I put Tyler in his highchair and washed my hands while she ran the diaper to the pail in the garage and returned to wash her hands.

We sat down and Olivia reached for my hand and said, "I'm going to pray and I hope we can do this all the time."

I looked at her, "Of course we can. This is our house, our life and our family. Prayer is welcome here."

"Bless us, oh Lord, and these, your gifts, which we're about to receive through your bounty. You have made each of us whole and complete and brought our family together to celebrate our lives together as a family. There

*is no limit to our love and thanksgiving, Father. Thank you
for these and all of the blessings we enjoy. God bless all
of our loved ones, comfort and provide for those less
fortunate. Amen."*

I looked up and leaned over and gave Olivia a kiss on
the lips. "That was nice."

I sipped my water and we watched the sunset over
the desert. Even Tyler seemed content. We rested our feet
on our coffee table and enjoyed after-dinner coffee with
some cognac. Olivia said it was okay with my meds and,
boy, did it taste good. She lifted my mug, inhaled deeply,
and said, "That smells good, but it would curdle
Mommy's milk." I hadn't realized she wasn't having any.

Once I finished, she put Tyler on my shoulder and
rocked him gently. I didn't know babies snored. My son
was sawing teensy-tiny little logs against my shoulder.
Olivia nodded toward his bedroom and I rose with him. I
put him in his crib, pulling his blanket up as Olivia
looked on.

"I'm sorry but I'm really kind of lost here. What do
young, new parents do in the early evenings?"

Olivia replied, "I guess I dunno. I suspect they fight
and argue about money and other insignificant things.
Which reminds me, at some point, we should talk about
finances."

"When Mom called earlier, she said that Daddy was
asking her about Tyler's baptism. She had that mom
tone, 'You know it's a sacrament and he gets introduced
to the family and the universal Catholic family. It's
important to me and I'm glad it's important to your dad.
Because it's important to him? I know it's important to
you, Olivia,' and she laughed at herself mocking Ophelia.

"I agree, let's get him baptized. I'm surprised you
didn't just do it earlier as a matter of convenience."

"I wanted to, David, but in keeping with the Macias
and Mexican-American family traditions it's going to be
one hell of a big blowout party after the church
ceremony. You ready to deal with that?"

"Only because I have a strong, beautiful woman at my side, proud to introduce our boy, our son, to the church and the world."

"If it's okay with you, I'll let Daddy set up the dates with the church and let my mom go frantic with me about who to invite and what to cook and stuff. I'm going to give you a kitchen pass to just be a spoiled hubby-guy and get off easy.... Oh shit, David. I promised Mom and Dad I would call using the live camera app on the tablet so Mom and Dad can see you and talk to you up close and personal. Are you okay with that?"

"I contributed to giving them a grandson, so they probably won't hurt me."

She laughed, "Let me get my tablet out of the office and plug it in here at the table."

"When were you supposed to call?"

"Like...10 minutes ago but it's okay; they can figure out that we had a long day."

Facing Her Parents

Olivia made the connection and Ofelia answered. There was a stunning resemblance between Ofelia and her daughter, "Hi Mom, I love you!"

"I love you too, my darling."

"I have both of my boys at home and David's excited to say hello to you!"

"Olivia, surely he knows you talk nonstop about him and I've seen his pictures."

I laughed, knowing Ofelia would hear it and gave Olivia the shame-on-you gesture and she blushed and she laughed—joined-in by Ofelia's laugh that sounded just like her daughter's.

Before I got into the picture I said, "Mrs. Macias, good evening!" Ofelia was grinning from ear to ear. "Hi, David! I'm thrilled I finally get to meet you."

"We didn't quite get the order of things right like a wedding and then the baby, but we have everything else right. I'm going to love and honor her forever and proclaim that and make those vows before God in church!"

Her mother got weepy. Mrs. Macias looked off-camera, "Roberto, you talk!" She turned the camera toward Olivia's dad.

"David! Bob Macias, here. I need to thank you for something. No, two things. Thank you for our beautiful grandson and thank you for loving our daughter and treating her with respect and dignity every moment since you've known her. She stood up to the grilling I gave her. She's never lied to me, and I believe 100% that you're the man she believes you are."

Wow. I didn't expect that from her dad and it caught me on my heels. "Mister," and he cut me off.

"David? It's Bob. And after you're married and I'm 100 years old, maybe I'll let you call me Dad. For right now, Bob is okay," and he laughed.

"Bob, Olivia probably told you that I have four
names: David Francis Bernard Callan. Your grandson's
mother is Olivia Maria Christina Macias and she'll tack-
on Callan if she wants to."

He was just listening, giving me enough room to trip
myself up, perhaps? It didn't matter. I wasn't nervous
but had nothing to hide.

"I know how badly you want to see your grandson,
Bob, and I'm all for it. We'll be newlyweds, soon. You *will*
consider babysitting so we can do the things that
newlyweds do, won't you? That's what grandparents do,
right?"

He laughed and said, "I might hide your son from you
so I can enjoy him as much as you do!" Olivia grabbed
the iPad out of my hands.

"Hi Daddy! I love you!"

"I love you too, sugar. Please tell David we are going
to pray he gets better and stronger. I forgot to say it. But
I know you'll tell him and you know I mean it with
everything in me."

"Thank you for saying that Daddy and he's right here
and heard it."

"Thank you, Bob. With all the love and support I'm
feeling at the moment I already feel like family. Olivia and
I will make plans so you and Ofelia and can hold and
play with our beautiful boy!"

Ofelia said, "Where is he? Tyler?"

I jumped up and lifted Tyler from his highchair,
seating him in my lap with his head resting against the
bottom of my ribcage.

Olivia was staring at me as if I was the first diamond
she ever saw or the first truly gorgeous sunset. Her dad
and I hit it off right in front of her and she said,
"Someone wants to see his *abuelo* and *abuela*!," and I
filled their screen with Tyler's face as he looked around.

Bob and Ofelia chattered away at him, taking turns
appearing on the camera.

"Okay Dad, I've got to go because I have two boys I have to get to bed. One of them needs a little extra TLC and the other needs a breast-fed meal! We'll talk soon."

"Okay honey, love you."

Off camera, I said, "Ofelia, goodnight!"

She replied, "Goodnight, you lovebirds! Kiss my grandson for me until I can do it myself!"

"Will do Mom!"

"Will do, Ofelia" and Olivia closed the connection.

"David, if that could have gone better, I don't know how." and she gave me a kiss. "I think I do want a sip of wine. You okay? You have frownie-wrinkles."

I laughed, "Frownie-wrinkles?"

"Yes. Something's on your mind. Mommies know this!"

"Fine honey-great…. This could have waited, but I think you would like me to let you know when and why I may get frowns. I need to get something onto the table so you can help me sort it out."

She just finished pouring the wine and using the heel of her hand to reset the cork as she replaced the bottle into the refrigerator. She was nonplussed.

"What's that?"

"My apartment and my lease and the stuff I had there. In the bigger scheme of things is it's not that important I guess but it's nagging me a little bit."

Olivia sat down across from me instead of next to me and she put her hands out, palms up, and I rested my hands on hers. She wrapped her hands around mine and said "You know that man you just talked to on the tablet? You don't have a lease because my dad paid it off. All of your stuff is in our garage 15 feet from where you're sitting except for the stuff that I thought might be damaged by heat like your stereo and records and stuff. All of that is in Tyler's closet. See? Good things happen when Daddy's willing to talk to Mommy about an-y-thing," and she made a funny face at me.

I shook my head, "You blow my mind. If nobody told you today, Olivia, I'm telling you that you're freaking amazing."

"I'm not freaking anything. I'm just in love with you, ya dope." She sipped her wine and I felt her playing footsie with me under the table and it felt good to feel light-hearted and playful with Olivia.

"What does tomorrow hold in store?"

"I think you should get a lawyer to check into your motorcycle accident, David. I know you're not about money and all that. But if you consider that anything you get could go into a trust fund for Tyler. It's the most unselfish reason. That probably sounded weird, but whatcha think?"

"I agree. That's the same conclusion that I came to thinking about all of it. I just hadn't done anything about it. Can we brainstorm on that in the morning?"

"In the morning, Tyler's getting his dad a homecoming present."

"Yeah? I don't know how much walking around I can do, shopping, and I don't want to be a burden."

"Oh no this won't be any burden. It's kind of 'drive-thru' shopping. Tyler's getting his dad a present with four wheels. Since it is rumored he's a family man and the family already has a truck, Tyler likes the idea of something a little family oriented. I'm hoping Tyler will think more along sedan or something."

"Chuckster has my truck. Maybe I can put it in storage for Tyler," and I tried to keep a straight face. I couldn't.

Olivia's wondered, "Will you hate me if I ask you to get rid of it... give it to Chuck? Sell it? Trade it in, honey? Or I can find a garage to rent, maybe?"

"Don't fret over a silly old truck. Let's donate it to the St. Vincent de Paul chapter at church so they can deliver groceries in it. Hell, I don't care."

"Thank you. I just.... We have money, David. Something nice and family-oriented? You okay with that?"

"Olivia, what I think we need is a sedan or SUV, especially if there's a chance we're living in Abiquiu carting babies around." I knew I skewered her attention with the plural. I waited for the reaction. It wasn't lost on her.

"Babies? *Babies, plural?*"

"Well... Yes. The prototype turned out perfect. Are you telling me we only get to make one?" I smirked.

She was on full adrenalin, now, grinning as big as I'd seen her grin. "Just *how many* of these babies do you think we should have, there, cowboy?"

"Depends on the size of the bunkhouse and number of bunk beds but the exact number is... Hmm.... is as many as my wife *wants* and that's my final answer." She shook her head smiling.

"Right answer. And?"

"And I think I might be up for a practice round right about now or soon, cowgirl."

"You're two-for-two, battin' a thousand, cowboy. Take me to bed and own me. Convince me, again, that you're stud-worthy," and I did as soon as Olivia returned from putting Tyler in his crib.

She woke early and breastfed the baby and they both dropped back to sleep. I slipped out of bed, headed for the kitchen and started a pot of coffee. I hadn't noticed drapes covering the main sliding doors to the patio. When I pulled the cord and they opened, I gasped. Driving in, I saw the condos were terraced facing the road but the backside of the hill was sloped. From left to right, the vista was the greenest, most beautiful desert-landscaped golf course you could imagine. The gated entrance to the condos now made sense and answered my curiosity why there was a second road leading to somewhere I couldn't figure out. It led to the clubhouse and restaurant.

I opened the sheers and stepped outside. This was completely different air than in the Bay Area. This was dry, nothing citified or salted about it. Back inside, I poured myself a cup of coffee and set an empty cup out on the counter for Olivia unsure if she was taking caffeine or not. There were decaf teas in a cupboard and I laid out several of those.

I walked into Tyler's room and lifted a few of the box tops of my stuff.

Vanessa had picked out all the furniture in my apartment so I was going to either donate that somewhere or suggest to Olivia we could run an ad and sell it at one price for the whole lot. I was more sensitive about the truck than I let-on with Olivia because it was a reminder of Vanessa and I'd feel better not seeing it. I wanting to look ahead.

I heard a voice in the hallway saying, "Peek-a-boo! Where _is_ he? Where is <u>Daddy</u>! We're gonna find him, _aren't we_, Tyler. WHEEEEE! There's Daddy!!" and Tyler was giggling in her arms.

"Let's go give Daddy <u>big</u> smooches!"

I had to put my hands on my hips and just look at the two of them, I was floating on air watching my family approach me, smiling at me, loving me. Olivia held Ty to my cheek so I could get a good slobber-kiss. He cooed and she held him to my cheek and I leaned in for it and kissed him. Olivia retracted him and came in for a third pass. I intercepted her and kissed Olivia, tenderly.

"Hi, Gorgeous."

"Hi, Lover."

"I made coffee but I'm not sure if you're doing caffeine so I have some decaf tea on the counter. What can I get you?"

"Coffee is fine but I'm only going to have one cup."

"I love cooking breakfast. What do you feel like?"

"I'll go easy on you. There's some non-fat yogurt in the box and if you just slice a banana into a bowl with a cup of yogurt, I'll be a happy girl. I'll be an ecstatic girl if you get some English muffins from the bread box on the other counter and toast one. I'll split one with you! Maybe a single piece of French toast for Tyler. I think he can handle it."

"Comin' up!"

"The toaster's behind the cabinet door next to your left knee."

"Thank you cuz I don't want to curse in front of my son because I'm an impatient boob opening 14 cabinets and not finding the toaster," and Olivia laughed.

"No cussing around the greenhorn, cowboy."

"Then I'm going to ask the boy's priest for special dispensation until Tyler's about two."

"You don't have a foul mouth...at least not what I consider a foul mouth, anyway, probably because you lose your job if you let out a string them over the air."

I fetched butter and got her yogurt and banana ready, knocked out the piece of French toast. I joined my family at the table. I handed Olivia a napkin and bent over to kiss my son and stroke his hair.

"I still need to say he's beautiful like you, Olivia."

"We both made him David. He is little Mr. Us, David, and ours forever!"

I was grinning at her for a reason and Olivia asked, "What!?"

"I was thinking we could take a shower together." She was cradling Tyler and used one hand to point at his tiny forehead.

"You see this little boy, David? This is what we got the last time we took a sex-filled shower together. Are you sure you want to risk it?"

"Well in light of new information I think we should never ever get out of the shower," and my beautiful Olivia laughed with me.

I pointed at Tyler with my half-eaten muffin. "You're one lucky little dude, Tyler! We might have named you *'Faucet'* or *'Counter!'*

When our embarrassed laugher subsided, Olivia said,
"Sure, we can have a shower together and I think our
son will think that's just fine if we do." I stole a couple
teaspoons of Olivia's yogurt.

We made our way back to the bedroom put the rails
up and moved the pillows so Tyler could have his space.
"Halt! I'm issuing a Dad-o-Gram. Tyler, you will join
Mommy and Daddy for our first family shower together!"
Olivia loved it, and laid Tyler on the bed long enough to
get the two of them in the buff. Olivia turned and was
standing there just like God made her, holding our
naked child. We just looked, taking each other in, in our
own home.

"Let's put him in a towel, honey, so there's no chance
of him slipping out of our hands."

"You're playing in my mind again, David."

"He's our treasure," and I kissed her neck.

There's no describing that experience, the three of us
like the first family on Earth. It was profound, the aura
that we bonded as a family unit in the shower washing
each other. We were aware it was a memory in the
making, experience we'd cherish and recall.

We dried Tyler and got him into a jumper. She
handed him to me, and I put him in his crib with a bottle
of water. When I returned, Olivia was coming out of the
bathroom. I intentionally used a finger to hook the edge
of Olivia's robe, slipping her out of it.

When she turned to me and closed in, she could feel
how on fire I was for her. She bent down and slid a
bureau drawer out about four inches and rested her foot
on it. She put her hands on the counter and I
repositioned myself. She was wet with anticipation and
desire. As I entered her, she used her hands to push
herself back into me, taking all of me inside of her in a
long, slow thrust.

As we made love, my eyes looked at our reflection in
the big mirror as we let passion have control of our facial
expressions. Our rhythm was slow as could be, rocking

gently, lasting forever if we could but urgency overtook our pace and drove us to a shuddering, breathless finish.

I then turned her around to me and kissed her, leading her to the bed where I lowered a bedrail with a hand, pulled her atop me, and scooped her robe from the floor, blanketing her backside with it. Her head was against my chest. Content. At peace. Nestled and cocooned by love at its fullest. We fell asleep like that.

I awoke when I felt her body sliding up mine to pin me down to kiss me with the same fiery passion we'd shared. She put her palms on my cheeks, "I can't know, even imagine being happier than you make me, David."

"It's effortless, Olivia. I can't do enough and I know it. I'll never hold back and give you everything I am, to old age and beyond." She sighed and rubbed my sides and chest. She propped herself up, "I'm going to feed Tyler so he'll be sleepy when we're car shopping, okay?"

"M-kay," and Olivia rolled herself away and slipped into the robe and returned with him and disrobed.

I slipped out of bed and onto the little patio, adjusted the Jacuzzi's jets, and slipped in. My head was back, my arms outstretched, eyes closed, legs floating in the circulating bubbles. I didn't move when I heard the door, probably because I couldn't. I kept my eyes closed.

I felt Olivia slip into the water with me and she touched my chest, whispering, "Here. Fresh lemonade," and I felt a straw at my lips.

"Mmm, you are my goddess, indeed." I heard the plastic tumbler settle on the cool-deck and Olivia's movement brought my head up, my eyes opening.

She was positioning herself to wrap her legs around me and take me again, but I reversed her move. I spread her legs and pointed her g-spot toward the water jets. The forceful pulses of water hit her right where I hoped. She moaned, loudly, as I kissed her neck and nibbled at her earlobe. I reached around and fondled her breasts and her nipples got hard despite the hot temperature of the water. The jets were pummeling her *womanlies* and she couldn't escape because I controlled and held her position, moving her into and away from the jets.

Her orgasms were explosive and massive, firing off like stuttering geysers as her fingernails dug into the underside of my thighs as the involuntary thrusts overtook her. I lost count but know she had ten or eleven orgasms. I turned her around toward me and put the lemonade's straw to her lips to bring her back from the pleasure-driven exhaustion. She drank half the glass.

She turned around to me and wrapped her legs around me, so I guided myself into her and she let out an "Oh.... Oh, easy, David, easy," and I knew why. She was a furnace. She was taking deep, slow breaths and filling her cheeks to puff them out. Once her breathing allowed her enough control to speak in a full voice, she said "Where the hell did you learn *that*, cowboy?"

I reached backward over my shoulder and got the tumbler of lemonade, putting the straw in reach of her lips, again.

She took a long drink, "Ooh...."

"I improvised. I've never been in one of these things in my life."

"Are you kidding me?"

"Nope, I'm a bubble-newbie, Olivia," and she splashed me.

She pointed at me, "If you ever do that to me again," and I got defensive.

"*To* you, not with you?" I said, teasing her.

"If you ever do that *to* me again, David Callan, I'm going to chain you to this spa."

She backed herself off of me and turned 180-degrees and I pulled her against my chest, crossing my hands across hers. She nestled her head between my neck and collarbone. We were still. I kissed her neck, softly.

"I think I'm wrinkling; time to get out, cowboy."

The star jasmine aroma filled our lungs and it was a gorgeous morning as we stepped inside and she headed to the bathroom.

She sat at the vanity brushing her hair and said "I don't think I want to be contacted by all those creepy, ambulance-chasing injury lawyers. Is it okay with you if I turn the motorcycle thing over to Daddy? He's used to gnarly legal shit and I think he will screen all of the crappy stuff out so we don't have to spend much time dealing with it."

"If he's willing to do it I'm more than fine with that. Absolutely fine with that. Besides, getting Tyler's daddy a new car with a primo baby seat sounds much more fun!" Olivia looked at me in the mirror and saw me grinning with my hands on her shoulders.

"That robe fits you perfectly, David, you sex machine, you!"

"My wife, my incredible wife gives me everything in exchange for the great sex I provide at her *every* whim and request."

She shot me a promiscuous grin, "Don't look for that to stop anytime soon, cowboy."

"Pfft. Ain' no way."

"Any ideas what kind of sedan or SUV you're interested in?"

"I like Fords but can't tell you why I like them. We can look online and see all of the actual units that are on the dealers' lots. We pick the one we want, stop-in at the closest dealer and give him an ultimatum: he can bring it in for us on a dealer trade or we can fly to the dealer who has it and drive it home. We tell him, 'We've got cash. Wanna sell a car, today? Or are we buying this same car from someone else?'"

"You make it sound easy, David."

"It was taught to me by one of the salesmen at the station whose uncle is a car dealer. He said it works 100% of the time."

"You open to suggestions?"

"Yeah, I'll drive anything, honey," and I meant it.

"Would your price reduction thing work with a Mercedes dealer? I think you'd love what I have in mind."

"Uh, probably not. I don't know if they wheel 'n deal on Mercedes. Honestly, Olivia? I think a Benz station wagon's just lame, I'm sorry."

"Not a wagon, an SUV. I saw a few TV commercials. I looked online and really like one, a 350-something." She grinned, "I don't think you'd feel any less manly behind the wheel of a Mercedes SUV."

"I'm fine with that, sweetheart. Let's check 'em out." I heard the baby and he grinned when he saw me.

"Hey there, little me. Atsa big boy!" and I raised him above my head before I put him against my shoulder. He began drooling baby-goo-saliva on my shoulder which made him giggle and I didn't mind a bit. He was Olivia and me in one cute, smart, loving little human being.

"I think he likes you, David. But only because you love his mommy."

"Boy do I. I'm going to go out and get one last cup of coffee before the coffeemaker shuts itself off. Want anything?"

"Not particularly. I'll be out in a few minutes."

I looked up from the kitchen table where I had been making silly faces at Tyler in his highchair. Olivia was wearing white shorts and white sandals with a red and white-striped blouse opened at the top a couple of buttons, and with her hair in a ponytail. She looked like she had just stepped off of a yacht.

Less than three hours later, we were in our Mercedes M-350 SUV with all the trimmings. Olivia was into forevers (why she picked me, right?) and heard that Mercedes Benz' lasted forever. It was white with a dove grey leather interior and killer sound system. We took turns driving it.

Olivia's phone beeped with an incoming text.

"Dad sent me a picture of a lawyer's card and texted, 'This is the guy David needs to call.'"

I made the call an hour later while Olivia was feeding Tyler. They put me right through to Mr. Gibson on the mention of my father-in-law's name. Gibson asked me to describe the accident. He told me the call fell under 'attorney client privilege' since he was now accepting the case, should I agree. I agreed, and he said he would email some releases to get all the police records, anything regarding the incident.

Less than fifteen minutes after the call, I filled out the forms he sent in the secure, online version that makes an electronic signature, and it was out of my hands and out of my hair.

Olivia was glad. I was glad.

At Olivia's urging and with her help, I got the truck paperwork located and we ended up donating it to the Catholic Church, just as we discussed.

Gwen

We were on our way home and I needed to get away from her for a little while to carry out a little labor of love. I never drove off without telling her where I was going. I had nothing to hide nor would I ever except. where little surprises for her were concerned. Like now. I needed her to agree to be dropped off.

"Honey, would you be okay with me calling Stephanie and seeing if I can stop by the station for a while? I'd like to head over there." If it fazed her it didn't show.

"I'm surprised you didn't bring it up before now, David. I didn't want to push you to do it but I thought it would do you some good to reconnect with all those people that care about you."

She turned in her seat with an expression of compassion and caring.

"Hey, cowboy. I know that Stephanie and Vanessa were tight and I have absolutely no problem with that because I love you. You got crushed by the same thing I got crushed by."

"I gotta do this. It's long overdue."

She held out a pinky finger and I took my right hand off the wheel to take hers in mine. "We're in this for life unless you tell me otherwise."

"Ain't happenin', cowgirl. You are my one and only my forever-love," and her pinky gave mine an extra squeeze.

"It's fine if you wanna drop us at the house and go to the station. Surprise 'em! They'll flip-out!"

"You sure?"

"Mama said."

"I'm not going against what Mama said. I never want to sleep on a couch because of something I say or do. I like my mommy-cuddling," and I gave her my silly grin.

"Good. Mama won't have to take her hand to your backside."

I let that one slide.

"One more request honey? Will you go out with me? I'd like to take you out on a dinner date and you can pick the restaurant. Think special occasion, like 'Family Homecoming.' Can we do that?"

"Anytime," and she saw my expression change. "Aww, baby, you meant tonight. Of course we can! There's a special place I wanted to take you, anyhow. Tonight it is. And if you're nice to me? I might even make myself pretty for you."

"Prettier is impossible. So is more loveable. I won't mind if you show up in a bedspread. But I'm in the mood for a coat 'n tie 'n slacks. I'm told I 'clean up' real good?'"

"Who told you that!"

"Flirty gay guy in college."

We loved laughing together, something about us staring at each other when we did it.

Not far from my apartment, I'd seen what looked like a 'finer' jewelry store on the corner of an upscaled shopping plaza in Scottsdale, proper. There were just three cars near the building. I walked in and knew I was in the right place. This place didn't cater to first-timer $99 wedding ring buyers. 'Upscale' would have been insulting."

A pleasant woman rounded the corner of a display case, pushing her glasses up into her hair as she extended a hand, "Hello. My name is Gwen."

"Hi, Gwen, I'm Dave."

"What brings you in, Dave, or are you just browsing around."

I grinned a conspirator's grin, "I'm here on a mission," and she liked the humor.

"The love of my life has a very desolate, empty-looking place on her beautiful left hand."

"So your mission, now *our* mission, is to change that."

"Right."

"In a big way or a small way."

"In this case, a little bigger may be the better way to go. Earthly. Not other-worldly."

Gwen laughed and smiled, "Good answer, David."

"Now you sound like my Olivia, Gwen."

"Ooh, Olivia. If she's as pretty as her name, I may know the very neighborhood of rings we'll explore."

With no customers in the store, Gwen had seen a brand-spanking new Mercedes pull into the lot. She knew whatever was going to go down wouldn't be difficult if she had the goods in one of her display cases. I followed her to such a case.

"Gwen, we have a child. At the risk of sounding weird, is there such a thing as an engagement ring with an extra stone, an extra little stone?"

"There's not a rule book, David. Wait to you see all of the rings that aren't just a single stone. Do you have a boy or girl?"

"We have a son named Tyler."

Gwen's eyes got big as saucers and she sighed. "David, I know why I thought I recognized you. I listened to your newscasts every morning when you were at KFCG. And I'm so terribly sorry for your tragic loss."

"Thanks. I got a second chance, I have a beautiful bride-to-be and the child we created, together. I'm grateful and happier than any guy should be."

She placed a black velvet cloth across the top of the glass case. On each side of it, she placed two trays full of rings. There must have been 80 rings, total.

"Right there," I said pointing. "That's it."

Gwen laughed, "I haven't shown you anything. Point it out!"

I moved my finger right over the top of it.

"You've got the mojo, Gwen, had it when you pulled the second tray. I'm left-handed and you put the tray next to my left."

"Most lefties wear their watches on their right wrist, just as you do. So I was tipped-off," and she returned my conspiratorial grin. "It's a tip-off."

Gwen removed the ring from the tray and wiped it with a jeweler's cloth before placing it on the black velvet. It was an emerald-cut diamond framed in yellow gold. On one side of the ring, inset in the gold, was a small, dark ruby. Pretend the rectangle's the trunk of a person's body and you're facing them.

"Hold out your hand, David."

Gwen slipped the ring onto the end of my pinky finger. It only took a second.

"Take it off of me, please. I don't want to smudge it," and Gwen complied and placed it gently back on the black velvet."

"It this still the one, David?"

"No contest. I'll take it."

"David, the sign out front, 'Pierson-McArdle Fine Jewelry'? I'm Gwen McArdle, the owner." She picked up the ring and looked at the tag.

"Nice to meet you, Gwen. And I'm impressed you're helping me, personally. Thank you."

"You looked needy and I took pity," and her eyes twinkled as she kidded me and we chuckled.

She removed a small tablet of paper and a pencil, and a sizable calculator from the counter right behind her. She scrawled "$14,580" making sure I was watching. She hit the calculator and picked up the pencil. She crossed out the fourteen-five number and wrote "$10,150 + tax."

"Because you're you, David."

"I think you and I will be seeing each other again. I want a pendant for her, too, Gwen. But today, the ring's everything."

"Let me get a box. Bring her in for sizing and make sure you ask for me when you call. I'll size it while you wait. I grew up in this store."

"I can't thank you enough," and I handed her my credit card.

She was back in a minute with five boxes in her two hands. "You get to pick out the box, too, David. But I'd bet you'll pick the one I would!"

White and heart-shaped, red velvet inside. "Can't be any other one that this one, Gwen."

"It's unanimous," Gwen said, nodding. "Suggestion if I may?"

"Sure, Gwen."

"Take a picture of your receipt with your cellphone, David, and leave the original with me so she won't find it. I'll slip it to you when you bring her in for sizing."

I took her advice, the ring, and couldn't get home fast enough.

On the way home, I called Stephanie's cellphone. She picked up.

"David! What's doing?"

"A couple things, Stephanie. First, I came in to see you this afternoon. That's the story, because I was getting a little giftie thing for Olivia.

"I gotcha covered. You said a couple things."

I squirmed a little.

"Vanessa's folks added me to the hospital's short list for family medical information without even meeting me. I never reached out to them. I want to. Need to. I have some things I want and need to tell them."

I think that came out of left field because of Stephanie's long silence.

"Tell ya what. The way to do that is, pick up a sympathy card and bring it in. I'll help you write it and give you the address. The personal sentiment? You tell them just after they've received the card. You'll say you're going to follow-up with a call. We'll make that happen, David."

I'd never heard her more sincere.

"Thank you, Stephanie. I gotta bolt, I'm pulling in," and we hung up just as I cleared the security gate.

The Right Way to Ask

I called out as I came into the kitchen from the garage, "Where's my family?"

Silence.

I walked into our bedroom and Olivia was in a tube top and jeans, barefooted and sleeping. Tyler was on the mattress, snuggled into the warmth of Olivia's cleavage. I slipped out of the bedroom, quietly closing the door.

I flipped on the TV and muted it, settling for the golf tournament, kicked off my shoes and put my feet on the "Journal of Nursing" magazines on the coffee table.

It wasn't long before I heard a hallway chant, "I think Daddy is in the building! Yessir, I do, Tyler. Let's find _Daddy_! ...YEA! There's Daddy!" Olivia had him in her outstretched arms and spun around with him, slowly, bringing him in for a landing in my lap. Over the back of the couch, she bent and I turned my head to kiss her.

"How'd it go?"

I laughed. And lied. "Well, I got a surprise. Chuck was 45 miles away doing a required visual on the transmitter, and Stephanie couldn't stay very long. No biggie. Couple of people rolled up and we talked a bit. BUT!"

Olivia had snuggled up next to me.

"But what?

"But I love-love-_love_ the new car my wife bought for me today!"

"That boy in your lap bought you a Mercedes, today. He has his mother's good taste," she said, her eyes twinkling. I gave her an Eskimo kiss.

"I really haven't gone out to dinner very often, David, I mean, casually with other nurses, yes. But the place we're going tonight? I've gone there alone when I did need to get out.... It's safe...close and they have great food."

"Nothing wrong with that. Why the build-up?"

"I don't want you to be weirded-out if the hostess or server recognizes me. It's Tyler they remember, not me.

Everyone makes a big deal with our handsome little cowpoke," and she laughed.

"Uh...from hanging out in the lounge?"

"Seriously, David? Hanging out in a bar with Tyler on my hip? Uh, no. From having dinner-for-one, ordering a shrimp cocktail, Caesar salad and a Diet Coke time after time."

"That actually sounds good, Olivia."

"We can go anytime. We don't need a reservation."

"Scottsdale? Phoenix? Tempe? Where are we headed?"

"Somewhere out there," she grinned.

Tyler was wearing a little outfit that made him look like he was wearing bow tie, blazer and slacks. Olivia was in an elegant-looking sundress with a white background and small clusters of wildflowers of purple, teal and orange. She was a knockout in it, especially in contrast to her tanned skin. Pale orange lipstick and earrings, and of course, her white sandals were perfect complements to the dress. I was shaking my head admiring her beauty when she walked out of the master bath.

I smiled and she knew why. She was turning me on.

"Like it?"

"Mmm, yeah."

"If you behave at dinner, I'll take it off for you later and...Hmm. I can't remember if I'm wearing a bra or panties. No worries, you can let me know," and she came over and gave me a delicious hint of later.

She whispered, "I'm going to bring you here for dessert."

"You're lookin' pretty tasty there, too, cowgirl. I may want seconds."

I took my jacket off and put it over the SUV's console after we got Tyler settled in his car seat and we headed for the restaurant. I was rolling down our usually deserted street, curving around with the security gate just coming into view.

Olivia looked over, "Turn left just before you get to the gate, baby."

I was clueless and looked over at her.

"Gotcha. We're going to The Hideaway, the formal dining room at the country club."

I laughed, "You're too much, Olivia. We could have saved at least 20 cents on gas and borrowed the neighbor's golf cart to drive to dinner, honey."

"Not so. If we are stylin', then you're taking me in the royal coach."

I stopped short of the turn, leaned over and kissed her. Then proceeded.

The Hideaway was as nice as any formal restaurant I'd been in, San Francisco, included. One side of the dining room was picture windows overlooking the lakes on the golf course, with a Western view for sunsets. Without even knowing it, Olivia had set herself up perfectly for my big move.

We could see our big patio from the windows on the other side of the dining room.

"How did you manage this, Olivia?"

She whispered across the table like it was one secret agent to another, "Don't tell anybody. We're members here."

I burst out laughing which startled Tyler and started him crying and thought other may be staring at us. They weren't, so Olivia removed a small blanket from Ty's bag, threw it over her shoulder and tucked his head underneath it so he could breast-feed a few minutes. He wasn't awake three minutes when he was finished.

We were the youngest people in the country club. The food was out of this world and I intentionally left food on my plate.

"You're not going to finish your dinner, David?"

"I wanted to leave room for dessert. I'm having two, tonight. One here and one at home," and she looked at me, tenderly.

"I'm stuffed but you know I have wifey-rights to as many of your desserts as I want for the rest of your natural life."

"And everything else I have. Without argument."

"Right answer, cowboy."

Our server came up to the table and asked how everything was. Olivia spoke up "The sea bass was really extraordinary, just delicious."

"And yours, sir?"

"It was terrific. The shrimp cocktail and Caesar were perfect, as Olivia promised they'd be, and I loved the sea bass, too. I just didn't eat it all because I wanted to save room for dessert."

"Dessert menu or do you know what you'd like?

"I'd like the lady fingers topped with strawberries."

"And for you, ma'am?"

"I'll just share his, thanks," and the server headed toward the kitchen.

It was going to work perfectly into my plan.

"Excuse me, honey. The men's room?"

"Left side of the main lobby."

I got up and smooched her, and got our server aside. I slipped her a fifty.

"This is a tip for having champagne and flutes arrive as soon as I'm on one knee, proposing, which will be just after a bite or two of dessert. Can do?"

"Can do," and she was grinning, "Congratulations!"

I returned once I was sure the ring box was in my pocket and the server's arrival with dessert coincided.

Olivia sucked in a breath, "What a beautiful dessert."

I used a big soup spoon to get a bunch of strawberry and a bite of lady finger onto it and held my hand under to catch any drips as I reached across the table to offer it to my Olivia. She opened her mouth and I gently let her mouth take it off the spoon.

"Mmm!"

She got it down, reached for her water goblet, and took a sip.

"I may want more of that, David!"

"You know the best thing about lady fingers, Olivia?" I said, taking her left hand in mine.

"No. Tell me, my love!"

"I'll show you," and I stood up and took half a step to her. I quickly got down on one knee and I pulled out the white, heart-shaped Victorian-looking ring box.

"Olivia, the best thing about lady fingers is finding the only lady's finger in the world on which I would like to place a wedding ring.

Her napkin was already up on her face, catching the tears. I opened the box, showed her the ring in the box, and gently removed it. I poised the glistening 2½ carat diamond ring next to her fingernail. Her hand was trembling.

"Olivia Maria Christina Macias, will you marry me, marry me so that I can spend the rest of my life loving you and Tyler, be the man you want me to be, and the best father I can be?"

She was nodding behind the tears. Everybody in the place knew what was happening as soon as I went down on my knee and there were already whispers about the size of the stone because it was very visible in the restaurant's dramatic lighting.

She leaned over and kissed me. "Yes, David Francis Bernard Callan. Yes, I will be your wife, happily and proudly and always."

I slipped the ring on her finger and people politely applauded.

There were tears here and there around the dining room. Our server led the line of other servers, arriving with a champagne bucket, the server behind her with chilled crystal flutes, and another with fresh strawberries on a tray. Once in place, all the other servers raised flutes of what must have been ginger ale and, in unison, said, "A toast to the bride and groom!" and everybody in the place clinked glasses with their silverware and said "Here, here!"

I kissed the back of Olivia's hand, "I love you so much."

She leaned down and kissed me gently on the lips as I rose to take my seat, sliding my chair next to her without losing contact with her hand.

She held up her left hand with the back of it toward Tyler, "See that, Tyler? Daddy busted a move on Mommy and we're getting married!"

I was the happiest guy alive. "We're doing this, cowgirl!" Even Tyler grinned.

"You bet we are, cowboy."

"And?"

"And whenever and wherever and however you want, Olivia."

Our server came up. "Congratulations to you both! That was the most exciting and romantic thing that's probably ever happened here!"

Olivia answered, "I know you remember me coming in a lot by myself. This is the guy I was aching and grieving for, Candace. We'll never be separated, again. Thank you for being part of this incredible evening."

She blushed and turned to me, "Mr. Callan, after you pulled me aside to arrange the champagne? We—some of the servers and me—decided we'd start sneaking pictures with our cellphones. I think we've probably got twenty or thirty pictures, most of them as you proposed and just afterwards. I'll burn them onto a CD. I'll tell management you left it here in the restaurant and leave the CD in an envelope for you."

Olivia was gracious and sincere, "Candace, that's amazing and thoughtful! Please. Please do that."

"Would you like to see?" and before we could say yes, Candace got between us and showed her the pics she, alone, took. They were crystal clear and looked like the work of a pro photographer.

"Olivia and I will be back frequently and when we are, you'll be our server. Fair enough?"
"Thank you, Mr. Callan."

"You took care of my Olivia when I couldn't. That makes us friends. Call me David."

"Thank you, David.

The valet brought up the SUV and we wound our way up the hill toward the condo. She stared at her ring all the way. She looked over at me just in time to see the blood drain from my face.

"Olivia?"

"Are you okay, David??"

I stopped and put my forehead on the top of the steering wheel.

"Olivia, I just walked out without paying our check."

I didn't see anything hilarious. Olivia sure did. She was losing it, laughing.

"Come here, you!" and she flipped up the console and hugged me and nose-to-nose said, "They don't give members a check. It's on our monthly membership bill, honey."

"Okay, I'm a dope. I did take care of Candace, though."

"You're *my* dope, and with this," she said holding up her hand, "...you are _my_ dope, forever." Olivia looked up to the rearview mirror, "Don't look, Tyler. Mommy's gonna give Daddy a big, wet, let's-have-sex kiss!"

Tyler was already out like a light from the ride. We got him out of his seat and went inside and put him down in his crib. Olivia walked up to me, confrontationally.

"No girl deserves this, deserves you. And I got you. Do you know how humbling that is? Do you know how grateful to God I feel right now? Do you know how many things were so against any of this happening and working out okay?"

I was nodding my way through it and put my arms around her.

"Olivia, you...we went through a lot to get to this moment. We're a long way from done. We're just getting going," and I held her and held her.

I was getting out of my clothes headed for the bathroom. Olivia stopped, put her hands on her hips, turned around and said, "Hey! I have a question. Why does my engagement ring fit so perfectly!??"

"God intended it that way. I dealt with Gwen, the owner. You'd like her and get to meet her when we look at wedding rings. She went out of her way for me and, personally, wants to size your ring."

"Can we, David? Just a teensy bit smaller, like a half-size would be perfect."

"I'll call her tomorrow...because, if it slips off, I'll lose my mind."

"I never want to take it off. You already know that, right?"

I moved close to her, slipped the straps of her sundress off her shoulders as I kissed each shoulder.

"Mmm, you'll take this off for me, won't you?" and Olivia was standing barefoot, earrings-only in front of me just seconds later.

I loved her body, padded perfection. She undressed me, scampered down the hall to put Tyler in his bed, and began her own version of sexually wearing me down and out as I had done with her in the whirlpool.

As we lay there thinking about the superb the day and evening, I asked, "What are we doing tomorrow, what's in store, on tap?"

"I figure it's banking day. I'm going to haul out a bunch of stuff and lay it all out for you, where we are on finances. There's a lot you need to know. First and foremost, David, we're set.... Um...well-off for our age."

"It wasn't ever a concern or issue for me, Olivia. I believed—and still do—that we could achieve any goal we set," and she smiled. "My financials are all accessible by my phone and I don't spend much on anything, really. No debt to speak of, and fine on cash. But that'll keep until tomorrow," and I hooked her neck with my elbow and kissed her.

"Oh, Tyler and I have a well-baby clinic appointment at 1:30."

"You mean *we,* don't you? *We* have a well-baby clinic appointment? Unless you don't want me to go."

"You mean you'd go...will *go*?"

"Well, if dads are allowed and you don't mind?"

"Mind? I'm *jazzed,* honey. Of course it's okay, but you may be the only male there; like OB-GYN visits, the men usually bail unless they're bossy wives order them to be there," and she laughed.

"You know I'm all-in. What's better than hanging out with my son! I don't have to go to work, I don't play golf, and I don't hang out in bars. This is what the happy dad, family guy, does right? And I'm loving it!"

She rolled her eyes at me and laughed. "You are a real piece of work," and she held up an index finger, "a <u>lovable</u> piece of work, but just unbelievable sometimes."

"Believe it. I'm trustworthy... loving...and don't forget humble!" I raised my palms to the sky and hunched my shoulders, "And you're stuck with me for a little while."

She furrowed her brows in mock seriousness and said, "Yes, as you wish, my 'Foreverness,' we're going long-haul."

We grinned at each other like fools, the grins turning into soft smiles, and then gazing into each other's eyes letting the love ooze over the silent tenderness.

We went to sleep in each other's arms, showered together and got dressed. I'd already promised myself to attack the unruly looking rosebushes while she got the financial stuff out and arranged on the table.

"Let's get after this finance stuff," she called out to me. "I'm not in a hurry. It bugs me the dining room table's covered with paperwork and folders. I'm a little OCD about wanting to put it away."

I put the bag of clippings and trimmer in the garage and joined Olivia at the end of the table.

Olivia took a deep breath, took my hands in hers and said, "Here goes," and grinned at me. "We can label this discussion full disclosure, David. We aren't hurting. In fact, we're pretty well off just from my end, alone. I told you Daddy has a home on a little piece of property he calls his ranch. That's true. I told you he works for a rich white guy on a very big ranch and that is also true."

Olivia looked me dead in the eye. "My dad's got bucks, he's loaded."

"Yeah, well I fell in love with his best asset," and it drew her smile.

"Daddy was a pro rodeo cowboy when he was young, a bull rider and famous in those circles. The rich white guy hired my dad to work on his ranch, raising prized rodeo bulls that bring seven figures. My dad became part of a working beef-cattle ranch that featured an extraordinarily profitable rodeo animal operation. They started making money hand over fist. My dad proved his worth and handled increased responsibilities given him. One of the perks he was given early-on was profit sharing."

"I'm interested in the 'famous' part as a cowboy."

"He won everything he entered on the big money circuit for five-plus years running. Cowboy of the year twice, and more bull riding trophies and belt buckles than you can imagine. He was a phenom, David. They put him into the Hall of Fame Cowboys Association and Museum as soon as he was eligible to be voted-on."

"That's an American success story if I ever heard it."

"That's not the half of it, David. Today, his profit sharing entitles him to a piece of the ranch and he gets a lot of income from it. The house that I told you he built? It's 3,700 square feet, David, and looks like a full-sized hacienda. I don't know why my mom and he have to knock around in such a big house but that's what he wanted, what he could afford and that's what he built. It's his most-prized possession other than me and my mom."

"Olivia, when I flew to Denver and saw you in something other than scrubs for the first time? You were wearing very expensive clothes and all the trimmings. And I saw you in another outfit, also very expensive, lavishly accessorized. I knew you weren't making that as a student nurse. It was obvious you came from money, and it was also none of my business. I didn't ask because I didn't need to know. You were, you <u>are</u> my life and that has nothing to do with money. Ever, and it never will."

"David!"

"What?"

"DA-VID!"

"O-LIV-I-A," and I laughed and made goo-goo eyes at her.

"I was going to tell you that I make $50k from a trust but I don't, because that's going to change. There's a $25,000 increase."

"HUH? For WHAT??"

She got up and walked to me. I put my arms around her waist. She looked down at me.

Something was making her tear-up, and they were coming down her cheek. Now she was going river-strength, almost convulsively crying.

"Please don't hate me. Our Tyler was born on the 29th of December, one day after your birthday," her sobbing intensified, "I'm a terrible mother! One day after your birthday and you never knew it until this instant because I didn't tell you," I hadn't seen her cry this hard, "and, and...and I'm crying because I think I'm getting my period!"

"Honey." I put my knee out and had her sit on it. I pulled her close and rocked her with my arms crisscrossed around her chest. "That's awesome! It's a bond my son and I will always have. Tyler and I will share that and nobody else can change it"

She was still sobbing. I was still rocking her, stroking her hair.

"Look at it this way: With the extra 25 grand, Tyler can afford to pay for my birthday cake <u>and</u> his!"

That made her laugh in the midst of a good cry and she slapped me on my shoulder, "Don't make me laugh, I'm sad right now and you're wrecking a good girl-cry!"

I pouted at her.

"Oh, you POOR baby. Come to Papa," and I cooed her just as I would Tyler. It was a warm moment. Her head came back to rest just under my jaw. She was regaining her composure with my help—kisses to the corner of her eyes.

I got up and got her a glass of lemonade, in awe that we had a refrigerator that made ice accessible without opening the door. I know, I know. I lived meager without apology. Knowing they exist and experiencing the reality of modern conveniences are different stories.

"If need be, I will scrounge for money while you care for our child, Olivia. I swear and promise that you will never want for anything."

"That's my point, David. We will *never* need money. Dad set up a trust fund for me and from that trust fund I'm gonna be getting $50K a year plus the $48k base giving us $98K in December. Even as a *new* nurse, I was making $7,000 a month. I was grossing $11,000 a month and daddy was picking up the taxes on the trust fund. I only paid taxes on the seven grand which were negated when I bought this condo."

She explained, "Our house payment's about $2,200 a month but that includes the country club membership. There's a big golf tournament here every year and if we rent out the condo for just that one week, we'll make about 6 grand. We can decide if we're going to keep the condo as a rental or as a winter house or whatever you want to call it. Or we can just sell it. I don't really have a charge on it. Think about it and let me know and I'm happy to do what you want to do with it."

"I love this place, Olivia. It's beautiful and it's perfect for us right now. I've even gotten sentimental about it. You brought me 'home' here, and because of you it *felt* like home."

"David, I really want you home-home, in New Mexico where Mom and Dad to spend some time with Tyler and you and me."

"And your ortho nurse practitioner certification?"

"My family, first and always, David. It's not so important, now. As the only child, I'll eventually own our New Mexico ranch. In fact, Daddy worded the trust so he could turn it over to me while he's still living. It feels like we're going to be heading that way. Are you comfortable with that?"

"Well...sure. Why wouldn't I be?"

"Because it's a big change. Because you haven't been there, seen it. And Taos is your only close hope of staying in radio, baby."

"Olivia, should you want to continue getting your certification, this stays as our home and/or we buy or build. If we relocate to New Mexico, we see how things fall into place and rearrange anything to better suit us. Lots of choices, Olivia."

"Are you sure you're okay with all of that...of this?"

"Once upon a time, I fell in love with a beautiful girl with the most beautiful name in the world: Olivia Maria Christina Macias. She loved me. She loved me so much she made a baby with me, for us, and chose to take care of him all by herself until my professional life got going. Drama and consequences aside, it all worked out for us."

Olivia was listening, intently.

"You had faith, in us and in me, that your someday-wish would come true. You loved me so much you gave our son my names, Tyler and David. The love of my life gave me a life, gave me all of her love, gave me a son, gave me a family, and gave me an extended family in New Mexico. I'm humbled and grateful to God with every breath I take. 'Okay with all of this?' Yes, my incredible love. Yes, my sensuous lover. Yes, my wonderful mate. Yes, my most intimate friend and confidant. Yes, my playmate. Yes. My hopes and dreams have come true because of you. I'm yours for the literal taking, anywhere," and I got choked-up.

I sipped at the lemonade and chewed one of the ice cubes to clear the lump in my throat. Olivia sipped some, too, never taking her eyes off mine. She started a widening smile.

"Spoken like my one and only, my forever-love and husband." She pulled my hand across the table and kissed every one of my fingers.

"Let's do this, Olivia."

"Okay. Then let me just lay one more number on you. We have almost $120,000 in savings and about 90- or 100K in checking."

I heard myself whistle.

"New checks are arriving with your name on them and we're stopping by the bank later today for you to fill out a signature card."

I was staggered by what I just heard. "Olivia, a hundred thousand dollars in our _checking_ account?"

She blushed, "Yeah. Maybe I should move that off to a college fund or savings account for Tyler or something."

"It's fine, I wasn't criticizing, I was just...kinda shocked."

"David? If you want to be a kept man? I'm giving you my blessing and permission. But I, your keeper, will kill you and eat you raw if you screw this up!" She laughed.

"Olivia? I'll shovel bull-poop for 2 bucks an hour at our little New Mexico ranchito before that happens. You're laughing because you know that's the last thing I would ever want to do. I would never want my son telling his friends 'Yeah my pops is a bum living off my mom's money but he's cool and my mom digs him," and that made Olivia laugh even harder.

"I don't care if I have to work as the receptionist at the only religious radio station in Taos, Olivia. I'm going to be doing something as long as it's not getting the shit kicked out of me by a mad bull or cow on the ranch." She was laughing hysterically envisioning all of that, so much that she handed me Tyler cuz Olivia was freaking him out.

"Mommy's a funny girl, huh, Tyler." She was laughing so hard she couldn't breathe. That made Tyler pee. On me.

I grabbed the tissue and handed it to her so she could wipe the laughing tears from her eyes. She grabbed a dry diaper to dab me as I was bouncing Tyler up and down in my arms gently to keep him quiet and a happy boy.

"Okay, cowgirl, it's my turn. I was under contract at KFCG. I got paid weekly and was making about $140,000 on a yearly basis. Because I got hurt, my disability is based on 50% of my annual wages. So I'm currently getting about $6,000 a month until I am evaluated as not being disabled. If it's determined I have permanent, long-term damage, it's negotiable."

Olivia rattled off the numbers rapidly and was writing them down.

"So your $6,000 a month, David, my $4,000 a month from the trust fund, my seven grand a month, plus the 50k lump sum. Or I have severance and vacation coming in if we go to New Mexico, which should be about $10-12,000. So that puts savings at about $132,000.

Your $70k is going to drop off sometime in the near future. Fifty-thousand drops on December 28th or 29th. The way I see it, David. We don't have a worry in the world as far as money goes."

"Olivia the only worry I have is that, *now*, I feel like a 'Cheap Charlie' about the ring that I put on your finger."

She showed me her left hand, admiring the ring: "This is the ring you picked out with me in mind, David. If it had been 1/10 of a carat cubic zirconia on a plastic band it would mean no less to me than what I'm wearing now and I would have knocked-out any cowgirl or cowboy who criticized or made fun of it. So don't even go there, cowboy" and she pulled me to her for a very slow and wet kiss.

All I could do was mumble and say, "Well, I paid cash. We don't owe anybody anything for it."

"I need some water. Want something honey?"

"I might share yours."

As I returned to my chair at the table, I said, "Olivia I've got an idea. But it's going to depend on your answer to a question. If you change your mind, then we should probably hang on to the condo while you pursue your orthopedic specialty. You-slash-we don't have to make that decision right now. The condo's only going to go up in value and we can swing the monthly payment without even feeling it. All that furniture in storage from my apartment can be donated to a homeless or women's shelter as far as I'm concerned. Is that okay with you?"

"I'm fine with that honey. How about somewhere for single mothers?"

"Super. You've probably got the connections from the hospital and just let me know what I have to do as far as signatures or whatever to make that happen. I know what I paid for all of it and I know I still have receipts. Those can be some nice deductions for us. Olivia?"

"Yes, love?"

"I'm brain-cramped. Please tell me something good."

"I'm horny."

"That's seriously good," and off to the bedroom we went.

As we lay in that magical afterglow that lovers universally share, I looked over at her. She turned and looked in my eyes, pushing my bangs away.

"I'm going to say something very un-masculine. I don't know when we're going to talk about a wedding day but I'm excited about it. Please let me know when I can marry you, 'k?"

"You're not escaping, going any-damn-where, David. I've been doing more than thinking about it. When you were at the radio station... or supposedly so, sneaking around to get my beautiful engagement ring, my mom and I talked about announcing the engagement."

"Olivia, if we find ourselves anywhere near the Nevada state line, you're toast. I'm goin' all hubby on you!"

She saluted. "Noted, sir."

We got dressed, ready to run errands like groceries and stopping by the bank to do the signature card thing. On the way out, Olivia rolled down the window and checked the mailbox and was sorting through the mail.

"It looks like your forwarding order finally hit, David: let me see...you, you, you, me, me, you and you. Here you go, cowboy, from your adoring fans at places who want their payments and stuff."

The bank was a non-issue. I never thought I would have fun at a bank and the grocery store with a woman and a small baby, but I actually did. We laughed and talked all the way through errands that I really didn't relish when alone. In fact, I was surprised at how many groceries we ended up hauling home. The groceries were almost put up when the phone rang and I happened to be closest.

"David?

"Yes."

"This is Bob Macias. How are you?"

"Never better, in love with your daughter and taking great care of your grandson, Bob." He laughed

"You better be."

"Let me get Olivia."

"No, hold on, I'm calling to talk to you. I want to send you some papers for legal representation about the motorcycle accident. This guy comes very highly regarded and doesn't work cheap. It won't cost you anything out of pocket. He gets a percentage of the settlement and he's going to go for the throat. I'm not going to mention the figure that he thought he could get, but what you're signing is to give him access to all the police reports and records and stuff. I'm enclosing his business card but I didn't give him your number. I told him you would call him because you had a lot of things going."

"Bob, that's a huge load off, right now. I can't thank
you enough."

"How *is* Tyler today, anyway?"

"We're going to the well-baby clinic in just a few
minutes. Everything should be okay. He's doing all the
normal baby stuff, nothing out of the ordinary."

Olivia called from the kitchen, "Is that Daddy?"

"Sure is, honey."

"Then let me speak to him, you dodo," she said, as
she came walking out toward me

"It's man-talk, Olivia, you may not understand it,"
and I begrudgingly handed her the phone and did the
mature thing: I stuck my tongue out at her.

She took the phone, reciprocated with her own
tongue.

"Hi Daddy... Yeah, like David said, we're going to the
baby clinic, just routine stuff no big deal. David's getting
set up with his physical therapist tomorrow and I'm
thinking they'll be doing three sessions a week or so....

Is Mom around? ...Of course not.... What's she doing,
today?"

I heard Olivia laugh. "She's going to buy a car by
herself!? Without YOU!? ...You know Daddy, I need to
teach David 'Happy wife, happy life,' don't I!

Oh! Daddy! I forgot to tell you David and I got *our*
new car, a Mercedes-350 SUV, a white one with all the
goodies. I think it's beautiful. It'll sure look nice on our
little road when we get home.... Oh, okay Daddy. Love
you bunches! Bye."

"David this is too funny. Can you believe my mother
is going out to buy a new car all by herself just because
she felt like it?"

"I don't really know them but yes, that's funny."

Well Baby Clinic

We were sitting in the waiting room of the well-baby clinic and Olivia's cell phone rang. She plopped the baby in my lap and grabbed her phone.

"Hey Mama how are you! I heard you were car shopping today... Oh no you didn't!! Really? You're kidding. ...You're not kidding. Here, say that exact thing to David that you just said to me!"

"Hi, it's David!"

"Hi David. Ofelia."

"Hi Ofelia, how did your shopping, go?"

"Excellent! I'm very excited and my daughter told me I have to use the exact words I just told her. I just bought the new white Mercedes-350 SUV!"

I looked at Olivia.

"Ofelia, we bought the exact same thing two days ago here in Scottsdale!"

"Jesus, Mary and Joseph, David, REALLY??"

"Ofelia, think about it this way. You picked Roberto out of all the men in the world to marry all those years ago, right? Uh-huh. Well, Olivia picked me out of all the men in the world to marry, didn't she! ...Yes! So that means you and your daughter have great picker-genes! That can only mean one thing: *Olivia and I need to make a little girl!*" and I swear, everyone in the baby clinic's waiting room was laughing their asses off.

"Olivia!! I'm talking to your MOM," I pleaded as she was ripping her phone out of my hand and beating me with it.

"I'M SORRY MAMA! No, Mama! STOP CRYING! I'M NOT PREGNANT AGAIN! ...NOT. And I may never let him near me again!! ...YOU'RE NOT LISTENING, MAMA. I'M NOT PREGNANT WITH A BABY GIRL!"

I was now on my side, lying on the other chair laughing uncontrollably. Olivia was kicking my feet in a tantrum, which only made me laugh harder.

Her mom was *convinced* we were pregnant and expecting a baby girl. The room was <u>done</u>. Even the receptionists were losing it, laughing.

"Mama, *I have to go.* I'm so embarrassed I wanna die or hide right now and I <u>can't do either</u>! Bye, Mama!"

Olivia was fuming. Everyone else in the room was splitting their sides. The more they laughed, the more pissed Olivia got. The only thing that saved us was a door that opened, "Tyler Callan? Tyler?"

As we were about to go through the door into the hallway toward the Doc's office, I was getting thumbs-ups with people still wiping tears from their eyes from the laughter.

Olivia stopped in the hallway and turned on me. "My mom BEST not think I'm *knocked-up with a little girl* or the next time you get laid will be on Tyler's 21st birthday."

She was REALLY gonna hate this: the doctor was standing right behind her and heard every word. His door had opened right behind her and even he was smirking.

"Ms. Macias, I'll be happy to call your mom and tell her whether you are or aren't, uh, 'knocked-up' or not." And the doc winked at me.

Olivia's head was down. Chin on her chest. The angry whisper came as if from a monster in a B-movie, "David Francis Bernard Callan? You <u>better</u> find out the address of the nearest sperm bank because that's going to be the only way we will bring another child into this world anytime soon."

As subtly as she could, using only her clenched fist with her wrist as a spring, she popped me in the zipper. And scored. "OUCH!"

She turned around and we went in and sat down, putting Tyler on the table.

First words out of the Doc's mouth?

"Mr. Callan, I can give you the sperm bank's number if you need it." He had to go there. I was going down, again. Losing it. I loved this doctor.

Olivia buried her forehead into my shoulder and began slugging my good arm. The MD couldn't contain himself and we both laughed as she pounded away. It worked. Olivia actually chuckled.

"I love him and this is what I put up with, Dr. Keslin."

"You two are fine! Let's see how Tyler is."

He got examined and we waited for lab results. Perfect health. Happy, bouncing baby boy, son of a man with a nearly-bruised testicle.

I had Tyler. Olivia held onto me as we left. On the sidewalk, "Can you take him a minute, honey?" and she did.

"Can we please have make-up sex?"

"We better. You owe me, cowboy. You owe me big-time."

Olivia was rooting through her purse with purpose. And closed it with a "Shit! ...David? David, could we stop at the pharmacy a minute. I need some Midol, baby."

"Sure. Ty and I will hang out in the Benz and play with the stereo."

"I love you!"

"I love you, too. I think it's just up here on the right," and it was.

I pulled into the *Handicap Parking Only* spot and dug out the temp hanger from the console. Olivia kissed me again and hopped out. She was back quickly with a small sack.

She opened a pill bottle and popped two capsules. "This should keep me from being a crying mess because of cramps. I'll try not to turn into a dragon. But in case I do, I have an already-sorry present for you." She dug her hand into the bag and pulled out a single orange Popsicle.

The True Beginning

"Orange popsicle?"

"Yep. Half for you and half for me and Tyler."

"I love orange popsicles, Olivia. They're my favorite."

I went to work on mine, sucking it. Olivia gave hers a lick to wet it and ran it across Tyler's mouth. She hadn't buckled-up yet and sat sideways in the plush seat, her back against the passenger window.

"You don't remember, do you, David."

I held up my popsicle, "This?"

"The first time I ever saw you, you were on an ambulance gurney getting rushed into the closest empty trauma room at St. Dominic's. A passing RN saw my student uniform and said, "Come help, now!" and I followed him in. He and I cut away your clothes as fast as we could so the rest of the team could see you and your injuries, start IVs and start treating your injuries."

"The RN stepped back and I didn't know what to do, so I just stood quietly beside him. He looked over, 'Good job... uh,' and I could see he was looking for my name."

"Macias, I'm from USF."

"You jumped right in and were a huge help. You're going to be a great nurse."

His name was Victor.

He asked, "Where are you supposed to be right now? I'll fix it with your supervising RN."

"Home, actually. I have to be back for grand rounds."

"That Victor guy offered me a big secret. He said, 'If you have clean scrubs, there's a staff lounge with recliners. You can shower and nap without worry of being late from your commute or oversleeping,' and I took his advice. But I was wide awake at 3:30am."

"I took that shower, changed, and wandered down to the Ortho ward. I told the RN at the nurse's station, 'I was in ER and worked with Victor on Mr. Callan when he came in. Can I look-in on him, please? She said, 'Sure, he's due meds. Why don't you come in with me and you can sit with him for a few if you like. You look tired, honey.'"

"You were a mess, David. You were restless. When you tried to toss and turn, you yelped in pain. It was awful. The RN hit your IV with Demerol, said something to you and you said one word, 'Ice.' The RN turned to me, looking for a name tag, 'Would you get him some....'"

"Macias, I'm Macias "

"Doorway next to the nurses' station. Plenty of ice chips or you can even get him a popsicle. I think he'll tolerate it okay."

"You opened your eyes, David, and I was sitting right next to you. Our eyes met. I said, 'Hi, I'm Olivia.' Know what you said? You were funny. You said, 'Hi, you're pretty," not 'What happened? Where am I?' You said, 'You're pretty.'"

"So, what did you say to that?"

"I said, 'Thanks. I have something for you, a popsicle,' and I finished unwrapping it and broke it down the middle so it would be easier for you to manage. 'It's orange, Mr. Callan. I hope you like orange.' You said, 'Yes, my favorite,' and I told you, 'Mine, too! The freezer gods were nice to us. Here, let me help you.'"

"You tried to hold the stick and get the end of the popsicle into your mouth, but your grip couldn't manage the popsicle stick. I wrapped my hand around yours and said, 'Let's try it together.' You got tears in your eyes. I got a lump in my throat, David. For a second, it didn't look like you were in pain, but I knew you were, and a lot of it. I kept helping, and you mumbled something. 'What,' I asked."

"'Yours. Melting,' and I told you 'I'm okay, Mr. Callan.' You corrected me, 'David. I'm okay David.' It made me smile. I said, 'Here, take a bite. I think you'll be able to get the rest of it in your mouth.'"

It was like she was talking about her experience with someone else. I could only imagine my expression was blank. I had no recall of any of it.

"You were on your side so I wasn't worried about you choking on the melting chunk of popsicle in your mouth. To cheer you up, I picked up the melting half-popsicle and acted like I was looking to make sure no one would see me. I was tired and needed a sugar blast. I bit half of it right off the stick and giggled."

"You mumbled. 'Your favorite. Mine too. Now my favorite nurse....' And you just drifted off to sleep with a smile on your face, as much pain as you were in, you were smiling."

"At grand rounds, I was kind of hiding. I didn't want them to ask a million questions, how you recognized me, what I was doing there at that time of night. And then, wow, I was assigned to your case, David."

"You were hitting on me in the ER the first night you saw me?"

"Not at all. I was empathizing, caring for and about you, pressed into service by somebody."

"You came up to my room on the ward," and I was teasing her. "Professional follow-up. I saw you come in. I was curious and wanted to follow-up. Closure. Educationally, so."

"You flirted with me about popsicles, then fed me one? That's a little phallic, yeah?"

"The official version was, I relieved your pain under supervision of your RN, upped your sugar level for strength. The unofficial version was hell, yeah. My job was on the line. I didn't think you'd complain or report me." She grinned.

"You shameless flirt! Okay, here's the home version: Aspiring nurse is pressed into service and does so to earn student brownie points. For closure, checks on patient upstairs, *with permission.* The guy thinks I'm hot and comes onto me with a popsicle pickup line, 'Orange, favorite flavor, favorite nurse.' I'm liking it and so I *spend a night* with a broken guy I've just met, who won't...hell, can't touch me, I have to touch him. And he falls asleep on me!"

We exchanged loving glances as I adjusted the mirrors, unfamiliar with their controls and the conversation paused.

"Olivia, never ever change. I love you, that was completely funny and cute. Let me get you home so you can lie down. I'll take Ty if you like."

"He's okay. Mind if we just order pizza or something?"

"I'll bring you the Chinese and pizza menus. Girls' night to pick."

I kissed her, and put the Benz in reverse, and we left the pharmacy. We rolled into the garage a few minutes later.

I took Tyler, "Let me feed him, then he's yours. I just need a nap, honest," and I handed him back.

Once I was sure Olivia was sound asleep, I called Bob Macias.

"David, that you?"

"Yes! How are things at the ranch?"

"Going well, just the usual daily and weekly pains in the ass but rolling along."

"Bob, we haven't discussed Thanksgiving. I don't know if Ofelia and Olivia discussed it, but... Can you get away from Abiquiu, come here for Thanksgiving? I want you to see your grandson. But I also think Olivia needs her mom and dad right now. Tell you why. Everything has been focused on me, all the attention, worry, concern, my needs and health. I'm sick of the pampering."

"Her mother and I talked about it, wanted to get a sense of what Olivia might want to do. Ofelia and I decided we'd make our plans around your wishes, if we're included in them."

"As far as I'm concerned, you're not only included, Bob, I don't want Olivia to have a Thanksgiving *without* you and her mom."

"You're more than welcome to come here, stay here. We have plenty of room. Olivia said you were here to close the deal on the condo so you know we wouldn't be cramped with 4-1/2 people in 1,758 square feet of house."

"We're on the same page, David."

"Okay, if you're willing, here's my plan. Hands down, you're the head of the family. Maybe say to Ofelia, 'I think it would be very special if you and Olivia made Thanksgiving dinner for our grandson at his home. We can stay in a Scottsdale hotel or with the kids, Ofelia.' Bob?? Do you think that would fly?"

He laughed, "That's perfect, great minds think alike. I'll tell Ofelia I want to get away and that the only place I want to go or do is to see is Tyler and Olivia and you. I can't imagine her saying no. Bank on it!" and he laughed, adding, "You're good, son! Damned, good."

"I'm a words guy, Bob. Thank you. I...we owe you."

"Nonsense. We're family, and this family doesn't keep score or hold grudges, okay?"

"Good to know. I'm excited you're coming. If you have a pen handy, my private email address at work is dfbcallannews at kfcgfm.com."

"Got it, thanks. I hafta run, David. Busy workday. See you, David."

"Bye, Bob."

What a guy. Then again, Olivia was from his genes and upbringing. She and her parents were like hitting the trifecta.

I pulled some pork chops out of the freezer to thaw, assembled the ingredients and utensils for cooking them, and began washing veggies for our dinner salad. There was fresh asparagus in the drawer of the fridge. Quick and easy.

I put on my headphones from work and turned on some Sting and Police music, just kickin' back on the couch with my eyes closed. She thought I was asleep and quietly sat next to me, slid my way and tucked herself and Tyler under my outstretched arm. I kissed her on the top of the head. "Feel better," I asked, removing the headphones.

She shook her head, "Lower back, headache, cramps. Usual stuff. Mmm, what smells so good? I thought we were ordering take-out?"

"I've got supper covered, baked chops, asparagus, salad."

"Mmm, sounds good, David."

"If it doesn't taste or sit right, I'll put it away and make or get you anything you want."

"I don't know why it's so bad this time."

"Because you have me to lash-out at, honey," and she looked up with her sad eyes and whispered, "I love you.... What were you listening to?"

"Sting...Police."

"Ooh, Mommy wants some. Share, please?"

I picked up the remote from the table without disturbing her or Tyler and brought up the speaker levels. Perfect.

A soulful ballad I loved was playing. I stood and helped her up and stepped around the coffee table with Olivia's hand in mine. I held out my arms indicating a dance and she gently put Tyler down against the back of the couch and used her feet to push out the coffee table. And we danced.

"You smell good, Olivia... You feel good... And we need to dance like this more often. Ask me anytime you want to or just grab me. You belong in my arms," and she looked up and gave me the Olivia smile that, from the very first, made me erase every thought that didn't center around her.

 Olivia's phone was ringing, from the sound of it, in her front Levi's pocket. I reached down, "Let me honey."

"Hi, Olivia's phone, David."

I pantomimed to Olivia, 'your mother,' and put the phone on speaker.

"Hi, David. It's Ofelia. Is Olivia around?"

"She's in my arms dancing with me."

"No, really, is she there?"

Olivia spoke up, "Mama, he's not kidding. This goofy, lovable man I'm crazy about just asked me to dance when my monthly-moon has me all out of sorts. What man does that?"

"A brave one, I think," and the three of us chuckled.

`I covered the mouthpiece and whispered softly in Olivia's ear, "What're they doing for Thanksgiving? Your call. I'll back whatever you decide." She smiled and gave me a thumb-up 'atta boy.' "Mama, you have a plan for turkey day, yet?"

"Your dad and I talked about Thanksgiving," Ofelia said.

"Mama, I hadn't forgotten about Thanksgiving, I just haven't done anything about it."

"Let me tell you, I want to do something about it, Olivia. Roberto really needs a break and I thought we could fly down there if David doesn't mind; it's only like an hour flight. We can get nearby hotel and I can come over and make Thanksgiving for my grandson."

"OH MY GOD, MOM, REALLY??"

"Yes, really!"

"Mom? David will not tolerate you staying in a hotel. You'll stay here where you belong.

"That will make the cooking easier, for sure, Olivia."

"Mom, you'll blow his mind at our traditional, Abiquiu-style Thanksgiving dinner. There's nothing on your table that my David won't eat and love…. He's sitting here with two thumbs up grinning like a fool that you and Dad are bringing Thanksgiving here!"

"Ofelia. I'm humbled and grateful that you're coming, and Olivia's right. I won't permit you to be in a hotel. Our home is yours, too, and I insist you're here so you can spend all the time you and Roberto want with Tyler, Ofelia. When I was young, I heard other kids talk about their grandparents and wished I had had some…known mine. This is important to me and I love you for it."

"We can't wait, David. Bob wants the phone, David."

"Sure, put him on… Bob, good evening!"

"Hi David. Ofelia's right. I need to get out of here for a
couple weeks but you may get tired of us in the house for
that long."

"Bob? There is *no time limit* on our end. If you want to
stay a month, stay. It's open..."

The animated excitement in Olivia's voice was
genuine, "DADDY! YOU'RE COMING!!!! I'm over-the-top
happy." Tyler wailed at exactly the right time, hearing
Mommy's excitement, I guess.

"Hear that, Daddy?? Tyler's excited, too!"

"We are too, honey. David, be good to my Olivia!"

I laughed, "I can't be anything else. She loves me too
much."

Olivia's eyes were loving-me-up.

"I'm gonna get dinner going on," and I kissed her as I
put the headphones on the coffee table and went back to
work in the kitchen. "It'll be about 90 minutes."

I nuked some water and got out three jars of baby
food-- strained beef, peas 'n carrots, and applesauce. I
set the tray with the food, a bottle, bib, napkin, paper
towel and spoon on the coffee table. When he was
finished, I let him crawl around on the floor a minute or
two before Olivia brought him to the highchair while I
put the finishing touches on our salad.

Olivia was at the table, "If you hand me something, I
can help."

"Okay," and I set the tray of raw pork chops near her,
then three bowls: flour, egg, and seasoned crumbs. I put
a roll of paper towels down.

"Easy peasy. Dip and flip in flour, then egg, then
crumbs. Back onto the tray. Next one. Paper towels are
for your hands."

She smiled, "Got it, cowboy."

The 14" iron skillet was finally hot and I seasoned it
for the chops. The oven was preheated and water in the
steamer was at a near-boil. Once the chops were
browned and finished-off in the oven, I grabbed the
asparagus spears out of the box. I washed the

asparagus, steamed it al dente, then set it aside to whip some chipotle mayo for the cold spears. You could have cut the pork chops with a fork.

Half an hour later, Olivia was praising the meal and took a glass of wine. I joined her and we chatted about Thanksgiving. My phone rang.

"This is David... Yes, hi.... I'm glad you found it. I know your pro shop's open early. Would you please leave it with them so I can swing by early and get it in the morning? ...Good deal, thank you. ... and goodnight to you."

"Candace's pictures?" Olivia asked.

"I'll swing by on the way to P.T. unless you don't want me to. I was going to do some running around. I want to stop by the Mercedes dealer after P.T. and use one of the coupons for the complimentary wash," and the plan was solidified.

Dinner clean-up was easy and the only thing I really wanted to do was lie down with Olivia while she nursed.

"Thank you for liking my dinner."

"I liked it because it was delish—right down to the chipotle on the cold asparagus spears, honey."

After she finished nursing, Olivia handed Ty to me. I put him on his own bed and he slept through the night. Olivia wore a t-shirt and panties to bed and we snuggle-cuddled as usual. I caressed and kissed her. She drifted off after she pulled my arms around her to spoon.

Morning was unremarkable. The CD was at the pro shop, I had a zip drive in my pocket from a sneaky little mission on the computer in Olivia's office, and the SUV seemed revitalized with a wash. I was so focused on me; I didn't know what Olivia was up to.

Olivia picked up her phone, scanned the contacts and hit the call button.

"Women's Reproductive Health Group, Cindy."

"Hi, Cindy. I'm one of Dr. Beauchamp's patients and an RN next door. Do you think you can get me in kinda soon?

The receptionist paused, "We had a cancellation for 11, tomorrow, if you can make it."

"Yes, I'm off. That's great!"

"Your name?

"Olivia Macias, M-A-C-I-A-S."

"Found it! You're Tyler's mom! How is he?

"Doing great!"

"And what is Dr. Beauchamp helping you with in the morning?"

"I'm not sure, cramps? Tubal pregnancy? I dunno."

"You know he's the best and we'll get you taken care-of."

"Thanks, Cindy. I'll see you tomorrow."

Nothing's Too Good

"This is David."

"Hey, sexy."

"What's doing?"

"I got an invite to grab a bite with Sheila at the hospital. Think a girl can hitch a ride with you to therapy?"

"I'd could probably use your moral support. I just got off the phone with Tammy. Tommy's under the weather so Tammy's going to work me out. I've seen her in action. I think that girl's *into* inflicting pain."

"Not me, cowboy. Where you're concerned, I inflict pleasure. I'm your joy-toy!"

"Down, girl! I'm driving!," and we laughed.

"I gotta go. Your son is calling for the milk wagon!"

"I love you."

"I love you muchly!"

At the photo kiosk inside the drug store, I installed the zip drive and brought up the text of the love poem Olivia never saw. I had used a font that seemed to coincide with romance and printed the page so it would fit in a 5x7 frame which I picked up on the way out. I also printed out some twenty-odd color 5x7s taken by the wait staff at The Hideaway. Olivia was going to get quite an I-love-you, today.

I hit the hospital lot about 12 minutes before my P.T. appointment. Two hours later, I used the SUV's Bluetooth system and called Olivia. "On my way home, honey, need anything?"

"I think we're good on everything. How did it go?"

"I'm a little stiff and sore, so that whirlpool may take on new meaning for me, today. How's our boy?"

"Feisty! What did you *do* to him this morning??"

"Uh... just loved him up. Nuttin' special."

"See you in a bit. Be safe."

"Love you, Olivia. Kisses."

I wheeled into the garage and sat there until I could get the poem in the frame, centered in the pink matte, which looked nice. I grabbed the bag with the photos and headed inside. Olivia and Ty were at the table.

"The Hideaway pictures are really cool, lots of keepers," I said, handing them to her. "I got 5x7s so we could pop some into frames for us and your parents," and gave her my best cartoony grin.

Olivia was slowly laying out the pictures on the table. "Oh David, you were right. Some of these are precious." She looked up at me, "My Cinderella night."

I put my hands on the table and gave her a loving kiss, then kissed my boy. "You sure have a pretty mommy, Tyler." I managed to keep her from noticing the other bag with the framed poem and made my way down the hall, and slipped it under her pillow.

When we put Tyler down and headed to the bedroom, she said, "You getting in the spa?

"Can we lie down for a few, first?"

We were on our sides, eye-gazing at each other. She repositioned and moved her right arm and made a little startled-like noise followed by a quiet, "Wha.... What's this?"

Olivia loved wildflowers and I had found a wildflowers border online for the poem.

She looked at me.

"Da---vid?"

Her eyes went to the poem. She started reading it, aloud.

"For My Olivia, Strings of Kites"

Around me, you're sparkles and aglow.
I'm alive'r by your woman-ness,
healed and strengthened by your nurse care,
bordering trouble with your profession
should our love collide with it.

Take my hand to common ground
to that in-between niche where
deepest friendships flourish and
lovers may have stolen away
to languish in their first kiss.

Arriving where we can play,
Exhilarated, laughing whilst watching
tangling strings of kites,
kites that bob and bump
in their wind dance, overhead;
a hand to warm, sunset to watch,
anticipating swirls and circles
just before a poem on the sand, and then
to see reflections in each other's eyes
of another day to play.

We can. There's promise.
Trust enough to take my hand and
allow yourself to feel,
to know by your soul informing you
that nothing's been surrendered,
that it's safe and healthy
as my own soul's wings wish to soar,
thirsting for its dance on earthly legs,
my tattletale soul whispering
there's but one partner
my soul will embrace
and she is you.
Come to me. Come to me and dance,
for, I sense you are my now
and in my many tomorrows.
Please come to me, Olivia…. David

"David, this is incredibly beautiful." I could barely
make out her eyes as she looked between the poem and
me. Her eyes were tearing-up. "When did you write this?"

"I wrote it at the Denver airport when I knew, realized how deeply in love I was with you. It was the second or third time I felt that I'd never had feelings for any other human being in my life like I did for you. So it was validated...for me, anyway. I knew we were meant to be together."

I looked down because my own eyes were wet, "And then you were gone, before I could ever give it to you. Before I could read it to you. The words...they haunted me, these words so full of love turned on me and hurt as my life so suddenly became empty. And now, I'm nearly in tears because you're here beside me, in our home with our son. I have your love and now you have my deepest thoughts about you on paper. I knew. I knew it was you, Olivia. I wouldn't settle for anyone else. My someone was you."

She'd been quietly sobbing as I spoke.

She lifted my shirt and pulled it off and wiped her face with it. She kissed my arms and chest and face, lost herself kissing my mouth. She reached down between my thighs and held me as I swelled into her hand, stroking me slowly, as she slid down the bed and took me inside of her mouth, and when I piqued short of breath with a slight gasp, I pulled her up immediately to kiss her.

We lay there, silently. The room seemed to have a heartbeat we could feel but it was our own heartbeats in slow unison.

"That poem is your heart, David, the heart I loved then and now."

She brought her left hand into view. "This ruby is both, my big David and my little Tyler David. I want to give you another child, add another gem to our lives. Will you help me put another ruby in this ring, in our lives with me, David?"

I rolled and brought her body on top of mine, looking straight into her eyes.

"I will give you the world if you ask. And if you would have me bring another child into the world with you, then, you are giving *me* the world. Yes. God and Nature will answer this hope as a prayer, do their thing. I love you."

We fell asleep as close as two people could be, physically and spiritually.

Party of Five, Please

David was still in the back of the house when I dialed Sheila and was surprised that she picked-up. Nursing supes are busy people.

"You sound great, Olivia! You coming back to work in this lifetime? I could use you!"

"I wanna, but this Mommy thing is kind of cool and I'm getting into this home life thing with David."

"Are you all right?"

"Very. I need you to cover for me, though. David's in therapy this morning and I'm being seen and don't want David to know or worry."

"Seen for?"

"Not sure. Beauchamp's my gynecologist. I'll let him figure it out, but no cancer symptoms. Just our girly-curse stuff, Sheila. I told David we're gonna do lunch together today, so, if you run into him, *improvise!*"

"Easy enough, Olivia. I hope everything checks-out okay."

"Thanks, Sheila. I'll try to track you down to say hi."

"Wear your track shoes, they're busting my buns."

"You got it. Bye, Sheila."

This next call was payback of sorts. I found the business card I was looking for in David's wallet: Gwen McArdle, Managing Partner, Pierson-McArdle Fine Jewelry.

"Thank you for calling Pierson-McArdle Fine Jewelry. How may we help you?"

"My fiancé gave me Gwen McArdle's card and said I should give her a call about my engagement ring."

"Gwen's here and I think she may be available. May I have your name, please?"

"Olivia Macias-Callan."

"One moment, please."

"This is Gwen McArdle, hello?"

"I'm Olivia Macias-Callan..."

"Oh, I know who *you* are, Ms. Macias-Callan!"

"I guess my David's hard to forget, right?" and I laughed.

"Impossible. I've got to tell you. He marched in here and knew exactly what he was looking for and nothing was going to keep him from getting that giant emerald-cut diamond for you!"

"It took my breath away when he proposed."

"It's a stone and setting that commands attention, for sure. I promised David I would size it for you, myself. Would you like to set that up?"

"Please. I think it's a half-size or less from fitting perfectly. But there's something else you can help me with. I want something for David."

"A watch? Maybe a ring or something?"

"No. Do men wear pendants? His birthday's at the end of December and I thought I'd get him a pendant with a picture of our son in it. Gold? Maybe an inch by a half-inch? Something like that?"

"May I call you, Olivia?"

"Please!"

"We don't make them, Olivia, but they're out there. I can find and get the right one in here. If you have a secure email address he can't access, I can send you pictures and pricing of what I find."

"Perfect."

"Olivia, there's one particular way I recommend we do this."

"I'll follow any advice you have, Gwen."

"An outside source is going to want to sell you a chain with it. Not good. Not good because cheap, poorly made chains are the way pendants get lost. So we'll find the pendant and I'll help you choose the color, weight and style of chain you'd like for it. Most important, I'll personally attach it to the chain. It can make a difference."

"David said you are wonderful. I agree and thank you. Your email address is on your card and I'll send you an email so you have mine."

'That's wonderful, Olivia. And I really want to see that ring on your finger, and that handsome son of yours and David's!"

"Well, there may be a modification in the next six months to year, but I'll tell you about that when I see you! I'll get David to set up the fitting appointment with you. And this discussion never happened, right?"

"It did not, Olivia. Take care of that man, honey. I knew he was a keeper when I met him."

"Thanks again for the help, Gwen."

"I'll get to work it, Olivia. Take care."

David came out and I got Tyler's highchair and his face cleaned up.

We each got a kiss from big daddy, "Ready, Olivia?"

"Yep. I'll grab his bag if you're on the stroller."

"We're outta here."

David parked near the P.T. entrance knowing I could make my way to Sheila wherever she may be. I had logged miles in this facility. David removed the stroller and I got Tyler in it and his bag, on it.

"You girls have a good time catching up...Take care of Mommy, Tyler," and David waved at him.

"I can't wait to see her and get the gossip," and I left him with a wet kiss and grinned, "A promise for later!"

Beauchamp got me right in, made a big fuss about Tyler, insisting to hold him and talk to him. The doc and I exchanged small talk about the hospital's goings-on related to the staffing issues.

"So what's going on, Olivia?"

I explained and he did a pelvic, took a smear, some blood and urine.

"I need a favor—could you run those, stat?"

"Sure thing. You and Tyler can hang out in here and I'll circulate among the other treatment rooms. He looks like you, Olivia, one pretty little boy."

I thanked him for a remark that may have seemed forward or out of bounds, but Beauchamp was that Catholic dad of nine kids who adored him, and everyone

who knew him thought he could be 'Father-of-the-Year'
on a daily basis.

Twenty-five minutes later, I worried when a tech
rolled-in a sonogram cart, followed by Beauchamp just a
minute or two behind.

"Olivia, there's nothing to worry about. I'll show you.
As good a nurse as you are, you'll know the diagnosis
and treatment."

I laid back as the tech lifted my top and put the
lotion on my lower tummy, turned on the machine, and
began slowly combing the lotioned area with Dr.
Beauchamp looking on.

"LARRY BEAUCHAMP! Tell me that's not a live
sonogram! Not mine!!"

He was smiling that reassuring smile for which he
had a patent.

"Congratulations, Olivia. I'm thinking your twins will
be along in early-to-mid August," but I was a crying mess
and only caught half of it. He comforted me. "You're
young and healthy, have given birth before and it'll be a
breeze. I'm writing you for some prenatal vitamins, so
stop by the pharmacy."

I finished wiping my face with the tissues and said,
"David and I were going to try for another baby at some
point. He'll go out of his mind!"

"Well, you've got two-fers."

I couldn't believe I kissed Larry Beauchamp on the
cheek. He blushed, "I'm happy for you, too, honey."

I called Sheila from the hallway and assured her
there was nothing wrong, false alarm, and promised her
we *would* do lunch soon. I headed for the P.T. area and
made a quick stop into the ladies' room where I changed
Tyler, used the toilet, and fixed my makeup from losing it
in front of Dr. Beauchamp.

David was sitting patiently in the waiting area,
finished with his therapy.

"I'm hurting! Tammy's rough!"

We headed for the SUV in the lot.

"I told her to be rough on you! It's my evil plan to work you harder to get you back to 100%!"

"No need. You loved me at 1% so I figure you'll probably keep me if I'm 60%."

"Yep. Sure will. I just have to find a place for a 60%-er in my life."

"Psst! Look in your bed, tonight, beautiful."

"David? Can we get that fitting for my ring scheduled sometime soon? It was a little loose, spinning around on my finger while I was doing some chores, today."

"Sure, I'll call the owner, Gwen McArdle. That's who helped me."

I was surprised I could pay attention to anything. I was happy, no, way beyond happy even though life seemed like it might be coming too fast.

We had a large enough house, enough money, time, and most importantly, enough love to be a family of five. David was gonna shit himself.

We no sooner got home than David called, "We out of Coke? I gotta have one."

"I'm sorry honey, I guess we are."

"I'm gonna run down to the convenience store and grab one. I'll bring you one!"

"I'll pass. I don't need anything to drink," which my internal voice translated into preggers-Mommy, "*There are three of us in one body and we're watching all intake until September 1st.*"

David rushed out.

Phone. It was the security gate, UPS requesting access, delivery for Macias, 122. I buzzed him in.

Doorbell. I forgot about the steaks. There were two sealed Styrofoam chests. UPS-guy said, "I'll need a signature, please, line 12," and he handed me his electronic clipboard.

"You're probably not supposed to do this, but I really don't think I can lift those. It's like ten feet. Pretty-please?"

"Sure," and he put them beside the refrigerator without incident.

"Hang on," and I took out a tumbler, it the ice, and filled it with the last of my homemade lemonade. "Your thank-you. Homemade."

"Ma'am, I can't stay."

"Didn't expect you to. Take the glass. Really. And thanks." He was polite enough to take a sip, compliment and thank me, and leave quickly just as the door opened from the garage and David walked in.

"Saw the UPS guy."

"He comes over for a jacuzzi when you're at therapy. He was bummed we couldn't hook up, today."

"Well at least he bears gifts," David said, pushing one of the ice chests with his foot, and we were grinning at each other. Then kissed.

"Oh, I got you something for your back, Olivia," and he set the bags on the counter, and reached into one.

"My back? What's wrong with my back?"

"It sounded better than saying I got you something for your cramps and he smirked. "Close your eyes," and I did.

"Open, please," and he was offering me one of those giant, one pound milk chocolate candy bars."

Reward time! I put my arms around his neck, "The only thing sweeter and better and tastier in our kitchen than this right now is you," and I tousled his hair and kissed him. A preggers girl is going to turn down chocolate? I unwrapped it and broke off two chunks, putting one in David's mouth and one in mine.

"None for Ty, Olivia?"

"It'll turn his tummy over, honey. Can you start on getting the coolers open, please?"

I slid-out the wide freezer drawer and put all the frozen veggie packages and other things on the counter. Freshly butchered, world-class beef would take priority in this house.

David started handing me the meat neatly taped in white butcher paper. They were labeled with a grease pencil. Roasts, ribs, ground beef, and the steaks were labeled by cut: "NY Strip" "Filet" "T-Bone" "Sirloin."

All but two packages were in the freezer and I knew why. They were marked "BB." David handed them to me with his 'Hmm, Curious' expression.

"Oh, yum! Prime stew meat! We're having this, to-NIGHT, David. You'll love it!"

"How do you get 'Prime Stew Meat' out of 'B.B.'"

I put on my innocent look, "On the ranch, 'BB' is 'Butcher's Best,' the parts that fall away as the best prime and steaks are trimmed. Maybe it's a thing with beef producers. It's been called that since I was little and probably before. We'll do stew because we can use a lot of those veggies that came from the freezer. Let me pick what will go in with the 'Butcher's Best' and I'll make the best stew and camp biscuits you ever ate, cowboy!"

"Sounds good!"

He was gonna kill me. This was my payback for him at the well-baby clinic.

I popped another chocolate square into our mouths and we finished up in the kitchen, leaving the BB out to thaw along with the selected veggies.

"Tyler's fed and I'm going to put him down. Come hither, my prince," and he followed me down the hall, giving me a playful slap on the butt.

"Housefly, honey. Missed. Sorry."

"It's okay. UPS-guy usually works 'em over but good!"

David said, "You *brat*!" and startled tickling me and I shrieked.

I was laughing and yelling "NO FAIR, NO FAIR, I HAVE TYLER!" Tyler was loving it and I bounced our little guy on the bed and he laughed and loved it, too.

I turned to David, put on my serious nurse face and said, "Mr. Callan, it's time for your hydrotherapy. Please meet me in the jacuzzi!" and he undressed me as he kissed me as I did, him. Tyler was happy with his rubber nipple plug on the bed. In the Jacuzzi, David was enjoying himself with my pair of the real things and I was languishing like a queen with my man. I stared at the ceiling, thinking, 'I'm glad his heart's perfect, cuz this is gonna just undo him when he finds out we populated my womb.'

We dried-off, dressed and headed for the kitchen with Tyler.

David grabbed a beer and took Tyler outside. I was going to check on dinner when Gwen called.

"Got it. Got a locket that's almost exactly what you described and I picked out the right chain, 18 karat and 20 inches is the perfect length for him."

"Sounds weird, but could you mail it in a padded envelope? David hates bringing in the mail for whatever reason, so that's my chore, alone."

"Easy. I won't use a company shipping label just in case. I'll insure it and send it next-day. Pay me whenever. It's no biggie, Olivia."

"If you can take a card over the phone, I can do it this instant," I told her as I was scampering back to the bedroom to grab my wallet on the dresser.

"The boys are on the patio, watching the golfers, below."

"I'm ready when you are," and it was done in a jiffy.

"It's all 18-karat and something to behold. It's $1782.63 and free shipping for you, Olivia. If it's not perfect, I can return it. No sweat."

"Gwen? I always feel like I owe you."

"You certainly don't, Olivia. You and I 'clicked' and I think there's a long-term friend thing cooking, here."

"Me, too! Speaking of cooking, I have dinner on the stove. Gotta run!"

"It'll arrive tomorrow, Olivia."

Dinner was in the crockpot and the beef stew, with a little red wine in the gravy base, was making the house smell heavenly. I got one of Tyler's plastic bowls out, strained out some of the vegetables from the stew and mooshed them with a fork.

I had David get some big stoneware bowls out. They were my grandmother's. Coincidence? Made by Louisville Stoneware Company, where David was born. I portioned our stew into the bowls and got a couple warm biscuits from the oven and honey butter from the refrigerator.

"What do you want to drink, Olivia?"

"Ice water's fine," and he appeared with two.

We talked about our day and about three bites into dinner, I frowned, looked David's way and intentionally mumbled... 'Sad.'

"What?"

"Oh...I was just thinking. At 5:30 yesterday morning, this poor bull was getting his balls cut off and tonight, we're *eating* the poor _bull's_ _balls_, and he's one hurting steer," and I pointed my spoon at David, "and probably cussing-up a *storm* at us!"

Slow-mo. David froze and his eyes opened as big as cantaloupes. He dropped his spoon and blew a mouthful of stew back in his bowl with a wounded rhino's "ARRRRRRRRRRrrrgh!!!"

I scooped Tyler up and was already on the run to the bedroom to slam the door so he wouldn't get me but I was too slow.

"You are DONE, Olivia, you are so done," he startled to tickle me as I got Tyler down onto our bed. Now, there was no escaping David with him on top of me.

"I'm gonna tickle you until you PEE, Olivia."

Through my laughing from tickle-torture I told him, "Payback for the well-baby clinic, David. Gotcha, cowboy," and best? Tyler was squealing and laughing as David eased up on me and I rolled him over and kissed him, "It *is* the best stew you've ever eaten though, honey, right?"

"Yes, because you made it, Olivia."

"Good. There's plenty for leftovers," and I did my best hurting-cow, "MOOOO-OOOH!" squeal and then he really tickled me.

I loved the boy. What can I say. David could paint me with motor oil and I'd probably thank him and love him all the more for it.

"Let me up, cowboy. You can ride me later. We have a kitchen to clean and a son to love-up a little."

We worked in harmony and restored the kitchen to gleaming before relaxing on the couch, Tyler content between us. Happy family. Terrific life. I was trying to envision how five of us going to snuggle like this on the couch. David caught me giggling with my hand over my mouth, imagining a 9-foot couch with toys between the cushions, uncomfortable as hell, noisy....

"What's so funny?"

"You reacted like they were *your* balls in the stew," and I rolled over and lost it, laughing so hard I had to lower myself onto the rug.

David picked up Tyler, put him on his lap, looked his son in the eye and said, "Ty? Your mother is seriously tweaked. I wouldn't trade her for the world? But she's tweaked."

I felt moodiness coming over me like warm syrup had been poured over my head. I climbed onto the couch, and lifted David's arm to put around me.

"You okay," he asked, sensing something.

"Just needy."

"I'm here for your 'needy.' How can I best accommodate your current neediness?"

"Can we stretch out together in the bedroom, David?"

"Let's do it," and he extricated himself from me only to hold the baby in one arm and help me up with his free hand.

We settled onto the bed, meeting in the middle.

David looked over at me, "I'm taking requests."

"A perfect score would be some soft music and just lying here with me for a little while," and he retrieved the sound system's other remote from a nightstand drawer and put on a soft, instrumental jazz mix.

"Doable. Easy," and he took off his tee. I had only turned down the spread to expose the pillows. David's hands exposed and explored all of me.

Making the Call

Over breakfast in the morning, David brought up the call to Vanessa's parents and I knew he was uncomfortable about bringing her up around me.

"David, let me put your mind at ease. We can talk about anything and everything. Vanessa, included. If there's any discomfort about that, don't attribute it to how I feel or might feel about it. You were close, intimate, and she was tragically killed."

He could only look at me, expressionless. I moved over to sit in his lap, "You're my guy. Always were, always will be. Make the call when you feel ready."

"Now. I'm gonna call now cuz I gotta get through this and don't move a muscle. I want you right here," and I kissed his forehead as he grabbed his phone and dialed the number Stephanie had given him. He put the call on speakerphone.

"Hello?"

"Mrs. Sorensen, this is David Callan."

"Oh God, David, it's so good to hear your voice. We've been worried sick and praying for you."

"I'm on the mend. I got out of the hospital and am undergoing lots of physical therapy. Mrs. Sorensen…"

"You can call me Sally, David. My husband's golfing with his buddies and is gonna hate himself for missing your call."

"I'm sorry I missed him, Sally. Look, Vanessa and I spent a lot of time together, and you know we were very close. I've been grieving for her and it took me this long to get the strength to call you."

"She spoke of you fondly, David. How kind and caring you are."

"You need to know that, in my recovery process, I found and reunited with the mother of my child. Vanessa was aware of that relationship. It didn't mean I was insincere with your daughter. I was always candid and

truthful. She was kind and generous and wonderful to me. I want you to know that I'll never forget her, Sally."

Mrs. Sorensen was fighting-back tears, "That's the way life is, David. We're not in control of as much of it as we think we are, and it can jump up and bite us. More importantly, David, I'm glad there's someone there who loves you and is beside you in your struggles, and that you have the kind of love only a family environment can bring."

"I assure you I do, Sally, and thank you for saying that. Please give Mr. Sorensen my sincerest condolences."

"I will. God bless you and yours, David."
"Goodbye, Sally."

"Goodbye, David."

He was quiet a moment, "I couldn't have done that, made that call without you, Olivia."

"David? If you want or need to call the Sorensens, again, then call," and I put my hand on his cheek and kissed him. Can you watch him a few minutes? I have some stuff to do in the office."

"Sure."

I went into the garage and got the locket out of the envelope. It was prettier than Gwen could have ever described it. I palmed it as I went into the office and ran a quick print of a picture of Tyler and sized it for the locket. Perfect.

I walked back into the kitchen, "David, could you take Ty over to the couch? I have something I want to show you."

He scooped-up the baby and sat down. I walked up behind him and kissed him on the crown of his head, then, bent down to whisper.

"This is a quiz. If you pass, you get prize."
"Ok."
"Who's your girl?"
"Olivia's my one and only."

"Who loves you more than pizza and gorgeous horses?"

"My cowgirl, Olivia."

"Okay, last question."

"If you could spend every minute with Tyler nearby, would you?"

"24-7."

"Perfect score. Close your eyes and put out your hand, palm-up. No peeking!" and I slipped the chain over his neck and put the opened the locket, placing it in the center of his palm.

"Okay, you can look."

He was soundless as I moved around the couch to sit beside him. He looked at it and me.

"It seems your favorite jeweler knows your tastes, David!"

He kissed me, "It's...you're astonishing."

Tying the Noel Knot

It wasn't David's fault, because I forgot to remind him. Six days before Mom and Dad were flying in, David came in with flowers for me.

"Busy tonight, beautiful?

"If my guy David says so, I sure am, cowboy."

"Good, because I forgot about getting your ring sized and I figured we'd run over there after dinner. Gwen McArdle's expecting us, if that's okay."

"Fine, darlin'."

David had only taken off the locket for the jacuzzi and shower, wore it constantly. He would occasionally hold it toward me and mouth the words, 'Love this. Love you." I was glad Gwen was going to get to see it on him because he was in a V-neck, form-fitting sweater and the locket lay just above the 'v' in plain sight.

It was dark and the store's interior lights were very bright from the street. Tyler was groggy when we put him in the stroller. With the blanket intentionally over his face, he'd pass out again, soon. It didn't seem there was a single customer in the place and the door alert chime sounded when we walked in.

"Mr. Callan! Wonderful to see you, David! And your lovely Olivia!" Gwen said, with an outstretched hand that took David's.

"Gwen McArdle, this is my Olivia, Olivia Macias, soon to be Olivia Callan."

"It's nice to meet you, having only spoken with you on the phone about David's beautiful locket. Your beauty exceeds David's description, honey," and I felt myself blush, "and our undercover baby is Tyler, whom I've heard so much about?"

I lifted the blanket and he didn't stir despite the bright lights. I gently replaced it.

"That's gonna be one good looking guy! Congratulations."

"Thank you," David said, "and the locket is exquisite."

"I've got to say, David. When Olivia, here, contacted me? She knew exactly what she had in mind for you, and even though I'm in the business, that locket is gorgeous on you."

David instinctively grabbed it.

"I don't mind you two collaborating and conniving as long as it's all about me, but, seeing you hadn't even met? This stunned me, Gwen. Truly. I love it."

"Olivia had a picture of it in her mind's eye. All I did was find the exact match. It looks sensational on you, David."

"Thanks," and David let the locket fall back into place.
"Well, let me see your finger, Olivia. I'm dying to see that ring on you," and I shifted my purse to my other hand and extended my just-manicured and polished fingers. Gwen gently took the underside of my left hand.

"I love it, Gwen. Tonight may be the only time I'll ever remove it except for you to clean it."

"It's stunning on you and the fitment's perfect; fitment, meaning the size of the stone and mount relative to the size and length of your finger."

"I get looks and comments, constantly, Gwen."

"Come back to the lab with me and I'll get it sized."

Gwen had already staged a couple of chairs for us, which we took, and I slipped off the ring and put it on the velvet cloth. Gwen measured my finger, wrote down some figures, and went right to work.

Over her shoulder, Gwen said, "David came in, Olivia, and sat down after he let me know he was wanting to see engagement rings. Four trays hold 120 rings. Just as I set the fourth one down on top of the display case, David said, 'That's *it*! I see it.' Now that I see it on your finger, he was right. It is perfect, so much so you could model it in a magazine ad."

David was all smiles.

I told her, "He explained the little ruby, that it's our son. In fact, Gwen, we talked of adding another ruby when another baby arrives, God willing."

"Easily done. David and I discussed that, as well. In fact—did you tell her, David?" and I looked to see him shake his head with a serious expression.

"Well, he enrolled in the *Next One Coming* program," she said as she pivoted on her jeweler's stool."

"I don't know what that means, Gwen." As Gwen turned back, she was laughing and had a beautiful gift box in her hand. "It doesn't mean anything, except that this David whom you adorably call 'my David?' told me you're going to try to have another baby and he thought you should have a 'placeholder' for the ring." Gwen handed the gift box to him, "All yours, David."

He took the box. My heart was racing.

"Olivia, when you read that love poem I wrote to you, you said I had put my heart on paper. I thought I could do better," and as he lifted the box lid and pulled away the gauze.

He said, "I love you."

Gwen had backed off a little to watch what was unfolding before her.

I sucked wind, couldn't help it.

It was a pendant necklace, yellow gold. Dangling from it, a heart-shaped ruby a little bit bigger than an M&M candy. Dark, rich red in the shape of a heart, the facets allowing the ambient light to illuminate it.

"DAVID! MY GOD, WHAT HAVE YOU DONE!" and my water pump started and ran my makeup all over my face as David was carefully taking it out of the box by its gold chain.

He leaned forward, kissed my forehead, looked at me and said, "Perfect. And the necklace ain't bad either, cowgirl."

He looked into my eyes, "You have my heart. You are my heart," and I saw Gwen reaching for a tissue.

I was on his shoulder wailing, "Oh, David. Oh, David," and sniffling. "Gwen? Now? Now do you see why I love this man so much?" Gwen was sniffling. Tyler joined the party making happy noises, too.

Gwen got a mirror out of seeming nowhere and set it on her workbench so I could see my ruby.

My life was not going to be long enough to play 'Top That' with my David and have any hope of winning— except for scrambling his brain when he learned I had two more Macias-Callan original creations on-board. He was my cowboy who was gonna park his horse in my barn, his saddle on my fence and his ass in my bed with his arms around me and the kids, including the ones he hadn't met yet.

We got home and I was drained. I wanted bed and now, said the body.

He slipped under the covers with me, and I rolled to talk to him. He surprised me by rolling me up onto his chest. He liked my nakedness full-length atop him. It was sexy. I liked it, too, kind of a bonding thing.

"Mom emailed me. Their flight arrives Tuesday, the 26th and they can stay until December 16th. I'm glad they can stay that long. You okay with it?"

"Absolutely, Olivia. They're family, we have room, done deal. I don't know if your dad's business slows down over the holidays or what, but they can stay as long as you and they want, Olivia."

"You not just saying that?"

"No, I'm meaning it. They're walking in cold on a man whose life is wrapped around their daughter and they don't know him from Adam. On top of that, they have a grandson they're dying to get to know. I'm anxious to know how it feels to be a member of a family at-large."

"Marry me, David Callan."

"I will, Olivia Macias."

"Sooner the better."

"Sweetheart? We can get married in our living room the night your parents arrive," and he kissed me, gently and deliciously.

It sounded funny, so I giggled, "Don't count that out!" and I rolled off of him and pulled him onto his side to spoon with me.

"Let's. Let's get married right here in the house while they're here, David! We can decorate a tree as a family and have a little Christmas thingy with my parents and our friends and, BONUS! Tie the knot!"

"I don't know why not, Olivia. Plenty of beef balls to go around and another package of them in the freezer!" and I hit him with a pillow.

"Touché!"

"Guest list?"

'Let's see, Sheila who's married to a radiologist named Clark...Tommy and Tammy Trang from P.T.?"

"Seeing them in action, Olivia, something tells me they're probably a hoot when they're together with a little booze in them, for sure!"

"How about Stephanie, Chuck, and Sandy Tuttle from the station—you okay with seeing them?"

"I have to see them. They have to be here, Olivia. In their own ways, they've gone over and above for me and I've been a shit friend, not even in touch. I know Norman's usually busy over the holidays but I need to invite him."

"Okay, quick headcount. With Mama, Daddy and us, that's eleven."

"Can I go kinda off-grid, here, Olivia?"

"Of course, baby."

"Can I... we invite Gwen McArdle? She's one-of-a-kind, Olivia, and I think she might accept the invitation."

"I'd bet you a hundred bucks she not only accepts but would bust a plan to be here with us.... So with her, David, that would be thirteen which is a great number for a house gathering."

Mom and Dad were arriving day after tomorrow. David's expression was between smirk and boyish grin.

"I don't know what's gotten into you, and I'm not complaining. Our lovemaking is incredible, lately. I thought you might wear me out. But you know what? I want more, I want more of you... You don't even have to ask me. I'm here for the taking and you know it."

I only had one answer for him. I moved around the table while he was still seated. I took his hand and put it up my skirt, between my legs right over my g-spot just long enough to affect my breathing and let him feel I was moist. "Follow me, cowboy, I have a present for you..."

For the last week and today it was all about sex and I wasn't ashamed to admit how much I was enjoying it. If I weren't already pregnant, our chances of getting pregnant would be pegging the meter. As we lay quietly, he reached over and just held my hand, rubbing it softly. I looked over at him, "How would you feel about going on a picnic tomorrow?"

"That would be swell."

"I've got enough stuff in the refrigerator we don't even have to go shopping. I want to have a long talk with you David and it's a good talk. Nothing down or bad or shocking or disturbing. It's just time that I had this talk with you. I want you to look forward to it because I think I can open your eyes to a lot of things, give you closure you deserve. Our relationship will soar even higher."

The look on David's face was if I had just pulled a rabbit from a hat and I think I had.

"Olivia, with that build up? We can start this picnic tonight and keep it going for the next 24, baby." He made me laugh, again.

"I just want to be out in the sunshine with you and Tyler and enjoy the day. And if we happen to find a secluded spot, oh well!" and I tweaked his little soldier.

"Come back here please? Mommy needs to be held," and I kissed him urgently and rolled over on top of him and started grinding against him until he was fully stiff.

As I straddled him, I found myself getting wetter and wetter. He positioned me to have my shorts and panties off in no time... He was pounding and pounding against me, deep thrusts as my hips answered his thrusts. He exploded inside of me, yelped involuntarily. Both of my hands pulled his butt cheeks with all my strength to take him as deeply as I ever had, holding and holding and holding him there.

I wouldn't let him out of bed all afternoon. He was giving and giving and I felt insatiable. I wouldn't let him stop, wouldn't let up until I had completely exhausted him. We lay there naked and cuddled. "I needed you like that today, David. I really needed you like never before.

The next morning, I joined him in the shower and took him voraciously and hungrily, there, and then took him back to bed where I encouraged him to ravage me and even manhandle me a little and he did so with perfect restraint and force. It was new territory for us but David enjoyed it. I purred.

Come to Jesus

The day's weather was built for a picnic at the
McDowell Rocks Park. We had two big quilts on the
ground, Tyler's playpen and ton of toys, a big umbrella
for shade, food, drink, just picnic perfection. It was time.
I reached under a corner of a quilt for my small spiral
notebook.

"I didn't want to rely on just my memory, so I have
notes. It's important to me that you *hear it* from me,
David, so I'm gonna be reading some of this," and I raked
my hand through his hair, kissed him and asked,
"Okay?"

He kissed me softly, whispered, "Okay."

I sighed, glanced at the notes.

"You didn't ask me how I remembered the popsicles.
I'm not sure I would have told you. Could I be more
forthcoming? Sure. Should I have been? Yes."

"I nursed you back from hell only to put you through
hell, *again*. Nothing about having sex with you that first
time was about a fling or a sleazy, on-the-job version of a
one-night-stand. I wanted more of you than that. My
willingness to risk my job was a conscious choice. Before
it happened, I knew it was going to happen. I would let it.
Whether I seduced you or you seduced me, I regarded it
as normal step in developing that one, possibly long-
term, special relationship. The poem's proof you felt it,
knew it, too."

He nodded, caressing my leg.

"So far so good, David?"

"'Course."

I got choked up, which sat David straight up and he
put his arms around me.

"I didn't walk away from you. It took every bit of my
strength and resolve to <u>tear</u> myself away. Did you need to
hear I was carrying your baby just when the biggest
career break of your professional life was being put right

in front of you? Aw hell no, not this cowgirl. I <u>loved</u> you and I wasn't going to lay <u>that</u> shit on you!"

David grabbed tissues out of the baby bag.

"Was I going to abort, terminate at the same time I'm professing and living by my Catholic faith like I had since forever? Not this Catholic cowgirl. Not me."

"David, my superstar love, I hated it. Loved you and hated it."

"One of the many reasons Arizona was regarded as a top RN Ortho environment in the country was what they did for newly graduated RNs. If you graduated #1 in an accredited university's nursing school class of 50 or more, and there were more than sixty in mine, Arizona would give you a starting job and guarantee your entrance into their Ortho Nurse Practitioner program once you amassed enough regular RN hours and experience. Even pregnant."

"That's how the condo came about, David. Daddy bought it so Mama could live with me during my 3rd trimester. She saved my ass, my nursing career, and even got Daddy to pay for some extra in-home help once our Tyler was born and Mama had to go home. Mama lived in Tyler's room and the nanny lived in my office. At six months, I was allowed to enroll him in the Employee Nursery Program at work."

"Childcare is expensive. Newborn childcare is horrifically expensive. The hospital's Employee Nursery Program was completely free. A male janitor could enroll his child...the lab director...anyone. The hospital knew it would keep us loyal and turning down aggressive offers from headhunters and other major health facilities with professional recruiters."

"David repositioned me so my head was against his chest, his arms across mine. I could tell he wasn't reading my spiral notebook scrawl and scribbles over my shoulder.

"When Daddy found you, and just a few miles down the road, I broke down crying so badly that I was on all-fours, finally burying my face in the rug. He was as gentle as he could be when he related you were with someone. But what did I expect: I walked and you were going to just sit around and wait and wonder about me for the rest of your life? We had the first, worst and only screaming match, ever. Even he yelled that I had done you dirty by running off and not telling you."

"I listened to you every day at KFCG and I hate country music."

"There were times I had the phone in my hand wanting to call the station and ask for you or leave a message. After what I had done to you, and running off with our child you knew nothing about, I was going to barge in and destroy the meaningful relationship in your life? Screw things up with you and Vanessa?"

I turned around to look at him. Tears formed and came from his eyes.

"David, my sweetheart, my darling, my love, I don't believe God willed Vanessa to die so we could be together. My God's not that cruel. I'm not that deserving. Vanessa wasn't some sacrificial goat. Charlie wasn't killed in a chopper crash on his 2nd day in Afghanistan to teach me a lesson or punish me because he wasn't the right guy."

"You and me, David? You and me are *it*. We're real, the real deal. One of the most lasting gifts you've given me is the faith to believe in today and the tomorrows as you like to refer to the future. Life is in two places, here and ahead, not behind. We have the same vision and focus."

David lowered me to the blanket, "What you've just done is break the last chains of my anguish, my guilt about Vanessa, telling me why you suffered so much to put me and my career first. That's the most selfless and bravest thing I've ever known anyone to do."

He was gently giving my hair long strokes with his fingers.

"I'll exchange marriage vows with you, Olivia, and mean every syllable. I used to think that I was made for you and that you were made for me. Since we've come back together, I know it, with no room for doubt. I was made for you and you were made for me."

We kissed as the sun was beginning to hide behind the red rocks.

"Let's go home, Olivia. I want to go home and lie down with you and Tyler, hold and love you both."

Roberto and Ofelia

Olivia dressed Tyler in a little sailor suit. Olivia dressed me in a Ralph Lauren casual shirt, slacks and a pair of nice deck shoes. She wore a sundress that, with her tan, made her look like someone's dream of a Hawaiian princess. Mine.

"Hold still, honey. I'll be right back."

I stepped onto the big patio and approached one of the potted plants and plucked a medium-sized red-orange hibiscus blossom and returned to the bedroom.

"For your hair, my queen," and I smiled.

"This will look great, David!"

"Yes, it does," and she handed me Tyler while she went into the bathroom to fasten the flower.

She smiled at us. Tyler's head rotated around to see her, "Beautiful, isn't she, Tyler!" and he made some repetitive loud noise as his little fist hit my shoulder three or four times.

"See, Olivia? He doesn't lie!" and we made our way to the SUV I had washed and vacuumed.

We managed to get good seats to watch the passengers to come out of the concourse through security. Olivia and Tyler were playing patty-cake. I was just people-watching. There.

"There they are, Olivia," and she startled, stood up and looked.

She squealed, "It's THEM! How'd you know?"

"Video chat, and your dad's thousand-dollar Stetson hat, maybe," and Olivia laughed.

She screamed and waved, "DADDY!" as I waved and called, "Ofelia!" and they spotted us just as they cleared security's turnstiles.

Olivia glided across the tile floor to her parents with me on her heels, squealing, "DADDY! MAMA!" and her mother took Tyler.

Ofelia was ecstatic, "LOOK AT THIS BOY!!!" and Olivia was in her dad's arms. It was really a heart-warmer, seeing their expressions when they first saw Tyler. And I captured it on video.

Olivia let go, grabbed her dad's hand and led him to me, "Daddy, this is David, the only other man I love in my life."

I extended my hand and he opted for a man-hug, saying, "Hello, David. This is what family does. We hug."

"Thank you for coming, Bob."

"David, I'll say this. She looks happier than I've ever seen her," as Olivia looked on, eyes dancing, and Ofelia swooning and bobbing and bouncing with Tyler,

"Mama, let Daddy hold him," and as the transfer was being made, I said, "He's solid stock, great breeding!" and Bob laughed.

"You bet, and I know that when I see it!"

I turned to Ofelia. "My feelings are going to be hurt if I can't give *you* a big hug, because Olivia had her work cut out for her today, trying to make me handsome for you!" and Ofelia opened her arms for a good long embrace.

She held me at arm's length. "A mother can tell, David. You love and respect our daughter. We couldn't be happier for Olivia. And you made us a beautiful boy, David, as handsome as you!"

Once at the SUV, we stowed the luggage and stroller. Bob and I sat in front, Tyler, his *abuela* and Olivia sat in back.

"I feel like you're driving *my* car, David," Ofelia grinned.

I looked at her in the rearview, "I am. I'm your chauffeur!"

Olivia went beyond herself making a giant brunch for our arrival at home. I offered to go straight to The Hideaway but Olivia explained she was excited to be cooking for her mom and dad.

"You seem to be getting around pretty good, David!"

"I really am, Bob."

"Daddy, his physical therapist says he and his doctor are amazed but it's because of his determination. He's really busting his butt, trying."

"Thank you, honey," and I shifted my gaze to Bob, "Look. I've never done a hard day's work in my life compared to a guy like you. I work inside a building, behind a microphone."

Her dad looked *pissed*. Pointed his finger at me. He was stern.

"I don't want to *hear* that, David. Do you know how important the news and the weather are to a rancher? It affects grazing, feeding and...hell, survival out there. You don't think we monitor the stock market's commodity trading and futures? Livestock illnesses? Feed shortages and prices? There are untold billions of dollars and jobs at stake and the info we get from guys like you is critically important to us, David."

"Now I'm humbled. Thank you. Sitting alone in a room like that, I find myself wondering if I'm helping anyone with anything at all. Still... I miss it... working."

I laughed to myself, wondering how I'd someday tell him, wondering *if* I'd tell him how unsanctimonious his office was when they told me to 'fuck off.'

"Well, we appreciate you, David," and he gave me a little reassuring punch to the upper arm. It hurt like holy hell. The guy's fists were steel. My muscles were overcooked vermicelli.

Olivia had done stellar job with Thanksgiving decorations, using things like colorful fall leaves she hot-glued in groups and placed on white napkins on tabletops; there were gourds and squashes in groups among our potted plants and, of course, the obligatory pumpkins, and some air freshener that *wasn't* pumpkin-spice (because Olivia knows I think that odor is vile) but outdoorsy. My Olivia was perfect. Never missed. Her parents were going to be impressed as soon as they walked in.

I insisted on handling the luggage, alone, as Olivia led everyone into the kitchen. I hustled Bob's and Ofelia's bags into our bedroom and laid them on the bed. We rented a queen bed and put it in Tyler's room, and put his crib in Olivia's office. She filled that closet with our most frequently worn stuff so her parents had room. I wondered if she was going to hold them to the naked-only rule for the jacuzzi?

I saw and heard Tyler practicing his made-up language while he was sitting on the counter facing his grandmother. Ofelia and Olivia had iced tea. Bob had a bottle of Coors with a shot glass and bottle of tequila next to it, with cut limes and a salt shaker.

They were standing around the kitchen's island and Olivia had a big tray of veggies, dips and crackers out for them. I grabbed a stick of celery and dragged it through some homemade dressing Olivia liked to make.

"What would you like, honey?" she asked.

"I'm going to join Bob for a shot and a beer."

"Olivia told me you're a tequila guy, David."

"I spent a bunch of time in Mexico and one of my local buddies really educated my tastebuds for it. Love the stuff."

"I don't drink often or much, but it's a shot and a beer if I do."

"We're celebrating, Bob. Life. Tyler. Two couples who love each other immensely." I picked up my shot glass Bob had brimmed, "Cheers!" and even the ladies clanked glasses. Olivia looked over at me and she had that internal glow thing going on, just couldn't be any more beautiful.

I stepped around Bob to be next to Olivia and held her left hand. "Another one, Bob? I'm going to!"

"Sure, thank you. I can feel myself relaxing and it feels damn good."

After the shot, I looked at her mom and dad as I raised Olivia's hand in mine, showing the flat topside of her hand.

"I asked your daughter to marry me, twice. The first time was in hospital pajamas and from a wheelchair, in a beautiful courtyard garden area at the hospital. I told her she is my forever-love and I can't live without her."

"The second time was more traditional, when we had dinner at the country club's restaurant just down the hill and I got on bended knee and asked her to marry me. Properly. When she said 'Yes,' I put this ring on her finger. The ruby is for our son, as much Macias as he is Callan. More children, someday God-willing, more rubies will be added."

Mom and daughter were getting misty.

"If you don't mind, I would like to know, hear, that I have your blessing for her hand in marriage, to have and to hold her and provide and care for her and our children always, in a Catholic home that's filled with love. She will never be alone or cold or hungry or needy of anything as long as I live and breathe, nor will our children. I pledge this to you before God and Olivia."

Bob looked at Olivia a long moment, then me.

"David, her mother and I tried and tried to have a child. Ofelia miscarried a couple of times and it all but destroyed her. Ofelia said my love kept her going. She told me she didn't know if she go through the fear that would accompany another. She did. Our Olivia was our blessing for never wavering from our faith. Ofelia and I are happy to entrust her and Tyler to you, son. We are honored because Ofelia believes you have the kind of love that will sustain our daughter through the tough times, son," and he hugged me and held on a long time as the women wept.

Roberto looked me square in my eyes, "You have our blessing and without reservation, David."

Ofelia lightened the mood. "I smell something wonderful in the oven, Olivia!"

"Yes, Mama, and your nose knows what it is." It was a layered, baked dish of rice and lobster and rice and shrimp, and rice and red snapper, with oysters throughout the layers, and Spanish seasoning. Paella was a specialty of Spain. The wealthier the Spaniard, the better quality of fish and shellfish in the casserole. Olivia had baked bread, with sunflower seeds and rosemary, and whipped the butter soft for spreading. The paella had been baking on low heat for hours.

The dining room table had already been set, two unopened bottles of wine at the ready, and hot pads in place for me to place the huge, heavy skillet coming from the oven and from which the portions would be served as held by tradition.

Bob was at the head of the table, Ofelia at the foot. Olivia and I were sitting across from each other, and I had Tyler next to me in his chair. Bob uncorked the wine and the goblets were passed for filling. The room stilled.

Bob looked over at his daughter, "Olivia, please," and she and the rest of us crossed ourselves.

"In the name of the Father and of the Son and of the Holy Spirit. Bless us, oh Lord, and these thy gifts which we are about to receive from thy bounty, through Christ our Lord. We ask your blessing on this family, and that you keep us humble to serve you and to love you, always remembering and attending to those less fortunate. Amen."

My boy beat his spoon on his highchair's tray about halfway through without interrupting the reverence and love filling the room.

"Thank you, honey—beautiful! If I may," and Bob raised his wine glass...."

We raised ours.

"I just want to offer praise and thanksgiving to God for one of the happiest days of Ofelia and my lives. We are here for you in every way, David and Olivia, always. Cheers!"

And we drank our wine.

"Thank you, Daddy. Will you serve, please?"

"Sure, honey," and we passed our plates to him as Olivia rose and walked around to me and kissed me on the head.

"Help me a second, please?" and I said "Excuse me," and followed Olivia into the kitchen. She spun and kissed me without holding back. "They love you, are showering you in it and I hope you can feel it because that's their way."

"Yes, I can feel it. It's the same flavor as your love when you immerse me in it. Olivia, when I tell myself my life can't get any better, you prove that it can."

She smiled, and as she curtsied, "Tis my pleasure, my king," and I kissed her as she rose to open the refrigerator door and grab four glass bottles of sparkling water on a small tray.

"David, there's a tray in here with lemons and chilled glasses. Grab it, please," and we went into the dining room and set waters out for all.

People would pay $75 a plate for Olivia's paella and bread. It tasted like it was a recipe right out of a gourmet magazine. She hadn't consulted anything when making it. It was all in her head. Olivia wasn't just an A-student in school, she was an A-student in life, everything she attempted. I found myself shaking my head wondering how and why I had won God's top-shelf woman.

"Let me help you clear, Olivia, so the men can rest. They ate *a lot*," she said, grinning at Bob.

Tyler looked me, pounded his spoon on his tray and yelled, "Da-dee, Da-dee! Da-dee." We looked at each other as the room stood silently still.

"Did he just...." Olivia asked in wonderment.

And I grinned, nodding. "He sure did, honey!"

Everyone was stunned with happiness.

"That's my boy, Bob!" and he grinned and held up an upraised thumb.

Ofelia suggested we men have a seat on the patio so we'd be out of the way of the ladies doing the kitchen work. Olivia grinned and laughed as she said to her mom, "David's highly trained and loves table-clearing and kitchen clean-up, don't you?"

I looked at Ofelia, "I enjoy it. It buys Olivia and me time with Tyler."

"Tonight, David," Ofelia said, drawing a bead on me with her eyes, "you are off duty! You men go outside and we'll do this."

Bob and I retired to the patio.

Ofelia said. "Your dad's job seems to be taking more out of him."

"You've had a long day, Mama. You and Daddy are in the master bedroom. David put your bags on the bed and we made you plenty of space in the closet."

While outside, Roberto surprised me with a small, thin cigar about the size of a long cigarette.

"I really don't smoke but I figured this was a special occasion. Join me, David? I dip these in brandy at home and keep them in a little carrying case."

"Love to," and he struck a wood match against the patio's concrete and got the ends of our smokes going with a bright red glow. We didn't really say much. Too much paella. We finished the smokes and headed inside.

My future mother-in-law took the baby, lifted him and smothered him with kisses before putting him in Olivia's hands. Then, she came to me, "Good night, David. You are wonderful and I love you because my daughter does!"

"Goodnight, Ofelia. You know now, more than ever, our home is your home, too," and Olivia's mom squeezed me and kissed both my cheeks.

"I'll be there soon, Ofelia," Bob said, and Olivia walked her mother back to our bedroom.

Bob looked at me, "So when? When will you marry?"

"Yesterday, I told Olivia I'm fine if we get married in this living room while you're here. Honestly."

"The way Olivia loves you and worships the ground you walk on? She will make an excellent wife and home for you and your family."

"You know I'd fight and die for her, Bob. I'm not going anywhere. By the same token, I'm not one to wait around. I don't have any hesitation or reason for getting married as soon as we can."

He stood.

"Olivia's strong and smarter than most. She deserved to be loved and taken care-of, David. We worried she never would. Today, you erased all those worries. Honestly, truly, welcome to the family. And you can call me 'dad,' Bob, or whatever. I'd be honored because I'm going to consider you the son I wished we might have had in addition to Olivia," and he bear-hugged me, again.

"I'm beat. Need the bed. Goodnight, David."

I looked at him a very long moment. "Goodnight, Dad."

Olivia and I were dead and crawled off toward bed in our makeshift bedroom. I shut and locked the door as Olivia was slipping into a beautiful negligee, looking at me.

"They're just as wonderful as you said they'd be. Can I tell you something good?"

"Uh-huh."

"I love you and that's never going to change," and Olivia walked over into my arms and I kissed her as she began undressing me.

After we made love, she confessed, "I told mom we're getting married the 12th of December, David."

"I told your dad I had no reason to hesitate or wait. He'll probably think I'm a goof for not mentioning, 'Oh, yeah, it's December 12th if you aren't doing anything,'" and Olivia laughed.

"He's not like that. He's smart enough to figure out I hadn't told you the plan, yet."

"How 'bout we do a house and tree decorating thing about the 10th. The tree will be fresh, and you and your mom won't be rushed decorating for the wedding."

"Thank you, you answered questions I hadn't even voiced yet. I have one for you."

"Yes?"

"Will you please make love to me until you can't possibly continue?"

"Only for a lifetime, Olivia. Yes."

"And?"

"Best offer I've had tonight."

Olivia slipped the negligee back on and scampered out and into the small guest bathroom. She slipped the nightgown from her shoulders as she came back in and came to me. Nothing was rushed. Nothing was verbalized. It didn't need to be. We made love as passionately and as attentively to the other as we had of late. I fell asleep looking into Olivia's eyes.

The smell of coffee brewing awakened me and I walked out from the now-bedroom that was just off the kitchen. Bob was reading on his cellphone.

"Good morning, Bob. Smells good."

"Hi, David. I make it strong so you may want to add some water."

"I like mine strong, too."

"I feel bad that Ofelia and I put you out of your bedroom. She and I would be fine with the room you are in!"

"Olivia wouldn't stand for it and neither would I, Bob. That master bath may be my favorite feature in this whole house, and we wanted to give you the convenience of having it right there for you! You're not putting us out at all."

"You mind doing something, David?"

"Not at all. Whatcha got?"

"Grab your cup. Let's have our coffee on the patio!"

"I love this time of day."

We slid the sliding glass door open noiselessly and covered the six or seven steps to the table.

"I need to talk to you, son. Privately. Strictest confidence kind of thing."

"Go ahead, Bob. I'll keep your confidence, whatever it is."

"I found out I have prostate cancer and it's bad. I found out last week. Ofelia doesn't know and I don't want to ruin her Christmas or Olivia's, but I wanted you to know. You know, for like, the future."

"I have something you absolutely must keep confidential that I'm going to tell you."

"Jesus, David, you're not sick, too, are you??"

"No, Bob. At dinner tonight, you'll learn we're having a Christmas party with our closest friends. There will be a dozen or so people here, and the house will be decorated for Christmas. Dad, and I mean you, Bob—Dad, we're going to get married on the 12th of December because you and Ofelia are here. We really don't need a big wedding. And before you ask, this archdiocese allows marriages in an 'appropriate' place outside of a Catholic church, itself. We'll be married by a priest, and it'll be recognized by the Church."

Bob said, "That's what Olivia told her mother, so I kind of knew. Ofelia was exhausted and couldn't remember any details."

"David, I was worried.... A Catholic wedding is very important to us. We believe in our faith and raised Olivia to believe and participate in it with us."

"There's no need for worry, Bob. You will see Olivia as a bride in a Catholic wedding on December 12th. Your blessing was more important than you know."

"You just lifted a great burden from my heart, David. It was not my place to tell you or her to hurry up and get married. She'd figure it out, and I don't want her to know until she has to."

"Understood."

We both heard Tyler sound off with his new war-cry of "Da-dee! Da-dee!" so I knew Olivia was awake. We went inside and sat at the island until our bedroom door opened and I stepped over and met Olivia and Tyler in the doorway to the bedroom and kissed them. I took Tyler and put him in his highchair. I poured an OJ for

Olivia and set it in front of her, kissing her hair as I set it in front of her.

She said, "Thank you, David," and I went to the cupboard and got some baby cereal and a bowl out, and went to work getting his hot cereal ready.

"Daddy, Mom and I are going out today for something special." Olivia looked over at me for support and I knew she was going to tell him.

"Since David and I are going to get married while you're here, I think a dress for that occasion might just be the thing I need," and Olivia was grinning like a school-girl as she pirouetted, mimicking a ballet dancer.

Bob jumped up and stepped around to her, "*Mija*! My beautiful Olivia, I'm the happiest dad in the world right now. You're my one and only. Get the dress of your dreams, honey, or else my success in life has been meaningless if I can't provide this for you."

Bob didn't have an arrogant bone in his body. Proud? Yes. Confident? Very. Generous? Very. This wasn't showing off, it was showing... showering love.

"I told Mom we are not coming back without one. But don't get your hopes up. You and David don't get to see it until our wedding night, the 12th!"

I objected, "No fair!" Olivia glared at me and gave me the stink-eye. Then she stuck her tongue out at me. Discussion over. Her dad laughed.

"What's all the commotion!" we heard Ofelia say, coming down the hallway, "...and where's that handsome grandbaby of mine, huh!?"

"David, would you get Mom some coffee please. Just cream."

"Coming up," and I set it near the empty stool. Ofelia went around the table and kissed Bob, kissed Olivia, and kissed Tyler as she took him from Olivia's arms, and then kissed me and pinched my cheek. "How's my almost son-in-law, today? I heard you all talking."

"I'm excited."

"We are, too, Ofelia!"

"Daddy, David? You guys need a plan. Because I don't really have an inkling of how long this is going to be, today."

"I think we'll be okay, honey," Bob said.

"Okay, bacon and waffles coming up," Olivia said and launched into high breakfast production mode. I hit the shower in the guest bath, Bob and Ofelia stayed with Olivia. We enjoyed breakfast, got everything in shipshape. Bob kissed Tyler goodbye and the women and Ty blew out of the house.

"Know what I'd like to do, David? I'd like to go to the casino! I saw some pictures of the Scottsdale casinos, online. You don't have to stay if you don't want to, but I never get the chance to go. Can we do that?"

"Sure! It's not far at all, and it is definitely beautiful."

With a stop at the ATM for Bob, I dropped him off at the main entrance of the casino.

"Stay as long as you like. I have to go downtown and that may take an hour or two, but I'll swing by here when I'm through."

A handicap parking space opened up right in front of the County Clerk's office.

"How can I help you, today?"

"I'd like the forms for a marriage license, please."

"Yes, sir, got them right here. Are you going to be mailing them or walking them back in?"

"We'll bring them in. That way, if there's a problem, we can fix it right here."

"Okay. I'm also giving you name change forms in case your wife is changing her last name to yours, okay?"

"Yes, thanks, she wants to do that. And could you throw-in a name change form for our son, too, please?" He obliged.

"They need to be notarized and most banks and credit unions do that for free."

"Also good to know. Thanks for your help, today."

Asking on My Knees

I was compelled to spring another surprise on David. Gwen McArdle had given me her super-secret cellphone number and I used it.

"Olivia!"

"Gwen!" and we laughed for no reason.

"I needed a hug today and you call me just when I need it most, Olivia!"

"Anything I can do?"

"Not really. Big dollar client, one of my jewelers screwed up and we're gonna take a little hit on a make-good for him. That's all. So what's new and exciting in the love nest; I swear you and David should be a reality show."

I cracked up.

"But you wouldn't qualify cuz what you two have going on is so *un*-real, Olivia. What's up with you?"

"My mom's with me and I'm pulling into a parking spot just outside your door. We're supposed to be wedding dress shopping. I'll tell you, inside."

Gwen giggled.

"Get in here, girl!"

I made my way in as Gwen waved me to the back and we entered her office.

"Mama, this is my friend, Gwen McArdle, who owns this store. Gwen? My mom, Ofelia."

Gwen pulled a couple bottled waters from her small fridge for mom and me, "It's a pleasure to meet the mom of this amazing woman, Mrs. Macias. Talk to me, Olivia!"

"Today, Gwen, I'm after a ring for *him* because I'm going to get down on my knees and propose to *him*."

"Oh, this is getting better and better. You have something in mind or do you want me to put my brain to work on it?"

"In my mind, I see an 18-karat gold band, a wide one and there's a middle part that is nothing but shimmering diamonds and the outer edges are like ruby baguettes or something."

"Nice touch, to complement the ruby on your own ring."

I leaned forward and picked up two tissues out of the box and handed them to Gwen who accepted them but was obviously wondering why. I pulled two more tissues and gave them to Mom.

"Yes, the ruby in his ring symbolized our child. On our wedding night, in front of our friends, I'm going to give David his wedding present."

"And that is?"

"Information, Gwen. I have a big reveal planned. I'm pregnant with twins."

I should have warned my mom this was coming, because she screamed, "Dios Mio!," crossed herself and squealed, "Olivia, praise God, child!"

Gwen screamed and I mean screamed and jumped right out of her chair and ran around the counter to hug me, "Olivia, oh, oh my God, Olivia!" and now we were all crying. It took at least ten minutes for us to come back down to Earth.

"David proposed to me in a garden at the hospital and I knew, I felt sure it was coming. My coworkers were hidden but watching. They streamed out screaming on my signal. He was in hospital pajamas, couldn't get down on a knee and didn't have a ring. He felt like he short-changed me. Then, there was the second proposal when he gave me the ring he got from you. Now that we're going to have *three* children, and three's a charm? I want to have a third proposal. From me. With a ring. On my knees in front of my parents."

"You *are* a reality show, Olivia, whether on TV *or not*. Check that, you're a fairy tale romance."

"We got off to a really bad start, Gwen, and I disappeared...pregnant, and he didn't know. I'm not going into that right now, but we have this chance and we are fighting to let our love happen without anything threatening to remove it or take it away. I want to propose."

"Okay, Olivia. This is serious. Let's get out there and see what we can do."

We must have looked at 500 rings or it felt like it. "Wait a minute," Gwen reflected, "one of the rings is coming back to me," and she picked up the last three or four trays we had seen.

"This one."

It was a wide, 10mm, 14 karat yellow-gold band. There were small, brilliant cut diamonds inset 360-degrees, with a single row of baguettes on each side. Gwen mentioned that kind of inset was called *pavé* like paved.

"I'll replace the diamond baguettes with dark, beautiful rubies. If I can't find them, I'd suggest we use a semi-precious stone, garnet, dark red and it shimmers beautifully."

"Do we have time for all that, Gwen?"

"For you and David and your *three* children we do, Olivia," and she hugged and kissed me. "I'm thinking it'll be done late Friday or Saturday. I have a great source for ruby baguettes."

"You're a miracle worker, Gwen."

"With your ovaries and David? I say you're the miracle worker, Olivia" and we giggled and hugged.

Gwen turned her attention to Mom, "This is one incredible woman you raised, Mrs. Macias."

"It was easy. She is very smart and always did as we asked. Never a problem," Mom said, taking my hand and patting it.

I thought Gwen and I were done but she motioned me to sit and returned to her high-backed executive chair.

"I want to give you something, Olivia, but you need to hear the story behind it."

"Gwen, you don't need to give ..."

"Nope, nope, nope. Wait until you hear," and I eased back in my chair.

"My dad's big break came in the late '90s. One of the hottest young players in major league baseball was here. He was a national heartthrob besides being the best hitter in the big leagues. He was here for Spring training with the team, and came in to talk to dad about an engagement ring. Remember, Olivia, it was the 1990s."

Gwen continued, "This 22-year-old guy bought a $4 million diamond from my dad that made national newspapers everywhere and we were mentioned in all the articles. Every ball player started coming in her buying-up every expensive diamond we could get our hands on. Earrings, necklaces, didn't matter what. They wanted it from McArdle's. Dad went from one other jeweler and a tech to nine jewelers and three techs in an instant."

"Holy shit, Gwen!"

"We got big-time rich overnight. So Dad buys this wild-ass Italianate mansion I live in now and gets a hair-brained idea: Since the players are transient, and now we're on the map with all of the richest who come to Scottsdale, Dad bought a limo I still have. A presidential, it's called, because it only seats four or five, but luxuriously so. He hired a driver to pick these people up and bring them in and take them home, and even make deliveries with it."

I couldn't help laughing and the opportunity to tease Gwen.

"So my new bestie is a spoiled rotten rich kid! Yikes."

Gwen howled, reclining her chairback to the max.

"Well, you outted yourself, Gwen. At least I know never ever go shopping with you for anything!"

She sat back up.

"That's why I love you, Olivia. You just bring so much joy and laughter to me. But to the point. The limo is yours for your wedding. In fact, if you need it to haul stuff or pick up anyone, I retain a driver to keep the thing maintained and beautiful. Both are yours."

"Gwen, I... I."

"Say, 'Thanks, Gwen,' then shut up and ask for the limo when you want or need it."

"Thanks, Gwen. Can David and I go to a drive-in tonight, and... you know? Break it in?"

"Hell, no. Next question," and we were laughing ourselves silly again.

Mom didn't get the veiled reference to having sex at a drive-in movie and looked to each of us with a puzzled expression.

"I'll call you as soon as I finish David's ring."

My mom surprised me, "Olivia, you don't know the cost of this?"

Gwen deferred to me.

"Mama, Gwen and I are friends and want to stay that way. So she won't hurt me. If she tries? I'll tell the world she slept with the Chicago Cubs... and their bat boys!!"

Again, my mom crossed herself, shook her head, mumbling, "That's not right...." as Gwen and I were laughing ourselves into streams of tears.

It took a few to get composed, again.

"We're not doing anything traditional. No best man or bridesmaids, Gwen. If we had? I'd have asked you to be my Maid of Honor, Gwen."

It set her back on her heels.

"You mean that much to me, Gwen. Love you," and I hugged her as we headed to the doors and I left.

New Names

I got home to find my boys sitting at the kitchen island, Tyler with crackers and juice and David with what looked like sparkling water with some papers in front of him. I kissed Tyler then gave David one on the lips with an "Mmm, my favorite man!"

"Find the dress!??"

"Tried, huh, Mama," and she played along and nodded.

"The major department stores are way backed-up on getting the dresses in on time and then getting the alterations done. You'd have to be able to fit into one already on the rack and with little or no alterations needed, David. It was frustrating," and Mom knew to nod in agreement.

"What's all that, David?"

"Olivia, there's two name change forms, here. One is for you and the other is for Tyler."

She looked up at me and just stared.

"You think we should change his name?"

I looked at her and for the first time ever, gave her a dictum. "You opened that door and I thought you gave me your blessing. I'm not *thinking* we should change his name, Olivia. We *are* changing his name."

"David, that sounds heavy-handed and forceful, like you're excluding me, which you have never done and I'm uncomfortable. It hurts. His names are both yours! I DON'T UNDERSTAND."

I hurt her enough to make her cry. I quickly smiled at her, pulled her close, and said tenderly in her ear, "Our son's name is going to be Roberto Tyler David Callan, and we can call him Tyler; I have gotten used to it and he just seems like a Tyler. I want my boy, our son, to be named after your dad."

I held her away from me and put up my dukes and smiled at her, "Do you want to fight me about this?"

She cupped my fists, capping my hands with hers and spread my arms apart. She put her hands upside my cheeks and said, "I love you David, I love you so much. Thank you. Daddy won't know what to say. I don't either. If that was our first fight, it was a draw. All three of us won. I love you."

Tell me something good."

"There's a man standing in front of you quivering, hoping you'll get into the jacuzzi with him."

"This girl in front of you, cowboy? You are her chocolate, the hot fudge kind she can never turn down or say no to... And she melts in a Jacuzzi."

"My sweet tooth is raging. Let's go play in the water, baby."

The water soothed her hurt feelings, relaxed us, and we were cautious about making much noise with our intimacy.

"I'd love to take Bob up and get the tree tomorrow morning if that's okay with whatever you have in mind, honey."

"That's actually perfect because Mom's been after me to keep looking for a wedding dress. You guys get the tree, and Mom and I will find some kind of something to wear when you marry me."

"Judging from what you look like in the altogether, I don't think you need much else, honey."

"You've got an exclusive on my body, there, cowboy. I don't think I'd go messing with that if I were you. I'm only wearing a dress for my parents and your friends' sake."

Our Tannenbaum

We packed a thermos and some snack crackers, an axe and some tie-down rope. I checked the glove compartment of the truck for my tree-cutting permit and it was right where I'd put it. Bob and I kissed our girls and Tyler goodbye and headed out.

Once we passed the huge Indian casino and resort hotel, the scenery of Arizona high country held Bob's attention.

"This reminds me of Abiquiu, David."

"It's not as high, only around 5,000 feet above sea level, here. It gets dusted with snow but not bad. We'll go just past a little town called Payson and the approved tree-cutting area is about a half-hour from there."

I reached down and turned the radio onto KFCG.

"Do you like country-western music, Bob?"

"Love it. It's usually what we listen to in Abiquiu. Olivia's weird," and I laughed and looked at him, "...because she likes all of that old school Mexican music, especially mariachi, if you can believe it."

"I haven't heard it around the house."

"She probably doesn't want to piss you off, or have to translate, or lose you," and Bob laughed, hard, and I joined-in.

"This is KFCG, the station where I work, Bob."

"Good signal. Strong, and I like the music!"

"We're in the top ten of all country stations in the U.S. as far as audience size, at number 4 right now, I think!"

Bob whistled.

I looked over at him, "Keeps our paychecks big!"

There was a sign, 'Payson 14 Miles.'

"I need to make a stop in Payson, David."

"No prob, Dad, I could probably use a potty-stop, too," and he looked over at me like there was more to stopping than just a restroom.

Entering town, he said, "Just drive around, I'll know it when I see it," and we started covering the downtown area. I turned left onto Old Pine Avenue and Bob yelled, "Over there! Park right there!" he said, pointing to a dirt patch next to a good-sized area with a big sign, "Boy Scouts Christmas Tree Lot."

I looked at him as I set the parking brake.

"For over twenty years, David, I have cut our Christmas tree. What Ofelia doesn't know is that for twenty-plus years, cut means trimming the trunk to fit the stand and shaping the branches *after* I buy it from the Boy Scouts."

I laughed my ass off.

"All this time, you bullshitted her?"

"You're a smart kid for a former orphan. I say 'former' cuz I've already accepted you as my son. So this is a *family* tradition, David. You need to pay *serious* attention here, son. I am teaching you this hallowed, annual family tradition. We get the tree here, we trim the bottom, then we drink beer. Lots of beer. Then we go home and put up the tree. It helps the scouts, we get a nice tree, and we risk no injury unless it's from falling off of the barstool."

I loved his sense of humor and was laughing so hard I almost pissed myself because my bladder was convinced we were stopping at its urging.

Bob and I agreed on the perfect tree and paid the scoutmaster. He thanked us, and Bob asked the guy, "How long have you been working with these kids?"

"Since my own son was about 11. But he's in college, now. Made it all the way to Eagle Scout!"

"You should be proud! Here," said Bob, as he peeled off a couple of hundred-dollar bills, handing them to the Scoutmaster. "I'm a cattle rancher. Do a steak cookout for them or something."

"You don't have to do that."

"You're right, I don't, but as they say? 'Tis the season' and my son, here, and I have been very, very blessed. Merry Christmas and thank you for helping young people all these years, sir," and we got in the truck while the scouts used their knot-tying skills to secure the tree.

He referred to me as his son to a total stranger. Growing up without a dad, this was the first time I felt I actually had a dad. I felt tears coming.

"Hang on a sec, Bob," and I walked about 20 feet into a small thicket of brush and trees and took a leak just out of public view.

"I had to water the bushes." Out of Bob's view, I also had to wipe welling tears from my eyes with my shirt.

"This is an 1880s town, Bob. Let's head downtown. I figure there's an old-West type saloon or two with ice-cold beer."

He glanced over with a serious expression.

"Tradition," he grunted, then paused and burst out laughing. "See?" he said, "You're already getting it. Family tradition's a good thing. _Now_ I know that when I'm long gone and Tyler is 40 or so, he will cut his own tree just like you and I did, today," and we both smiled at the thought as I wheeled the SUV into a parking spot in front of The Wild Appaloosa Lounge.

It was smoky, dark, with the jukebox wailin' Waylon and half-a-dozen beer taps sticking up from behind the center of the old wooden bar. A fifty-year-old blonde with store-bought boobs said, "Hi and Merry Christmas, guys. Whatcha havin'?"

"Got pitchers or just glasses?"

"We have 32- and 64-ounce pitchers."

Bob looked at me, "Pick a flavor," and I knew he liked Coors.

"Sixty-four of Coors, please."

We followed that big pitcher with a 32-ounce pitcher, just listening to music, people watching and talking about nothing in particular until Bob looked at his watch and said, "Okay, we just arrived back from our trek in the woods loaded the tree and got it tied down. Time to head back. I hope there's beer at home!" and he winked.

He started for his wallet. "My turn, Dad. You got the tree, and steaks for the scouts!" He let me pay and give the blonde a generous tip and we drove home and got the tree put up.

A couple beers later, we were both on our respective mattresses while the women were doing whatever women do when they shop. I was formulating a hangover in my sleep.

A Ring and a Dress

The men were happy to take Tyler as we ventured out to actually find a dress.

"Mama, I don't need or have time for a *new* traditional wedding dress!"

"Olivia! Listen to me. You want some soiled, ill-fitting, used rag somebody else wore?"

My mom was trying.

"Mama? The used formals and gowns shops only take stuff in new, unsoiled condition. No rips or tears, no buttons or clasps or pearls or even sequins missing! God will take us to the right dress at the right store," and we were nearing the first stop.

God delivers. There were three used formal and gown shops in the metro area in a loop of about 60 miles to get to them. We went to the closest, first, in Scottsdale. They boasted they had the largest wedding dress selection and were sorted by size. We pulled about six or seven dresses – ones we removed from the rack that got a closer look. As soon as Mama pulled out *my* dress, I took in a sharp breath. It was stunning and looked like it would look good on me: white, sequins and pearls on lace, low cut, wide shoulder straps, and a bell-shaped white satin dress covered with white lace and heavily beaded.

I motioned toward the clerk about twenty feet away.

"May I try this on, please?"

"Certainly, I brought a fitting room key. This way please."

The fitting room was no joke, like 8x10 with mirrors everywhere and a bench seat in the middle, where mom sat. I went behind a changing screen and got out of my clothes while mom took the dress off the hanger and unzipped it, and handed it to me over the screen. As I gently got into the dress and got the straps up, I was hoping my milk-laden breasts wouldn't keep me from seeing the dress zipped. It was going to have to fit over nursing mommy-boobs on our wedding day. And it did.

The woman who must have had it originally must have been very chesty. The bust hadn't been altered.

Mama sniffled and said, "Santa Maria, Olivia, you are the most beautiful bride I will ever see!" I was looking at myself from 50 different angles. We were a perfect match for each other. I walked around in it, barefooted and it flowed perfectly with me as I moved.

I was looking for the tag and never did see it *or* the price. The label said, "Angelique Gowns, Luxembourg" and nothing else.

"That's the one, Olivia."

I turned quickly around to her, "Yes, Mama, I think it *is* the one!"

Mama helped me get it on the hanger just right, and get the dress' protective cover back over it. We excitedly walked it up to the counter and Mama put the hanger on the place provided next to the register.

"That's the Angelique," the clerk said. "That's a gorgeous gown! The girl who bought it new paid a fortune for it and I have no idea why she didn't keep it. It's none of our business and we don't ask."

Mama winked at the woman, "It's here because it was meant for my Olivia. Ring it up, please."

"Right away, Mrs. Macias." She knew Mama's name. Of course.

I turned to Mama. "You already paid her something or gave her a card, didn't you!"

Mama smiled, "Your father's card, when we walked in," and Mama winked. "It's our gift to you, my precious baby girl." I hugged her for all my worth.

"Thank you, Mama."

"When are you getting married, Ms. Macias?"

"The 12th."

"12th of...?"

"December, in fifteen days"

"Wow. Okay, you need this. Justa minute," and the clerk rooted through a drawer.

"This is a gal who does top notch alterations and fitting work. She even makes gowns from patterns. Being December, she may be able to get this perfectly fitted to you in time for your wedding."

We got to the car with it and got the dress in, okay.

I dialed the seamstress' number, "Sewing and Alterations, Nicole."

"Hi, Nicole. My name's Olivia and Scottsdale Preowned Gowns said I should call you immediately."

"They have some really beautiful stuff in there."

"Yes, I just bought my wedding dress in there and I need a rush job—but there's not a lot of sewing needed. At least, I don't think so."

"When would you need the dress?"

"We're getting married December 12th."

"If it's a relatively small job, I can turn it around for you, but you'd have to get in here for a fitting."

"How soon can you get me in?"

"I'm open 10-7 daily, if you just want to drop-in. I'm in a small strip mall at Purple Ridge Boulevard and Hewitt Road, near Manny's Shoes."

"May we swing by, now?"

"Sure. It's quiet. I'm just sewing, as usual."

"My mom and I and the dress are on our way."

Nicole got me into her changing room and I put on the dress for the second time. For the second time, I felt like royalty in it. My lips were trembling as I was saying silent prayers Nicole could get it altered in time.

I walked out and Nicole's lips were holding a bunch of straight pins as she motioned me to the 3-way mirror. With her marker and pins, it took her all of ten minutes.

"You're a lucky girl, Olivia. The girl who wore this dress last must have been built similar to you. I can turn this around in about 72 hours. It's $175 if you pick it up, but for $300, I'll come by just before your ceremony and all but sew you into it. It will look and feel custom-tailored, Olivia. Sound fair?"

Mom and I exchanged nods, excitedly.

"We'd love it if you could come. It's early evening, December 12th at our home."

Nicole pulled a book from under her counter and flipped it open, finding the December 12th page.

"I'm available," and Nicole seemed as happy as we were.

Mom said, "I would like to pay you now, in full, please."

Nicole politely said, "That's really not necessary."

"I insist, because we appreciate what you're doing for us. Besides, you may need Christmas shopping money," and Mom shined her infectious smile at the middle-aged seamstress.

"How am I going to keep David from seeing it, Mama? "She looked at me like I was *loco*.

"Your maiden/matron of honor keeps it for you. Without one, the cleaners. You take it to the cleaners, they clean it, you get it out to be altered, you take it back to the cleaners and have it cleaned and you don't pick it up until your wedding day or the day before, child. I'm sure Nicole will hold it if you ask, honey."

Come

In the morning after all of our respective routines, Olivia told Mom and Dad we were going to be in the office for a bit. I sat beside her as we had the CD of pictures from our engagement and she stored them in the computer's hard drive. She brought up a graphics program and we decided on the picture for our wedding invitation.

The front of the invitation was a beautiful script font.

"On the 12th day of Christmas
my true love and I
will exchange
wedding vows of forever-love."

She used a photo of two gold wedding rings and superimposed Christmas a sprig of holly with red berries.

The left panel on the inside of a card was a beautiful picture of Tyler and Olivia and me at the country club engagement dinner. The right panel of the card read:

"You are cordially invited
to a Christmas party
in the intimate setting of our home
where we,
Olivia Maria Christina Macias
and
David Francis Bernard Callan
will marry.

We both loved it and Olivia grabbed a bag off the corner of the desk and pulled out the card stock she had selected from the stationary store. In a jiffy, she printed 25 invitations: 13 for the guests and the other dozen as keepsakes or for guests invited as afterthoughts.

We hand-addressed all the envelopes and agreed to call everyone personally to tell them something important was coming to them and to open it immediately.

"Hi, this is David Callan.

She interrupted, "OUR David Callan??"

I laughed, "Yes KFCG's David Callan, the best voice delivering the worst news. Can you connect me to Chuck in engineering please?"

"Sure can," she said laughing, "I hope we get to see you again soon, David! You sound great, just a minute."

"Engineering, Chuck Aundrin."

"Hey, it's David."

"The ghost of David Tyler speaks! Things okay?"

I laughed. "I'm great How about you?"

"I'm great too but I'll be a little bit better once you get your butt back to work."

"That may happen sooner than you think, Chuck, but I'm calling you about something important."

"Okay, go."

"December 12th at my house. I need you there at 6pm without fail."

"The 'without fail' part makes it sound serious. What's up?"

"A Christmas party. Well, it's not just a Christmas party, it's that combined with a wedding. My wedding and Olivia's. I'm going to marry Olivia that night right at home."

"Holy shit, you're doing the deed!"

"I have to. There's nobody else I want to spend the rest of my life with but her, and you of all people know what I've been through. Will you please be there?"

"I *will* be there, David. I will be there even if the transmitter goes down!"

"Well don't go that far, Chuck, because Sandy is going to be here, too."

Chuck, my solutions guy, always had the right answers, "I will hide his cell phone so he doesn't get the call David."

"We have an invitation on the way in the mail to you and I sent it to work so please look for it because it's kind of cool. Olivia made them."

"I'll look for it. Also, since it's at your house, send me an email of what you want for music and I'll burn it on a CD and bring in a portable set-up, David."

"Oh man, I'd appreciate that. Will do. I'll talk to Olivia and have it to you in the next 24. Can you get me over to Stephanie?"

"They just got off the air-sheesh, why am I telling you that because you know that. I'm sure she's in her *cubi-hole*." The rest call them *cubies* some call them cubicles but Chuck-good old Chuck-called 'em *cubi-holes*.

"Thanks buddy."

"You got it."

"Steph, Steph, I have a call for you some guy who said he banged you in the restroom of a to-go pizza joint, which narrows it down to an NFL stadium's crowd."

I was glad Olivia didn't hear that one, because even though she knew 'the wild thing' happened with me and Stephanie, our wedding was the last time and place in the world I wanted it brought up; in fact, I never wanted it brought up again.

"Very funny, dickweed. I'm getting you a puncture repair kit for your inflatable doll for Christmas... If I really know him, put him through."

"He's been on with us the whole time, Steph" and Chuck laughed.

"Hi, it's David!".

"Hey asshole! Come back to work. I'm trying to keep my shit together doing all this stuff by myself."

"That's a very different way to say hello and lure me back to work. Also good to know that you are still saving your potty mouth for the 22 hours a day you're off the air."

"I gotta get serious, here. I want to invite you to a party on the 12th at my house."

"Lotsa parties this time of year, David let me see what the 12th looks like and get back to you."

"No can do. Steph, before you even look, I'm going to marry Olivia in our living room the night of our Christmas party. The 12th. I want you there. You *have* to be there."

She got quiet and became her away-from-radio self.

"You amaze me, David. You just amaze me because guys just don't bounce back from that header you took with Vanessa. But you did come back, and strong, and I know that you did because of the woman Olivia is."

"It would mean the world if you could come, Stephanie. Please?"

"I'm *all* over that! Getting to watch *Studley Dudley* walk the plank into domesticity and go down, hard? Hah! Crash Callan takin' the dive! Damn RIGHT I'm there."

"I was kind of hoping you'd come alone rather than dragging your man of the week but you know you can bring somebody if you want to."

"I'm not going to bring anybody because they just wouldn't get it. We're friends, this is personal, and as real as it gets. I'm really happy for you, David."

She paused for a minute.

"David?"

"Yes."

"As a friend, I love you to the moon and you know that."

"I do, Stephanie, because nobody would have held my hand through what you have. On a cheerier note, Chuckster's coming and I really want to invite Sandy. Is he in?"

"I know he's here but I'm not sure what he's doing -hold on, I'm going to put you on hold while I check with his secretary." She was back in a flash.

"Yeah, he's just coming out of a meeting with sales so hang on a second and I'll warm-transfer you."

I heard the live feed on hold and it wasn't too long before I heard Stephanie's voice.

"Hey Sandy, this bozo on the line is insisting we cover his wedding and I think we should. Go ahead, sir, Mr. Tuttle is on the line."

I laughed.

Sandy said, "I know *that* laugh! David how the hell are you?"

"Sandy I'm getting married and I want you there."

"WHEN!"

"On the 12th at my house, at a Christmas party and you just *have* to be there. Please tell me that you'll be there, Sandy."

"I'm absolutely going to be there David because I'm going to bend your arm and step on your foot to get you back. Now that you'll be married with married man responsibilities, you'll need a steady job and my God I've been holding onto your slot long enough. I just have to figure out how to get you back in the booth," and we both laughed.

"I love you guys and I can't wait to come back to work. You've got invitations coming in the mail."

"You got it, David."

"No problem, David. We love you."

"Okay, bye guys."

Olivia was sitting next to me just grinning and glowing.

"I'm batting a thousand honey."

"Did you call Norman Lydell, yet?"

"Yes. I wasn't going to bring it up until you asked. His mother's like 98 years old and he's arriving in Chicago on the 10th. He wants to be with her for her last Christmas."

"Oh, David, I'm sorry, honey."

"Okay…. Your turn Olivia."

"Gwen McArdle."

"Deal!" And she dialed.

"Hi my name is Olivia Macias for Gwen McArdle and it's important.

"She's on another line.

"I'll hold if that's okay—Olivia Macias."

"I know you're acquainted. You'll hear a little beeping tone which means you're holding and the call will automatically connect once she hangs up."

"Thank you so much."

"You're most welcome."

"I love Gwen, David. She is just *so* cool."

"She was over the top when I went to get your ring honey. I'm glad you want her here, too!

"Gwen McArdle, who is this please?"

"Hi this is Olivia and David. We've got you on speaker phone!"

"Hey there, love birds, how are things?

"This is David. Things are better than you know. I want to invite you to our wedding!"

"Wedding!? You're gonna do this?"

"Yes, at a Christmas party we're throwing on the 12th."

"The 12th! That's kind of soon."

Olivia took over, "We want to get married while Mom and Daddy are in town and we don't have any reason to wait, Gwen. It just makes sense. Please tell me you can come!"

"I don't think I have anything on my schedule but let me check my planner a second. I'm clear and available; there was a cocktail party originally for that night and I decided I wasn't going to it, anyway. You don't actually think I'd miss your wedding, *do you*!?"

"We were hoping and praying you wouldn't. We're going to be thrilled to have you and you can bring someone if you'd like."

"I'm divorced and not seeing anyone because I'm married to my work. I will absolutely be there for you kids."

"You're the best and we love you. Watch for a printed invitation at your office, Gwen."

"That's right-you don't know where I live, do you? I'm at Paradise Valley Retreat, about a mile down the road from you!!"

"If you drink too much, we're still sending you home in a cab! Anyway, look for the invitation. We love you, Gwen!!"

"I love you kids too, thanks. I'm excited."

"Bye-bye."

"Holy God David. Paradise Valley Retreat. Those places start north of 3 million bucks."

"Scottsdale, honey. And her dad established himself catering to the upper end decades ago. I bet it's her folks' place she inherited."

"Yeah, and how ironic her hours are probably so long she never gets to spend time in her house. Please promise me we won't ever be like that because I kind of like our little love shack."

I kissed her. "Who's next?"

"Sheila. She wasn't my supervisor when I started. She got promoted right after I got there but we took an instant like to each other so she never treated me like an underling. I want to invite Sheila and her husband. Those two are like us and never go anywhere without each other."

"Make the call baby."

Olivia dialed into the hospital switchboard, "Sheila Larkin, please, but I don't know where she's assigned today. My name is Olivia Macias, an employee of hers."

"Just a moment please."

"5 South, this is Richard."

"Richard, they rang me to you because I'm looking for Sheila Larkin. I'm an employee, Olivia Macias."

"Just a sec. She's on the other side of the nurse's station." He put his hand over the phone and we heard him say 'Sheila?'

"Sheila Larkin. May I help you?"

"This is Olivia and you can only help me if you attend my wedding on the 12th, Sheila!" and the nursing supervisor squealed.

"David and I are getting married right here at the house."

"That's one I'm not missing for the world and I'm going to make sure my husband isn't on duty or on call. Even if he is, we'll do whatever it takes to be there, Olivia. This is the b-e-s-t!"

"An invitation's on the way but there's only like a dozen people. You are on our very short list, Sheila!"

"Olivia I am honest-to-God happy for you. You convinced even *me* that he's the one. We'll be there, girlfriend!"

"Love you, Sheila, thanks."

"Love you too. Duty calls," and she disconnected.

"David, you get to call the Trangs."

"I could just wait and see them and hand them the invitation."

"Too risky. Let's give them a call and get it done."

"You got it."

"Physical therapy please."

"Physical therapy, this is Ladonna."

"This is David Callan. Is either Tammy Trang or her husband Tommy available, please?"

"Tammy should be back from her break any second now. May I ask what this is regarding?"

"Yes, my wife's a nurse and I'm a patient of theirs. The Trangs are also personal friends of ours."

"Justa sec."

"Hi, this is Tammy!"

"Hi Tammy, David Callan."

"Hey, lazy bones, when are you getting your butt back in here!"

"At my next appointment, smarty pants."

"So what's up?"

"What's up is you and Tommy are going to attend our wedding on the 12th at my house." She started shrieking

"I so happy for you guys, like, complete awesomeness!"

"It's on the 12th so I'm going to bring the invitation into my appointment. Can I count on you guys to be there?"

"If we got something going on that night it's over and we're coming to your house to your wedding!"

"Bring your dancing shoes. I'm going to be blasting the music.

"You got it. I'll let Tommy know and he'll be verry happy for you, also!"

"Thanks, Tammy."

I put the phone down.

"Okay, David. Cross your fingers and hold your breath on this one."

Olivia dialed the number, "Yes may I speak to one of the hospital chaplains, please? Thank you."

"Hi, I'm Olivia Macias, a nurse on a leave of absence. I'm trying to reach Father Terry. Is he in today?

...I'm against kind of a timeline here. Do you think you could have him call me as soon as possible, I mean it's not life and death but I do need to hear from him?

...Olivia Macias, M-A-C-I-A-S, and it's on record there; just use my home phone of record, that's fine.

...Yes, that's it, thank you so much."

I had time to slip out and get David and I some iced tea, "Here, honey," and he smooched me for the effort.

The phone rang almost instantly. Phone karma. We were getting instant access and attention, everywhere.

"Hi this is Olivia.

...Yes, Father Terry. You'd probably recognize me from coming to Mass at the hospital because I work there. We've got everything all set to get married on the 12th of December but we don't have anybody to marry us. We're getting married at our house. Can you help us figure out how to get an available priest?

...Is it possible to put the hurry up on that paperwork?

...You're kidding. You can?? You will??

...I'll be down this afternoon to pick it up or, if we can fill it out right there, I'll bring my fiance with me.

...4:30, okay see you then. Thank you, Father!" and Olivia jumped up and down.

"Looks like we're going to have ourselves a wedding there, gorgeous."

"You're done, cowboy. You are *so* done," and she took my by the hand. We snuck around the corner of the office and into the bedroom. I was well done, so well done by Olivia that I needed a nap. Her libido was mindboggling.

I drifted off, didn't know Olivia went outside to make a phone call.

Olivia hit redial and spoke very quickly. "I just spoke to Father Terry. Is he available please? ...Thank you."

"Hey Father Terry, I have to be quick. It's Olivia Macias again. David and I have a child out of wedlock and I just found out I'm pregnant with twins. My parents are here from out of state, no one knows about the twins, and I want to be married. If that has any sway on hurrying up the paperwork.... Uh-huh... Yes.... please. Thank you, yes, this is under the seal of your confessional, Father. We're doing the right thing just going a little bit about it the wrong way. ...You *can* help us out?

...You're going to make it happen?

...You will??? Oh, Father Terry! Oh Terry, you're the greatest guy in the world...uh...uhm... besides the one I'm marrying!! Thank you. We'll be down later for the paperwork. ...Not a peep.... Okay thank you. Goodbye."

I sat down next to David.

"You can't hide tears from me, you know."

"Just silly girl stuff. Happy kinda tears. I'm okay. My mind just went 'sentimental sot' on me."

David and Fr. Terry hit it off. We filled out a few papers, handed him one of our invitations with the address and directions, and we were set.

"Is Tyler baptized, yet?"

David and I looked at each other and gulped. "Well... uh...no."

"I'd be happy to do that for you as well."

Olivia jumped into my arms and then threw them 'round Father Terry, whispering, "Let's baptize Tyler with the twins, please?" and he whispered, "Okay," as I turned back to David.

Prepping for Turkey

It had become morning routine. Bob had the gourmet coffee ready to pour by the time I got up.

"Mornin', Bob. How did you sleep?"

"Very well, and you?"

"Same. Toast or muffin, Bob?"

"I'll pass. I grabbed a banana and an orange. I'm good," and I opted to spread peanut butter on two slices of bread as my morning repast.

"I need a lift to the home improvement store in your truck this morning, David. Something I have to pick up."

"Sure, what time do you want to go."

"They're open now, do you mind if we get over there and back?"

"Not at all. I just need shoes. Be right back."

Olivia stirred when I walked in. I knelt on the bed and kissed her neck softly and she responded by reaching for me with her eyes still closed, "Hey, handsome."

"Hi, gorgeous. I'm gonna run your dad over to the home improvement store cuz he says he needs something."

One eye popped open and she looked at me and she said, "I know what that 'something' is. Fifty bucks says it's a smoker, cuz we don't have one and that's the only way he will eat turkey!"

"Jeez, I don't know how to use one. Not a clue."

"You'll know by the end of the day and get your first bird smoked in time for Thanksgiving. Dad's got it down to an art. You'll learn from a master, baby."

"If that's all we're getting, it shouldn't be long," and I kissed my Olivia and headed into the kitchen. I sat down and wolfed down the bread and grabbed my cup to take with us.

"All set?" and Bob gave me two thumbs up, "Let's do it."

Yep. Smoker.

"You never get the smallest one. Here's why. We're gonna do a turkey, yeah? Well, we're also gonna do some of those long sausages. The smoke from those, combined with the smoke from the mesquite is going to produce the best turkey you've ever put in your mouth, David."

"My mouth's watering, already!" and we were back inside of an hour.

On the ride back, Bob said, "Ofelia got excited because Olivia said there's a small chain of pretty good-sized Mexican grocery stores here in Phoenix."

"Yes, we like to go there because they have a great deli, an excellent produce department and a bakery that makes fresh tortillas. They have stuff I've never seen or heard of. We love it."

"Olivia told her mom they have big bags of mesquite, too. So we'll have the girls pick that up and you will be a master smoker by the end of tomorrow, son."

The women were up and buzzing when we got home. Bob and I unboxed the smoker on the patio and went right to work assembling it. We came in and Bob said, "Olivia, our Thanksgiving is going to be exactly like the ones you grew up with on the ranch."

She went to her dad and gave him a big hug, looked in his eyes, "Daddy? Have you ever *not* taken good care of your baby girl?"

"I better. You mother would whack me. An' besides, I love you, *mija.*"

"Mom and I are going to run over to Romero's after we make a list. With all you brought from the ranch, we know to get the mesquite, some produce and spices and stuff, right Mama?" and Ofelia nodded.

"Olivia! Put on the list, we need lamb's quarters for the *quelites.* Maybe they'll have them, I dunno."

"Bet they do, Mama!"

"We're having lamb and turkey?"

"Olivia, help your man, will you?" Ofelia said chuckling and patting my hand.

"Lamb's quarters are delicate little greens, David. Do you know *quelites* from your time in New Mexico?" and I didn't.

"It's a hot dish of lamb's quarters with green chiles, bacon drippings and a sprinkle or two of apple vinegar. Very *tradicional* and very New Mexico, honey."

"We can make *quelites* substituting other greens for lamb's quarters, but I hope they have them," and they did.

Olivia and Ofelia came in from the garage with five sacks of groceries, kissed Bob and me, and said, "The charcoal's in the back of the SUV, David."

I'd never seen anything like this mesquite charcoal. It was a brown, 40-lb bag with huge chunks of what looked like burned-down forest wood; pieces 10-18" long and as big around as a softball.

Bob saw it and commented, "Perfect, David. This is wonderful. Just right."

The turkey was on the counter in a pan under a towel, thawing. A 14-lb tom, a range bird, meaning no artificial anything. Without all the chemical additives as the turkey was raised, the breast and legs were a little smaller than the 14-lb. name-brand birds, but the flavor was remarkably different if prepared correctly.

"David, please, while we're getting these groceries out, grab that menu from under the magnet on the refrigerator, honey, and read it to me, please.

"You got it. Here we go:

Ceviche *Atun*

Blue corn stuffing

Sweet potatoes con tequila

Quelites

Blue corn tortillas

Cranberry-Pine Nut tamales

Sunflower seed bread... Olivia, isn't that the same one you made for me when we first met, honey?"

"Sure is! I brought it to you in the hospital." For dessert that memorable day, we conceived Tyler behind the locked bathroom door, I recalled with a blushing smirk.

"Never forget it, honey!"

"Thank you, David, and oh, they had the lamb's quarters, look!" and she held up two rubber-banded bunches of leafy greens. "These are great!"

"What's *atun*?

Our appetizer. You know what ceviche is, I know you do David, we've eaten it together. *Atun* is Spanish for tuna. We picked up a nice piece of line-caught fresh tuna that I'll use for ceviche."

"Spoil me at the table, Olivia, but please, please don't ever make me so fat I have to go to the gym."

"Are you asking me for one of Tyler's plates and spoon?," she razzed, and she laughed.

"And I'll love you more for it, sweetheart," and I patted her butt.

Did he have to bring up girth, fat, body size? I was going to be a building made out of jiggling flesh by the time I got to my last trimester with the twins. It wouldn't phase him. He'd look at me and treat me as if I was 124 pounds in a string bikini. Men don't usually do that, but my David would be incapable of doing anything else.

"Mom, can you do without me for a bit? I didn't rest well. Do you mind?"

"I'm a machine and this is nothing, *mija*. Get rest. David, take her.

"I'm getting a little overheated and I don't know why, David. Take a shower with me?"
"Sure, honey? You okay? I'm worried."

"Fine, just run down," and I grinned at him out of Mom's view.

We made our way to the shower. I set the water warm and then gradually started making it cooler for her. We even got a little playful.

"I think I know what I need, David. Sex. I need a big dose of you!" and she grinned and kissed me as we hurried out and down the hall to our room, skirting around being spotted by Ofelia or Bob or Tyler.

We made love with a small fan on. Slowly, sensuously, and both climaxed.

"*Dr. David's Miracle Cure* work?"

She looked over and grinned, "Oh, yeah. Is this treatment every four hours or what, Dr. David?"

"As needed. No limit."

"Mmm, good. Then c'mere."

Turkey Day

Bob and I were at it early, arranging the mesquite in the wood box of the smoker. I had an electric charcoal starter so we didn't have to use fluid. It took a little longer but was fine. Bob said he used a propane torch on the ranch and got the center pieces lit and stacked on the others. Ofelia joined us on the patio with her hot chocolate.

"David, at the ranch we are doing this all day, the day before Thanksgiving. A lot of our hands have nowhere to go or it is too far to travel for them to get back and they cannot afford to be away very long. We've fed everyone who's ever shown up."

Ofelia chimed-in, "The ranch Thanksgiving is an incredible amount of work. Olivia grew up helping, so you might just get a little tummy on you! There are 80 hands, working cowboys, spread out over nine square miles of ranch. In general terms David, the ranch is about 2 miles wide by 4 and a half miles long, both hilly and flat. You will come and you will see."

"I can't even picture that in my mind, Ofelia." She gave me a toothy grin and said, "Well, you are part of a ranch family, now! That means, you show up? You work, too!" She paused and added, "Cowboy," and Olivia and her mom, howled.

"WAIT A MINUTE. Ofelia? When Olivia calls me that, I thought it was a term of affection, like sweetheart, but she's making fun of me??" Olivia started to answer but her mom's hand came up, "Ah! Ah, child!"

"David, when she calls you 'cowboy,' it is affection, big love and more, *mi hijo*. Compared to our crew? Just let me say you'd maybe last ten minutes as a ranch hand, that's all," and Olivia and her mom tittered.

I wasn't going to win, and Olivia was hiding her eyes. "Well. Your mom could have said nine minutes. Or five, honey!" and we busted out laughing.

"David Callan, Ranch Wimp," I added.

"Not so," admonished Ofelia. "David Callan, Mr. Macias' son-in-law, and that will bring some instant respect in two counties, David. You'll earn the rest," and she winked. "I'm sure of it."

"Well, back to Thanksgiving, there. You were saying?"

"My crew of ladies and I make these very same dishes except we have a grill master we hire to turn large turkeys on the outdoor spit over mesquite we've gathered. We will serve all day and the hands can come in and eat as many times as they like. We don't have cake. We have cobblers and pies! Apple, cherry, blueberry, pecan, banana cream and strawberry."

"For you, this may seem like a lot of work here in your house. For Roberto and for me this is a holiday. Relaxation and how better could it be done with all of us, here to enjoy it."

"I'm sure someone's handling the ranch feed."

"Oh, yes. I'm the only one missing and I've had a couple of my ladies over 15 years and they step in and supervise. It will go fine. Just like here. It will go fine here but don't expect pies.... Although Olivia said you *love* cherry pie.

I went stone cold silent and looked at Olivia. She kept a straight face.

"Ofelia, I'm sorry but please don't go to all that trouble. I'm really *not* much of a cherry pie fan," and I turned to give Olivia an accusatory look and Olivia burst out laughing.

"I think mama was testing you. Well, I was testing you to see if you would look at her and tell her a fib and you didn't! You passed the test, cowboy!" and the women hi-fived each other, then rubbed their hands on their aprons and got right back to it.

My David

David woke up and stumbled into the kitchen and didn't know what he was looking at. There was a 40-quart aluminum pot on the stove and 12 feet of the counter supported containers and bowls of ingredients. Mom and I were in aprons and Mom was the first to notice David watching. Bob was having a patio having a cigar watching the golfers.

"David if you don't get out of the kitchen, I'm going to put you to work! Your work is outside, on the turkey! But my Olivia said you need to learn some things in here. I dunno if that's good or bad. Just remember: I am the *madron*, in charge. I give the orders. You follow them and you won't get your butt cheeks popped with a towel!" and she put her hands on her hips and laughed.

"Olivia, you would let your mom *do* that to me?"

She pointed an empty corn husk at me, "David I would *make* my mother do that to you. Besides, you get the fringe benefit of getting one of these tamales when they're done, but only if you help. If you don't help, you don't get any and I mean that."

"Is that fair, holding me hostage over a tamale? I shouldn't have to wait until tomorrow, after waiting for you my whole life?"

"You're right. Okay. You screw up or don't help? No sex 'til June. THAT should be worth rolling up your sleeves and getting your ass over here like, *andelé*!"

"You have a cruel little girl, Ofelia. Stingy and selfish."

Olivia tried to glare at me, but her upturned lips were a grin and the glare came out as sexy. She couldn't help herself.

"It would take three days, David, for someone to make Christmas tamales on Thanksgiving morning and still get Thanksgiving dinner done at the same time. Mama and I have it down to a science, my love!"

Now, *Ofelia* turned around and put her hand on her hip and gave me the *stink eye.* "Apron or scram, *mijo,* you choose." And Olivia and her mother cracked up. It was a happy time with a happy family, something I had never experienced.

"Okay, apron but in a minute. Let me take Bob a beer, peek at the turkey, and hang out with him a few minutes". Tyler was pushing big plastic blocks around on his highchair tray. I grabbed two beers by their necks and scooped-up Tyler and a couple of the blocks. I still had a couple of fingers available to slide open the glass door.

"There he is! Your *abuelo*! Say, 'Hi, Grandpa! Hi, Grandpa!' and a grin overtook Bob's face as I set down his frosty beer. I used my foot to kick out a chair and sat, keeping Tyler in my lap and putting the plastic blocks on the table for him to bang around.

"Thank you, son! You were reading my mind. I was just enjoying my cigar, a man's guilty pleasure. I only like the one kind and don't have one very often but when I do, I really like it. How's your day going?"

"Physical therapy kicked my butt yesterday and I'm still suffering. That's why I grabbed a little nap.

It was mid-afternoon. Olivia and Ofelia worked their tails off and it was time for our Thanksgiving meal.

All of the serving dishes were on a side table, with dinner plates at the far left.

Once we were seated, we joined hands and Bob said the blessing.

Orphanages serve Thanksgiving meals but, at the end of the day, it's institutional. You don't get an extra roll or more mashed potatoes or yams. I realized that's why I was being more quiet than normal.

Olivia kept looking across the table at me with questioning eyes. I'd wink and pucker my lips as if sending a kiss across the table.

Our family Thanksgiving was extraordinary. I enjoyed the traditional New Mexico dishes, immensely.

We finished our desserts and coffee. I wiped my lips with the cloth napkin and cleared my throat for attention.

"I've never experienced a family Thanksgiving in a room so full of love. Bob? Ofelia? I can't describe what it means to have you here." I needed a sip of water to continue. "You accepted me as family and today I've never felt it more. And with that, I'm ready for a cigar with Bob!"

When Bob and I sat down on the patio. I noticed his brand of cigars we was smoking and made a mental note so I could get him some for Christmas.

Speaking of Christmas, Olivia wore a traditional watch but mentioned she thought about getting one of those fitness watches with internet access that hooked into her phone service. So that was going to be easy. Tyler was going to get big trucks and cars so he and I could play with them on the floor and fill them with dirt outside.

I had no clue what to go to Ofelia. I was going to rely on Olivia for help. My first thought was a pair of really nice leather sandals because she was wearing some. It looked like she could use a new pair. Olivia told me I had a good eye and that would be a wonderful present she would love. Olivia knew a couple places in Scottsdale that were likely to carry them.

Three's Indeed a Charm

Bob and David rejoined Mom and me. We were relaxing at the table when Mom looked at me and said, "Should we teach him to play and take his money?"

"I'm game."
David had a quizzical expression.
"Cards, David. We live on a remote ranch. In the evenings, Bob and I like to play cards and all different kinds of table games. When Olivia was little, we taught her how to play hearts and other card games. You know how to play hearts?"
"I think I've played maybe once, so honestly, no."
"Good get your piggy bank because we're going to teach you."
David got his butt handed to him and lost all of his pennies. We had a rollicking good time. He was a good sport, a cheerful loser. Bob and David had a couple beers, Mom made some tequila screwdrivers for herself, but I passed on alcohol, opting for some flavored bottled water. David started to get up from the table and I motioned 'Stay put' with my hand. My parents wondered what was up. Dad shrugged his shoulders at Mom and David. David knew we were all about surprises and heard that train a-comin'.
I walked over to the refrigerator and reached up on top of it to retrieve his unboxed ring. He would have seen a box up there and been curious. I palmed it and came back to the table and stood in front of him, until he pulled his chair out a little. I nudged his knees apart with mine, so I could move in close.
I got down on both knees in front of David. I took his left hand with my right, and with my left hand, used my index finger and thumb to show him the ring.
"David Francis Bernard Callan, will you marry me... in our home on December 12th... while my mother and dad are here... in front of our closest friends? Will you

have me and hold me until death us do part, because I can't possibly live without you with as much love I have for you now and will always have for you."

I thought my mother was going to have a heart attack. Daddy just grinned and shook his head. David looked like he was in a trance for a second. They were all in tears.

David held out his left hand and spread his fingers, looked me in the eye.

"I will," and I had no trouble slipping the ring on his finger as he took my hands lifting me into a standing position and kissed me.

I heard Bob ask Ofelia, "Were we like that?"

Ofelia replied, "Of course we were, Roberto. Olivia didn't arrive on the chuckwagon, honey!"

David couldn't take his eyes off the ring. Before my parents could ask, he held it out to them, explaining, "I don't know why but I envisioned our son as a ruby and put one into her engagement ring. I'm thinking that the rubies in this ring are a promise of more children one day? More grandchildren for you?"

I nodded behind the tissue I'd grabbed, handing one to Mom, too. I returned to the refrigerator where I had stashed a bottle of champagne, grabbed it, grabbed the half gallon of orange juice, and put them on the island, turning back around for frosted stems I'd put in the freezer.

I made mimosas and served them, joining my parents at the table, and accepting David's beckon to sit on his lap.

"CHEERS!" my dad yelled, and we clinked glasses and drank. We were all a little tipsy by the time the champagne was gone. I don't think anyone noticed I hadn't refilled my glass with champagne. It was OJ, only, from the start.

We all trundled off to bed, David stopping to scoop-up Tyler and put him down in his crib which he was learning to like.

David pulled my nude body up onto his, all five-foot-six of me trying to cover his six-one frame.

I looked him in the eye and said "You know what? I got the best tamale in the whole batch. I got you, the sweetest and tastiest treat of my life."

"We're a thing, Olivia, and we're gonna do this thing."

"Gwen—I'm assuming it was Gwen—did a bang-up job on this ring, honey!"

"You don't even know what I put her through, and she just shines, comes through, never says 'No,' or 'Can't,' she just makes magic happen. We've gotten tight. I think I have a non-hospital bestie, honey!"

"She a super lady, sharp as a tack, successful in business, and can still turn a head or two, I imagine."

"Imagine?"

"She's attractive. Not my age group, but ten or ten-plus years older? She'd get swarmed."

"She never gets out. All work and no play makes Gwen a dull girl, David."

"I bet we can change that up, a little, Olivia." "Really?"

"Sure, I like the heck out of her, too!

"Tell me something good."

"Sit up. I think I'd like to rock your world."

We lay in the stillness completely perspired and exhausted in our favorite tangle of arms and legs.

"David?"

"Yeah, baby?"

"I love us like this. Help me keep it like this."

He kissed my neck.

"Should be easy." He grinned, "You're a willing accomplice."

The time had flown by. It was time to take the plunge. David winced when I said that. He much preferred 'take the leap,' like leap of faith. We were ready and it was tomorrow.

Vows and Wows

The Hideaways van had been running foodstuffs and tablecloths and utensils up the hill since 7am. A full wet-bar was set up on the patio, kind of a cool thing using a garden hose to provide cold water and a line tapped into the kitchen's hot line for the other spigot. Very small occasional tables with candy dishes were integrated with our furnishings, just big enough to rest two or three drink glasses.

We gathered in the kitchen and had coffee and juice, a banana and cereal for Tyler. The general mood was ecstatic. I was convinced Tyler could feel it. We'd start breakfast as soon as Fr. Terry got here, then go over the vows and the order of things.

A hairdresser would come about 4-ish for Mom and even trim-up Dad and David if she thought they needed it. My hair would be done last because consideration had to be given to the round halo of white carnations, gerbera daisies and gardenias that would be pinned into my hair, with red and white silk ribbons, trailing.

David seemed fidgety.

"You okay, David?"

"I'm fine. Little nervous thingy going on."

"Me too, I just happened to notice your fidgets before you noticed mine," and I giggled at him.

"I have something for that, justa sec."

David got up from the table and walked into the garage. I heard the truck door open and shut, and he walked back in and joined me at the table.

"Here, honey, take two of these."

I thought two aspirin or something were going to drop into my hand. It was a tiny note.

"Happy Wedding Day, my forever-love," and he brought up a beautiful small box that he'd kept out of sight under the table, set it on the table, and slid it to me.

"OH, DAVID," and I started sobbing and stepped around the table, the box in one hand and my other arm around his neck, holding him and kissing him. I removed two, quarter-carat, ruby stud earrings with 18kt white gold posts.

"My hands are shaking, David. Will you put them in for me, please?"

"Sure."

David held my earlobe, inserted the stud and I moved my head so he could put on the locking back. Then he did my other ear.

"Olivia, those are just beautiful, honey," Mom said.

"They are, Mama. And so's this man's heart I'm stealing, today and forever," and I turned and kissed him.

"I have something for you, too, but you'll get it in a while, baby."

"I have everything I ever wanted."

"And soon you shall have my wedding gift to you."

The doorbell rang and it was the seamstress, Nicole and my dress arriving. She had thoughtfully put the dress in an opaque, full-length garment protector so no one could see what it looked like. It took Nicole about ten or twelve minutes to put stitches here and there into the dress and it felt like a second skin. It was comfortable, and I could move and breathe in it.

Mom had gotten an ivory suit, skirt and blazer, with a dark red silk blouse and ivory scarf gathering the collar to the neck. She wore scarlet flats to match. There was a dark red corsage in the refrigerator next to my floral halo of gardenias, white gerbera daisies and small white carnations, and 18" red and white silk ribbons curling down onto my back. We dispatched Dad to get both.

Gwen walked up to me grinning, "I've never seen a more beautiful bride, and I may be prejudiced, but that ruby heart David gave you jumps out accentuating the beauty of your hair, face and gown, Olivia."

"Thank you, Gwen. I'd like to send David's locket over to him. I'd be honored if you gave it to him."

"You sure you don't want to give it to him, honey...see his reaction."

"I have his heart right here on my chest. I'd like to be next to his heart, in the locket, when I become his wife."

"David came up with the ruby heart idea, size and chain, Olivia. He's discriminating, knew exactly what he wanted without compromise. He won't be deterred in providing for you, and with all the men I do high-end business? David stands above the rest in what's driving him to get something that will please you. Today, that ruby has never been more beautiful, Olivia."

David and Father Terry were in the office where David had on his black tuxedo pants and white pleated shirt with dark red studs and black shoes. His deep scarlet bow tie matched his cummerbund. He pinned on his own boutonniere; a white rose accented by a live, berried holly sprig. My gold band was in his pocket.

I retrieved David's locket from where I had hidden it, in the toe of a pair of boots. The locket had pictures of the first time he saw and held his son. It was in the main, right panel. I argued with myself about the left panel, 'What would David want, there.' I was 100% sure he would want my picture there. No doubt. No question. He loved me that much and if he carried me in his heart as I knew he did constantly, he'd have me in his locket.

Gwen had prepared a gorgeous cardboard box with a printed design and ribbon, she included a small blank card and matching envelope, fine stationery with linen in it, so I could write something to David. I did:

"David, my husband, my life and my forever-love—
We're with you and love you, always.
Tyler 'n Me"

I wrote, "To My Husband" on the front of the small envelope and pressed my lips to leave a kiss imprint. I put a kiss mark on the card.

Our friends were having a nice time, talking, having some cocktails, and enjoying the plentiful hors 'd oeuvres on trays circulated by white-jacketed servers from The Hideaway.

Dad got our flowers and Mom secured my ribboned halo, and just before I was about to pin-on Mom's corsage, my dad said, "Please," and took it from me. As he pinned it on my mom, he said, "Ofelia. I love you as much as the day you and I were doing this as kids. Thank you for our life and our beautiful baby girl," and my dad kissed my mom gently enough to keep her lipstick intact. He turned to me. "Olivia, I don't know if I'm ready for this, giving you away but I know you have found someone we are proud of, confident that David will love and care for you. I love you, *mija*."

"You're making me cry, Daddy!"

"I know, I know. I think more tears are coming in a minute."

It was 5:55. Father Terry told David it was time and slipped out of the room to come to the master bedroom to let us know. It was our cue to exit through the jacuzzi door and slip around the edge of the trellis to go to the patio and await our entrance behind the drapes which had been closed just seconds ago. It was silent with anticipation on the other side of the glass.

The sound of cathedral bells rang out from a CD Chuckster played as the drapes were drawn back. As the door was opened for us, we could see the Christmas tree twinkling and everyone was standing, every face beaming, with cellphones raised to photograph me. Streams of compliments were coming from everywhere.

I met David's eyes as he walked out from the office, through the kitchen and into the living room. Again, the pictures and muffled praises.

I could almost feel David's touch just in the way he was looking at me. We approached each other, close, and he whispered, "You are ravishing, my love."

Fr. Terry took his place and motioned us into position, whispering, "Hold hands and face your friends, please."

"With God and his people present here tonight, I will begin in the name of the Father and of the Son and Holy Spirit," we all said, 'Amen.'

"You're not just witnesses here, tonight. You are endorsing and celebrating the Roman Catholic Church's conferring the sacramental act of pure love upon two as they become one in marriage, Olivia and David. And what a better time. Advent, the coming of the Christ-child promised, foretold in Scripture of the Old Testament written thousands of years ago, about a season of celebration far into the future. So let's get these two married!" and there was a smattering of applause.

"Who giveth this bride away?"

My dad cleared his throat, "Her mother and I do."

"David, would you and Olivia please face each other and I will begin your Simple Rite of Christian Marriage."

They were the vows everyone who's been to a wedding recognizes. Fr. Terry blessed our rings, and we placed them on each other's fingers, looking into each other's eyes, as we said with slow deliberation, 'With this ring, I thee wed."

"I now pronounce you husband and wife. You may kiss your bride, David."

David's eyes were misty as he leaned down and kissed me, and then lifted my heart-shaped ruby and held it dearly and kissed it. Then he kissed each of my earlobes, right on the ruby earrings he'd given me. Then, loud enough for everyone to hear, "You are my forever-love, Olivia Maria Christina Macias Callan," and then he leaned me back, movie-style and gave me a kiss with the cumulative passion of our whole love story in it.

I whispered to David, "Garters, honey," and he knelt and raised the right bottom of my dress slowly, revealing the blue garter I wore and slid it down and off, handing it to me. Then, he raised the left side of my dress, revealing

another garter he slid down, removing it and handing it
to me.

I yelled, "Stephanie!" and shot the garter like a
rubber band right at her glass. I took the other garter
and yelled, "Gwen! Catch!" and did the same.

Our friends went wild, hooting and cheering and
clapping. Chuckster cued music, "Beautiful," by Gordon
Lightfoot, its lyrics, "I think that I was made for you, and
you were made of me," as David swirled me around in
our first wedded dance. We chose David's favorite love
song he heard in Mexico in the days volunteering at the
orphanage. It was "Te Extraño," by Luis Miguel, the lyrics
speaking volumes about the heights and depth of love
one can have for another. My mom came to David who
took her in his arms, and I got a big hug from Dad as he
began to dance with me. He whispered, "Your mother
and I have loved this song forever, *mija.*"

Chuckster and David had put thought and time into
choosing romantic, danceable music for the CD and it
showed.

Only Mama and Gwen knew about the twins. It fell
on Gwen to get the SUV rigged for the reveal. Even if she
didn't do it herself, she ran a business and was a
seasoned pro at delegating to get things done. She didn't
fail.

A couple of printed signs had to go into the SUV with
the items we'd use for the reveal. Gwen had her
advertising person design and print-out hi-resolution
signs printed on a plastic, canvas-type material.

Gwen locked up the SUV and entered the party
through the doors on the big patio and slipped the key
back in her interior pants pocket where it would stay
until she could sneak through the kitchen into the
garage and move the SUV to the curb and lock it.

David and I were handed stems and he raised his to
toast me.

"My bride and my mate and my forever-love, you
found me hurt from a motorcycle accident. I lost you and

hoped against hope when another serious motorcycle accident delivered me into your care and loving hands. Yes, I lost you once but you found me twice. I will never forget the hurt of that loss, and I will never lose you again. It's forever-love, Olivia, and it's ours."

We tilted our champagne flutes toward one another until the slightest touch and sipped, followed by a little kiss.

"My husband, David? You never doubted me that our love was meant to last a lifetime. You had faith I loved you when I was gone and knew I would be back. No woman is loved like I am loved. I have pledged all of my life and all of my love to you in front of the most meaningful people in my and our lives. David? You got me. Cheers, cowboy!"

And I didn't just kiss him lightly, I kissed him for all my worth. Everybody in the place was hooting and hollering and clapping as the pictures continued.

He picked me up in his arms and swung me around as he was kissing me. We had agreed to change clothes but my wonderful David, my husband David, asked in a whisper, "You look like a goddess, Olivia. If you want to keep your dress on, then do it honey."

"No, honey, let's party with our friends, baby! But don't be surprised if you come home from work one day and I'm cleaning the house in this dress."

"I guess my reaction will depend on what you are wearing or not wearing underneath it." And he kissed me. We excused ourselves, went into the bedroom and changed, never taking our eyes off of each other.

"We did it!'

"I know, huh!!"

"Can I just tell you that you're awfully pretty, Mrs. Callan?"

"You may, sir, and you don't ever have to stop." I grabbed his hand and led our way back into the living room where the atmosphere was crankin' and the alcohol was flowing. Spotted, a cheer went up and David did a most curious thing. He walked up to my mom and picked her up and spun her around and gave her a great big kiss.

"I love you, Mom." He looked in her eyes much like he looks in mine and said, "She is so much like you, and you and Bob gave me this gift, this lifetime love. If you would call me your son, I would be humbled and proud, always."

"You'll never be anything else, David. You make her world so happy," and Mom kissed David lightly on the mouth. "Thank you, son."

Despite the raging party, I had work to do.

I went over and grabbed Gwen and said, "Come to the bar with me, G.!"

Gwen said, "Olivia, no one is ever going to forget this Christmas or this party or your wedding. It's all a fairy tale dream we witnessed and participated in."

"My God, are you a little tipsy?" I giggled.

"That, I am, my fairy-tale princess friend!"

We walked onto the patio and enjoying a moment alone. "I'd like the white wine please, Gwen? "

"No thank you I'm good on my drink. Everything is set for the big reveal. My driver got it all handled."

"I needed a partner in this and you came through for me just like you have every time."

"You would do the same and more for me, I know you would," and Gwen clanked her glass against mine. "Cheers, Mrs. Callan! You are now officially off the market."

"I was never really on it, Gwen. I had it bad for him from the start and I'm sure I always will. I think he really was made for me."

"Oops, forgot to tell you."

My attention piqued.

"When you and David are ready to leave, the driver's going to take you to your honeymoon suite."

"Gwen, we're not going anywhere, we're staying here."

"Not according to your parents and me. We changed that plan so you get to leave and we can throw rice and confetti at you! You and David aren't the only ones who know how to pull off a surprise."

I was dumbfounded.

"Don't worry about Tyler. He's going to stay here with your mom and dad. I've got two nights for you in a grand master suite with unlimited room service. It's prepaid so party like it's your Christmas wedding!" I wasn't believing my ears.

My cheeks were getting wet, "What can I possibly say, Gwen...."

"Just thank you and thank you parents. We packed your bags and already sent them over. Your clothes, toiletries and makeup are already there."

It was time.

"CHUCKSTER, MUTE THE MUSIC. MUTE IT PLEASE, CHUCKSTER.

We're thrilled you came, but there's more!" I let out my best woot-woot cowgirl yell, and everyone applauded.

"I'm going to give David and Tyler a father-son Christmas present tonight so they can be comfortable with it by Christmas morning!"

I grabbed a bag from under the table nobody had noticed and removed some duct tape and a long strip of dark cloth, tucking the bag back under my arm.

I turned to my husband, "David. I'm going to blindfold you."

The room went quiet.

"Okay, I'm game."

I blindfolded him and secured it with duct tape to ensure he could see absolutely nothing.

"Under NO circumstances can you take off the blindfold. I WILL TELL YOU WHEN YOU CAN!"

"I'M NOT GOING TO MESS UP GETTING MY PRESENT EARLY!" and people laughed.

"OKAY. EVERYONE! Grab your drinks everybody and follow me." I led David carefully out the front door and started down the sidewalk with everybody following. My mom had Tyler in her arms. I motioned Mama to hand Ty to me.

I had David by the hand and Tyler on my hip with a bag in my hand as I approached the passenger side of our Mercedes SUV and opened the passenger door. "David get in the car. I'm gonna hand you a shirt. Put it on, and buckle up, baby!"

Loudly, David said, "Okay Olivia, but now this is freaking me out a little." I kissed him and whispered, "You're fine, cowboy, it'll just be like 3 or 4 more minutes, tops."

I shut his door and opened the rear door, "Honey, I'm putting Tyler in his car seat."

I trotted over to the assembled guests and my parents. "Okay everybody- head over to the SUV by the passenger door behind David-but not too close. When I raise my hand like this and make circular motions, start taking video footage RIGHT AWAY toward the back seat's passenger door because it's going to be over in a few seconds."

I heard someone whisper, 'Must be a puppy.' Boy were THEY gonna be surprised.

I kept my back to the crowd and took off my overshirt revealing the back of a gray-backed t-shirt to the crowd. I waved my arm in the air in a circular motion and barked, "DAVID!! TAKE OFF YOUR BLINDFOLD AND GET TYLER OUT OF THE SUV, NOW! HURRY!"

David pulled off the blindfold and jumped out of the car, immediately, doing a quick 90° to his right to get his son. There were three baby seats attached to the back seat. The middle one had Tyler in it. In bold orange brushstrokes, the seat on the left held a placard that said "COMING" and the seat on the far right's placard said "SOON".

I was standing right behind David and yelled, "TURN AROUND, COWBOY!" My t-shirt had a Minnesota baseball logotype on it that said "TWINS" with a bold orange, hand-drawn arrow pointing toward my tummy. David was wearing a matching Minnesota Twins shirt but without the arrow.

David looked down at his tee, at the car seats' placards, ran to me and kissed me, ran a lap around the SUV screaming and jumping up and down with Tyler squealing, and then ran over to the little patch of front yard grass we had and laid down and began weeping, finally turning over onto his back laughing, as I caught up to him, knelt down beside Tyler and him and he pulled me on top of him.

"Merry Christmas, Boys!" and I kissed him.

A second later when it all sank in, everyone on the street started cheering and dancing, clapping, howling at the moon and laughing.

Our raucous celebration moved into the house. Chuckster got some rock 'n roll cranking at high volume, people were throwing back drinks and getting louder.

David and I were dancing in our Twins shirts, still getting photographed. "David, look!" and he did. Sandy Tuttle was dancing with Gwen McArdle.

My nursing supervisor, Sheila, had a huge goblet of wine in her hand and was barefoot. She was snuggled husband-Jim's lap in the huge recliner. David's physical therapist, Tommy Trang, was dancing with his coworker-wife Tammy in their color- and pattern- coordinated Hawaiian shirts. Stephanie and Chuckster were kind of dancing around outside on the big patio, probably smoking a joint. Or three.

I had Tyler in my arms and was dancing with him and David. Mom and Dad were right next to us 'old school' dancing and keeping up just fine.

Tyler was squealing every time we spun, having a great time. I put my arms around David's neck and said, "Merry Christmas, my forever-love. I'm delivering our twins in August."

"We're going to need that time to come up with quality middle names," and he bent me over backwards and kissed me dramatically like in the movies. Again, everybody howled and cheered.

"I got this. Kundegunda Monica for her and Methodius Steven for him."

"I'm going to make you rethink that when you're sober, my most worthy husband."

David chuckled and then his expression and aura changed. He took my left hand and brought it to his mouth and kissed my engagement ring. "Two more stones on the way."

David was pretty well oiled and blurted out, "EVERYBODY LISTEN-UP PLEASE! Just when I think I've had the happiest day of my life, Olivia gives me yet another and another and another. There aren't a lot of people here tonight because Olivia insisted that she only wanted people here whom she most cared about. You are our short-list so let's keep the party going! Stay as late as you wish or even all night! Mama Macias and I will be putting out a huge breakfast in the morning and you are invited to that as well!," and Ofelia laughed and shouted back, "For my new son, anything!"

I made my way to Gwen, "I think it's time we scram and figure out what newlyweds do on their wedding night," and I winked at her.

"One kick-ass wedding and party, Olivia. And your double-barreled reveal? You're my new hero, everything-flavored hero!"

I had to laugh because I had never seen her cut loose nor had I seen her on the way to getting completely trashed. She kissed me and wandered off, grabbing Sandy by the shirt, and pulling him to her as I grabbed David's hand, "Ready, cowboy?"

"Take me away, Mrs. Callan. I'm yours." We made our way to plant a kiss on Tyler and my parents and slipped out. We shouted, "Good night! We love you!" eliciting farewell and congratulatory shouts and waves.

David and I were making out in the back of the limo and didn't notice we were arriving. The car slowed to a stop. The driver stepped out and opened the doors and David and I almost fainted. We were standing in front of a 7,100 square-foot Italianate mansion. It was Gwen's, could only be Gwen's.

The driver rang the doorbell which was answered by a uniformed maid who invited us in. I turned to Olivia and picked her up in my arms and kissed her.

"Congratulations, and welcome. Please," as she held the door open.

"It's my only chance to carry you across the threshold. All three of you!" and he kissed me. He set me down about 10 feet inside of the door.

"Welcome to the McArdle home. I am Elena. My husband, the chef, and I will be taking care of you for the next 2 or more days. We've prepared the grandmaster suite for you. It hasn't been lived-in for some 20 years, as, she chooses to live elsewhere in the house. You have full access to the house including the library, which has a stocked bar and if you would like me to show you the entertainment room, I can show you where that is as well at some later point. We have an intercom system you will find on your nightstands and inside of the grandmaster suite bathroom as well.

David and I could only stare at each other in shock. "Thank you."

"If you'll come this way, I will show you to the suite."

We approached and went up the curved curve mahogany staircase to a set of double doors leading into the 800 square foot master bedroom.

Elena opened both doors and revealed a massive chandelier and a handtied Persian rug that must have cost half a million by itself. Four candelabras had 16 new tapers burning. There was an iced champagne bucket next to the bed and two flutes on the table beside it, plus a basket of fresh fruits. There was also a meat and cheese, bread and crackers platter as nice as the ones we had gotten from The Hideaway. They were beautiful.

"The orange button panels are your intercom. There are more staff members in the house and we are here for you, 24 hours, including food and meal service from the fully stocked kitchen. You will never be disturbing anyone. You are the sole reason we are here and are happy to serve you, especially on your wedding night and honeymoon, Mr. and Mrs. Callan. So welcome and please follow me. The driver will bring your stuff up, immediately." Elena curtsied and wheeled around and left, closing the big double doors.

"Pinch me, Olivia."

"No David, pinch me."

"When I was sneaking around behind your back with Gwen, she told me the story of how her old man got so rich and in a hurry. It was major league baseball money, during spring training year after year, that paid for all of this. I'll let you her tell you the story one day."

The suite was expansive and jaw-dropping, right out of *Architectural Digest.*

David walked me toward the canopy bed, "If you'll excuse me, Mrs. Macias-Callan, I have a marital obligation to attend to," and he stepped around me and started undressing me slowly, kissing my neck and behind my ears.

"Our stuff's on the way up. Hold up a minute, Cowboy."

He grinned, "My wife thinks of everything...." He looked around the suite, "and so does her new bestie. Look at this place, Olivia!"

"I think it suits us quite nicely, cowboy...er, Mr. Callan, my studly mate."

David was fascinated with the room and looked at every inch. I had to admit it was the most palatial thing I had ever seen in my life. I'd seen memorable magazine pictures of museums and mansions, and this one belonged with the best of them.

Being a radio nerd, David was fascinated with the intercom like a damn little kid (I thought it was cute). I laughed and said, "It's okay, Elena gave you permission to play with it and they will certainly answer you because that's what they get paid to do." He realized I was ribbing him and he was taking it well.

"There *is* something I want to ask her...I wonder if Gwen is sleeping here, tonight?"

"Good question, honey. That never occurred to me. I guess I assumed she would stay at our house in one of the bedrooms since we're not there and maybe give my folks a hand with Tyler. But I don't know."

"I'll try to ask Elena in a way that doesn't sound nosy," and David pressed the orange button he was dying to push.

"This is Elena, Mr. Callan."

"Olivia and I were thinking we'd like to eat in the dining room in the morning. Is it okay to wear robes?

"Yes, robes and even pajamas are fine. You have the options of the dining room, the glass enclosed garden patio or the outdoor gazebo."

"Will there be anyone else dining in the morning or do we have the house to ourselves?"

"Gwen is here in her regular living quarters, Mr. Callan. I don't know where she'll breakfast. It may be in her living quarters, a distinct possibility. "

"Thank you, Elena, sorry to bother you."

"No bother sir. Would you like more champagne sent up or anything else?

"Come to think of it that might be nice. And some ice for the bucket please."

"On the way, I'll attend to that personally. "

I was irked. "David, I can't believe what you did that just now?"

"Did what, Olivia!??"

"David, this isn't a hotel! This is Gwen's house and you just asked her to bring you some of Gwen's champagne! I mean it's not like you're going to get a bill or tip anybody for it! Why didn't you just order caviar while you're at it!" I was laughing and disbelief as I said it.

"I screwed up, majorly, didn't I."

"Sure did, cowboy, but everybody falls off the bull right out of the chute sometimes. But I love you because you're human and I'm a forgiving kind of cowgirl," I told him as I started removing the studs from his shirt.

I pushed him onto the bed and crawled over on top of him and kissed him. I rubbed my nose against his to let him know that he was not in the doghouse on our wedding night.

"I didn't mean to react like that. It just hit me funny (thank you, Tilly and Lilly in my tummy!). I'm sorry. Forgive me?"

"Yes, do you forgive me for being a clueless dope?"

"Always, you're my lovable dope and I have forever to work on your few flaws I've discovered."

"I knew I married you for lots of reasons and that's one I love. Tell me something good?"

"Wedding night is an action verb and I think there's too much conversation between two people quickly approaching nudity."

"In a minute sweetheart. Remember: the dope you married just ordered champagne and it's on its way up."

He made me giggle. I love it when he makes me giggle.

There was a small chime that sounded. David hopped up and grabbed a robe and opened one of the double doors for Elena, who came in with both the ice and the champagne, icing the bucket and putting the newly uncorked bottle in the silver bucket.

"Thank you, Elena, and we will be sure to replace this for Gwen when we next see her."

"No need, sir. Call if you want any hors d' oeuvres or munchies later, all right? We have bottled water and soft drinks, and of course, a full bar."

"Thank you, Elena. My husband and I are so impressed," I told her, looking into his eyes at the word 'husband.'

David shed the robe and brought the near-empty bottle of champagne into bed with us and handed it to me. I chugged some and handed it back to him so he could kill it. We were getting a little tipsy. I was completely relaxed and surprised I had any energy left at all. I had all the energy that mattered for my David on our wedding night.

About 5:45am, I was startled and jolted straight up in bed and made some kind of a noise that awoke David. He threw his arms around me immediately, "What is it, what is Olivia!?"

In an instant I knew and clunked my head against his shoulder.

"The 6th-sense mommy thing, David. Something in me sensed that Tyler wasn't here and it freaked me out. I'm so sorry, honey," and I clunked my head down onto his shoulder, momentarily.

I plopped back down onto my pillow and stretched out my arms and put one arm underneath him. What was I going to do when I had three little ones all begging for a spot in our bed? Thank God for my blessings is what I decided.

"I don't know what kind of mattress this is David, but I never want to get out of this bed."

"I never want to get out of this bed as long as the woman next to me is in it. I'm David Callan, and you're?"

"Married. Very, very married and have two belly bombs—Jose and Hose B. that are dropping in August. My name is Olivia Callan."

"We probably shouldn't be doing this, Mrs. Callan."

"Oh, but we should Mr. Callan, because I have it on good authority, a Catholic priest's, that I'm married to you."

"Oh yeah, since when?"

"Formally and legally, since December 12th."

"And informally?"

"Since the 1st of forever."

"Hmm, well whaddya know."

"Come closer, a lot closer, cowboy. I'll show you everything I know, if you can handle it."

David and I thought we had quite the shower suite but the grandmaster in this mansion had the equivalent of a full spa that included a professional beauty salon chair and hair dryer.

David and I took every advantage of the amenities, got on some pajamas and a couple of clean robes. We opened the double doors and ventured down the mahogany staircase, just exploring. We saw double doors that might be the formal dining room and walked in.

It was a baseball museum. Everybody who was anybody from the last 20 or 30 years, players, coaches, announcers-had signed or given Gwen's dad something and everything was displayed. Signed pictures and baseballs, signed bats, and a jillion different framed pictures of Gwen's dad next to players, some now in the baseball Hall of Fame. Among the photos were shots of Gwen as a young girl, standing next to her father. She was very pretty albeit with an air of prim 'n proper seeping from the pose.

A Surprise Guest

After we got our eye-full, we snuck out just as we had snuck in. David spotted a corridor with lots of windows and bright light coming in and had a hunch. We followed the hunch and went down the corridor and, sure enough, it led to the gardens with a gazebo and the very last room which was the garden view dining room. David and I walked in and sat at one end of the massive the table that six place on each side, one at the head and foot for a total of 14.

I don't know how Elena knew we were there but she entered within ten seconds of us sitting down.

"Good morning, Mr. and Mrs. Callan. We print out menus from the foods we have in the house week to week. Here's the breakfast menu for this week and you're welcome to order anything you wish from it, in any quantity. May I start you with coffee or tea? Perhaps a mimosa or just champagne?"

David said yes to the coffee and I asked for water and a grapefruit juice.

"I'll be right back with that."

"I don't know how Gwen does it, David. I'd be lonely as hell in a place this big. Can you imagine being a little kid at the wrong end of a table that seats fourteen with only her mom and dad in there??"

"Maybe it's the memories that keep her here, Olivia. But it would feel like living in a warehouse to me."

I no sooner finished the sentence than the doors swung with some oomph and in walked Gwen in one of the house robes. Trailing behind her, holding her hand, was Sandy Tuttle. He was in a robe.

At noticing us, Gwen sucked wind and blushed the color of a radish. She immediately turned to Sandy and said, "The jigs up, Sandy. I guess we got caught!"

My sweet David effected the most innocent look I had ever seen on his face and said, "Caught? Of course. You were caught without a ride home, Gwen. We took your

car. I know Sandy to be a nice guy and he gave you a
ride and in exchange you gave him one of the bedrooms
because he had been drinking."

"You *are* a <u>smooth </u>one, David Callan."

"I have to be because that man with you pays me
huge money to say the right thing at the right time,
Gwen," and everybody laughed.

"I'm a business woman, David. Here's the non-
bullshit version: Sandy is a hell of a good dancer and I
love to dance. He *did* offer me a ride and I *did* offer him a
bed and it was MY bed. So build a bridge and get over it!"

David and I laughed but even Sandy was taken by
surprise when Gwen planted a big wet one on his mouth
in front of us.

"May we join you honeymooners for breakfast?"

"Only if our family can move-in, Gwen," David teased.

"Gwen," I implored, "In YOUR house? You're asking
me permission to have breakfast in the dining room of
your own house?" Everyone found that funny also.

David looked at him, "Sandy, that's Olivia's way of
inviting you to sit your ass down."

After Gwen and Sandy got settled in their chairs next
to each other and across from us, Gwen said, "I'm telling
you. That was probably the most romantic wedding in
the most romantic setting I have ever experienced. The
Christmas decor, the holiday mood, and love saturating
the air?"

David and I looked at each other as lovingly as ever.
"It was pretty special all right."

Sandy laughed, "I think it's the only wedding I've
attended with the bride carrying twins that the groom
knew nothing about!" Smiles and giggles went up and I
was shaking my head.

Gwen, again. "David, under the penalty of suffering
the fires of hell, did you tell Sandy that there was
mistletoe out in the garage?"

"Nope. He's the big boss where I work and I don't tell
him anything, I ask. He found it on his own. Olivia

suggested it, actually along with the mistletoe in the laundry room for adventurous secret smoochers."

Elena returned with the beverages and took our breakfast orders. Yogurt and bran for me, pancakes and bacon for David, cold cereal, toasted bagels and fruit for Sandy and Gwen.

I found David's foot and slipped out of my sandal to apply some pressure to his foot as I said, "Gwen you have done so much for us in the relatively short time we've known you that we'd like to do something nice in return."

"Olivia, I may not like where this is going," and she cocked her head and smiled, "...because you two are the king and queen of surprises!"

"Gwen you will love where this is going-more like where *you* are going. We are going to haul your butt out of that jewelry store and take you to our Abiquiu, New Mexico, ranch where you and a plus-one will be our guest. We're going to teach you how to ride a horse, how to stand in a stream and catch a trout and then cook it on a stick over an open fire, and how to relax under the stars after eating the best barbecued steak 'n beans you've ever had in your life."

From the look on her face, it didn't seem to register with Gwen for a long moment.

" I'm floored... I mean it sounds wonderful, like one of those 'dude ranch' experiential vacations. I've never even considered anything like that!"

"Neither has David. So you will be losing your greenhorn status with somebody very near and dear to both of us!" and I patted David on the knee. I felt David's foot rubbing the top of mind in complete acceptance of the notion.

"You'll be at our Macias family ranch but you can count on Daddy to take you on a horseback or helicopter tour of the big ranch."

I had her, was on a roll and feeling a little devilish so I stared right at Sandy and continued, "and Gwen, as far as the plus-one? It would probably be best if you brought someone along so the two of you could earn your spurs together!"

Whatever happened between them must have been awfully good because Gwen looked right at Sandy and said, "Will you go play cowboy with me?"

In the spirit of the moment, Sandy said, "As long as I don't get the business end of a branding iron put to my butt, yes. It sounds amazing."

"You probably won't get that, Sandy, but I can't wait until you get to savor bull's balls for the first time!"

I spit my orange juice, "DA-VID!"

"You fed them to me! You're not going to feed them to HIM?"

Sandy was mortified. Gwen's jaw dropped. "You ate bull's balls, David?"

"Not knowingly. The Macias Gang snuck them in on me in the form of stew when I was ravenous."

Gwen considered that for a long moment and looked at me. "Olivia?? Is that how you got him so fertile?" and Sandy spit his mouthful of coffee back in the cup. We were splitting our sides laughing.

We all quieted down basking in the glow of a good time.

Gwen smiled then leaned over and kissed Sandy on the cheek. She reminded me we had another night in the house, insisting we use it, and we thanked her profusely. I told her we needed to run one little errand with the car if that was all right and she said she didn't have a problem with that. I could arrange it with Elena.

We were going to the liquor store and buying champagne to replace what we drank. Too, I had never been without Tyler for 24 hours so I wanted to stop by the house and hold him.

It was David who approached the topic of loneliness in such a big house.

"Gwen how do you just knock around in this giant place by yourself?"

"David, I don't know what I would do if I sold it, wouldn't know where to go. People think I stay for the nostalgia and family thing but before all this quick wealth happened, I was much happier in a cozier home. It's like living in a gaudy furnishings warehouse or museum. It weirds me out but I'm so tired from work I just come here and fall into bed. My dad actually set up a trust fund to keep the staff. So the gardens are attended and the house is kept in good repair, and there is housekeeping and food service help at all times... It's like a luxury resort hotel for one. How fun is that...." She continued.

"I'm going to tell you something. I don't invite people here or host any galas, fundraisers or benefits of any kind. I keep to myself. I invited you because you're so special to me. Both of you. I hope you'll come over for dinner now and again or just come over and hang out because that just doesn't happen here or in my life. This feels good and I want more."

Again, out came my funny boy, David. "Olivia's parents taught me how to play hearts and took all my money. We could teach you how to play and maybe take this place off of your hands to settle your losses."

Sandy said, "You're a bastard, David, and I've never seen that greedy, conniving side of you." We all cracked up.

"I need all of you to remember that I'm going to be kind of moody and bitchy as I swell to the size of a Thanksgiving parade balloon with little Lucy and little Ricky inside of me, growing by the hour."

"Do you know the gender of the babies yet, Olivia?" Sandy asked.

"When I have my next sonogram, we will confirm it. But I know it's a boy and a girl. Just know. I said we because I want David there. We're not going to have any big reveal party about that. We'll just let our friends know and, as you saw at the wedding, we have a small circle. Word will spread like wildfire at the hospital but I expect that."

"Well one of your guests from the station, namely Stephanie, isn't known for keeping things on the down low, is she David."

"Wowie, you can say that again and when I tell her about you and Gwen, tomorrow, Sandy?? It's news and that's what I do, right?"

Sandy paled, turned red, and nearly choked, covering his mouth with the fine linen napkin. "Now, you <u>are</u> a rotten bastard and I may kill you, rope you and drag you at the ranch until the meat's knocked your bones."

"Hey wait a minute," I objected, "You're going to make me a widow with 3 children?? To try that, buster, and before you leave the ranch my daddy will make you a steer instead of a bull and you might be the star attraction in the next pot of stew!" Either that or you will get a red-hot branding iron on each cheek. We were gasping for air and tearing up from the laughter.

It quieted and Gwen looked kind of pensive. She studied each of the three of us carefully. "There hasn't been joviality or laughter in this house in decades and I'm loving it. When I ask you back, no is not an option. In fact, it's an open invitation. When you show up unannounced, the door will never be locked. I love you guys."

We had a terrific breakfast and Gwen and Sandy, after kisses all around, went their way.

David walked over to me and knelt down and lifted up my shirt and kissed my belly. I heard him whisper, "Time to check on your big brother and grandparents."

He kissed my tummy again.

Olivia's Catered Dinner

David took my hand and we intertwined fingers as we walked down the hall, taking in the beauty of the gardens and the rainbows from all the sprinklers in a misting spray over the flower beds and grassy areas.

The suite's doors were wide open. We could tell either Elena or a housekeeper had been in and cleared glasses and the empty champagne bottle. Two clean stems were next to the silver champagne bucket that was freshly replenished with ice and the unopened bottle continued to chill. I guessed it was Elena who had opened the sheers and drapes on all the windows admitting sunshine that may have been blinding but for the reflective tint on the window, tint that was as much for security as it was for subduing the rays.

We got out of our robes. David thought we would take a shower but we didn't quite make it. The bed was too inviting and so was my husband. I invited myself to have him as an after-breakfast newlywed bride's indulgence. My trick. His treat. And mine. And it wasn't even Halloween.

I snuck up behind him and put my arms around his waist, slipped my palms past the elastic waistband of his pajama pants and kept going down, finding him, and running my hands over and around him. He looked up at the ceiling and sighed with a guttural moan.

David put his hands gently around my wrists and turned, putting me in a twist much like a dance move where I was facing him, still holding me. David scooped me up in his arms. Our lips found each other's. He shuffled me over to the bed and dipped down so my outstretched hand could yank the bedclothing down to expose the coolness of fine linen sheets that would greet my back upon my landing.

He stepped out of his pajamas. I lifted my arms so he could take off my top. paying attention to my 'girls' with his kisses, mouth, and tongue. David could tell I was a steam engine ready to be engaged, my desire, eating me alive. He was ready, big, full, and I guided him into me, immediately and easily.

David was rocking with me gently. As always, was tender and affectionate, with heightened awareness to everything that would bring me pleasure at an accelerated rate. My body responded to him as if he had a set of master keys opening every nerve and pore. We timed it perfectly, waves of shivering and convulsive reactions coming from all of my triggers being pulled.

We lay quietly in the bright morning light. He was playing with my hair, lifting tufts, running his fingers through them and then letting them fall only to lift another tuft and do the same.

"I need to call Mom and make sure things are okay with Tyler and them."

"Here you go, honey," and David handed me my phone.

"Hey Mama, good morning! I'm going to put you on speaker."

"Good morning, and good morning, David, I know you are right there!" and I could have sworn Mom's was a naughty chuckle.

"How ARE you, my son?

"Ofelia, I'm crazy in love with your daughter still, and the four of us got a good night's sleep. Can you believe we have two more grandchildren on the way for you!"

"David, she didn't really have to tell me because a mother knows these things. She had the glow of a pregnant woman which made her extra beautiful in her wedding dress. I'm telling you, in my heart and in my soul, I knew maybe before she did, which only made me more glad and thankful to God."

"Mom we're going to swing by the house, later. I just wanted to check in and make sure everything is okay! I do <u>not</u> want you cleaning up that place!'

"There's nothing to clean! It's spotless. All your
friends started picking up the place before they left.
Sweeping. Mopping. Dishes. Everything."

"No way!'

"Yes, way! The party wound down and everybody just
started picking up, so I started wrapping all the uneaten
food and giving it to your friends to take home. So, we're
good."

"Mama, I'm sorry you went to all that trouble, had to
do all that."

"I didn't have to, I wanted to. Your friends are very
nice and were very loving and kind to your dad and me."

"Is he there?"

"Your dad is on the patio enjoying the morning with
his grandson. Tyler really seems to be getting to know
him because I see your dad making him smile and hear
them constantly making happy noises and giggling."

"Doesn't surprise me at all, Ofelia," David replied.

"I can't thank you enough, Mama, and I want to tell
you how beautiful you looked last night but the pictures
are going to show that!"

"Oh no, mija, there was only one beauty in the room
and it was you. You made a beautiful bride and
everybody in the room took deep breaths of wonder at
your beauty. If you don't believe me, you can look at the
pictures!"

"I'm going to ask Gwen if we can invite you to her
house for dinner and there's a 100 percent chance she'll
say yes! I wanna make a southwestern style dinner to
thank Gwen and open our wedding presents over here. I
don't think she'll have a problem with it. Does that
sound good to you? You won't have to do a thing because
I want to cook. I feel like it!"

"It sounds wonderful honey."

"Okay I'll get back to you Mama."

"Love you, Mom," David said.

"That's beautiful music to my ears, David. Thank
you."

I called Gwen.

"Well if it isn't Mrs. Callan! Good morning!"

"I just want to tell you how amazing your house is. In fact, we would like to invite you over for dinner tonight!"

Gwen laughed and said, "Well that's a first."

"I would love to cook for you in your kitchen and invite you and your new love thing, and my parents over. I thought we could bring the wedding gifts from the house and open them. May I invite Elena and her husband?"

"Sure! They'd be thrilled!"

"Sounds like plan and a party to me! Let's do it! We are in the house if you want to meet in the garden dining room. I think the idea is sparkling!"

"Hold on a sec, David wants to say hello."

"Gwen, I never got a chance to say thank you because I know you had a hand in all the goings-on that I didn't know anything about. You worked your butt off and our wedding was flawless because of it. And then, the gift of your home? There just aren't words, Gwen."

"I didn't do it alone, had some willing accomplices. Didn't Olivia tell you; she is my new is my BFF!"

"Well at least she's consistent...being an excellent people picker. I mean, look at the guy she married!"

"Ev-ry-one was looking at him last night; he was one handsome dog! Anyhow, I just told Olivia we are in the house. We'll see you in the dining room in a few minutes, okay?"

"Nice! See you in a few."

"I don't need to talk to Olivia again. Just come on down when you're ready."

"Okay Gwen, thanks."

While we were getting dressed, I had to tell him. "Honey, your reaction was epic when you realized we were going to have twins!"

"Speaking of, have you seen my t-shirt? I want to wear it to breakfast!" "Good call, I'll wear mine, too!"

"Epic? My wedding night and I'm having babies, too!?? I went berserk, baby, running around like an idiot with our friends all shooting video of it. Then I'm crying face down in the grass? You got to save that video so that in 30 years you can have me put into the looney bin and be done with me."

"We will be my mom and dad's age in 30 years. You think I will be done with you? You should have seen my dad kiss my mom while I was getting dressed. He told her our wedding reminded him of when they were kids. It was so tender that my tears threatened to ruin my makeup. He thanked her for our life and for the gift I was to them both. David if we can love each other half that much at their age? Then, my *God*, we've been blessed."

"I agree Olivia. I wish I could have seen that moment."

He had his sexy little grin face on, "At the rate we're going, I also see us in 30 years as being dirt poor because we have 14 children and 40 grandchildren."

I smacked him on the tee-shirt's word 'Twins. I smiled, running my fingers over his cheek bones.

"Is that so bad, David? All we would need is a bigger pot and more beans, honey. They would all be good and loving people because they came from us."

"It's like you are my conscience Olivia, always making sense of things with your perspective on life. I actually visualized a huge bean pot and us making sure everybody had a full bowl before you and I shared what little was left, honey. That perspective? It makes me a better person. You make me better in ways you don't even know."

I went nose to nose with my husband and whispered, "Have you ever considered that you have all the right ingredients inside of you and I am just a catalyst? Huh?"

"No," and he burst out laughing, "I hadn't considered that. I felt an incredibly strong attraction to you the first time you and I were alone in that hospital room. I can't explain it."

"Then don't. It's not broken, cowboy." I spotted him grinning and I said, "What!"

"Okay QUICK! We have a boy and a girl-name them!!

"Cami and Carlos"

"Two boys!"

"James and Kyle."

"Two girls!"

"Renee and Amelia. How did I do?"

We left the suite hand in hand and started down the staircase toward the dining room.

"Judging on my gut reactions, Olivia, you got huge points on Amelia and Renee. Cami, which I assume is Camille, I love. Boys names? Carlos made me think of Carlos Santana who I like but I don't know that I'd want a son whose name makes me think of somebody else. I love Kyle and I love James *big* time. Can you guess why?"

"Gospel?"

"Not primarily although it could be subconscious."

I thought and thought. "I'm drawing a blank, David."

"Your dad, Roberto *Santiago*!"

"Aww, Da-vid! See how you are? How did you *know* his middle name?? Have I ever even told you...or said it to you?"

We turned the corner and walk down the beautifully sunlit corridor with all the windows facing the gardens, windows catching some overspray from the wind hitting the sprinklers' output.

"If you have or did, I don't remember but I actually looked him up on the internet. I found out he was in the Hall of Fame Cowboys Association and Museum. They listed his full name."

David got serious to the point of somber, "When I was looking for you, Olivia. It was an awful time... But that was then, huh? Look at us now," and he had pulled himself right back out of the dark cloud.

"Okay. Mommy says James is absolutely a must if we have a boy and what do you think about Jamie if it's a girl?"

"Love it!"

"We've got a bunch of names down. Now, we only need middle names and I'll leave that up to you because there's too many for me to even consider," and he laughed.

We came around the open doorway of the garden dining room and spotted Gwen.

"Hey good morning, newlyweds. How are you?"

"We're fine and just named our future children as we walked downstairs."

Gwen applauded, "Marvelous! Are you going to give it up, share?"

"Let's wait for the ultrasound!"

"Gwen, I kinda sprung it on you. Look me in the eye and tell me if you're not cool with the dinner idea; it's okay for you to tell us no. I just thought you might like a home cooked meal in your own house, not one prepared by staff."

"I just committed to more gaiety and people in this luxurious prison, Olivia, don't be silly! This is a swimmingly good start. Tell you what: after breakfast, let's go in and you can scope out the kitchen and everything in it to see if there's anything you need, like utensils or pots or pans or anything. I'm ashamed to say it, but I can't tell you where the spice rack...spice cabinet...See? I'm a mess. I don't know my ass from my elbow about my own kitchen!"

"Understandable, you only collapse here to return to work and collapse here again. That's old news, Gwen! We're reinventing you! The kitchen looky-loo would be great. I'm assuming you like Mexican food?"

"I consider a margarita Mexican food and anything that follows afterward is fine! I do like it."

"My proposed menu is New Mexico-style beef enchiladas, cheese enchiladas and a taco bar, with New Mexico style salsa and made with homemade blue corn tortillas which you may not have ever even eaten."

"Blue? I haven't heard of them, Olivia."

"They're a staple and tradition in New Mexico and hard to find elsewhere. Mom brought 25-lbs of blue corn flour in her luggage. David and I are set for a while. If you feel like putting on an apron, tonight, I'll teach you how to make blue corn tortillas and everything else!"

"I would love that!"

"Super. We're going to hit the Mexican market later and swing by the house to take Mom and Tyler with us. We miss our little boy!"

"Everybody adores him! If your two babies are half as cute as he is, you all are going to make a magazine cover for some perfect family publication."

We ordered and got breakfast. Gwen called for the car to be brought up out front.

"If you're wondering, Sandy stayed last night but was out of here pre-dawn to get home and pickup his golf clubs. He had a tee time at one of the Scottsdale resorts with a client. I'll text him about dinner."

"Super! We're gonna get going, Gwen," and I moved around the table to kiss her. David gave her a wave, "This is an incredible experience for us, Gwen. Thank you!"

"It won't be your last. In fact, why rule out slumber parties! I have an incredible home theater. We could do midnight movies."

"Olivia? I think you're turning Gwen into a party girl," and I snickered. "You're her friend. Tell her to get on the pill," and he patted my stomach. We laughed. Gwen gave David the finger, and then burst into laughter.

As we headed toward the driveway, I asked David, "Honey? Remind me to pick up a fiesta-styled cloth apron for Gwen. I bet there's nothing but institutional white stuff in there. I'll get one for Mom and me, too."

"I don't get one?"

"You got $12.99, cowboy? You can have one," and I kissed him as he opened the limo door for me before the driver could get to it.

"Do you mind if we have a little heart-to-heart on the way, David?"

"No, what's on your mind?"

"Justa sec," and I told the driver, "Please drive around about ten minutes before taking us to the condo. That okay?"

"I was told to drive you to Alaska and back if you asked," and he laughed, "Sure, I'll give you a little time."

"David, we have a full and wonderful life and a love like nobody knows. I worked hard studying nursing and I feel guilty. I have all that ability and all that knowledge and I'm not helping anyone with it, not a soul."

"Olivia if that's troubling you, look at me and say 'David, I'm going back to work. And then I kiss you and say oh, wow, cool! And I also say I'll support you 100% every way I can."

"Really? Honest-to-God?"

"I'm not intentionally keeping you pregnant forever, Olivia," which hit my funny bone, "although it might seem like it. Truth: we haven't been married long enough for me to lie to you and I don't think we'll ever be married so long that I feel the want or need to lie. If you want to work, call the hospital right now and tell them when you want to start! And I mean it.

It was like mental fireworks going off in my mind, a huge celebration.

"Oh David, David, David. I love you so much!"

He pretended to be serious, putting his hand on my lower tummy. "You only have two boobies and can't nurse forever. We have a growing number of mouths to feed! Remember that huge bean pot discussion we had?"

I couldn't help to just grin and stare at him.

"You were recognized for excellence before you even graduated, honey. You answered a calling. Because we have had a little pause doesn't mean it's a stop sign in your life. We are green lights and I mean green lights all the way!"

I couldn't help kissing him all over making little squealy girl noises like I do when I'm ultra-happy.

"What about you, David?"

"I want to go back to work and assumed you'd support that. Do you, will you?"

"Of course."

"I just feel a little bit weird that in a 24-hour business I can't adjust my schedule to help you and our kids as far as logistics of pick up and drop off and making lunches and all that good parenting stuff you're going to teach me. In radio, morning drive is where the audience is and that's where the big bucks are for the on-air people."

"I don't think you're going to take much teaching because I think you have it in you, innately. And if you work so hard you're never home? I'll tune in so the children will know what Absent-Daddy's voice sounds like."

"Oh no you don't. No pool boy or delivery guys for you! You won't want or need them cuz I'm gonna keep you busy and exhausted," and he laughed, contagiously, drawing my own laugh out, easily. "By the way, Olivia, good eye at the wedding party, spotting Gwen and Sandy!"

"Yeah, who'd have guessed!"

"Not me that's for sure," he said.

"Think about it though, David. He's very successful, well-to-do, loves life, plays golf and socializes a lot. I'm sure he would enjoy having an attractive and sharp woman on his arm often, or at least, every now and again!"

"I agree. That hookup could be amazing, IS amazing."

"I almost lost my shit when she asked him to play cowboy with her!"

I doubled over laughing holding my stomach, "Oh my God, way too funny. I think they may have still been a little drunk. Those may have been Bloody Marys and Screwdrivers at breakfast!"

"Olivia...imagine him chasing her around the bedroom wearing a straw cowboy hat and a pair of boxers yelling, 'Yee haw.'"

"Oh my God, you had to go there."

"Tell you what, when we go to the liquor store, why don't you tell me the name brands of some traditional beers popular in New Mexico and we'll have them on ice at dinner."

"It's easier than that. The Mexican market sells 'em all. They even sell my favorite tequila you can't find anywhere else but in Mexico."

"You have a favorite tequila?"

I grinned, coyly, "You *do* have a lot to learn, cowboy."

"Okay...driver. Yes, driver. I almost said, 'Home, James.'"

He looked at me in the mirror. "Would have worked. That's my name."

Ten minutes later we were at the gate and Mom buzzed us in.

She met me at the door with Ty and he immediately squealed and smiled, reaching for me. I kissed his cheeks, "Hey, hombre! Mommy missed you!! Have you been a good boy for *Abuela*? Yes, yes, I bet you have. LOOKIE! It's DADDY!!" and David took him and kissed his forehead.

"Hey, Slugger! Did you miss Daddy, too? NO?? Well, no beers for you tonight!"

David smooched Mama and walked to the kitchen island.

"Hey, Dad, we're back."

"Your dad is lying down for a little bit."

"Oh, okay. Sorry about the noise. We missed our little man."

"He's been good, not a problem at all," Ofelia said, "just like when Olivia was his age," and she smiled warmly at me.

Graciously, but kidding, Olivia said, "Of course I was perfect, David."

"Mom, can you pull out some meat for the enchiladas and tacos tonight?"

She gave David a wary look, and me a pleading expression.

"You know what I want to use, Olivia. I'll pull out something else for David."

I knew what she meant and spoke up, "Let's get this settled."

Ooh, this was my David's 'Big Boy' voice.

"I like balls," and mom and I lost it. So did David.

"That should have come out differently, but you know what I mean," oh, was he making it worse, "I'm fine with eating prepared bull's balls. I'm not fine if I've never had them before and I'm told I have a mouthful of them!" And now both mom and I were fighting for our breath.

Mama looked at David, innocently, "You've eaten _unprepared_ balls, David?"

Destroyed by laughter were we. Once I could speak again, I said, "The upside, David?? Your payback is the look on Sandy's face. We'll tell Gwen in advance."

Mom faked a serious expression, shaking her finger at David. "Mister Sandy better not spit _my food_ back onto his plate at _my_ table!" Again, three adults were incapacitated by laughter. I pulled the "BBs" package from the freezer and set it out to thaw.

"I told Gwen I'd show her how to make the tortillas, Mama. We'll get there early to do that, and you and Daddy can see this crazy huge mansion she lives in all by herself! And she hates it! She's lonely in there!"

"I would like that. I've only seen pictures of mansions."

"Mom," David said, "it's beautiful beyond belief. The way Olivia and Gwen are getting along, it will not be the last time you are welcomed there, either. I swear."

"Then let's get busy, Olivia. Pen. Paper. Ingredients list so we know what to get at the store," and I snapped to it and complied. David put Ty into his highchair and gave him the choice of a baby biscuit or a rubber nipple.

Tyler went for the nipple. David tried to mutter it under his breath, but I heard him.

"Atta boy. Just like your old man."

"What was that, David?"

"Just Tyler and me checking out how good lookin' his mama is, Olivia," and he winked. "I think your son's gonna be a boob man, Olivia. At least, that what he just told me."

"BACK TO WORK, CABALLEROS! ANDELÉ! THESE CATTLE ARE YOUR PAYCHECK!"

Daddy's booming work voice scared the shit out of all of us and he was laughing because he got us good. His voice had picked up the reverb of the hallway.

"Your laughing could wake up the dead! Look!"

We all looked at him as he pointed.

"Look! The bottom of the Christmas tree! There's hardly anything there. Ofelia. We need to fix that!"

"We will too, Dad," David offered weakly.

"All the stores are open way late, here, this time of year. It's not like home. We have plenty of time," Olivia said.

"Well, your mom and I already took care of you and David. But I think Santa Claus might need some help with Tyler, right Tyler?"
He had been staring at Bob, intently. Our son was nuts about his granddad

"C'mere, cowboy! Your *abuelo*, your grandfather, needs a hug," and as soon as Bob extended his arms, out came Tyler's arms with a smile and a squeal. Bob noticed that we all noticed.

"He's just kissing the foreman's butt for a good job on the ranch, you all. Happens all the time," Bob said with a smug look.

David went there, "Your cowboys holding their arms out to hug you, Bob?"

"Da--vid!!"

"Only the lonely ones, David," and Dad winked at David. I couldn't help giggling because David just learned my dad had a little smart-ass in him, too.

"Oh. Speaking of packages, I have an overnight package coming in from the ranch. Important. It's in a poster tube thing, okay?"

"They're good about getting things to us here, Daddy. It won't be a problem."

David snickered, "I have to warn you, Olivia and the delivery guy..."

"Don't _even_, Mr. Husband!" and I gave him the finger. Oops. Right in front of my parents.

Mom's eyes bulged and Dad shook his head, "That's my cowgirl. She's been doing that since she was about twelve, David, and I'm sure you're used to it by now."

"I think that's the first time I've ever seen her do that!"

Bob continued, "I guess I'm okay with it.... She had to be tough with a bunch of cowboys constantly showering her with attention that she didn't always want or welcome. I let it pass...well, except the time she gave the priest the finger in church for bringing up unmarried girls getting pregnant."

Now my eyes were as big as saucers. Mom put her hand over her mouth, then crossed herself. Dad laughed his butt off.

"Balls. I'm feeding you BALLS for supper tonight, David Callan. But if I was you, I'd check my bowl verrrrry carefully. There may be an added surprise."

"Not nice and not fair, Mrs. Callan. On behalf of my three children and I, we object to spousal torment via food."

"Three children? I'm carrying two you don't have access to and one who's car seat is in the SUV that I drive. But complaint acknowledged. Tell me something good!"

"You're the most beautiful woman I ever fell in love with and made babies with and married, Olivia."

"And?"

"And if you come kiss me right now? I'll make you a believer."

Olivia appealed to her parents, "See? See how he could always do that to me?"

I went around the island to him and put my arms around his neck.

"Proof's in the puddin', Cowboy," and he almost made my parents blush and yell 'Get a room.'

Ofelia broke it up, "Enough, you two! We gotta ingredients list to do…. Olivia, blue corn tortillas we'll make there, cheese enchiladas, beef enchiladas, and a taco bar?"

"Yes, Mama, and I'm going to do some chili verde salsa with cilantro and tomatillos. David, while I'm thinking about it, do you mind getting the wedding gifts and loading them into the SUV."

"I'm on it, baby."

"Your chili is better than mine, *mija*. I love it! Are we doing dessert?"

"I don't think so, Mama. Probably just drinks. Oh, and we're gonna pick up five festive aprons: for David, Sandy, Gwen, you and me."

"Done. On the list."

"Mom, add a bottle of *Viuda de Romero*. They have the reposado and I want to pour David and them some shots," and my mom knew I had an agenda and snickered, shaking her head.

Our loaded-down caravan passed through the subdivision's gate and then got buzzed through Gwen's gate. We drove around to the side entrance near the garden dining room and saw the door that led directly into the kitchen. Elena awaited us and I introduced her to everyone. We got all of the groceries in and at Elena's excellent suggestion, put the wedding gifts in the dining room.

"Tomás, my husband, cooks for Ms. McArdle. He's been preparing your food and will help any way we can today and tonight. Just tell us what to do!"

Tomás waved a hand from the other side of the kitchen where he had been apparently putting some things on the worktables.

"I heard you were making tortillas, enchiladas, and tacos, so I thought I'd get a head start on getting your utensils and stuff out in advance. Let me help you with those groceries."

"Thank you, Tomás. Elena? Would you call Ms. McArdle and let her know we're here, please?"

"Right away, Mrs. Callan."

"Elena?"

"Yes, ma'am?"

"I've heard you call Ms. McArdle 'Gwen.' Please, and I mean *please* call me Olivia! I love the sound of my married name, but I'm a country girl from a cattle ranch, not used to all of this. I'm Olivia. Okay?"

She blushed and said, "Okay. Thank you... Olivia."

"See? Was that hard?"

"No ma'am... uh...Olivia. OLIVIA," and we all laughed as everyone was bustling.

"Okay," my mom, barked. "I am the kitchen boss, my daughter's the chef! Let's get this going and we'll have a great time, tonight."

"Oh, and Elena?"

"Yes."

"You and Tomás are getting a paid night off, tonight, if and only if you accept my invitation to party with us. If you don't like tequila, you will after tonight," and I couldn't stifle my giggle. "I cleared it with the lady of the house, and I insist."

"That's very kind," and she looked to Tomás. He grinned and put one thumb up.

"Sounds great, Olivia."

"Yes, I'm looking forward to your authentic recipes," Tomás said.

"David, since Tomás is now also getting initiated into the Callan family crazies tonight, would you throw him that apron we intended for Sandy?" David tossed it to him as he got out of his chef's white apron and donned the new one.

"Since you're not working, I expect you to be in casual, comfy party clothes at dinner, too, Chef Boyardee!"

Tomás laughed and said, "You got it, Chef."

"I think Tyler's ready for some sleep, honey," and when I looked over, he was out cold on my dad's shoulder.

"Uh-oh. Where to put him down's the thing…"

"I made room for the playpen in the SUV. I'm on it, honey!" and David trotted out and swiftly returned.

I let out a cowgirl hoot, "Yeow! Team Callan! I shoulda married that guy. WAIT! I did!"

David set it up in the dining room just clear of the kitchen's door and came back.

I approached him, "Kiss, please!" and he accommodated.

"You're the bestest hubby!"

"I'm a rookie but I'm trying, cowgirl."

"You don't have to try all that hard. I'm in love with you!"

I kissed him back.

We no sooner got underway than Gwen came bombing into the room and we all cheered.

Gotcha, Sandy

"Ladies and gentlemen, our principal Chef Trainee for the Evening," David announced, "Gwen from the McArdle Bed 'n Breakfast of Scottsdale!" and he ceremoniously slipped the neck loop of the brightly patterned apron over Gwen's head with a smooch.

"Oh crap, I gotta get outta these shoes. Lemme run to my room."

As soon as she left, I looked to Elena. "Elena, you refer to Gwen as being in her, quote, living quarters. That grandmaster suite's amazing. So, what are her 'living quarters' as you call them?"

"It's a full-sized apartment within the house, Olivia. This place is almost 7,300 square feet and gives her the creeps because of its very size. Echoes. Shadows. So she's got, I guess, around a thousand square-foot apartment that's beautiful, inside. Two bedrooms, 1-1/2 baths."

"I think I'd do the same, Elena."

"THERE!," Gwen said, announcing her reentry. "Tennis shoes. Mucho better!"

"Okay, Mama, put her to work."

With the festive aprons, it looked like we were prepping for Cinco de Mayo.

Tomás noticed Mom unwrapping the meat and strolled over. "BBs?" Tomás inquired.

Mom froze and looked over at me. I bailed her out.

"Tomás, it's 'Butchers' Best' from my parents' ranch!"

"Looks like bull's balls to me," and the Coke David was drinking came right out through his nose and the laughter started him choking.

"Rocky Mountain Oysters," Tomás said.

"Tomás? Tonight, they're 'BBs' because we're going to pull a fast one on Sandy who, by the way, is David's BIG boss at work, okay? So, hush-hush about the bull's balls until we prank Sandy."

Tomás shook his head, "You guys are just plain mean and I love this. Shall I whip-up a white sauce?"

Everyone lost it.

I responded by pointing at Tomás. "Tomás? You were nice and polite, before. NOW? I like the hell out of you!"

A big laugh went up again and my mom used her butcher knife to tap a big pan like a bell being struck twice, "This is a working kitchen, people!"

Sandy strolled in from the dining room door about a half hour later. "This looks like a restaurant kitchen with all the hustle and bustle!"

"It is, boss," David said. "Ready for your assignment?"

"You bet, but keep it simple. My microwave oven and I have our differences."

"First, your uniform, Chef," and he caught the apron David removed from himself and threw his way to put on.

"This is as simple as your microwave, Sandy. Knife, cutting board, limes, bowl."

David retrieved the bag of limes from the refrigerator. "Just halve and make wedges. They're for tequila shooters, later."

"Got it."

"Music! I need music!" and it was my mom doing the demanding.

"My mom runs a foodservice operation and there's always music on for the staff, guys. Tomás? Elena? Is there a radio or anything in here?"David pointed to an obscure corner. He had spotted a small CD boombox on a chair. I strolled over and found a Spanish radio station playing campesino and Norte music.

Gwen was getting into the tortilla making with Mama, and everything else we asked her to tackle.

"You look like you're having fun over there, Gwen!"

"You guys should open a cooking school. We'll use this place and I'll be your first student," Gwen said, grinning.

A cheer went up. Everything was coming together much easier than I expected, because mom was overseeing the efforts as I instructed everyone on their next move.

I grabbed a metal spoon, tapped a pan twice, "Listen up, please. It's almost happy hour. Tomás, Elena, out! Get into your party clothes. How long will it take you to get home and get back.

Tomás spoke up, "We have clothes, here, Olivia. We're set!"

"Well get into 'em, we're not starting without you guys!"

Tomás saluted, "C'mon, Elena!" and she rushed over to Tomás and they scooted out a door I hadn't noticed before.

Gwen explained, "There's a little studio apartment I let them use; convenient and close to chill out, stay overnight, or get high or whatever. It doesn't get used so it's a fringe bennie for them."

"Jesus, Gwen, sign me up!"

"Too many stairs for a preggers girl carrying a double load, girlfriend.... Can I ask you guys a favor?"

"Gwen? In your own house. Cut it out! Name it and we'll claim it."

"I'm having a blast. I think there's no reason we can't turn up the music and eat and party in here! Less... well, less stuffy and formal, know what I mean?"

"Great call, Gwen! Why not!" I assured her, "plus, if my son... or HUSBAND..." and I looked over at David, "...spill or break anything, I won't freak out," and I laughed.

Gwen picked up the humor and served back an ace, "You're a house account at McArdle's, honey. I'd bill you!" and she threw her head back and laughed.

The enchilada pans finally went into the huge commercial oven, the taco bar items were in containers in the refrigerator, the blue corn taco shells came out of the frier perfectly and on a covered long baking pan.

Two people came in from where Tomás and Elena had exited.

David's jaw dropped. My own eyes nearly fell out of my head.

Elena's lips were electric-red gloss. She was in hip-hugger bell bottom jeans that were so low-cut, her belly button was showing with some extra skin below it. She sported a baby-blue satin form-fitting top, obviously braless with bullet-strength nipples pushing against the fabric. She had black flipflops on with baby blue leather straps. Sexy as hell.

Her ass was perfect. I hated her, hated her because my ass used to be that tight when I barrel-raced at the ranch in my younger years.

How the hell did her uniform just completely neutralize, camouflage...hide a body like that. It was probably the result of a strict regimen of biking or running, calisthenics, and weightlifting and yoga,

I wasn't concerned that David was taking it all in. He'd look and then drop it. I likened it to a Maserati going slowly by as he was walking down a sidewalk. He might look, even stare but for a second, and then it was history. It was the same for anything, whether it was cars, yachts or bombshells like Elena. She had the whole thing working overtime at once. Elena had the goods to model on a world-class level.

If jealousy could be in the air, David might have been worried about me.

Without his little cooking hat and apron, Tomás was a hella specimen of man-godliness, himself. Black, wavy-shiny hair, olive complexion, dark and inset eyes, heavy five o'clock shadow and a white cotton shirt, generously unbuttoned, revealing some chest hair and musculature. It was obvious he was in the gym 3-4 times a week. He, too, came from the land of perfect ass-dom. Oh, God, I hoped he wouldn't catch me looking, especially after a couple tequilas. 'No calories in an eye-feast, Olivia,' I told myself.

I greeted them, "There you are! Sidle up to the bar. You can help yourself or I'll assist!"

"Thank you, Olivia. It was nice of you to include us, and thank you, Gwen."

"Tomás, this is going to happen a lot more around here. David and Olivia are teaching me how to live again, reminding me what feeling good really feels like!"

"Cheers!" It came from Daddy, who downed a shot of tequila.

Gwen turned, "Sandy? You know how Olivia and David always say to each other, 'Tell me something good?'

"Yep. How could you not notice. They make the rest of us look like amateurs."

"Sandy? Tell me something good." It caught him off-guard.

"Uh...." and even through his burn-tan, you could tell he blushed, "Okay. I'm going to the BACON-A show in Vegas and would like you to go with me, Gwen."

"Bacon, what!?"

"It's Broadcast and Cable Operators National Association." The room went still and silent.

David chimed-in, "It's huge, Gwen. Our ownership group provides Sandy with 1st-Class air and a premium hotel set-up, because he's there making deals. Do it, Gwen. Go with him. You'll have an absolute blast."

"I'd love to, Sandy!"

Everybody cheered and hooted as Gwen moved up to him and he kissed her. I caught Tomás and Elena checking it out, looking ecstatic that Sandy and Gwen seemed to be a thing that was going to continue being a thing.

I produced some blue-corn chips and poured some of my special salsa verde from a full pitcher that had been chilling a while.

My mom bragged on me, "This salsa is my Olivia's creation! Everyone in Abiquiu begs her to make it."

I was ready for a mixed drink, and announced, "DRINKS! DRINKS TIME! EVERYONE! THE BAR IS OPEN! Tomás, get me a blender with some counter space, please? David, the limes and lime wedges please. I'm going to get some simple syrup going, here. Margaritas in 3 minutes, everyone."

We dedicated one of the stainless-steel tabletops to alcohol and snacks. The party was on.

David finished eating a chip, "Interesting name, Tomás... Don't tell me. Could be Italian but I don't think so. Not Greek, you don't look it to me. Spaniard, maybe?"

"Portuguese, born here, but my parents emigrated."

"I visited, once!" David said with a grin, dipping another chip.

"You're kidding! Nobody from the U.S. visits Portugal, of course I'm kidding about that."

"It was a self-discovery thing. I'm Catholic. Felt compelled to visit the shrine at Fatima."

"Yes, very holy and very beautiful. I'm from the wine country, Douro Valley, the Douro River area."

"Cheers! Here's to Portugal, Wine and the Virgin Mary, herself!"

Oh. My. God. I thought my mother would choke. Or have a stroke, or drop of a heart attack. She rolled her eyes, crossed herself, and rolled her eyes Heaven-ward again. I slammed a Viuda de Romero and ooh it burned so good!

Dinner was going incredibly well.

I stared as Sandy tilted his head to take his first bite of a completely overstuffed blue corn taco shell. Sandy had just begun to chew when, still staring at him, I mumbled, "Sad."

David was biting his lip so hard, he had to turn his head away so he wouldn't blow it until I nailed Sandy. From the way David's head was moving, I could tell he had already begun to laugh.

"Sad?" Sandy managed to say around a mouthful.

"I was just thinking, Sandy. Yesterday morning, this poor bull was thinking about which hot cow he was going to drill in the breeding barn...but just a few hours later, he got his _balls cut off_ and tonight? We're _eating_ his bull's balls in tacos_and enchiladas while he's one bleeding, hurting steer."

Sandy blanched, paused, then blew out his mouthful of taco so hard that everyone could hear the taco shell's shrapnel hitting our glasses.

We were nearly falling off our chairs laughing as he wiped his mouth and screamed, "You're kidding, RIGHT!??" which only made it funnier.

David caught enough breath to say, "Olivia's ranch is eco-friendly, boss. They use every part of the cow, and you didn't complain about eating them at the wedding party." Again, raucous laughter rocked the room. Sandy walked over to the sink and spread his arms putting his hands palms-down on the edge of a basin. I truly thought he might blow his groceries.

Gwen wanted fun and frivolity? She got it. I thought she probably wet her pants. She was trying to console Sandy while laughing at him, and how well do you think that went over?

Sandy recovered, and Gwen put her arms around him and said, "They got you, Sandy. It was just your turn in the barrel, honey. We all ate the bull's balls, tonight.... Sandy? Honey? Hold still! Is that a hair between your teeth? A cow-pubie??" and Gwen took off running as the rest of us watched Sandy just lose it. Gwen was bent over a side table with laugh-tears streaming.

There was more to come, unexpectedly, from Elena whose goddess-body had a little too much to drink, evidenced by an attempt to dip a chip into the salsa. The chip made it to her mouth. A good half-teaspoon of the chilly green salsa dripped off the chip and hit Elena's blouse right over her left nipple.

We dug into the world-class enchiladas. Tomás summed it up with, "Mother of God, my mouth's in Heaven." He paused and looked at Sandy, "So Sandy, I'm feeling a little, you know, manlier from the tacos. You?"

Our eyes locked and we burst out laughing so badly that I had to go take David's hand and walk him outside into the garden. Everyone was howling. Sandy was being a good sport and taking it all in stride.

We were only out there a minute or two before David turned and opened the door for me...only for us to see there was a wet spot the size of a tangerine on Elena's chest. I wanted her to like me, so no lactating joke. I'm sure David wished he might have stayed to watch whoever had the privilege of wiping off the salsa and having enlarged the wet stain in doing so. That woman was cutting-torch hot and would never, ever, over my dead body, find her way into our Jacuzzi. Even *with* clothes.

My drinking ended after a couple because of the twins (James and Jamie, maybe?). God that would be cool if it were a boy and girl and we could name them that.

Mom and dad were troopers and cared for Tyler the entire evening.

I needed air and gave David the high sign toward the doors. We stood outside a few minutes.

"This worked out great, honey. Good job," and my husband high-fived me.

"Even I can feel the house itself brightening up with a little zing of life happening in it, David."

Walking back in, everyone else seemed to have slowed down, all with a good buzz and stuffed from a gourmet meal any New Mexico restauranteur would have been proud to serve.

"David and I are gonna tackle clean-up. We wanna get Tyler off to bed and we have stuff upstairs to bring down."

"We got this, Olivia, really."

"I instigated all of it, Gwen. At least let us help."

Everyone, and I mean everyone went full speed and I was impressed at how fast we got the kitchen back to its pristine condition, with just the whir of the commercial-sized dishwasher now going behind the Mexican music still playing.

"Consider your aprons your graduation certificates from Olivia's Abiquiu Chef School! You all tied for #1 in the class," David said.

I had almost forgotten, "Oh my God, the wedding gifts. They're in the dining room! Gwen, can we take drinks in while we open them?"

"What's the Spanish, '*Mi casa es su Casa*,' my house is your, house?," she shook her head, "You don't ever have to ask, Olivia!"

The first box I grabbed was, coincidentally, from Gwen, about the size of a shirt box. Inside, there was a dustpan, and with drinks in us, it was all the funnier. There was a note taped to it. It wasn't a note, it was a gift card from a maid service for three heavy cleanings.

"Oh, Gwen! Gwen, this is overkill!"

"I don't know how you keep up as it is, Olivia."

"I have a magic weapon named David or I couldn't," and I kissed Gwen.

We opened a huge, electric ice cream maker from Tommy and Tammy, a vegetable and rice steamer from Stephanie, a nice vase from Sandy for which he received a kiss and hug and thanks.

Chuckster gave us a super-techie, stereo clock radio that David flipped over (he whispered, 'These things are like four hundred bucks. Wait 'til you hear the sound, honey). Sheila gave us a huge box with barbecue utensils and a rack to hold them, and Stephanie gave us a gorgeous down comforter. There was an envelope from Mom and Dad.

I pulled out the letter from the envelope, and five, crisp 100-dollar bills fell onto the table. "Woo-hoo, it's raining money," and I ran around and hugged them.

"Read the note, honey."

"Oops, I thought it was just paper hiding the money.

"Ahem, 'Olivia and David, your Christmas and wedding gifts were delayed and we're sorry. They'll both be here before New Year's. Thank you for choosing David. We are proud to have him in the family," and everyone at the table said, 'Aww,' and 'How sweet.'

"Mom? Dad? The best wedding gift, besides your love, is staying for Christmas. David and I would have been crushed to put you on a plane back home."

"It worked out as far as the ranch goes, Olivia. Another blessing! So, cheers, everyone!" and he raised his favorite Mexican beer.

We straightened up the dining room and got everything out of there.

We hustled upstairs and brought our stuff down, got everyone and everything loaded-up and hugged everyone goodbye. The Macias and Callan caravan headed for the condo where we all fell asleep within five minutes of face contact with our respective pillows.

The routine we were forming continued in the morning. Dad was the first one up and got the coffee going. I tended to Tyler and Mom wandered in.

I put out some yogurt, fruit, bran, and some muffins. "If anyone wants eggs or anything, holler," and I got no takers. Easy peasy.

My Dad looked at David, "The order of the day for me is shopping, Olivia. I know what I'm going to get and would just like to get it done! David, will you come with me so I can tell you what I'm after, because I think you may know who sells it and might have it in stock."

"If I don't know where it is, Dad, the internet will tell us and almost anything can be overnighted."

"Overnight! My tube! My tube should arrive today," and our magic karma continued: the gate buzzer sounded.

"UPS delivery, Macias?" And we buzzed him in.

"That's Daddy-magic, David. If you're as good a dad as MY dad, maybe you'll have some of that, cowboy."

"I can't fill his shoes, honey—well, boots. All I have to do is love and take care of Tyler's mom and Ty and he'll be a forever-happy camper!"

"Almost right answer, cowboy. I patted my tummy, "Don't forget *Tracy and Lacy*... or maybe it's *Luke and Duke*."

"I oughta start writing these down, Olivia. You're on a tear, honey."

Doorbell, and again.

"I need a signature please," and David accepted the tube to and handed it to Dad.

"Now, would you Christmas-wrap this please, Ofelia. You know what it is." Mom shot him a loving smile and nodded, "Yes, I do!"

Bob resumed his thought, "Getting back to what I was saying, David, I want to see and touch Tyler's gift, get it in a store, because it involves some assembly, that's all."

"We can go right now, Dad," and David looked to me and Mom for approval.

"I'm fine with that. In fact, if you guys take the truck, Mom and I can get a start. Tell you what, plan on going to lunch somewhere, and we'll figure out dinner when we call get back to Casa Callan. Sound good?"

"Gangbusters, honey."
"Are you good with that, Mom?"

"Yes!"

We put the hurry-up on getting out of the house to battle the retail crowds.

Men and Retail

"Bob, I know what I'm getting Olivia as far as a 'big' gift. She wants an internet fitness watch so she can calculate her walking and monitor herself. The big box stores have several models, and I'm good with any of them. What are you after for Tyler."

"A model train."

"Oh yeah? COOL! I never had one."

"Me, either. White kids had 'em and their dads would set them up running circles around the Christmas tree and presents. I'd like to do that for Tyler."

"You're doing it for me too, Dad. Orphans don't get trains and stuff like that for Christmas. It's more like a new shirt, new pants, and a ten buck toy or ball or something."

"I don't want to give you the wrong idea, David. We weren't too poor for me to have gotten a train for Christmas. My parents were just more practical than extravagant. That's at all. I would get something that lasted, like a nice cowboy hat I dreamed of wearing and looked at every time we were in the clothing store. But I want this for Tyler—and now that you've let me know— it's for you, also. The possibility of a long-lasting thing of you two setting up the train at Christmas, maybe. A tradition."

"Sure, we could do that."

"If you don't mind driving, I'll pull over so we can switch so that I can be running down places that have the trains in-stock."

"Fine with that, son. I like these older trucks and this one runs really good."

Before we even got back on the roadway, "Dad! Here's a place that has a fitness watch that ties in to Olivia's cellphone service and they also have model trains. Three different sets of trains. Want to try it?"

"Sure. Dial up the GPS and we're on it."

"No need, it's not that complicated. We can take the Loop 101."

The big box store had plenty of parking. It wasn't jammed, but busy.

"Let's find the trains, first. The watch is in the cellphone department."

There was an 'H.O' gage set which means miniature-sized cars and track, and two standard-size sets. I had one box in my hand, and Bob had another.

"You see any real difference, David? I mean, what to do?"

"I know there are a million different things that you can order for the H.O., from cars and locomotives, to extra track, even buildings. Some are powered with lights. I like the idea of the smaller size around the tree, Dad."

"That makes sense to me. He can get train stuff for birthdays and things from us and you, huh?"

I turned the box over. "Look, Dad. There's a coupon inside for a 20% discount from any cars and accessories ordered from the manufacturer if ordered 30 days or less from purchase."

"Yeah, they'll need the receipt. Tell you what, let's get this one and I will order a bunch of extra track pieces and some cool cars!"

I grinned at him, "You're not thinking of spoiling my son, are you?"

"Not at all. I would never spoil your son. I will just tell you that I will be spoiling *my grandson*, thank you very much," and I hi-fived my father-in-law.

I trotted to the front of the store to get a flat cart for the oversized box. When I got back, Bob said, "The box says we can have it set up and running in about an hour!"

"With the two of us, Bob, that means we'll be playing with the choo-choo in...what, an hour and forty-five minutes?" and we laughed.

"Prolly. You know how these things are, David."

"Okay, cellphones are over there, and the watch will be right there, too," and I aimed the cart in that direction. That department was jammed. Because the watches were in a locked case, we took a number.

"I wanna say Olivia told me you and Ofelia have the same cell carrier, Dad?"

"Olivia suggested we have three lines on one account to save money. My ranch phone is, of course, separate."

"You're saving *a ton* with three lines. You just made this easier. I'm gonna get Ofelia and Olivia an internet watch and they'll be able to chat with each other on it and even net-surf."

"That's awfully generous."

"I have one mother-in-law and a good job I'm probably returning to in the next couple of weeks."

"Yeah?"

"Yeah, Olivia said we have an appointment with my orthopedic surgeon, Dr. Drew, to evaluate my fitness for returning to work. And Olivia's dying to go back to work, too, Dad. They have an employee nursery where Tyler can go, and I get off at 1pm every day. It's not like Tyler will be dumped in there for 9 hours. Besides, Olivia will certainly swing by throughout her day and spend a few minutes with him like the other parents do. Employees even go there to have their meal breaks with their kids."

"That sounds like a great deal."
"Truly is, and no out-of-pocket to us."

Our number got called.

"Happy holidays. What are we helping you with, today?"

"I know what I want, a couple internet watches in that case over there."

"I have the key right here. Let's go!"

I made quick work of it and paid for the watches with my card so Olivia wouldn't see the charge unless she opened the statement for my old single-user account. I was going to swing back by and get the same thing for Bob so the three of them could hook-up.

"Where to, now?"

"One of those western jewelry stores in Scottsdale, David. I'd like to get Olivia some turquoise... earrings, necklace, I dunno. And Ofelia, too."

"I know just the place. Less than fifteen and we're there," and the bench seat enabled us to put the big train box just behind it. Leaving it in the bed was going to get it stolen in less than 10 minutes this time of year.

Bob found a gorgeous silver and turquoise bracelet for Olivia. It was about three inches wide with beautiful engraving work and several large and small stones. It was expensive and looked it. Knowing him as I now thought I did, Bob would have paid double for it for his...for our Olivia.

"I think I like the bracelet idea for her mother, but I kind of had a mental picture of a big silver and turquoise cross to wear around her neck, on the outside of her shirt."

It took several stores along the same sidewalk for Bob to find Ofelia's cross. It was every bit as pretty as Olivia's bracelet.

"If we hit one of the bigger retailers, we can get some clothes and stuff for Mom, Olivia and Tyler, plus some smaller toys for Ty. We'll do drive-thru lunch and head home so we can put the stuff we buy in the truck bed."

"Beautiful. Let's do that," and we did.

It was nice so we opted to eat outside at a great little fish taco place.

"Dad, I looked for Olivia high and low when she disappeared. I paid a law firm's investigator to help me find her and could only say that she was safe, and probably had money to keep me from finding her."

"Not so, David. You weren't hard to find at all. Truly, I didn't know if I wanted to kill you or even deal with you, but she pleaded with me to find out if you were married or engaged or anything. The P.I. that I contracted located and identified that Vanessa girl and got some pretty revealing shots of you two, pictures Olivia never saw and never will. Olivia swore and be damned that she loved you so much that she wasn't going to come barging in on your life and cause any wreckage. And she really worked me over to get information from me, the little I gave her."

"It was a rebound thing with Vanessa, Bob. And the very thing that made any future with her impossible? That's what got her killed. She had serious issues going on, and in the back of her mind, she always knew that guy, her killer, was out there."

"I hate talking about this David. It's Christmas, for Christ's sake. Can we please..."

"Yes, Bob, but it was important for me to tell you that I pulled out all of the stops trying to find Olivia. And when I called your ranch? They told me, literally, to 'fuck off,' that no stranger just calls up and demands to talk to the G.M."

Bob had to chuckle, "I understand. As far as trying me at the ranch? They follow my instructions. So, no apology or excuses, David. It's necessary."

"I wasn't looking for any.... I needed to have this talk with you, Bob. It was a lot of excess baggage I was dragging around," and I extended my hand for a handshake with my father-in-law. He accepted it graciously.

The Women's Side of Christmas

"With me going back to work, I'm thinking David's probably going to hit the nursing uniform places to get things that will fit me as I get bigger with these babies."

"He'd think of that?"

"Mom? You never want to underestimate how thoughtful and thorough he is. Anyhow, I grabbed two different shoes out of his closet. That's what's in the bag in the back seat. I want to get him some exotic-skin cowboy boots to wear with his jeans. I think he'll love them. The western store I like advertises they have the top six brands and 800 pairs in stock. It's unreal."

"That will be good for the ranch!"

"These are dress boots, Mama. No mud and dirt on this pair. I'll get him some suede rough-outs for that."

"Oh, okay."

Their sign boasted "Chester Bros. Western Apparel – Since 1970." As I parked, Mama said she thought she'd browse the shirts for Dad and David, an idea I liked.

The exotic skins choices were plentiful. I leaned more toward light tan and camel for David. I didn't see him in black or dark brown. Gray might be a possibility.

I grabbed a clerk, "I'm getting my husband some exotic skin boots, today. I brought a couple of his shoes to measure and get close to the right fit for him. Can you help me with that?"

"Yes, ma'am. We have an electronic measurement machine that makes it easy. It can see right into a shoe and determine the exact internal specs. You'll leave with boots that will fit him. It's a Chester Brothers guarantee."

"Things have sure changed."

"Yep, even in Western wear."

The clerk did his magic.

"Your husband's an exact $10^{1/2}$ and the boots boxes are arranged by size. Let me walk you over and get you in the exotic skins that'll fit him."

It didn't take long at all. A medium brown pair of ostrich boots with two-tone uppers was gorgeous. They were hand-made by one of the top three bootmakers in the US, in Texas, of course. I set the pair on top of the counter. "Whatcha think, Mom?"

"He'll love them for sure, Olivia."

Price was no object. Mom's eyes fell out at the register but I didn't care. They were hand-made and would last David a lifetime. The clerk offered saddle soap and polish, and I took them as stocking stuffers for him.

Mom said, "There's a big sale on nice shirts over there. Walk with me?"

We were back at the same register in just a few minutes with two shirts, each, for Dad and David. One of the shirts Mom got David was what she thought might be really showy with his boots and she was right. I was afraid, that, in his new boots and shirt, I may rip his clothes off instantly on seeing my cowboy *look* like a cowboy. I hoped Mom and Dad would be in the other room if I lost that much self-control. Tyler's conception would never let me forget my impulsiveness with regard to his daddy.

"Whatcha feel like for lunch, Mom?"

"Fish."

"Seafood?"

"Yes."

"There's a fresh seafood grill place on the way back home. They have great salads and shrimp cocktails, too!"

"You talked me into it."

Mom had trout almondine, rice and the vegetable medley with iced tea, and I had the baked whitefish in buttery wine sauce with broccoli and a green salad and tea. They baked their own scrumptious rolls and I took mine for Tyler.

We left the gifts in the SUV and walked in on the men who were lying on the floor near the Christmas tree. The model train box was self-explanatory.

"Hi, guys!"

"Oh, hi!"

"I see what David got himself, Dad," and we laughed.

"This is going to be so cool, honey," David said, as he carefully grabbed the base of the tree and pulled it out so the men could get the train's track assembled behind it.

Tyler was in his playpen next to them, going berserk because Mom and I were home. I reached a bag from the restaurant and held out the still-warm roll, "Look what mommy got you!" and handed him a piece I tore off for him. I took a bite. Oh, God, baked Heaven.

I was just about to ask the guys where they ate when I saw the fast-food bags on the island from our favorite little joint down the way. "Oh, mom, see those bags? That little place has the best fish tacos this side of Vera Cruz, I swear. And the burritos are big enough for two meals. I'll have to take you there, Mom."

They were so fixated on the train, we walked right behind them with the boot boxes and shirts and things. Since Mom and Dad were in the master, we hid them there. David respected their privacy and Dad wouldn't ever nose around in someone's closet. His own clothes would be the only thing he'd notice.

"I think this preggers lady needs to lie down. You good with Ty, David?"

"Sure! You'll probably hear the train inside of a half-hour."

"I may be out cold, honey," and I kissed my mom who said she'd handle Tyler and put him down on the master's bed so as not to disturb me.

I woke up and, sure enough, heard the train going and the boys laughing. I walked out and Daddy was holding Tyler, pointing at the train going around, while David was pushing the control that made the locomotive's whistling sound. Tyler was squealing.

"Anybody care if we order pizza tonight? I think we should take the night off from the kitchen." It was fine with everybody.

We were sitting around the table with our pizza and drinks and Mom asked, "How did everybody do, shopping today?"

David said, "I think the men's team did okay, don't you, Bob?" and Daddy nodded.

He said, "By the way David, can I borrow the truck tomorrow? There's a gift I want to go out and get, alone."

"Sure, Dad, no problem."

Mom said, "We got a lot done and really had a nice time together. Olivia took me to a nice lunch. We had fish and good coleslaw there, too."

"David, did you hear from Dr. Drew today?"

"I saw a call come in I didn't recognize and let it go to voice mail."

"He called me and asked if I could come to your orthopedics evaluation he's going to do after your therapy on Thursday. He wants to watch you do your P.T. workout and then he'll meet with us."

"Sounds fine to me."

"David, it sounds like he's going to release you!"

"That sounds finer!"

Everybody was into their second slice of pizza and we continued the casual conversation around the table. Dad looked over at Mom and said "Speaking of messages, I got one from the freight company, Ofelia. The crates should be here the day after tomorrow, the 23rd."

Mom replied, "Roberto, I think we were very fortunate those companies got the items done in time to get shipped here in time for Christmas."

David looked up, "Crates?"

"Yes, David, I'm sending you a life-size taxidermized bull and horse for Christmas," and my dad cracked up and the rest of us did too.

I was intrigued at what my dad might send that required two crates.

My phone rang and I wouldn't have picked it up except that it was Gwen, "Merry Christmas, girlfriend. What's going on?"

"Not a whole lot. We're just sitting around the table staring at leftover pizza and having a couple drinks."

"I caught you at a good time! Put me on speaker, honey!"

"You have all of us, Tyler included."

"Merry Christmas, everyone!"

And everybody at the table wished Gwen Merry Christmas.

"I would like all of you to come to my house for dinner on Christmas Eve. I want to pull out all the stops and put out a Victorian styled Christmas dinner which Tomás will prepare, and I have asked he and Elena to join us for dinner as well. If you have plans, I understand. I'm sorry I asked so late."

I looked at David. He could see I wanted to accept. Everybody else seemed like, 'Go for it.' It would relieve us from cooking and all the shopping, and I didn't want to do it alone or put my mom through it.

"Gwen I'm looking around the table and I see 10 thumbs up. We are going to be there lock, stock, and highchair!"

"Marvelous! I was so hoping you could come. Sandy will join us also. Cocktail hour from 6:00 to 7:30 and dinner promptly at 7:30. Is that too late or okay for everyone?

"Perfect, Gwen. That will give us the day in pajamas to destroy this place and reconstruct it, and we will be thrilled to come to the house!"

"Then it's on! I've got to run but I love you all and I can't wait see you in a couple days! Oh, hey. If you want to get there early and just hang out, use the theater? Come on! Any, and I mean any time's fine. Love you all," and the call ended.

I looked at everybody at the table and I said, "I can't imagine what that woman is going to do for a formal dinner. And that mansion? With the formal flatware and fine china that must be in that house? And Tomás and Elena in the kitchen? I think we are in for a big-time experience. God, I didn't even get her anything for Christmas yet."

David said, "I've actually been thinking about that. We're doing pretty good getting her busted out of that boring lifestyle of hers. What would you say to getting her a getaway in Sedona, a couple of nights in one of the B&B places on the creek?"

"I'd say we give that to Sandy and let him take her there."

David looked confused, "Then what about Gwen?"

"Other than business and money, what does *Sandy* love best?"

"That only leaves golf, Olivia."

"Bingo! We cruise down the hill to the pro shop. We'll pick out a nice pair of golf shorts and a couple tops in whatever colors coordinate with the shorts! I'm sure the pro shop's having a big sale and we get our member discount in addition!"

"Works for me. But with the getaway for Sandy, how do we know what dates to pick for them, honey?"

"No need. We'll just get the lodging and get them prepaid for a couple of nights and let them choose the dates."

I walked around the table to him and he pulled me onto his lap. "We're the bomb."

"I don't know about *that*...I'm just your other half," and he looked up at me and smiled and I took his face into my hands and kissed him.

The next morning, Daddy got David's keys. Unbeknownst to me, he headed out to buy David a pair of black sharkskin boots in his size. Mom had spilled the beans, so Daddy knew right where to go and used GPS to get there and back. We were off to physical therapy, leaving Ty with Mom.

I thanked Tammy for the ice cream machine they'd given us for our wedding present. Tommy waved at me and started putting David through his paces on the equipment.

"Olivia, how nice to see you!"

"You startled me, Dr. Drew!" and I spun around.

"There's a rumor you're coming back to work, young lady."

"It's no rumor. David and I talked about it, and I really want to keep up on my game."

"And I hear you are in the family way?"

I couldn't help laughing and blushing, "Yes, the ever-pregnant Olivia and that baby maker I am married to are going to have twins in August!"

"I couldn't be happier for you and I don't know if I've ever seen you look happier, Olivia. I truly miss you on service and hope you come back soon. I got spoiled relying on you. Between you and me, nobody can fill your shoes around here and I want you back."

"You're too kind, Dr. Drew and, well, you're getting all of me... Us!" and I patted my tummy, "Three-for-one!"

Daniel Drew was respected all over the region. I liked the way he treated his patients and he afforded as much respect and kindness to the entire staff, whether you were a nurse or a janitor. We ran into some very difficult cases and he went out of his way to tell me that I had proven my worth as a top-notch orthopedics nurse. I told him I was committed to get into the practitioner program as soon as I had enough hours to qualify. He promised the strongest endorsement possible in my being accepted.

"Let's walk over and talk to David. I've looked at his x-rays. I've been watching him a few minutes and his range of motion is good, no pain grimaces. I think he's ready to go, Olivia."

"He will be thrilled. I'm not the only one who's been itching to go back to work."

"Then let's go over and give him the good news."

David was on a stair step machine and we walked up behind him, Dr. Drew to the left and me to the right.

"Hey there handsome!"

"Look who's here, my favorite nurse and mommy on the planet and I have to add, my best wife!"

Dr. Drew even laughed.

"David," Dr Drew began, "I think we need to get you back into the mainstream so that's where I'm sending you. I'll see you in 30 days for a checkup but I'm writing the back-to-work release as soon as I get over to the counter."

David had stopped his exercise regimen and extended his hand.

"Thank you for everything you did, Dr. Drew."

"You're very welcome. Hang onto that walker we provided and if you need the cane then by all means use it. Let me know if you have any unusual pain, swelling or other issues, okay?"

"Olivia will be hovering over me. Seriously, you worked wonders, Doc. But can I ask—I have an inside job behind a mic. I guess I'm surprised I wasn't able to work, sooner."

"I didn't want you sitting still or in the same position for extended periods of time. Your injuries needed relaxation and normal movement routines throughout your dicier days. And I'm sure you didn't need the stress which I'm sure is everywhere in your business. I wouldn't let you risk aggravating your condition with any of that. Now? I think you're ready to take on the world, again."

I agreed, "He's right, David."

"Oh, I know honey.... Dr. Drew, I never had hard feelings about being kept away from work. It was just curiosity. Thanks, again."

"Yes sir! Have a great day, both of you and Olivia? Please get back to work, please?" And we all laughed.

Tommy and Tammy came over, elated. "We're still friends, right?"

"To the end. Thank you for all you've done to get me going," and we hugged them both.

A Little Girl's Meadow

The first truck to arrive called 15 minutes ahead of time and we buzzed them right in. David and Dad met them out front and David raised the little golf cart garage's door. It was the large cube's delivery. They lowered it on the tailgate of the truck and slid it into the empty space. We thanked them and they left.

I looked at my father-in-law.

"Let's get going, David, because Santa isn't coming to town, he's right here. How about a crowbar if you have it, or a tire iron? Claw hammers and screwdrivers? We need to be very careful prying this open."

I noticed the origin stenciled on the crate was an Amish furniture place in Pennsylvania. Dad and I worked on it painstakingly for the good part of a half hour because he said we could damage the wood or finish of the item, inside, if we weren't careful.

Once revealed, it blew my mind. I gave my father-in-law a look.

"What?"

"You just don't hold back, do you, Bob."

"Says the father of my grandson, with two more buns in my daughter's oven?"

We shook our heads laughing in agreement with each other and we agreed it was easiest for us to carry it around to the front door and ring the doorbell. Once we set it down in the vestibule, I dialed Olivia.

"Honey? Could you please pick up Tyler and carry him to the front door when we ring the bell, and don't peek, okay?"

"You got it, cowboy."

"Dad, I'm going to back off so I can get a picture of Olivia and Tyler when they see it. So, gimme a sec and then ring the bell, please."

"You got it, son," and he saw my signal and rang the bell.

The door opened slowly. Olivia had Tyler on her hip and gasped and put her free hand over her mouth. Her dad and I were standing behind the hand-carved, 150-lb. giant rocking horse made entirely by Amish hands and old school tools. It was hand-sanded and hand-painted and hand-finished. It was as beautiful as it was massive. It could have been a museum piece.

"C'mon, cowgirl! You said you were good in the saddle," and I patted the seat area.

I got a picture of Olivia holding Tyler sitting on the rocking horse, and video of her rocking our son and again, my bride lit me up full of love for her and our son. Bob high-fived me and I hugged him and then looked him in the eye. "You are absolutely the best." I had to hug him

"David, this will get passed down to your great grandchildren and theirs. They'll be rocking on this thing."

Olivia handed Tyler to me so I could take him as she climbed off of the huge hobby horse and threw her arms around her dad's neck, kissing his cheeks again and again, saying how much she loved him.

"Tyler can name him later, *mija*."

"Nope," Olivia said, in a matter-of-fact tone. Bob gave her a look.

"You're telling your dad no? With Santa coming?"

"Yep. I named him the instant I saw him," and Roberto looked over at me.

"David, I know where this is going," Bob said, as his smile grew and he nodded, slowly.

"His name's 'Shooter,' David, after Daddy's favorite horse. He's practically a legend and buried on our family ranch," and Roberto snuck a whisper to me as he changed angles so Olivia wouldn't see.

"She's *loco* or clairvoyant, cuz wait until you see what's in the next crate."

We got the horse into the house and set it in the living room.

I mentioned my stomach growling and headed for the table where Olivia plunked down two icy Coors. There was plenty of leftover pizza that we had for lunch. We were just relaxing, watching TV and chatting casually and Dad's phone rang again.

It was the other delivery. We heard him say "Yes, we will buzz you in the gate. Bring the crate to the front door, please. Use a hand truck so you don't mark-up the tile in here."

Twenty minutes later, the doorbell rang. A large pallet-looking crate was brought carefully into the house. Bob told the driver to put it in the kitchen.

"David, this one I think we need screwdrivers and a claw hammer," and I fetched two different sizes of each from the truck's toolbox.

Olivia didn't hazard a guess what was inside. I had no clue.

Working as carefully as we did on the hobby horse crate, Bob and I finally got it down to where the huge gift was bubble wrap covering layers of brown paper, heavily masking-taped.

It was obviously some kind of artwork in a glass frame, 30x48 or so. Dad managed to turn the frame toward himself so that once he got the edging and the bubble wrap pulled away, Olivia wouldn't be able to see it.

"Okay, Olivia. Move your chair right in front of this... like, four feet from it. David, help me slide this over." We got it positioned for the reveal to Olivia.

Ofelia had joined Olivia in position. We rotated the frame and the Olivia was dumbfounded. It looked like she was in shock and looked at her dad as tears began slow streams down her cheeks. I looked over the top of the frame, looking at the image upside down. Olivia's weeping increased.

Once I stepped around, I saw a painting of a serene meadow with a horse in the left corner of the scene next to a tree. The horse was grazing and the meadow was a solid quilt of yellow wildflowers. The sky was almost turquoise and scattered with billowing clouds. I couldn't help to get drawn in. It captivated me.

Bob said, "My horse? 'Roberto's Shooting Star' but I called him 'Shooter?' He's buried about ten feet from that tree trunk, David."

Olivia's mother looked at me, "Do you know what that is David?"

"I know it's beautiful, Ofelia. I'm guessing somewhere on the ranch."

"We named it "Olivia's Meadow.' Shooter was our prized stallion that sired most of the quarter horses that work on the big ranch and our own. Roberto used to ride Olivia up there on Shooter when she was a little girl. He'd picnic with her in the meadow when it was in bloom, with the blanket of yellow wildflowers and fresh lavender filling the air. He would unsaddle Shooter who would graze near that piñon pine, just like you see it. I took a picture I still have. I might even have the negative, still. I dunno."

Olivia had a pile of soaked paper napkins and tissues in front of her. She looked child-like with a faraway gaze. Her words seemed dreamy.

In a weepy voice, Olivia said, "David, I have that photograph in one of my boxes out in the garage. Daddy got the photo from Mom and went into town so I could have an 8x10 of it. It was the only photograph in my bedroom, on my wall next to my bed so I could just turn my head and look at it, and sometimes run my hand around its edges. Daddy would catch me staring at the photograph and tell me, 'That's your meadow, baby, Olivia's Meadow."

Roberto looked at Olivia and said, "This is a painting, *mija*, where the wildflowers will always be in bloom and Shooter will always be looking out for you while he grazes." Ofelia couldn't keep all of the moment inside and started to weep, too.

I was struggling for the right thing to say and looked at Roberto. I was profoundly moved.

"This will be the centerpiece of our living room. I'll have it professionally installed and get accent lighting with a dimmer."

Olivia looked up with her puffy eyes and rubbed my cheek, beckoning my lips to come close. She rested her forehead against mine and whispered, "I love you and this family so much right now, David. Thank you."

Her dad's voice broke the near prayerful silence in the room, "David, your joy won't be...can't be complete until you visit Olivia's Meadow with Olivia and your children. With your love for her? I think you will feel her spirit, there, as it was when she was a little girl." Olivia could only bury her face into my shoulder and weep.

Ofelia removed a large pitcher of iced tea from the refrigerator and filled our tumblers, setting them in front of us.

Roberto continued, "It almost killed me when I had to bury Shooter. He was my prized stallion and daily ride. He was 12 when Olivia was born and always gentle when she was around. He could sense I'd shoot him between the eyes if he harmed a hair on the head of my precious Olivia. He was almost 28 when he went down with pneumonia and there was only one thing to do. We took him up to Olivia's Meadow because he loved it as much as our little Olivia did. So the piñon pine was the place for him to rest, to the right of where you see him depicted in the painting.

"How far is it from the main complex?"

He turned to look squarely at me. "It's not on the *big* ranch, David. It's on *our* ranch, the one you and Olivia will eventually own. Mama, would you grab that tube under the tree for me, please."

Ofelia spun herself out of the chair and retrieved the tube from the corner behind the Christmas tree and walked over to Dad, who was standing at the kitchen island.

"Olivia, Ofelia? Would you mind clearing the table off completely and wiping it please," and they did so. He offered the tube to Olivia.

"Here you go. Open this."

I was over her shoulder as Olivia pulled the snug cap off one end of the tube. She pulled out a map and Dad opened a drawer to grab a steak knife as I was getting it unrolled and held down with salt and pepper shakers, a sugar dispenser, and the napkin holder on the fourth corner to keep it from curling. Bob brought the steak knife, his makeshift pointer, down on the map.

"David, this is our ranch. Here is the main house and barn, and a couple small utility buildings. There are grazing areas here and here and an artificial lake, here, for watering the livestock. Opposite that, northeast? That corner of the property is where Olivia's Meadow is located. Do you see the blue survey lines cordoning-off that area?"

"Yessir."

I was about to be glad that Olivia's arms were wrapped around my waist as we looked on.

"It's three acres give or take. The lower left part of those three acres has electric and water, and even sewer already into it and a crew is already laid-on to begin leveling a site so a home can be built there. Your home."

Roberto looked up from the map and looked right into our eyes. "It was always meant for Olivia to come home to. For your Christmas present, Ofelia and I deeded the parcel and homesite at Olivia's Meadow in your name and hers, jointly. The prep's nearing completion. Construction can commence when the winter weather breaks."

Olivia collapsed into my arms, resting her head against my chest. She was regaining her breath. I saw tears in my father-in-law's eyes.

"It is only right that Olivia and the love of *her* life *own* Olivia's Meadow, so that you and your children can picnic there as we did when she was a little girl. You'll have the deed in-hand in the next few weeks, arriving certified mail. It's already been approved and just awaiting the rubber stamps from the bureaucrats."

I kissed the top of Olivia's head as she repeated "Oh Daddy" a few times, almost imperceptibly. I grabbed her iced tea from the counter to help her throat get clear. Ofelia was a weepy as well. After I gave Olivia a sip of tea, I reached over and took my mother-in-law's hand in my own, "We will cherish this, always. As God is my witness, we will keep it in the family so your great grandchildren's grandchildren will know and enjoy this place, regard Olivia's Meadow as their home, too, Ofelia. Thank you," and I tenderly kissed the backs of each of her hands

Dad said, "David let's get this packing stuff out of the kitchen, huh?" Once outside, he said, "Even before the prostate cancer diagnosis, I was going to do this, David. The diagnosis only sped it up and whenever God takes me, I can go to my rest knowing it's done."

"It sounds like you're telling me it in an advanced stage. Is it?"

He shrugged his shoulders, "So they tell me. I couldn't put this off."

"Roberto, we will build that house and we will live in it with your grandchildren. The kids will romp and we will picnic in that meadow."

In that moment, I saw my life and Olivia's take a big turn. Eastward, to Abiquiu. Home to Olivia's Meadow.

I could manage the ranch finances and I'd ask Roberto to think about who he'd recommend I hire. Olivia? My life was our children and her world. I considered Olivia's options were without limitation from me. She would have total say over the house design. We'd have enough money to figure out future income streams.

In the spiritual sense, my faith told me we were being called and should answer the call. I didn't like questioning God, blaming Him or looking for motives. I'd been told and taught by priests and nuns who cared about me that faith was all about trust. Without parents and frequent foster parent changes, my faith was my only constant.

In the flesh? I trusted Olivia. She'd have 51% of the say. Period.

Most of our day was spent thinking and talking about going to Gwen's. Olivia and I tackled some housecleaning and we let Ofelia and Bob hang out and watch football. Between the cheers from the TV, I could hear Tyler getting into the action, too, sounding off whenever his granddad whooped or hollered.

Olivia organized some light snacks for mid-afternoon because we knew Gwen's dinner was going to be a feast beyond belief.

The four of us rotated through the shower, David and I showering together because it's what we'd become accustomed to.

Dinner Is Served

Gwen's subdivision was guard-gated 24-hours a day and we merely had to give our last name to get through. Curiously, Gwen's house had its own wrought iron security fencing and brick structures with electric carriage lights on each side of her own electric gate. Were I a multimillionaire jewelry magnate, I think I may have even added dogs as a deterrent to anyone thinking 'diamond heist' like we've seen in the movies. Whoever designed the elegant entry had done so without detracting from the view of the courtyard gardens and mansion.

Someone we didn't recognize answered the door, wished us a Merry Christmas, and welcomed us to the McArdle home. We stepped in and saw Sandy and Gwen approaching.

Sandy looked more handsome than I'd ever seen him, a white dinner jacket and what looked like black tuxedo trousers with a red casual button down shirt, and red rose blossom pinned to his lapel.

Gwen wore a white strapless dress featuring a layered, cascading cutaway down the right side, accentuated with a wide red leather belt and red 2-inch heels. She had a Christmas wrist corsage of tiny red and white roses.

What set off the whole outfit were the pearl earrings she wore. They were studs, but the 8mm size and opalescence of the pearls were unlike any I had seen. The pearls, themselves, were mounted in what looked like little 18-karat gold saucers.

My dad and my husband went full cowboy. My dad was very dapper in his gray Stetson and David in his black Stetson Mom had given him as an early gift just for this dinner. David wore a white silk shirt, black belt, and tight black jeans. He had run out and gotten a red string tie from the western store and he actually looked terrific, so good you would have never realized he was in jeans.

Daddy wore gray slacks and gray boots to match, with a black dress shirt unbuttoned at the collar. I took pictures of them before we left the house because I love these two men more than any other, and tonight, I don't know if I had ever seen them look better, together or separate.

Mama modified her outfit from the wedding with a red and white floral blouse and I bought her a red and white corsage for the lapel of her jacket. I had a dressy-looking green shift I accessorized with a red, white, and green- patterned, oversized silk scarf. I wore my green flats out of necessity. I needed my feet to be comfortable. We had Tyler in a little suit and he was adorable.

"There's my favorite family in the whole world!" said Gwen, and she kissed us all and wished us Merry Christmas, right down to Tyler's little chubby cheeks bracketing his grin. He recognized and loved Gwen.

"Tomás and Elena are putting the last touches on dinner and then they'll do a quick-change and join us. I have servers who will take care of everything else so they can enjoy dinner with us."

Whatever Elena was going to come out wearing or not wearing was going to be a visual stunner and that was a certainty. I would try not to let my eyes fall out of my head. David would keep his usual, nonplused, calm demeanor. I could take that to the bank. Tomás would be sexy in anything. I was sure he would not disappoint and was right.

"I've set us up for cocktails in the study, which you may not have seen, yet," and we followed. It was located next door to the baseball museum room David and I had discovered.

Gwen opened the door and it was more a library than study. There must have been a couple thousand books in there. The smell wasn't musty but more of well cared-for hardwood, meticulously and regularly rubbed-down with the right oils and polish. There were a couple small tables that had been pushed together and cocktail service had been set up complete with an ice bucket and bartender who greeted us.

For never having anyone over, I marveled at how superbly honed Gwen's entertaining skills were. It had to have come from the social engagements she had to make with clients and events of the charities she supported around town.

I opted for red wine and Gwen asked for the same. Daddy and David chose beers and Mama had champagne and orange juice, the former coming from a split.

We toasted each other a Merry Christmas and then David excused himself. We thought he may have gone to the bathroom but hadn't. When he returned, he was holding a box in beautiful Christmas wrap. It was the size of a hat box, and a smaller box in matching wrap that was for Tomás and Elena.

The gift card on top read, "Sandy and Gwen from The Macias-Callan Family."

David walked over to Sandy and said, "We figured you were craving more bull's balls, so Merry Christmas boss." He didn't see that one coming and the humor was well received.

Gwen said, "Let me put those under the tree in the dining room with the others," and she was back almost in an instant. We recalled seeing some small gifts under that tree but assumed they were decorations.

One of the servers walked in and rang a silver dinner bell, announcing "Dinner is served," and we carried our drinks as we 'processed' over to the dining room. I say processed because it could have been a Christmas parade with everyone so elegantly dressed. The Christmas spirit was working overtime, as well.

Once we reached the opened, massive doors of the dining room, the scene was a thing to behold.

Commanding immediate attention was a 10-ft blue spruce Christmas tree in the corner. It was trimmed in white garland with red, white, and gold ornaments the size of softballs. There were tiny white lights strung throughout, twinkling with the slow pace of a gentle snow.

There was a nativity scene on an occasional table. The figurines looked to be made of crystal, and each was 10-12" high. The manger was crystal, as well.

The chargers under each dinner plate were muted gold. The plate atop was Currier & Ives in red and white, a Christmas scene right out of Charles Dickens. Each place setting had a lead crystal water glass and a wine goblet, each with an inch-wide band of gold around the rim. There was a salad fork, hors d'oeuvre fork, dinner fork along with a butter knife and a regular knife-all, sterling silver and gleaming atop a crisply pressed white cloth napkin.

A door opened and Elena came in wearing white heels, red leather slacks that looked painted-on-tight, and a white tunic with red and green sash belts gently braided around one another. Her hair was in a ponytail brought forward and hanging over her left shoulder. Large white dangling earrings with gold hoops set off and sold the entire look. She looked like an haute couture Italian model.

Tomás had chosen a black houndstooth jacket, white shirt with a white silk necktie with sparse, pea-sized red polka dots. The sheen of his tailored gabardine slacks gave him that high-fashion 'Euro-hip' look, also.

They carried small bunches of flowers, approached each person's chair, each kissed each of us on both cheeks, and wished Merry Christmas. The tiny, hand-tied bouquets were set on our dinner plates. They were lovely, with small satin ribbons tied around each, one green, and one red, the smell of fresh lavender arising from the single sprig contained within.

Tomás looked to me and said, "The lavender is for you, Olivia. I have read about where you are from and I learned the lavender grows wild, there. I love it. So, for you, and I am a little embarrassed to admit, for me? We included it," and he nodded.

I smiled at his thoughtfulness, "You're right. It grows wild and is even harvested in our area back home." He leaned down to the small bouquet for a closer whiff, "Mmm, I love that." I gave him a peck on the cheek and it was probably his dizzyingly seductive cologne that prompted me to whisper, "You're so very sweet."

Servers started bustling in with bread baskets and small silver trays of assorted crackers, followed by large parfait glasses containing our appetizer of cold lobster and prawns. Small plates of fat stuffed olives, smoked salmon and capers with onions were placed next to the salad plates.

One of the servers came around holding bottles of red and white wines asking which we would prefer and filling the gold rimmed goblets with that preference.

Gwen stood and reached for David's hand to join her.

"David?"

"I think all of us are going to remember this Christmas for a very long time, and it was your wedding that will seal that memory with joy, forever. We wish you a Merry Christmas. Thank you for spending it with us. Cheers!"

We toasted and sipped. Gwen lowered the glass from her lips.

Gwen continued, "David, Olivia? It was seeing and feeling your love brimming over the top that made me realize I was missing out on a lot in life. And then that funny feeling overcame me when I met a tan, handsome golfer who could dance," and she looked at Sandy with real affection.

She raised her glass to Sandy, "Cheers, sweetheart," and the rest of us raised our glasses as Sandy gave Gwen a small kiss after sipping their wine.

Gwen looked back at us, "I can't thank you enough, but I can't tell you that I love you as much as any friend could. That includes you, Mr. and Mrs. Macias. Olivia's a blessing to all who encounter her." She had to dab her eyes with a napkin before she could drink from her goblet of wine.

Roberto rose, "Ms. Gwen, Ofelia and I are humbled to be guests in your magnificent home. Please know that you are welcome to stay at our family ranch in Abiquiu, anytime. Merry Christmas to you as well," and Daddy toasted Gwen and Sandy.

Dinner salads that were topped with hard-boiled quail eggs, contained strips of anchovy, pimiento and bell pepper, with a sherry and cream dressing, were placed in front of us and whisked away as soon as we finished. To clear our palates, small silver dishes were set in front of us with a mini-scoops of orange and lime sherbet.

Tasting the sherbet, Tyler thought he'd died and gone to heaven, and his facial expression with the first spoonful was so cute, David's cellphone came out to take a video of the second spoonful and reaction.

The turkey was brought out on a platter with mashed potatoes squeezed around the perimeter in a decoration much like that of cake icing. A high mound of roasted chestnut dressing lay up against the lowers of the turkey. I had only seen chateaubriand served like that. There were hot vegetables in those same surrounds and the turkey looked roasted to perfection, with decorative Christmas foils on the end of each leg. One half of the breast had been sliced down, as had dark meat from a leg and thigh. A wrapped carving knife was alongside the tray. It went without saying we were going to leave the carving to Tomás unless Gwen or Sandy was taking on the task.

The side dishes were just as notable: glazed carrots and leeks in a light, tart, citrusy sauce, a crab-stuffed deviled egg atop a small pancake sized circle of cooked greens, a small plate of roasted garlic; it seemed every corner of the garden had been visited. We praised Tomás and Elena for the elegant menu.

Dinner was relative quiet as we took in the dinner's fabulous offerings. The conversation was almost entirely about Olivia's Meadow and the painting.

We were so full we could only toy with our desserts of mincemeat pie and pumpkin sorbet. As servers gracefully worked around the table between each of us, clearing, Gwen rose and walked over toward the tree and picked up two boxes.

She returned to the table and stood behind David and me. She put her hand on my shoulder, handed me a small box and said, "Olivia, Merry Christmas, love."

I opened a small box and sucked-in a breath. The earrings, the stunning 18 karat gold and pearl earrings Gwen was wearing, were an exact match to the ones in the box.

"Only the best for you, Olivia— Mikimoto Akoya 8-millimeter pearls. And Ofelia, if you'll reach under your chair? There's a box with a pair for you, too," and Gwen grinned.

"Oh, Gwen, may I?" I asked, motioning to put them in

"I'd pout if you didn't, Olivia."

I removed my own earrings and put in the pearls. I stood up and hugged and kissed her. She whispered, "I got a good deal. There was a two-for-one sale!" Only my friend could get away with that and I laughed and I kissed her again.

"Mom! Put them in. Here, let me help you," and I moved around to help her.

They were dazzling.

Gwen rested her palm on David's shoulder, "Cowboy? You are one hard dude to buy for, because I think a string on a stick would satisfy you. Sandy told me that you're going back to work and when I found out your schedule, I figured out the perfect gift for a man with a working wife and a little boy."

As Gwen handed David the envelope, she said, "I still have some connections over there so enjoy these!" None of us could figure out that reference before David opened the envelope.

It was the San Francisco Giants letterhead, with seasons tickets.

"The San Francisco Giants baseball organization is honored to invite you and your guest enjoy an entire 6-seat box behind our dugout for the entire Spring Training season."

David held up the letter, "I'm stunned at how you could you do this?"

"Long story. There was a young, hotshot pitcher that baseball nation was going crazy about. He bought a giant diamond from my dad and it made all the papers which made us rich in an overnight sensation kind of way with players all over the league. Even pros from other sports were calling and flying-in to shop."

"Today, three guesses on who the pitching coach of the Giants is, nowadays? Of course, I don't know where his diamond ended up because I think he's had two wives since, but hey, he remembered us and we, him! He actually had dinner here at the house a few times."

"Your turn, Gwen," and it was Sandy. "Close your eyes, honey," and she complied. He motioned to the bartender who stepped out and returned with a leather golf bag bearing her name, with the most sought-after ladies' clubs in golf protruding from the top of the bag. To startle her, Sandy yelled, "FORE!" and her eyes opened.

We laughed and cheered, and while everyone's attention was diverted, I grabbed their present.

"As long as you're on a roll, Merry Christmas, you two!" and David held the box as Gwen removed the wrappings. She took out the two designer golf shirts and shorts and held them up, praising them. "These are *schwanky*, Olivia! Thank you!"

"Keep digging."

There were a dozen golf balls and an envelope.

"Here, Sandy. Open this please?"

Sandy slipped the paper out from the envelope.

"Gwen! It's three rounds at their country club— that gorgeous course we see from their windows at home!"

I stared at David, wondering what happened to the overnight trip and he gave me a wink that took my concern away like 'snap.'

Sandy turned his eyes toward David and me, "You don't know how difficult it is to play that course. It's challenging and very exclusive. They just don't let anyone on."

"That won't be a problem, boss," David said. "Members can't be denied and I'm going caddy and ride your cart with you with our own catered beer cart following us! The girls can ride together. It'll be fun!"

"Tomás and Elena," David said, holding up an envelope I had slipped him under the table. Please accept this with our love and friendship. Merry Christmas."

As if choreographed, each of the men rose and approached each other, meeting near Sandy's end of the table. Tomás accepted the envelope, and in euro-fashion, gave David a two-cheeked peck of gratitude.

"It's from the best wine provisioner in Scottsdale, Tomás. We hope you and Elena will find some of your favorites."

He rose and did a slight bow of deference. "My turn, David and Olivia," turning to turn-on his sexy smile at me.

"Elena thought we could do something very special for you. We would like to prepare and serve a gourmet meal for you in your home, for your family and six extra guests, or intimate with family-only or just the two of you? You and your parents while they're here? On the counter over there, is a large envelope. Elena and I developed your choice of four 7-course meals from which you may select or mix-and-match. They are the dishes we love most preparing."

Olivia and I were humbly grateful.

"Tomás, whatever David and I decide, two of the places at that table will be for you and Elena. We wouldn't have it any other way."

Gwen walked to the massive tree and reached around back to a branch to which a ribbon was tied, holding a dangling envelope.

"What you all don't know, is that Elena and Tomás met here and fell in love here, and eloped to Vegas. They never really got a honeymoon or anything. Until now. Happy Honeymoon and Merry Christmas, you two!"

Elena accepted the envelope, answering with a hug, and opened the envelope with Tomás looking on.

"OH MY GOD, GWEN," and Elena's butt found the chair in a hurry. "You CANNOT. You DID NOT do this!" Elena shrieked.

"Oh yes I can. And, OOPS! I did!" and she giggled.

It was a 12-day trip with Business-class air, an Italian Amalfi-coast cruise followed by four days at one of the most exclusive cooking schools in all of Tuscany. There was $2500 in cash in the envelope as well.

"You two have been here with me, easing the loneliness, pampering me beyond the things I ask you to do. You keep me and this place afloat. You deserve a cruise. I'll eat over at the Callan's while you're gone!"

Tomás, in shock, stared at Gwen, then wrapped Elena up in a kiss I can only describe as rivaling my David's most dramatic kisses. I got a picture of

Tomás holding her with the paper in his trailing hand.

"Don't think we've forgotten you, Bob! We all pitched in. Drum roll, please!" We all used our spoons to tap the metal chargers on the table.

"Day after tomorrow, the 26th, a chartered luxury van is picking you up and taking you to the Grand Canyon; it's 4-1/2 hours North. You have a dinner reservation for a view table at the historic El Tovar Lodge on the edge of the canyon, where you'll spend the night."

"The next morning, you'll have breakfast overlooking the canyon and then board a van to take you to your 2-hour helicopter tour of the canyon! You'll take the luxury van back and be here in Scottsdale by 7pm."

My parents looked thrilled. They wanted to see the Grand Canyon but felt there were too many other places they should see first. Further, Dad reasoned his...our canyons were beautiful enough for him.

Mom and Dad were humbled, and we applauded. After all, their presence brought on the wedding. We all felt we owed them in some significant way.

A Lazy Christmas Day

We slept-in because we decided to stay up and drink wine, wrapping gifts and making stockings into the wee hours. David lit the gas fireplace and we eventually decided to get to bed.

Dad was the first one up, and the glorious smell of cooking bacon he brought from the smokehouse at the ranch woke us all up. He had pancake batter made, an iron skillet ready for eggs. The table was set.

"Good morning, Daddy, Merry Christmas," and wiping the sleep from my eyes, I went over and hugged and kissed my dad. While hugging him, I looked over his shoulder and saw the Olivia's Meadow painting leaning against the wall on the far side of the sliding glass doors.

"You know that painting grabs my heart and attention every time I walk into this room, Daddy."

"Home is wherever your nursing and your family take you. Your spirit will always be there, in Olivia's Meadow. You owe your mother for coming up with the idea. She handed me an envelope with the photo to get it enlarged and found a Taos-area painter to make this a reality for you."

"I'm learning what a great partner David is for me in life Dad, and at almost every turn, I think we actually have that team chemistry thing that you and Mom have. We know our individual places and responsibilities, each with one foot in the huge common ground where we get life done, and the other foot committed to anchoring us to our family and responsibilities."

He was so embarrassed he changed the topic, "OJ for you? Grapefruit for you, honey?"

"Just water, please. I need to take the prenatal vitamins. I'll let my boys sleep a bit longer."

Dad and I sat at the island so he could remove and drain the bacon. He finished and washed his hands. As he was drying them, Mom came down the hallway,

"Merry Christmas, my loves," and I greeted her with a hug and kiss.

"Coffee, mom?"

"Oh, yes, thank you, honey," and Dad was already pouring it and getting some cream from the refrigerator."

"Your Dad and I would like to go to Mass, Olivia. We'd like you to come, too—Do you think David will want to?"

"Mama, the boy took an extended trip to Chimayo to explore his faith, and he returned to make a documentary for radio that aired nationwide. He'll go. If I know him? He'll want to wear his boots and hat! Plus, there's a group of Franciscan Friars at a nearby retreat center. They enlarged their worship space and I'm sure we'll find seats. I think it's at 11:30."

Dad and Mom looked at their watches, "So we leave here...when?"

"I think if we're there by eleven we'll be fine. I'll be in the baby room with Tyler, anyway."

"Ah, coincidence, that's where your mother and I will be, at Mass with our grandson," and he grinned.

I realized I almost gave away the surprise and David and Tyler shuffled into the room, but David had only seen the boots Daddy gave him.

"Merry Christmas, everyone! Did I hear Mass at the Franciscans' at 11:30?"

"That's our plan, cowboy. You in?"

"Family, Christmas, Mass, all in one? No brainer. We're there, aren't we, Tyler!"

David put Tyler down, held up his fingers and 'walked' Tyler toward the hobby horse.

"Okay, unless you want an omelet, I'm gonna put out a plate of fried eggs and big stack of flapjacks. If you want toast, that's on you!"

"Aye, aye, sir!" and Olivia saluted her dad with a grin that made him shake his head.

David nailed it when he got Mom and I the internet watches, and the one he snuck back to the store to get

Dad was worth the trip, too. David saw what he thought couldn't be anything but a boot box, but since he had already gotten a pair, he kept dismissing the notion of a 2nd pair. He was surprised.

"These are gorgeous," and he held Ty's hand as he leaned back to kiss me and kiss Mom's extended hand.

We got things cleaned up and were on track for making Mass on time.

David's phone rang, "Merry Christmas! Hey guys, let me put you on speaker, and he pantomimed 'Gwen.' On David's cue we shouted, "Merry Christmas!"

"Same! Hey I have two problems and I think you are the very people to help me out with both of them," and there was too much elation in her voice to be sharing a real 'problem.'

"I have half a ton of food bulging two commercial-sized refrigerators and no one to eat all of it."

"I'll gather as many homeless as I can and drop them off, Gwen, when do you want them there," David quipped.

"As long as you and your crew are coming and nobody has lice, get your butts here, whenever."

"Hey Gwen, I have a spiral cut ham I was going to warm and fix with all the trimmings, but it can keep. Lemme ask the family: Ham or Gwen's?" and my peeps yelled, "Gwen's!"

"Gwen, I knew the outcome before the vote," and we laughed, "I'm already craving a turkey sandwich with cranberry sauce on it! We're out of church, say, 1:15. Is 1:30 too early?"

"God know, we have leftover hors d'oeuvres and snacks and everyone can just wander into the kitchen at will. I'll have Elena get it out for us."

"Their honeymoon trip was one awesome thing you did, Gwen."

"Before you and David walked into my life, I needed those two and they were there. Now, they're beyond a support team. They've transitioned from working at and in the house to being part *of* the house."

David offered, "That's your perspective changing, Gwen."

"Quit being right, David," she said, razzing him.

"I have to get this crew moving, Gwen. 1:30-ish honey!"

"Come hungry. Please!"

The Franciscan retreat place was on property with little bungalows and lots of palm trees. Their church was modern architecture that seated almost fifteen hundred people. There was plenty of room for us in the cry-baby room. In fact, there were only four other adults and three kids in the room.

As a family, we went to Communion and walking back down the long center aisle, I was thanking Jesus for his birthday and how blessed I was in life.

We piled comfortably into the SUV, "I want to change, David. Stop by the house for a minute, honey?"

"I think I'll trade the boots for loafers, they need breaking-in."

Mom and Dad came in but kept their attire the same.

The afternoon was crystal clear, sunny and 67 degrees. As we approached Gwen's house, David laid on the horn and we soon cleared Gwen's electric gate. I smacked him, "Da-vid!"

"Five bucks she didn't hear it."

Elena answered. We rang out, "Merry Christmas" and entered the house. David said, mocking serious, "Did Gwen hear a car horn honk just now? It's important."

Elena smirked, "Impossible. She's not here! She flew out of here, pissed, because she couldn't find any of the nuts Sandy likes to snack on," and we both laughed.

"Pay up, buckwheat!" Olivia looked around me, "He lost a 5-buck bet, Elena."

"Is he good for it?"

"Probably not. But I'll take it out in trade," and I winked at her. She gave me a thumbs-up.

"I can't keep my husband out of the kitchen. He woke up and insisted on making skewers, like mini shish kabobs when he heard you were coming over. I think we're in the theater, today.

We entered a room that looked like a sports bar with six, 4-top tables plus a group of theater seats, three rows of six plush seats. The bigscreen, all 105" of it, was behind the bar.

Elena said, "Help yourself, everyone. Carbonated soft drinks, juices and mixers are in the gun, just like regular bars. I can help you with that or anything else."

David put Ty on the floor with a couple toys and he was happy. David wandered behind the bar. "What are you all havin'?" and he had drinks out probably as fast as would a professional bartender.

There was a loud knock, like knuckles on plywood, off to David's left. Elena pointed, "It's a pass window. Just unlatch it and you can slide everything Tomás hands you right onto the bar top. It's super heat resistant."

Tomás stuck his head thru the pass, "Hi everyone, Merry-merry! Here comes food!" and he wasn't kidding. The countertop was full of trays and condiments and bread and roll-baskets.

Sandy and Gwen blew in, "Welcome to Club Gwen! I don't think you've seen this room because I bet it's been five years since I've stepped foot into it."

Elena motioned to us, shaking her head, 'Eight? Ten?' holding up the corresponding fingers."

"Great to see you! Happy Yule!" and Sandy got answering sentiments as he set his grocery bag on a table.

"David! Didn't you tell me you and your dad hit a casino one day to kill some time?" and I thought Bob was going to choke on his brandy and cola because we hadn't told Ofelia. She looked unfazed.

"Just for a little while. I needed to run an errand and dropped him off, there."

Gwen walked over near a back corner of the room and hit a switch. The wall retracted and, as it did, Gwen hit an electrical switch that lit up a bank of six slot machines.

"Have at it, Bob—let me get you a bucket of tokens. We're illegal at Club Gwen's if we do real coins!" She slipped around the back bar with David and slid opened a cabinet.

"Li'l help, please? They're heavy."

David gave his dad a small galvanized bucket nearly filled with quarters. 'Tokens, my butt,' David thought, grinning.

Roberto hesitated. "I don't know…"

Gwen dismissed his hesitation with a wave, "Those machines are fun! Go ahead, Bob," and I saw my mom nod approval with a smile. My dad looked like a kid as he walked up to the middle of the bank and settled onto a stool. He was playing video poker and thoroughly enjoying himself.

"I'll make you a plate, Daddy."

"That's alright, honey, I'll come over when I need food."

"Did Olivia tell you about my big present, Sandy?"

"Not that I know of…."

"I'm cleared to go back to work!"

"Give it up, David," meaning, 'gimme a hug' and the men exchanged one, "That's as big a gift for me as it is for you."

"Do this for me, David. Call payroll so you can start at the beginning of the cycle and let me know what day you'll be in. Day or two advance notice is all I need."

"Thanks, Sandy. I'm more than ready."

Gwen walked over and sat next to Mom and chatted her up about the Grand Canyon trip. They got up, made some plates, and continued talking.

As silly as it sounds, I felt like sitting on the floor and playing with Tyler, just him and Mommy and his yellow dump truck full of colorful blocks.

Tomás bounded in, "I'm starved! I've been fixing it and now I really, really want to eat it." He dove into the turkey-bacon-tomato-onion skewers, and a couple shrimp skewers. A couple deviled eggs and some of the spinach found its way on his plate, and he laid two slices of fresh pumpernickel bread across the heaped plate as he took a seat at the end of the bar.

He called over to Dad, "Kick it's ass, Bob. Those things hate me."

Sandy fumbled with a remote and got a football game on the main screen, the 24-hour sports station on another, and a different game on the third, and sat at a table, alone.

Everyone continued to mingle, eat and drink, and I put a blanket down near the farthest corner from the slots and noise. I lay down to calm Tyler for a few minutes and he nodded-off quickly. I snuck away and joined Sandy.

"I'm going back to work, too."

"Do you feel good enough? I mean, eight hours on your feet carrying twins?"

"It'll help me get stronger, benefiting the pregnancy later when I'm the same size as the SUV."

"Nothing as beautiful as a woman with child and you know it, Olivia."

"Yep. And then there's the mom carrying twins with a 'Wide Load' sign on her butt," and we laughed.

I was curious, "How soon's your Vegas trip for the BACON-A?"

"It's always in late April. Rumor has it we're looking to add twelve to fifteen small stations to the group to expand our syndication base for programming. It includes news, too, which means more David in more markets and that's leverage for more income if he can keep drawing people in and keeping them on a member station."

"Does he know that?"

"We've done a good job of respecting the work and away-from-work boundary, Olivia. I rarely see the on-air talent, anyhow. So, no."

"Oh, then I won't mention it."

"Thank you. I didn't want to seem distant or discourteous to you on Christmas or any other time."

"We haven't even gotten our *shadows* near any form of inappropriate compromise."

I grinned cuz Sandy had set himself up, unknowingly.

Sandy looked at me, deadpan. "You fed me balls," and the deadpan changed into a wide grin.

"David and I did the unthinkable inappropriate when I was a student nurse. I risked everything and look! We got a Tyler out of the deal!"

Sandy chuckled, almost embarrassed, "Well, Olivia. David and I are hush-hush but I promise you. We'll use protection if we get to that point."

"IF you get to that point, Sandy? I'll wrap that $800 driver of yours around David's neck and grab the 3-wood to send your boys 210 yards down-range." We were rocking in our chairs, fighting tears, laughing.

David was right. Sandy was a great guy, relying on the 4-1-1 he had gotten from his beloved mentor and professor, Norm. Dammit. I forgot to remind David to call Norm.

I've been drowning my poor husband in all-things-holiday and Macias and the poor guy hasn't really gotten much David time.

I called Elena over and walked her out of Sandy's earshot.

"What're the chances David and I can sneak off for a little somethin-somethin?"

Elena threw her head back and laughed, "This place is *made* for that, Olivia." She nodded over toward her hubby, "He and I have been having sex all over this house since, like, forever."

"Think we could sneak into the grandmaster spa?"

"Door's open. Throw the towels and robes on the floor and I'll get a housekeeper to pick it up, tomorrow. If that's not enough, do him in bed. Both! Not a problem, Olivia."

"You sure?"

"Gotta scratch the itch when we can, Olivia," and we chuckled like naughty-talking high school girls.

"I need a good scratching," I murmured to her over my shoulder, "David, honey?"

He excused himself and walked over. Without a word, I took his hand and led him out and up the staircase, shooting him 'that look' all the way up. He started to speak and I whispered, "Okayed by house operations."

David stopped and kissed me just inside the suite. "Merry Christmas my love. If you hadn't figured it out, it's the best one of my life by a hundred-fold."

I stared at him as I started unbuttoning his shirt and pulled it off of his shoulders, kissing his biceps and shoulders. He was responding and replying by kissing my earlobes and down my neck as I reached for and found his belt buckle. I gave it a yank, freed it, and whispered, 'Shoes,' and he kicked them off. I knelt and reached up to slide down his jeans and boxers, helping him to step out of them. I teased him with kisses to begin watching him rise, and I stood.

I lifted my arms and his hands slipped my top and bra off in a single motion. He moved to kiss my chest and breasts and neck. He heard my breathing start going a little staccato and put his thumbs in the side of my pants. His thumbs caught my panties and both pairs went to the floor.

He pulled me into him, close as could be and we were both getting hotter. He backed me toward the bed and it was all I could do to get the comforter and top sheet pulled back when my knees found the back of the mattress. I got one push up onto the bed with my elbows before he was covering me, entering me, and lapsing into the familiar rhythm we knew would bring complete satisfaction to both of us.

The sound of my moans was bouncing off the walls and ceiling because David seemed to be driving into me with new energy and I was propelling my hips at him in sync. He reached down and started quick, pressured circles on my hot button to shorten my orgasmic fuse and the fireworks went off as we thrashed in fully-consumed passion. Still inside me, he rolled over bringing me atop.

He smiled. Me, too. We didn't need words.

When I regained enough breath control, I whispered, tenderly, "Tell you what, cowboy. I'm going in there to that jacuzzi and getting it going, cuz I think you have another round in you. Come with me and find out?"

He chuckled, realizing what I'd just said, and blushed.

"C'mon, cowboy, you're going in the trough with Mama."

We didn't end up having sex in the jacuzzi. We did end up holding each other and feeling loved by the other with nothing held back.

My lifetime love and lover said, softly, "Do we ever have to leave this jacuzzi, Olivia?"

"I dunno. Can we afford paying the babysitter overtime?"

We stayed like that a few more minutes until David helped me out and we took a quick shower.

When we got back to the theater, everyone in the room was fully engaged. Mom and Dad had roped Sandy and Gwen into playing hearts, and Elena was curled up on the couch with her head in Tomás' lap as he watched the game, running his fingertips lightly over Elena.

Mom noticed, "Your hair's wet, Olivia."

"I felt sick and had to lie down. My tummy went upside down, but I'm okay."

Now everyone had a look of concern.

"You're alright, *mija*?"

"Yeah, Mama," and I turned my attention to Gwen, "Before I left so abruptly, Elena suggested the grandmaster suite for quiet, I hope that was alright."

"Of course, honey."

David and I wandered over and tried not to make it too obvious that we were eating like starved wolves to replenish the energy we used making love. I'm sure someone noticed my pile of food, but hey, it was Christmas and they let me slide. Not a peep from anyone, nor even a glance.

I reached for a far-away roll in a basket and David put his hand sideways, up my butt.

"YEW!" It startled me and I blushed. I whispered, "What was that for?"

"Coming attraction, later.... In our *own* jacuzzi."

"You're a beast. It's on, cowboy. You, me, and the water-jets, only you're getting them where you just got me!"

"Nope. Virgin territory," he said, smugly. I grinned over my shoulder at my husband whom I loved more than the deviled egg I had stuffed in my mouth with my back to everybody, invoking the 'YO! I'm eating for THREE' rule exception to the expecting-mommy health regimen.

Goin' home time came. We helped get all the foodstuffs put back thru the pass window and got the room closed up. I asked David to take Ty and I walked all the way around to the kitchen to see if I could help there, but more, to thank Elena.

We said our goodbyes with hugs and kisses. Once on the road toward home, I looked at David and stroked the hair on his temple as he drove, "Those people are so amazing."

"I think we've made some long-time friends, Olivia, meaning Tomás and Elena, too."

"Oh, I agree. I was including them in my comment!"

Roberto's Burden

Back at home and everyone and everything settled down, Olivia helped her parents pack for their canyon excursion.

I looked up to see Bob coming down the hall toward me while I was on the floor with Tyler, playing with the train set, making the locomotive go fast then slow then fast, again. It was unusual that, when he was looking at us, at Tyler, really, he wasn't smiling.

Bob eased himself down to join us on the floor.

"All set, Bob?"

"Olivia and Ofelia made sure I am. Thank you, again, for the trip."

"You're welcome. I know you said the Payson area reminded you of Abiquiu a little bit but the rim is going to blow your mind."

"I'm sure it will," and he paused, "David, as soon as we're back here, I'm going to get an urgent call from the ranch, that I have to return immediately. You're going to make that call, David, fake it."

"I don't think I want to know where this is going, Dad, but I think I do. Prostate?"

"Yes, son," and Roberto patted me on the shoulder, got up, and wandered back down the hallway toward the master.

The doorbell rang and the van driver hustled the bags out to the van while Olivia and I walked Roberto and Ofelia out to the van. We wished them well, and sent them off with kisses, the last from Tyler holding his arms out and demanding to get himself in on some of that love from his grandmother and grandfather. We waved as the van drove off.

I took Olivia's hand to walk back into the house.

"You're a little pensive, David, like something's weighing you down. You okay?"

"Huh? Why do you say that?"

"Hmm. I'm a mom. I'm a nurse who's paid to notice changes in people. It just seems you're preoccupied, David. It shows because it's not something I see in you often—or ever, for that matter."

"No worries, I'm just quieting a few little voices in my head that I don't want or need right now.... Now, what were you asking me about the jacuzzi water temp?" and my grin convinced her of how enjoyable the next hour or so was going to be. I escaped that one, but only because she didn't press me, not because I fooled her.

Olivia and I had the house to ourselves the next thirty-or-so hours and it was revitalizing. We snuggled on the couch watching TV and streamed movies, wrestled with Tyler on the floor and bed, made a picnic lunch we enjoyed on our patio.

"I'm worried about Norman."

"Then call him, David."

"You're right," and I hit dial.

"Merry Christmas, Norman! ...Yes we had a great one. How's your mom? ...That's nothing but good news. ...Yes, the wedding was beautiful, Norm, went off without a hitch and Olivia gave me one HELLUVA gift. ...Twins! We're having twins in August! ...yeah, yeah, yeah, I'm just on a long list of people who owe you. ...Soon, I figure. Sandy wants me back in the chair and it's just getting the surgeon to sign-off on my therapy, is all. ...Yeah ...Yeah, I'm thinking a month out, maybe. When do you start back? ...That soon. ...Hey, I'll be in touch. Happy New Year, Norm. ...Will do, you, too. ...Goodbye."

"He sends his love, Olivia," and she smiled. Still, my thoughts kept going back to Roberto, wondering how he had kept it from Ofelia.

The Macias' trip time was over in a seeming flash.

Olivia and I were playing cards when Ofelia called us from the van ride home, "Oh, David, wait until you see the video of our helicopter tour. It was magnificent, so pretty, I've never seen anything like that!"

"Yes, David, and that lodge was beautiful, just beautiful. The El Tovar."

"Daddy, that's the best one, there," Olivia said over the speakerphone.

"It shows. They gave your mother and I lap quilts when we were sitting in oversized rockers on the front veranda? And I got a nice cigar at the shop, downstairs, and enjoyed it immensely!"

"I've got a nice dinner in the oven for you when you get here, but it'll keep if you want to unwind a little."

"I called because the driver said we'd be there in about 45 minutes."

"You should get a van like this, David. It's like a limo, I swear."

"I have enough mouths to feed as it is, Dad."

"I guess so, son, I guess so. Anyhow, like your mother-in-law said, we'll see you in about forty-five, son."

"Love you, Daddy."

"See you two, soon. We can't wait to see Tyler."

Olivia's skillet dinner of simmered chops and Asian rice was superb. We all went to bed with happy tummies.

As soon as Ofelia walked into the kitchen in the morning, I greeted her, excused myself from the table to use the bathroom. In the bathroom, I dialed Roberto.

Roberto was sitting right next to Olivia, so she was going to catch every word and nuance.

"Good morning, Miguel, Whatcha got? ...Dear God! ...Not your fault, not anybody's. I'll get there as quickly as I can."

I walked out of the bathroom as Roberto continued to spin the big but excusable lie.

"That was the ranch. Miguel thinks we may have a brucellosis breakout at the ranch."

"Oh, Daddy, no," Olivia said, looking troubled.

"Brucellosis?" I asked.

Bob looked at me, "It's a cow disease that humans can catch...usually spotted when we notice our cows delivering stillborn calves. Miguel thinks one of the hands may have picked it up, too."

He was shaking his head, somberly, "I have to get back," he said, turning to Ofelia. "I need to go, Ofelia, but that doesn't mean you have to. Let me get there and then you can make a reservation and come home, like, whenever. Let me get a jump on dealing with this."

Ofelia looked to Olivia who said, "He's right. Stay, Mom. You can't do anything and a reserved flight will be a fraction of the cost compared to Daddy's flight out tonight or tomorrow."

"I'll stay, Roberto," Ofelia said, agreeably.

He kissed his wife, "I'll get packed.... David? Can you get me a seat to Albuquerque, please? I'll have Miguel pick me up, there."

"Sure, Dad. I'm sorry about all of this."

I scooted into the office and logged on. There were 7 outbounds leaving Sky Harbor for Albuquerque. One was in 35 minutes. Too soon. Our place was 15 minutes from the curb and he'd need 30-minute check-in before departure. I searched.... I didn't want him on a cramped commuter jet. I found a 737 leaving in two hours and ten minutes and called the airline, requesting any seat, family-emergency basis. It was a hassle, but it got done. I was advised security screening was more involved for last-minute ticket purchases, but we'd still be okay on time, I hoped.

"Got him a seat," I told Ofelia and Olivia, understandably worrisome expressions on their faces.

"Bob!" I called from the hallway approaching the master bedroom, "I got you a seat," and I quietly closed the door to the master after I went in. He was sitting on the bed throwing the last few things into his carry-on. "I don't need my suitcase or clothes. Ofelia can bring them. I have clothes at the house."

I looked at him and would continue to look at him until he spoke.

"I'm bleeding in my pee, David. My legs are swelling, too, and I told Ofelia not to worry, I was just retaining water or something. My MD said to see him right away if those things began happening, because it means Stage IV. My legs swelled and the blood in the pee started on our trip, so I called the doctor from there. He said get in to see him."

"When Ofelia gets there, I mean, no cattle disease at the ranch?"

"And that's when I tell her, David. I beg her to forgive me for lying.... When's my flight?"

"About two hours. We leave here in an hour and fifteen minutes at the very latest, Bob. Security's gonna hassle you for no advanced reservation but we'll get you home."

He extended a hand, "Help me up, please, son," and I pulled him onto his feet. He hugged me. Then his eyes drilled holes in my own: "Soon, you will be the *padrón*, the head honcho, the head of this family and the ranch, David."

"Bob, I'm not a real strong 'stepper-upper.' I'm a utility player, team contributor. Olivia leads and I'm a great complement. That's what works with us."

"You don't know your capability until you put on that hat, David. Life can be funny that way, son. Sometimes it's a moment when life calls us to 'man-up' and we do it without hesitating. Trust me, you'll be fine."

"I dunno... But anyway, you're here, you're saying this to me, Roberto, which means you're alive and kicking. Tyler's *abuelo* is not a man who gives up on himself, ever," and it was my turn to hug him. "Let's get out there so you can calm the women's nerves." He led me down the hall, holding his carry-on and his hat.

We sat back down at the table.

"Beer, Bob?"

"Thanks, but no. I don't want to have to use the lavatory on the plane. I hate 'em."

"Good point, I hate 'em too."

We parked the SUV in a short-term lot near the runways so we could watch Bob's plane take off.

"The good news, David, is that they can get a handle on the brucellosis pretty handily, if that's what it is. I just hope we have too many hands come down with it."

I got back to the house and knew Olivia and her mom were really down in the dumps about Bob having to fly back.

Olivia's phone, rang. She said, "Thank you," burst into tears and said, "Mama, can you come out onto the patio a minute!" It couldn't be Bob because he couldn't use his phone in-flight.

The sliding glass door came open after two minutes or so, and in they came, Olivia angling to sit on my lap, with Ofelia next to me.

"David. What's tomorrow."

"The 28th"

"WRONG ANSWER, COWBOY!," and she got eerie calm, and asked or demanded(?) again.

"David. WHAT. IS. TOMORROW."

Maybe it would boost their spirits, some. I knew I had to throw in the towel and confess.

"It's my birthday. I guess that's the answer you wanted, my birthday," and she put her head on my shoulder and cried, again, whimpering, "I'm sorry. Dammit, I'm a terrible wife," and she looked to Heaven, "Sorry, God."

"I ordered your birthday cake from a cheesecake place, like ten days ago. It took them to remind me it's your birthday *tomorrow* and our son's, the following day. I'm a *shitty* mom and wife and...and..." she broke into sobs.

I cupped my hands over her ears gently to position her to look into her eyes, "You're my beautiful, loving wife, and the mother of my children and you're *not any* of those things, Olivia. And you're human, on emotional and physical overload, pregnant and between your ears? Between your ears you're trying to carry everything that's going on in our lives. Look, Tyler doesn't know it's his birthday in two days and you think I feel unloved or unwanted? Hah! My life has no context or any content without you two. I'm get my birthday wish every day that I wake up and find you and Tyler beside me."

Ofelia and I made eye contact and she said, "That's sweet and you're right, David. Olivia does that, tries to take on the whole load of her world and of those she loves," she said to Olivia with love and without reproach.

"I meant every syllable, Ofelia."

That seemed to dam-up the tears and Olivia's arms tightened around me.

Olivia's sniffles were subsiding, "If it's okay with you, I'm going to call Gwen and see if they'll at least join us for dessert. If they can come for dinner, I'd love to have them, but it's your day, David."

"I'm happy with you and Mom, honey, and the more the merrier as they say; sure, if they can make dinner or dessert-only, let's do it.... I'm curious, you ordered a cheesecake?"

"Yes. Your favorite kind of cheesecake."

"You sure? I have three favorites."

"Okay, cowboy. Tied for second are carrot cake cheesecake and plain cheesecake with strawberries. Your favorite is pumpkin cheesecake. The bakery only makes it during the holidays, so you lucked out."

I looked at Ofelia, pointing at Olivia with my thumb.

"I don't *ever* remember telling her any of that, Mom."

Olivia replied, "You remember I fed you lots of pain meds in the hospital and spent a lot of time with you, talking to you and listening to you? You told me *lots* of stuff, cowboy."

"Your memory is amazing."

"I think you mean the one in my tablet," and we laughed but Ofelia looked puzzled.

"Smaller version of a laptop computer, Ofelia," I said, and she nodded with an "Oh, okay."

During her conversation with Gwen, Olivia held up a thumb and then pantomimed eating. She finished the call and filled us in.

"We're on for dinner, too, both Gwen and Sandy, and she said she'll see if Tomás and Elena can come. I'll pick up the cheesecake unless I forget that, TOO!" and she pouted.

"Bring those pouty lips here. I'm gonna kiss 'em and turn 'em into a smile." As she closed the distance, she smiled, and I kissed her.

"He kisses you a lot, Olivia," Ofelia said, her eyes twinkling as she looked at me.

"He sure does, Mama. I kiss *him* lots, too!" Ofelia smiled, shaking her head.

"It's actually nice to see...affection... the attention you pay to each other. Roberto was too shy. It was always kind of private with us. I didn't mind, I didn't get shorted," and she chuckled and winked.

Make a Wish, Cowboy

I remembered what my father-in-law had shown me about the smoker. I hand-rubbed the prime rib, browned it in the oven, then threw it on the smoker. Back in the oven it went, or the meat would have been tomorrow's dinner.

Tomás and Elena couldn't make it, having made prior plans to go to a local club featuring a band they liked.

Sandy and Gwen brought my favorite cabernet, and had a few gifts with them.

Olivia chose romantic and intimate over a confetti-balloons-hats deal and I appreciated it. It was a candlelight dinner. It was news to me when Olivia told Gwen the flatware and china were our wedding patterns. Olivia winked at me right after she said it.

Tyler was the one in party garb, his bib, shirt and little hat all birthday themed. He sensed this was going to be fun and couldn't have been more happy or more lovable.

Sandy reached for the uncorked bottle that he'd let breathe and filled our goblets. Then, he lifted his.

"David, you've become my best friend. I see the professional you and the after-hours you and am impressed all the way around. Gwen and I think the world of you. Happy Birthday."

The cabernet was outstanding and worth whatever Sandy and Gwen had paid for it.

"My turn," Olivia declared. She rose from her chair and walked over to me, motioning that she wanted to sit on my lap. She put one arm around my neck and held out her wine glass, looking to Gwen and Sandy.

"Sandy, you're 100% right about this one. What you see is what you get.

What I got was a forever-love. I didn't regret and I don't regret giving him mine."

And then she turned to me.

"David, you are a gift to me every single day, cowboy. When I feel I don't deserve you, I remind myself that of all the beautiful and pretty and vivacious flowers in the field, you picked me. Happy birthday, my everything." She kissed me and we clinked glasses and drank the richness of the deep red, Carneros Valley cabernet sauvignon.

To complement the beef, Olivia's mom made a cauliflower casserole with sweet, not hot, green chilis that had a turkey stuffing consistency to it. Olivia made ratatouille, which I love, too. Our meal was colorful, festive-looking and mirrored the mood. The meal was epic, but I made it a point to save room for pumpkin cheesecake.

Ofelia began clearing the dishes, as Olivia said, "Gwen, gimme a hand getting the coffee going, please?" and she smooched Sandy on the cheek as she followed me into the kitchen."

Sandy and I made small talk as Ofelia made another couple passes, clearing.

The kitchen door opened with Ofelia followed by Gwen, followed by Olivia all singing 'Happy Birthday.' Olivia held the tray with the cheesecake and there was a sparkler hissing surrounded by candles around the edge of the cheesecake.

Gwen did the honors, slicing and plating the cheesecake. Olivia set it before us. Sandy got up and retrieved the two boxes they had arrived with.

I opened the first and loved what I saw. It was a canvas baby carrier with heavy duty straps that allowed you to carry your child against your chest or turn it around to carry a bigger child as if in a backpack.

"I love this!! Very thoughtful, you two. Cool, huh, honey!"

Olivia agreed, "Yep, and I'm gonna borrow it when you're not looking, too!"

Hmm, a wristwatch from McArdle's Jewelers? That was the size of the box they handed me next and even the weight seemed right. I was wrong. First, it wasn't from them and, second it wasn't a watch.

A small note was on top of the box, handwritten on a square of the wrapping paper.

"Daddy, Happy birthday. Save this for me cuz I'm gonna grow up and be a big cowboy someday, just like you. Love, Tyler"

I shook the box and the contents thunked against the insides of it.

Sandy, Gwen and Olivia were staring, ready to burst.

When I opened it, there was something that had been rolled in layer upon layer of gift tissue. It fell onto the table and I saw a Ford logo. It was a key fob.

"Wha...?"

Sandy, Gwen and Olivia laughed at my dumb-cow-stare alternating between their faces.

"Take a walk with me, cowboy?" Olivia said, holding her hand out as she stood next to me.

We went to the front door. She motioned and Sandy swung-open our front door.

It was Ford's top-of-the-line F-150, the "North Pueblo Edition 4x4" Two-tone, blue and a cream-beige, brush-guard and grille package, 20-inch wheels, exterior light bar package, and a medium cargo bed. Olivia had gotten the extended cab instead of the four-door. I used the fob and hit the unlock button and the truck lit up.

The seats were cream-colored leather, as big as any 1st class airline seat I had ever seen. There was a big center console and an instrument and electronics panel screen that was probably going to take a week or more to figure out.

I turned around and saw all three cellphones pointed at me, taking pictures.

"Sandy picked it up. I bought it over the phone like you taught me honey! We saved a bunch. The extended cab opens out from the inside. That back seat's plenty big enough for car seats and Tyler's is already in there!"

Olivia held Tyler up to her ear and had an animated expression. "Yes, Tyler? ...uh huh. Okay, I'll ask him." She turned to me.

"Your son wants to know if you like his present?"

"I love it, little-me. And your mommy, too."

"WAIT!" and Olivia again held Tyler to her ear.

"He said, 'What's your deal, Dad! We wanna RIDE in that bad boy," and Olivia took on a 'Well, why not?' expression.

"Let's do it!"

Olivia threw the house keys to Sandy who pulled our front door shut.

Olivia said, "How 'bout you and David and Gwen up front, Mom and me will sit with Tyler in back! I'll be getting plenty of up-front time. I insist."

I folded up the console so Gwen could sit with Sandy and me in front. The odometer had 14 miles on it at our front curb. Tyler was sound asleep when we got home, and the odometer had recorded 81 miles.

It had an incredible ride, as comfortable as any luxury sedan on the road. For what I'm sure Olivia paid for it, it better drive and ride like a dream and it *was* unlike anything I'd ever driven or ridden in. I got my Ford. My son got me my Ford truck.

Once back in the house, we put Tyler down and returned to the table to finish the cabernet.

I could only shake my head as Olivia thanked David and Gwen for being in on the truck surprise and getting it to the house.

Olivia said, "I like the blue way better but the North Pueblo 4x4 comes in red, too. Honey, I ordered a second one in red for Tyler's birthday, tomorrow, so you boys can share if you want to."

Everyone howled.

Gwen looked over, "I tell ya what, my place tomorrow for Tyler's birthday. Can do?"

I spoke up, "Unless Olivia has a plan...?" and she shook her head.

"Nothing in concrete, no. That would be nice, Gwen."

"Tomás can make a little cake, something specifically for Tyler to eat. You hungry for anything, special, Sandy?"

"Only attention," which drew chuckles, "I'm happy with anything."

"Come anytime, we'll eat at six. I have a shipment coming in early tomorrow so I have to head on home and get some sleep," and we thanked them profusely and saw them off.

"C'mere, cowboy."

"Yeah, cowgirl?"

"You really love your blue truck, David?"

"I don't remember having a toy truck as a kid, Olivia. I fixated on them. So, do I love it? Over the top, baby! Of course I do."

"There was a 4-door, but it was too long for the garage, honey.... You sure the extended cab is going to be okay?"

"Oh my God, yes, Olivia. You saw how there was plenty of room for all of us. I don't think any pickup looks like a truck if it has four doors. It's perfect."

"And?"

"And can I show you my gratitude in bed?"

"And?"

"And I've never had a better birthday. Even without the gifts. The ambiance, the meal, the love, the company. You always get it right with me, Olivia."

"It's not difficult. You're not difficult. You're not demanding or self-centered, David. It's easy.... Now, where did you say you'd like to thank me?" and David took his index finger and gently touched me in about five different places.

Tyler's Birthday

We got to Gwen's around four knowing it was no big deal getting there two hours before dinner. We arrived in style, in my truck, having stopped to top of the tank—which is when and where I discovered it had dual gas tanks. I ended the fill-up, got in, started the engine and an LED indicator read "Tank 1 Full. Tank 2 has 3 gallons." Olivia pulled the owner's manual and explained how to do the switch-over and I put another 23 gallons of premium in the newest pride and joy in my collection.

Sandy answered the door and complimented me on the carrier in which I had placed Tyler, facing me. It was my birthday present from him and Gwen.

"Gwen thought the garden dining room would be nice, and I love it."

"It's beautiful and fine, Sandy," and Olivia teased me, "David likes staring at the rainbows the sprinklers make."

"Yep. Tyler does, too. Isn't that right!" and Tyler yelped at the attention to him and grinned.

"We thought we'd have drinks around the kitchen island and carry them into the dining room when it was time to eat."

"Sounds like a plan," Olivia said.

Approaching the kitchen, we could tell seafood was the entrée of the evening.

"The Callans! Get in here and hug me!" bellowed Gwen.

We did, and I leaned down to let Tyler 'smooch' Gwen, but he wanted to go to her, extended his arms.

"I think he's taking a shine to me, David!"

"I think he's a cad, chases hot women who have money... You better watch your back, Sandy!" and they laughed at my humor.

"Where are Elena and Tomás?"

"In the apartment, changing. Dinner's in the oven and fridge, and Tyler's cake... well, I won't spoil the surprise."

"Wine? Beer? Cocktail? Name your poison," Sandy said.

Olivia asked for an OJ with a splash of soda water. I felt like a rum and Coke, probably from my subconscious memory that Roberto likes them. He was on my mind more than I could let on. That made me change my mind about the drink.

Gwen said, "I'm living large tonight, Sandy. I want a champagne cocktail. Mind getting a bottle? I'm sure there's some chilled in the back bar of the theater."

"I think I'll join Gwen with one of those, too," I said, "I'm drinking bubbly for my son, vicariously."

"Back in a flash," and he was, and nearly nailed me with the cork as it launched from the lip of the bottle of brut. He had the presence of mind to grab the sugar cubes and bitters from the bar and brought them, saturating the sugar cubes in bitters before dropping them into the filled champagne stems. It was the original champagne cocktail recipe and I admit I'd never had one like this but sure liked it.

Tomás and Elena came in, Tomás in a white cable-knit sweater and denims, wearing loafers without socks. Elena was in a flower-print dress with a scoop neck, a simple gold chain and gold studs in her ears. She wore white dress sandals.

"Hello all," Tomás greeted, "...and happy birthday, little Tyler! Oh my goodness, he's growing so fast!"

Sandy said, "What would you like to drink?"

"Mmm, tea, I think. Elena brewed some sun tea today and I think that's good for me." Elena moved to the cabinets and got two tumblers, setting them on the island before retrieving the pitcher of tea from the refrigerator. She iced and filled the tumblers. They toasted us and Tyler.

"I heard your husband had to fly back to work, Mrs. Macias," Elena said to Ofelia.

"Yes, it may be a serious thing at the ranch. I'm going home, tomorrow."

"Elena and I are sorry to hear that," Tomás said, "which makes me glad that I made such a special dinner for us, tonight. At least, I think it's special. I'll handle the dish from the oven, but even with drinks, I think we can manage the other food in the refrigerator and only make one trip. Please?"

We removed salads, a tray of antipasto and two of chilled, sliced vegetables in different marinades. David followed, wearing oven mitts, with a ceramic baking platter with an entire red snapper, filleted, and with tomatoes, onions, butter and wine, and other seasonings. It looked and smelled out of this world.

Elena engaged me, holding out an envelope, "Happy Birthday, David. I'm sorry we couldn't join you last night," and she pecked me on the cheek.

I opened the nice card and found a gift certificate for five premium visits to the local car wash.

"This is so thoughtful! So you know about the truck Tyler gave me!"

"Actually," Tomás said, "we saw it before you did. I gave Sandy a ride over to the dealership to pick it up for you. It's very, very nice!"

"Thanks to you and Elena, I'll be keeping it that way. Thank you."

We settled at the table.

Tomás said, "I didn't know you were leaving tomorrow, Ofelia, but I chose to make this with you in mind. In Spanish, its *Huachinango Veracruz*, which means red snapper Veracruz-style, baked in wine with seasoning and a few vegetables. Veracruz is one of the busiest fishing ports in all of Mexico and I would say this recipe rivals the best fish I've ever eaten! There, they pride themselves on preparing fish in many special ways. Enjoy, everyone!"

He was right. It was the best fish I had ever eaten, and Olivia said she'd never had better seafood. We told Tomás so. Tyler ate all we gave him and wanted more.

"It's flown in, and I picked it up, today. You'd have to go to Mexico and catch a snapper to get it any fresher."

We finished dinner and Gwen asked, "Tomás and I thought we could have dessert in the kitchen. Is that okay?"

"After all this? Of course," and we all helped with the clearing and wiping-up of the garden dining room.

We descended upon the kitchen island.

"Mr. Tyler gets the birthday-boy special dessert, and I have something else for the adults."

Elena and he moved to the freezer and removed four parfait glasses containing orange and yellow sherbet-looking scoops. As Elena set each in front of us, Tomás revealed a bottle of Cointreau and eyeballed the measure to drizzle over what he explained were mango and pineapple ices. There were vanilla wafers around the edges of the rims.

Tomás moved to the refrigerator and pulled out what must have been a 6"-high layered cake topped with one blue candle.

"For Mr. Tyler, we have sponge cake layered with freshly mashed bananas flavored with peanut butter in a sugarless whipped cream, and if you say he's allergic to peanuts, I'm going to cry. I'm sorry, I should have asked...."

"He loves peanut butter, Tomás," Olivia beamed.

"May I have the honor of giving him the 1st spoonful?"

Olivia nodded, "Sure! I think you earned it!"

Our cellphones came out to capture the moment with video and stills.

Tomás spooned-out a perfect bite-size for Tyler and we all started singing *Happy Birthday*. Tyler opened his mouth and when he tasted his birthday cake, went nuts. He loved it, and we all laughed. Tomás yielded the spoon to Olivia, and I held him as she fed him his cake.

Then, as only Tomás could to make the moment grander, he revealed more spoons, and had us adults open our mouths as he fed us each a heaping teaspoon, and it was glorious. "He must learn his birthday cake is for sharing," and he winked and chuckled.

"Presents! We need presents!" It was Gwen, who momentarily disappeared with Sandy. They reentered, sliding a deluxe, 8-foot rectangular baby pool, molded plastic and fancy, that would hold about 10" of water for baby to splash-in out on our patio. "Now you don't have to get in the tub or turn on the jacuzzi to play in the water with him. It's from Elena, Tomás, Sandy and me." We applauded.

"Olivia and I are giving his bedroom a makeover, converting it from an infant's room into a little boy's bedroom!"

"That sounds like fun, you two!"

"It seems the thing to do as he transitions to toddler. And yes, we're deciding on one of the hundreds of themes that little boys' bedrooms can be based upon."

"If it's anything but a Western theme, I'll be surprised," Gwen said.

"Safe bet, Gwen," I ventured, smiling over at Olivia and winking at my bride.

It was getting late, and they had really put on the dog to show us a nice time. Since she was leaving for New Mexico, Ofelia got extra-special attention before getting into the backseat of the truck with Tyler.

Awful Truth

Ofelia left, tearfully. She didn't want to hand Tyler back to Olivia and me and I couldn't blame her. Tyler had gotten to know and love her, and God knows she had showered him with love and attention at every opportunity, even singing him to sleep some nights in our room.

I got a text.

"Please tell Olivia while Ofelia's on the plane so she can't call. It's bad. I love you, son. Call you soon."

"Where you be, oh, wife of mine?"

"Laundry!"

"Okay, kitchen when you're done there, please?"

"Minute or two..."

I had Viuda de Romero on the table, limes cut, salt handy, and two glasses that could accommodate double-shots. I heard her before I saw her.

"What's all this?" she asked, as I patted my lap and she lowered herself onto it.

"First, we drink, then I talk," and I tried to sound calm and even, no emotion, not bossy.

"But..." and she patted her tummy.

"We drink." That drew a long look.

"To us," and I raised my glass.

She sipped and I shook my head, "Down the hatch."

She finished.

"Again," and I poured as she finished chewing the lime from its rind.

Again, the long look.

"Olivia," I was gripping both of her hands, "your dad is sick," and her eyes widened, "very sick," and her lower lip jutted out and she began to weep, "Cancer? What?"

"Prostate, Stage IV."

"Oh, David. Oh, no, Daddy...my Daddy" and she sobbed falling into and burying her face into my shoulder.

"When he left, it wasn't brucellosis. His symptoms worsened at the Grand Canyon and his doc told him to get home. I was in on the lie and the cover-up, honey, and I'm sorry. He swore me to secrecy and I respected his wishes. He wanted you to know on his terms and his time."

She was nodding, so I knew she understood.

"I had to tell you right now, while your mom's on the plane, because he wanted you to hear it from me, not a call from your mom or him. He'll tell her as soon as he gets her home. We'll call if we don't hear from them."

She pulled away to look at me, "What are we going to _do_, David!"

"Anything and everything we can, right, cowgirl?"

She used my sleeve to wipe away tears from each eye.

"Right answer, cowboy."

"And?"

"And shower them with love."

"And?"

"And I need to know if you forgive me for lying—it's been eating a hole in my gut, Olivia."

She held my cheeks with her soft hands.

"My dad asked you to protect me, look out for me, and you've never failed to do that. Forgive you? How can I _ever_ hold that against you."

I kissed her lightly on the lips and she opened her mouth and our kiss went on for a minute. When I looked at her, her eyes were dry but...glassy?

Eek, I'd just given my wife two double-tequilas. She was woozy. I moved my legs and she knew to stand up as much as I knew to make sure I had ahold of her.

"Woo! Whoa! I think you got me drunk, cowboy!"

"Guilty as charged," and I scooped her up, "and now were going back to our normal bed and cuddle with Tyler."

I put her in bed and got Tyler out of his rolling-walker seat and brought him into the bed between us. Together. It's how we'd get through life.

We spent a quiet New Year's Eve and Day with Gwen, Sandy, Tomás and Elena. Gwen had gotten us party horns, and we watched the New York City ball drop for the mansion's theater/club.

Tomás told us he was going to fix something 'simple' but filling for New Year's Day and our football watching. It was a whole salmon, stuffed with crabmeat. The guy deserved his own restaurant. What he had was a good life and was content with it. Why bother, I guess he thought.

Now more than ever, Olivia and I wanted and needed to latch onto something energizing, as in work.

I intentionally called H.R. on a Wednesday and told them Sandy Tuttle wanted me to report back to work on the first day of the next pay cycle. I figured it may be the following Monday and was correct.

When Olivia called, the chief nurse offered to let Olivia come in and look at the schedule so she could pick and choose among the available shifts. She wanted orthopedics, but if the only thing available there was graveyard shifts? Not a good prospect, I thought, but she'd see what was available and assured me she'd choose Tyler and me over a schedule that would make our family life complete topsy-turvy.

She reminded me, in her and our favor, there was a continuing national shortage of registered nurses and Olivia's permanent status at the hospital would override the shift preference of any temporary or traveling RN.

Peds. Pediatrics. It was the best schedule fit for us and how fitting for a mom carrying twins. She bumped two nurses onto working weekends, and landed 7am-3:30 shifts with weekends off.

Olivia picked up her phone.

"Hey, glamour girl! Wanna go clothes shopping with me?"

It had to be Gwen.

"I need to by some blimp-sized scrubs. It'll be fun because I'm going to be working pediatrics and there are

all kinds of cute and crazy patterned scrubs for peds
people, with Pooh-bear, balloons, purple dinosaurs.
...Yes, I start Monday. David does, too..."

On the Jobs

"...and the 101 merge with 17 North is clear. Time for news with my buddy-ole-pal, David Tyler, just back from his bone-crunch and baby-making vacation. All yours, Studley Dudley."

Of course, she'd say that on the air, but I got through it and the up-to-the-minute news.

"...and those are your top-of-the-hour headlines, David Tyler, KFCG. A personal note to all of you. I got bags and bags of get well wishes and cards from you after I got hurt. I could feel the love, you guys! So much, that I'm gonna share something with you. For Christmas, Santa brought my wife and I twins, who will arrive in August. So, keep listening and help me through this, guys!"

Being back in the saddle was the world. I felt worthwhile as a work-human, grateful I got paid for what I did and where I did it. I didn't have any post production to do, and when I got back to my cubicle, there was a sticky-note on my phone, 'Conference II, 1:45. Short meeting.' I could still be out of there and home before Olivia and Tyler, who'd be home by 4pm. Conference II was the huge conference room. This must be more than just me or the on-air talent.

Everyone yelled, "WOO-HOO! SURPRISE!" There were streamers, a cake, a huge banner, 'Welcome Back David' and people from different departments came up to welcome me back and congratulate me on the wedding and the twins. There was a baby-swing designed for twins, set up in the corner of the room with a huge ribbon. There was a big box in the corner, plain white wrap with a white silk bow. It was a green-blue down comforter and an expensive set of 800 thread-count designer sheets with green-blue swirls on a light blue background.

"I'm humbled, everybody. I have been through a lot since I saw all of you and I held onto one thing—well, other than Olivia—and it's you, my FCG family. I dunno what to say. Nothing but thank you," and I waved.

Sandy and Chuck helped me get the swing folded up and down to the truck along with the linens, which I put into the cab with the card and without the box. Chuck headed back inside and Sandy walked me to the driver's door.

"Gwen told me about Roberto, David. I'm so sorry."

"I have no idea how long he's got. Olivia may do a weekend turnaround to the ranch, just to let them know we're there for them. It won't affect my shift, Sandy."

"Would you be offended if Gwen and I went up to see them, sometime? Even if our visit time's limited, we could chase golf balls around some of the nice courses they have in the area."

"Offended? Not at all. They love you guys. Olivia can tell you the nicer accommodations around Abiquiu and Taos. Some are mighty nice, in fact. But I think you may have a fight on your hands about not staying at Roberto's."

"I'd feel better if we could come and go. Besides, Gwen's been taking golf lessons, one-on-one with a pro, is in a group lesson, and loves to go hit balls at the range! Oh, and be sure to tell Olivia she loves the outfits."

"Took to golf like a duck to water, huh?"

"Well, like a duck to a water *hazard* at this point but she really does love it. I think it's the first time she's ever had a suntan," and we laughed. He shook my hand and I zoomed off toward home and a crockpot dinner I would concoct in my head, enroute.

Short-ribs and some dry rub went into the slow cooker. Fresh broccoli and parslied potatoes would be an okay meal, along with using up the little salad fixins' we had.

I heard the garage door and opened the kitchen door, stepping up to get Tyler out of his seatbelts. "Hey, tiger!

Daddy missed you," and he beat on my forehead with his fist, yammering undecipherable baby-speak.

Olivia walked around the hood, "Hey, handsome," and I bent down to kiss her.

"Good day?"

"I'll tell you, inside."

I told her the menu and she thought it sounded delicious.

She sat down with an 'ooph,' and I said, "I have a non-alcoholic fixer-upper for you!" and I grabbed some soda water, a 7up and some homemade lime sherbet we'd made with our wedding gift from the Trangs. It was ice-cold, frothy, fizzy and looked so good I made myself one, too, and sat down with Olivia.

"Ooh, yum. Good, David," and Tyler was begging for sips of Mommy's cup, which he got. "Yummy, huh, Ty!"

"So, work. I love it, David. Not just because it's babies but because of the nursing care. I'm challenged. I think I could be damned good at pediatrics."

"Which would surprise no one, honey. You're a super-achiever because you work at it. Seeing yourself get better at something refuels you to keep on and on... Did it occur to you that you might like it long-term, I mean, it's way early, but did the inkling cross your mind?"

"I think so," and she laughed, "I have the clothes for it. The kick-ass scrubs I got, eight sets? They last, and I dunno about Pooh-bear or Disney princesses on the orthopedics ward. I know I like it now and probably would, later. Time will tell, honey. How are things at KFCG?"

"They threw me a little surprise thing in the conference room. On our bed, you'll find they got us a beautiful goose-down comforter and sheets to match. In Tyler's room, there's a contraption that, when unfolded, turns into a double baby swing for a set of twins. They had cake and everything. Blew me away!"

"Hmm, somebody besides me loves you?"

"I wouldn't go that far. I'll say 'appreciates' and maybe 'missed.' Oh, and Chuck and Sandy send their love."

"How are they doing?"

"Gwen's now a golf aficionado, playing and practicing anytime she can. And Sandy pulled me aside and said they'd like to get up to Abiquiu and see your dad."

"Aww, really?"

"Yeah, I told him we'd probably do a weekend turnaround soon as we could, and he mentioned going, sometime."

"Hear me out on this David. I'd rather have them up there sooner than later when Daddy's in really bad shape. I'd be fine with them going when we do. There's room in the hacienda."

"I'm fine with everything up to the accommodations. They need to be in a hotel, somewhere. Sandy mentioned they'd be golfing when not cruising around the area. I, personally, want quiet time with you and your mom and dad, Olivia. Just us, just family."

She cocked her head and smiled, "Um-kay. Done deal," and kissed her index finger before putting it on the tip of my nose.

Dinner was surprisingly good. We decided to try the new sheets and comforter on our bed. Olivia pulled a thin nightie over her head, and I was in a pair of tighty-whities when I slipped into bed.

We looked at each other and, in unison, said, "Wow." The sheets made it feel like we'd bought a new mattress. My girl was on her side as was I, just looking at each other.

"Life's good, David. Even when it's bad, it's good with you."

"It's because I have someone filling my world with love and my heart with happiness, so keep it up, cowgirl," and I smiled as I kissed her.

The next couple of weeks were unremarkable. We were in contact with Roberto and Ofelia every day or two.

Roberto had slashed his hours at the ranch, choosing to run things from his 'hacienda' as he called it.

Settling Up

I walked in from work, threw my keys on the island, popped the top on a soft drink, and my phone rang. My caller ID said "Bike Lawyer." The attorney calling about the progress on his case for my motorcycle wreck.

We exchanged amenities.

"David, here's what we got. And it's good. Very good."

"I'm all ears."

"We located and deposed the eyewitness who said you ran the stop sign. He had been in a bar over three hours when he gave his statement. So we subpoenaed all of the city and private business security cameras' video."

"What did that look like?"

"Seeing you get hit, fly through the air and slam onto the sidewalk wasn't pretty…pretty sickening, in fact. First, you didn't run the stop sign. You made a legal stop. Second, when you pulled out, you got hit by a distracted driver on a cellphone. Here's the payoff. It's true your bike was run over by a city water truck, right? But the vehicle in front of that truck is the one who hit you, a city water crew vehicle going to a site with the water tanker that was following it. We filed suit against the city and were legally required to show them what we had as far as evidence."

"And?"

"And how does two-point-six million dollars sound to you, which, if you accept the settlement, comes to $1,099,280. That figure is money in your pocket after our fees and expenses."

"I think I just peed my pants, counselor."

He laughed, "A drunk witness can lie or be confused, but the video doesn't lie. We had them hands-down. That represents damages to the bike, your pain and suffering, and monies so that you can afford any additional therapies or meds related to the injuries you received."

"I'm numb between the ears. So how does this happen?"

"Come in, sign papers and we cut you the check right then and there, knowing the city must and will cut the full amount payable to us with the power of attorney you gave us. When you walk in here, you'll walk out with almost a million-one-hundred thousand bucks in your pocket, David."

"Holy God."

"David? You deserve it. They hurt you, big time. So it was a big-time award. When are you coming in, because," and he started to laugh, "my wife wants me to get paid, too!"

"Uhm...tomorrow?"

"Has to be first thing, I'm in court from 11am on."

"8?"

"For us, 7am is first thing. Is 7am doable?"

"It's worth it. 7am it is. Thank you for all you've done. My wife's gonna shit."

"As your legal counsel, I strongly suggest flowers for her and something big for her, later," and we laughed.

"See you at seven."

I phoned Sandy, immediately.

"I need a sub in the morning. It's urgent but not bad. In fact, it's good."

"It better be good, David. Humor me."

"Calling my bluff, Sandy? Okay, but you absolutely cannot tell Olivia or Gwen."

"This is work-Sandy. Speak."

"Motorcycle wreck settlement. I'm picking up over a million in cash at the attorney's office at 7am." The pause was so long I looked to see if we were connected.

"Command decision, here. Take the day. Stephanie's got this for you."

"You're tops, Sandy, thanks."

"Strictly business, David. I take care of my peeps and you know you're one of them."

"Thanks, boss."

"Don't spend it all in one place."

"I already have. Don't tell Olivia."

The next morning, I kissed my sleeping bride and left for work long before sun-up as usual. Unlike usual, I had the day off and hours to kill, so I went to the lawyer's office building and parked. I reclined my truck seat, set an alarm, and slept like a baby until 6am.

I fired up the truck and found an espresso place with hot breakfast croissants. I sat and people-watched as I ate. About quarter-till, I opened the door and set my espresso in the cup holder.

Precisely at 7, I presented myself at the desk and was immediately shown into a conference room with a fat folder on the table and a grinning attorney sitting behind it. He rose and we shook hands.

"You're getting around better than I thought you would having seen that accident on video from three different camera angles."

"Something I never want to see."

"You saved me the trouble of offering. Down to business. You signed all the necessary forms with us. The only signatures this morning acknowledge receipt of the settlement and acknowledge that the case is closed as is our professional services contract with you in the matter." He spun two forms around that he had retrieved from the folder and took out an 18kt gold pen, "Here you go."

I signed them and handed him the pen.

"That pen's a personal thank you from me, David. Please keep it. You trusted an extremely important aspect of your life to me and we were both fortunate." He rose and extended his hand. "Thanks."

He handed me an envelope, "The check. Good luck to you, David."

I waited until I got to the truck to open the envelope, and my hand was shaking. Just like the man said: "Pay to the Order of David Callan... $1,099,280 and 00/100ths Dollars." My knees shook. I checked my phone to make sure there was no message from Olivia wondering why I wasn't on the air. Whew. All clear.

It was going on 8am. I drove to the bank where Olivia's and now my shared account was. I pulled out my ID and set it and the check on the counter when I got to the window. The teller's eyes almost fell out.

"I'd like to use this for two things. First, pay off the balance of our home loan." It took like no time at all.

"Okay, $173,251.15 applied to retire the loan. Your payoff will come to your home address, with a copy of the deed showing your home is free and clear. And next?"

"Pay off the balance of the truck we just bought."

"Just a moment, please... Alright, $58,588.90 retires that loan. You'll get your clear title in the mail in about 3 weeks, Mr. Callan."

"How much do I have left of this check?"

"$867,439.95, sir."

"Deposit that and cut a check for the same amount, payable to Olivia Callan, please."

"It'll take a just a couple minutes, Mr. Callan."

"That's fine. Where's your restroom?"

"To your left. I'll put the closed sign on my window so you can come right back to it."

On my way back, I skirted the stand-up desk with the blank bank forms and pens as you enter. It gave me an idea.

The teller and I arrived at the window at the same time.

"Please make sure the check matches the number I wrote down."

"Exactly. It's $867,439.95."

"Here you are," and she grabbed an envelope.

"May I have two more envelopes, please," and she slid them to me.

"Here you are. And Mr. Callan?"

"Yes," and I scrambled to find her name badge, "Cindi?"

"I was wondering why you weren't on the air this morning when I commuted to work. I live all the way out in Cave Creek, a long way from here, and love KFCG!"

She was all of nineteen, freckled, sweet, and made me blush.

"Shhh. I'm playing hooky, today, Cindi."

"Tell you what," and I reached for my wallet and retrieved a business card with my 'David Tyler' email.

"Shoot me an e-mail. In the subject line, type the word 'Payoff' so I'll know it's you. The next time we sponsor a big-named country artist, you've got two tickets—but for a price, and that price is this: Let me be Callan and stay Callan in your branch."

As hard as it must have been for her, she put on a serious face, "Of course, why would I call you anything else, Mr. Callan," and she winked. Damn cute. The world needed more like Cindi and we could use more listeners like her, too. She was fighting the urge to squeal and jump up and down. We were both floating on air as I walked toward the doors to my now-paid-off truck.
I stopped at the lobby desk and put down the three envelopes. On the one with Olivia's check in it, I used the gold pen to write, "You" in huge letters. On another empty envelope's front, I wrote, "I" and on the front of the next, "Love."

I wrote a note for the "I" envelope, "Our house is paid off." I wrote the note for the 'Love' envelope, "The new Ford's paid off." I added a note to the third envelope, "This is all yours, as am I. Every single penny. It's what's left over from the motorcycle settlement. xox David."

I cranked-up the rock and roll on the truck's kick-ass sound system, caught the loop and headed for the hospital. I'd never been up to pediatrics and only kind of knew what wing but not the floor where it was located. On arrival at the front desk, they directed me.

I practically waltzed down the gleaming floors and encountered double doors, "Authorized Visitors Only. Ring Bell." When the door opened, Olivia and I were both startled to see each other, and I smooched her.
"Surprise!" I gave her a little flower arrangement from the hospital gift shop in the lobby.

"You okay, honey?"

"I needed a day off for the love of my life!"

"Let me introduce you and show you the ward! Golly, this is so cool, David!"

She walked me around, politely introducing me and the last stop was the glass-windowed newborn nursery where it looked to be filled to capacity.

"Back row, see? Twins! Both boys, born last night!" I said, "You know I only love you all the more, now, right?"

"Back atcha, cowboy."

"Any chance we can sit down for a water or soft drink or something?"

"No prob. We take at-will breaks here; it's not real structured. The nurse's lounge is this way."

I was glad it was empty. We sat and I pulled out the 3 envelopes. She couldn't see what was on them.

"It's your lucky day," and I set them on table in front of her in "*I Love You*" order.

"Olivia, I love it when you read to me. Will you?" Delight was dancing in her eyes from sensing my level of excitement. She ripped open the end of the first envelope and retrieved the note, reading aloud:

"*Our house is paid off.*" She was really puzzled and started at me a second.

"Go on, honey. Envelope 2."

"*The new Ford's paid off.*"

Now she was shaking her head like, 'How?' and 'What the hell?' Without any urging, she tore the end of the 'You' envelope, reading aloud,

"*This is all yours, as am I. Every single penny. It's what's left over from the motorcycle settlement. xox David.*"

Olivia put her arm on the table and her forehead on the arm, weeping. She looked up at me, held up her index finger as in 'just a second,' scooped her cellphone from her pocket, dialed and put it on speaker.

"Olivia, it's a workday. You okay?"

"Not sure, Gwen, and David can hear you. We're on speaker."

"Is HE okay? Isn't he supposed to be on-air now?"

"Seems his boss found a good reason to give him the day off."

"Like?"

"Like, I think he and I both need to have our heads examined. Me? Because I'm so crazy in love with him. And him? Gwen? He just handed me a check, payable to me, with a note, *'This is all yours, as am I. It's what's left over from the motorcycle settlement. xox David."*

"Jesus, how much was the damn check."

"Only $867,439.95"

"HE HANDED YOU A PERSONAL CHECK FOR ALMOST A MILLION DOLLARS, OLIVIA!??"
"That, he did, Gwen."

"David?"

I had to stop laughing before I answered.

"Yes, dear Gwen."

"You have lost your mind, haven't you."

"Nope."

"You're sitting there laughing your ass off! You nearly got killed, could have been killed in that wreck!"

"That's right and it's the reason I'm laughing. Neither of you got it because of the staggering amount of the check. See if this makes sense. When that truck hit me, it sent me to the only place in the world I could meet Olivia, the love of my life and mother of my child, and soon, children. Without getting nearly killed, I would never have met her. You can't put a dollar amount on that."

"Oh Jesus Christ, now I'm bawling at work, David. Thanks."

Olivia was losing her battle holding back tears, "So am I, Gwen. See? See how he is?"

Sure enough, Olivia was bawling, too.

"I have to get my shit together. I have other people's kids to take care of."

"Well thank you for including me in your big news! Now that you're rich, Olivia, call me if you decide to leave him and I'll rent you a room!" and the unexpected joke turned from tears of joy to nonstop laughter.

"I need to work. Love you guys! Thanks for including me!"

I answered for Olivia, "We love you, too, Gwen," and Olivia hung up and stood up. With no one around, she kissed me with everything she had.

"I think I can suddenly afford to take you out on a dinner date tonight, cowboy. How about it? It would sure make this cowgirl mighty happy."

"Since you put it like that, sure."

"I'll pick up Tyler and take him, now, so you don' have to, honey." I kissed her, she pocketed her phone, we walked out of the lounge hand-in-hand.

I heard the garage door opening. I poured Olivia and I a glass of wine. There were five dozen red roses on the table when she walked in.

Her eyes got as big as saucers. I shrugged, "I've got a dinner date. Figured I'd get her some flowers."

Olivia waked to the table, grabbed a stem and turned to give me a kiss.

"They're awesome, honey. Let me get out of my scrubs," and she kissed Tyler before hurrying down the hallway.

She came out in jeans, barefooted, and a casual top, "Mommy's all better, now!" and she walked to Tyler who wanted to be held. She picked up her wine and kissed me.

"Gwen called me later in the day, about what you said? About the settlement coming from the wreck that brought us together?"

"And what did she come up with?"

"Oh, more tears. We talked about how some things can start out so bleak and then change into something blindingly bright and positive."

"Tyler and I talked about girls all day. I was explaining how fun it is to love them and surprise them and spoil them. And what a hot mommy he has. He liked that, big time," and Olivia blushed.

"Please remember to tell me that when our twins add fifty pounds to this frame, cowboy."

"I will and I'll be telling the truth. Once, you apologized to me. You were embarrassed because you thought your boobs were too small. Do you remember what I told you, because I do and it still stands."

She was quiet, listening.

"I told you I loved Olivia the girl, the entire package and not just a collection of isolated parts. That won't change." I smiled.

"If I don't go to our room and get ready for my dinner date this minute, we're never going to make it, because I'm wanting to jump your bones this instant, cowboy."

"We need energy, food, for that kind of thing, don't we Tyler!"

She went bounding down the hall and I followed with Tyler. I already had a pair of slacks and shirt on a hanger, figuring we'd be hitting one of Scottsdale's top dinner houses.

It was a Brazilian steak house that kept bringing platter after platter of assorted, grilled meats. The wine list was extensive, the dinner crowd was well monied, and the bill reflected the fine dining establishment it proved to be and lived up to the reputation it enjoyed.

Convergence

Three weeks later, David and Gwen were strapped into the seats in front of us when the 737's wheels lifted off the Phoenix runway. Just over an hour later, we touched down in Albuquerque and Sandy picked up the rented luxury sedan he'd gotten with all of his travelers' bonus miles. It was 80 minutes to Abiquiu at five miles an hour over the speed limit.

I called Mama from the car and gave her our ETA, 1030am. We didn't talk much. She told us that she'd listen for us but that a nurse's aide might open the door for us.

"I still have keys, Mama. If it's okay, we'll just let ourselves in," and Ofelia told Olivia which bedrooms we'd occupy.

'Hacienda' was the right word for the sprawling, 1-storey Spanish-style adobe home of 3,700 square feet that Roberto had built. Sandy pulled up right in front of the hand-carved double doors. Opposite the doors, was a circular garden and fountain that was larger than our jacuzzi. Sandy dropped us and our bags off at the hacienda and continued to their hotel.

Just inside, Ofelia met and kissed and hugged us. I grabbed one suitcase and the portable playpen and followed Ofelia and Olivia, arm in harm, down a tiled hall.

Ofelia opened a door and Olivia said, "MAMA!"

It was a nursery. Two cribs. Chest of drawers. Linen chest on the floor against a toy chest that matched. The lower wall was paint, with nursery wallpaper going to the ceiling.

"It's all your dad's doing, Olivia. He insisted. Tyler can stay in here or with you if you wish. Let me show you your room."

We were right across the hall and the bedroom must have been at least 12x16, with a small settee, oak furniture, indirect lighting, and a wall-mounted 48-inch

TV. There was a walk-in closet and bathroom with a small sink, tub and shower.

"The house looks great, Mama. Thank you for doing all of this."

"Roberto didn't compromise on the design. I have your dad set up in the living room."

Mom had done wonders, morphing a spacious living room into a hospital room-office and seating area. Daddy was at the desk, clothed in pajamas, an IV in his arm. He heard us and rose with the help of the IV pole.

"You're HOME!"

We smiled and laughed, "Yes, finally! You look good, Daddy!"

"I have my moments, honey," and he reached for Tyler whose arms were already wanting to be in those of his *abuelo*.

"You're getting BIG, you little cow-puncher! Let grandpa look at you," and Daddy raised his arms and Ty squealed and they both laughed as Daddy did it a couple more times.

"Do you like his room?"

Ofelia said, "I only showed them the twins' room, across from where they're sleeping. They haven't seen Tyler's room, yet."

Olivia and I looked at each other then back at them, "Huh?"

"Same side of the hall, right next to the twins' room, Olivia!"

"Tell them about later, Ofelia."

"Miguel's going to fire-up the spit outside and turn some beef. We'll have a nice dinner, then light the firepit because it will be chilly later on."

"What time would you like us to have Sandy and Gwen, here?"

"As soon as they wish. I was hoping they'd come in when you got here."

"Then I'll call, Ofelia, and tell them that!"

"There is already a plan for tomorrow, too. But it can wait until Gwen and Sandy arrive.

"Daddy, I want to freshen up a bit. Can you give me...us an hour or so? Tyler can stay if you like. It looks like he'll scream if I try to take him from you!"

Bob kissed Olivia, "Fine, honey. Thank you for coming. Coming home."

Olivia took my hand and led me down the hall. She passed our door and went to the door beyond the twins' room and turned the handle.

The 36x48" painting of Olivia's Meadow in our living room? A 24"x36" hand-painted and framed poster of it was hanging on the wall alongside a trundle bed. There was a dresser and double-door closet, and a small desk with a nice window and blinds. There was an artsy-craftsy aged wood plank on the wall, about 6"x24" and also hand-painted. It said, "Tyler's Room." Olivia and I could only shake our heads.

"Get used to it, David. This is your home in more ways than one."

"It's a little overwhelming."

"Mama, I need a little rest. David, come lie down with me, please? I need to cuddle. That okay?"

"Of course, Olivia," Ofelia said.

I smiled. It was always okay. She wanted and needed some mommy intimacy with me and I was more than willing to oblige. I saw her set an alarm on her new watch in case we drifted off.

She dialed Gwen.

"Mom and Dad really, really want to see you two... ..Uh, huh. ...I'm sure Mama has plenty of food, here, in fact, food and beer for all of us because they're doing a western cookout for us, so dress warmly.... ...I'll let 'em know, love you, Gwen. Thanks. I hope we didn't wreck your golf plans... ...That's sweet, thanks."

"She got to thinking about it, David. Gwen told Sandy she felt like a shit-heel for bringing golf clubs, that Roberto and Ofelia should be their sole priority. She pretty much told Sandy not to plan on golfing. He saw the light and was fine with it."

Knowing them, I wasn't surprised, nor was Olivia. "What better friends could we have, honey."

"I have you to thank, David. You found both of them."

"But you charmed 'em until they loved you like I do. You kept them coming back and made me interesting enough to like," and I chuckled at my own self-deprecating humor.

She pulled me down onto the bed with her and I kicked off my shoes. She pointed out the window, off into the distance.

"Olivia's Meadow is on the higher ground, up that way."

"If it's one tenth as beautiful as the painting, Olivia, then I'm blessed twice," I said, and she knew it would be a given.

I felt Olivia go limp, asleep. As I lay there, I thought of my religious sojourn in this area. Again, I felt some Zen-like calmness, at peace with one and all. There was something magical in the area that went beyond human knowledge or understanding. It was Spiritual with the capitol "S." Just before Olivia's alarm sounded on her watch, she turned and put her arms around me as she came-to.

"Still here, cowboy?"

I laughed.

"What?"

"I think you were pregnant the *last* time you said that to me."

"We make beautiful babies."

"So far, so good."

"That's you, David, the twins I mean. Mom and Dad don't know of anyone in either of their bloodlines with twins."

"News to me. I hope I don't have an unknown sister out there as ugly as me populating the world," and I laughed.

"Not funny."

"Orphan humor. If I have a sister, probably hairy, flat chest. Big feet...five o'clock shadow."

"STOP!" and she couldn't help laughing. "That's as near to a sexist comment as I've ever heard out of your mouth.

"Then I apologize to you and to a sister I don't know I have."

"Forgiven."

Olivia rolled off the bed and got out of her clothes for a quick shower. The stall was for one. I stepped in, passing her with a kiss as she got out, and we opted for sweaters and jeans. No way in hell was I showing up at the ranch without both pairs of boots, and I slipped into the black ones that went with my grey and blue sweater.

We strolled down the hall. Roberto was resting in his bed and Ofelia shushed us, pointing to the kitchen-family room area and we followed.

The kitchen was built for a restaurant. Big, commercial-grade appliances, and no expense spared. We sat around the island.

Ofelia started right in.

"He doesn't complain. He nearly punched the doctor when the suggestion was made he go to a hospice. He was going to be here, and only here. We take it one day at a time."

Her rest and nursing knowledge helped Olivia keep calm. Olivia helped me keep mine.

Ofelia smiled, "Seeing Tyler is the happiest I've seen him. You're a godsend."

"You mentioned plans, tomorrow, Mama...."

"After breakfast, Miguel and four hands are coming here on horseback. They're going to take you four to see the big ranch, 'Toro de Oro,' and then ride to Olivia's Meadow for a picnic that will be set up by the time you get there. You'll be back by early afternoon. Roberto has seen to everything."

I interjected, "Except me, Ofelia."

"Even you, son, especially you! Why *not* you?"

I laughed, "I don't know how to ride a horse. Hell, I fall off carousel horses, Ofelia!"

"The horses being brought for you are gentle enough for a 10-year-old to handle. You'll be safe, get the hang of it, and get some real dust on your boots, David."

We had soft drinks and took one to Dad.

"Roberto, they know the plan," Ofelia told him. Uncharacteristic of her, Ofelia continued, "David knows we're strapping him to the wildest stallion in the barn and slapping its ass to run off with him!" she said, with an evil gleam. Everyone was in stitches. After feeling sheer terror at the thought, I finally saw the humor with my green pallor subsiding.

We heard a chime and Olivia said, "Sandy and Gwen," looking at her watch.

"I want to see *el jefe*!" Sandy's voice boomed. "Isn't that the term for the big cheese in charge of a ranch?" and Olivia nodded as we all hugged and kissed. Mom led us to Dad.

"Sandy! Gwen! Welcome! Come in! Come in!"

Gwen leaned over the bedrail and kissed Daddy.

Sandy grabbed the hand without the I.V. and shook it, "Hey, Roberto! Thank you for having us. I hear your doing surprisingly well??"

"Day to day. Today's extra-great with you all here and especially with my grandson coming home!"

Dad was perky and loving the company. With his polished people skills, Sandy knew to ask Dad about the big ranch, and how he helped get it established. I was actually learning a few things, and Olivia was sitting at her dad's side resting her hand on his calf.

Dad looked at Sandy, "You and Gwen are going to get to see it all, Sandy. You're all going on a tour tomorrow with the <u>new</u> *jefe*."

"New *jefe*?," Olivia's face registering some concern if not a little shock.

Dad pointed right at my heart.

Sandy replied, "THAT guy, Roberto!? I *know* that guy. We're all in trouble," and my father-in-law laughed. "I forgot he's one of your hired hands." Sandy's expression changed, "One of the best, Roberto. In fact, while we're here, I have a little news in that regard. I'll save it for dinner."

I looked at Olivia and shrugged, clueless, and dismissed it.

Dad said, "We spared you, Sandy. No bull's balls tonight, I promise."

Sandy looked at Gwen, "Got the bag?" and Gwen produced and dangled a bag of marshmallows from her oversized, tooled-leather bag she'd obviously paid $600 or more for in the last two hours.

Sandy told him, "I heard it was a cookout and...well... I need my burnt marshmallows, it's a thing with me, Roberto."

Ofelia spoke up, "I'll put them in the kitchen and get out some skewers for us," and Sandy handed them to Ofelia who headed into the kitchen and came out with a beer for Sandy and glass of wine for Gwen.

"Mmm, thank you, Ofelia," said Gwen who took an immediate sip from the chilled goblet.

"It's a local winery and I like their white wines," Ofelia said, "Tell me what you think."

"Ooh, I like! I'll have Sandy pick some up to take home with us!"

"I'll give you the bottle so you can put the address in your GPS. It's maybe twenty or twenty-five minutes but they are small roads. The tasting room has plenty of bottles there. And sure, you can try some other ones if you like."

"Thank you, Ofelia. I'll probably make that stop on the way to the airport so we don't forget. We can each carry-on a bottle!"

It was as quick as his expression changing, Roberto just kind of sank all of a sudden. "I think I need a little rest, I'm sorry. Do you all mind?" and I reached over and took Tyler.

We let Dad rest, moving into the family room. There were good smells and muted noises coming from the kitchen and at least two people at work.

"This house is simply gorgeous, Ofelia," Sandy said.

"Built with rodeo money, fame and fortune, Sandy. It was his dream as a young bull rider. He said he built it just as he saw it."

"Tomorrow," Olivia said, "on the tour Daddy mentioned, we'll see some of the big ranch and then ride up to Olivia's Meadow where the crew will bring over a chuckwagon."

"Wait," Gwen asked, "chuckwagons really exist?"

"On the bigger ranches, yes. Hands can't be expected to be miles and miles away with rations strapped to their horses, drinking from creeks or rusty canteens, and living in pup tents. Daddy busts his butt to keep them comfortable with good food and nice, butane-heated tents. That's why they're fiercely loyal to him. They have always regarded my dad as one of their own, never some big shot who didn't give a shit. They'd kill for him if he asked."

From the look on Sandy's face, he agreed with me, chillingly so: Roberto probably *did* command the respect and loyalty to have one of his hands turn someone into mulch or hog feed.

"Neither Sandy or I ride, either Olivia."

"We have horses that have forgotten how to buck or get feisty with a rider, so gentle they'd be suitable for a kid's carnival, Sandy. When they're no longer working-horses for the ranch, we let the horses roam, keep them fed and vet-checked. You might even see a herd of them running on the big ranch if we're lucky. They have their own barn for severe wintering. They all have names and personalities and there isn't a mean one in the bunch."

You could feel the collective sigh of relief.

We heard commotion outside and I said, "That must be the gang getting the cookout set up."

"They've been out there a bit, David. They're actually almost finished. The meat's turning on the spit. C'mon, I'll show you."

Gwen said, "I'm just...just taken by how serene and beautiful this place is, Olivia."

"We appreciate it, too. Our license plates say, 'Land of Enchantment,' and now you see it and feel it. It's very real."

The brick patio was at least 20x40 and the spit was over a masonry barbecue, turning by an electric motor. The cook nodded to greet us and we waved. Chairs had been set up around the firepit and there was a big log surrounded by kindling waiting to be ignited. A self-serve bar was being stocked with ice.

We walked back inside and sat down for dinner. Daddy joined us at the table in a wheelchair with an I.V. pole. He led with grace, thanking God for our abundant blessings and asked that we remember those less fortunate. We stuffed ourselves and moved out to the patio where the log was ablaze and warming the chill.

I thought it was enchanting, too. "I'd forgotten the sky could hold so many stars, Olivia," and I took her hand and whispered, "This feels like home. I think we've arrived."

She looked at me with widened eyes and a smile that came from the warmest part of her heart, "We're home. I love you, cowboy."

"Okay, you two knock it off," Roberto said, teasing us.

"Daddy? He whispered he's home and can't wait until we get that house built."

"When I had the hacienda's plans done, you mother wanted something a little smaller. Well, 2,700 feet isn't a small house, but the builder had presented us with a plan she loved. I can show it to you – it's a beautiful house. I confess," and Roberto crossed himself, "my ego wanted big and bigger and so that's what we have," he said gesturing at the room, itself.

"It's awesome, Dad, and I'd be interested in seeing that plan," I said, looking for Olivia to endorse the remark. She did with a smile and nod.

"This is the most relaxed I think I've ever felt," Sandy said. Gwen nodded in agreement.

"Excuse me a minute, please?" and Sandy stepped inside. A couple minutes later, he reappeared holding six wire hangars and holding up the marshmallows he brought.

"Told ya. Gotta have 'em."

Ofelia gave Sandy a puzzled look, "The skewers were next to the bag, Sandy."

"I saw them, Ofelia. But hangers make barbecued marshmallows the real deal!"

Gwen chuckled, "You're like a little kid, sometimes, Sandy...and I love it!"

He bent down and kissed her.

"Okay, everyone take a weapon and I'll come around with the marshmallows."

I got four of them untwisted, ready to accommodate stabbing a marshmallow or two. Sandy worked untwisting his and Gwen's.

One by one, we got our marshmallows into the fire. Sandy was getting a marshmallow pushed onto a hanger, "This one's for you Gwen."

He knelt down next to her chair, hanger in hand with a marshmallow stabbed the end of it. He started shaking the hanger using only his wrist, quivering the hanger. There was an unusual noise as it shook. He held the hanger in front of Gwen at eye level.

Suddenly, Gwen put her hand over her mouth, "Sandy!"

She gently pulled off the marshmallow but Sandy was able to get hold of the ring that had been invisible behind it.

"I love this woman. Savvy. Smart. Fun. And it's unthinkable that I'd ever be away from her," Sandy told us, looking around the circle.

"Gwen, will you marry me?"

She hooked his neck with her forearm and went nose to nose with him and said, "You bet, Cowboy!" and they kissed. We cheered, stunned, but we were hooting and hollering. Then she looked over at Olivia.

"That was the right answer, wasn't it, Olivia... 'You bet, _cowboy_??" and Olivia was in a rolling laugh, "Yes, Gwen, it was perfect and I think you said it to the _right_ cowboy!"

"Gwen? Let me put this on your hand, please??"

We were all in so much shock, Gwen included, she hadn't even let him put the ring on her finger.

"The sunset and the stars, all of it... You sure you didn't just take advantage of me, Sandy?"

"Yes. I took every advantage I could but I don't hear an objection."

"I don't think you will," and Gwen put her hand on his shoulder and gave him a soft kiss. She got up to show us all the ring.

It was like one of the constellations, above. Sparkling everywhere with a center stone, round diamond that had to be 3 carats.

Gwen lifted her wine goblet, "All I know is, the box _better_ say McArdle's on it!"

Sandy faked a look of innocence, "_You_ know I can't afford to shop there on what I make," which made it funnier.

He explained, "Olivia was an unwilling accomplice. When she called you to go shopping for work clothes and you were gone for a few hours, I rushed into the store and got the ring. None of them know or recognize me other than on the phone, so as long as Gwen was gone, it was smooth sailing."

Gwen, now tipsy, asked, "Did he or she give you a discount?"

"Nope, he said there wasn't room for it with all the labor for the additional stones around the center diamond."

"Good! I'm looking up the ticket and giving that jeweler a bonus!"

Olivia looked at me and chuckled, "See? We're not the only ones who can fall in love in an instant," and everyone smiled and clapped.

The evening was surreal.

We parted ways. Everyone headed off toward their respective beds in agreement to be at the hacienda no later than 9am.

The morning was crisp and clear, with the vapor from our breaths easily visible as we stood sipping coffee, watching the hands bring our horses down the lane.

Miguel, Roberto's right hand, was riding lead and brought the hands and mounts to a stop. Miguel pointed at each man, "Pablo, Nico, Freddie and my son, Junior," and the men politely tipped their hats in succession.

"Don't be alarmed by the rifles and guns we carry. It's habit and also required by Toro de Oro because this is wild country. It's a year-round safety precaution."

"I imagine it's for more than snakes…like. coyotes?"

Miguel answered, "Yes, David, that and there are *lobos*, wolves in these hills and they are not to be messed with. We'll be fine today. Again, we're armed for everyone's safety."

The men dismounted and each held the reins of the horse that had been trailing. "Grab a horse, everyone, and the boys will help you get into the saddles. God gave us a beautiful day for a ride!"

I snapped a couple pictures of Sandy and Gwen, mounted next to each other. I was taking pictures of the 1st day of their engagement.

We made the lazy paced ride without incident, stopping along the way anytime someone wanted a photo or sip of coffee or water, or to duck behind a bush to pee.

It was quiet on the big ranch. There were only a few pickups at the main complex and little activity happening in the barns. Olivia told me Miguel had done an excellent job with the route, ensuring we'd have as much scenery as we first-timers could take in.

As soon as we reentered the Macias ranch, Miguel reined his horse to the right, heading up the fence line trail toward Olivia's Meadow. I could only imagine Olivia's anticipation, what was going through her head. I hadn't thought to ask her how long it had been since she'd seen it.

We spotted the chuckwagon, two ranch hands bustling to get a table loaded with serving dishes. There were two more tables and benches where we sat to eat.

"Miguel, it seems the only change is that it's more beautiful up here than I had even remembered," Olivia said.

"It's not your imagination, Olivia. See those stakes with the little streamers over there?" We all shielded our eyes from the sun. "When your dad started on your homesite, he started cultivating the area, tending to the natural landscape with the help of experts he hired. Soil enrichment and even some rodent and pest controls."

Olivia paused, the bread she was holding in mid-air. "That's my father. True, he spoils me but in quiet ways."

Miguel nodded, "That's him, Olivia, and he's the same when he does something kind for us."

Once we finished, the chuckwagon hands tended to everything related to lunch. Olivia grabbed my hand and we walked over to Shooter's grave. Miguel was close behind.

Olivia looked at the marker on Shooter's grave and told us his story.

"This young stallion was as majestic as he was fierce. I wasn't even born yet, but the oldest hands told me only the world's toughest bull-riding cowboy could break him to ride. They said Shooter threw my dad off his back again and again, even breaking his arm, once. But Daddy didn't give up."

"That's true," Miguel said.

Miguel continued, "Once Roberto broke him, you would have thought that Shooter was a puppy dog. 'Berto could walk around without the rein and Shooter would pace behind him about six feet. If Roberto stopped? Shooter stopped. If he skipped, Shooter kept pace. It was the craziest thing. I think my funniest memory of him is a bath that Roberto gave Shooter."

"After he washed him down and all, Roberto noticed he hadn't brought a curry comb from the barn. So he jogged over to get one, about half a football field. Shooter was jogging *beside* him, looking over at him and *Jefe* was talking to him. Shooter kept nodding. It looked like they were having a conversation as they ran." The fondness of that vivid memory softened the leathery lines of Miguel's face. "Me and a few of the hands laughed our butts off."

It drew a chuckle from all of us.

Miguel motioned to his own horse, "My horse *Chongo* is out of Shooter, one of his offspring. Most of our finest horses came from him or his bloodline," Miguel said.

Olivia turned to Miguel, "On the way back, I would like to walk around the building site. Then, we can save time by just riding down the hill instead of taking one of the trails, okay?"

"As you please. No problem, Olivia," Miguel said.

Miguel led us over to the building site on foot.

I asked, "What do you see, Olivia, as far as how the house will be situated?"

"I'm seeing lots of windows catching the afternoon sun, David, angled so we can enjoy either sunrise or sunset from a patio. I think the garage should face the trail. No circular drive, just the natural landscape beauty. Maybe a driveway to the front door wide enough for a couple traditional parking spaces. I guess I'm saying a driveway that looks like an upside-down L. What do you think?"

"I love your vision. We use the patio off the master bedroom a lot at the condo. I'd like us to have a patio off the master and see a small garden surrounding it. Expanding on my take, I think I'll like a very low, natural stone wall, maybe only ten or twelve inches high, around Shooter's burial site. I don't want to be morose or anything, but I have a hundred-year vision it's a family resting place, with like twenty graves or so. Ours included. So mark off and area and leave it like a quiet-garden kind of place. Next to it? Swing-set and teeter totters, definitely!" and I laughed.

"Those are wonderful, sweetheart. A family cemetery? No complaint from me. I meant my words to you, that I would love you forever and beyond."

"That's a scene even I could see for you," Miguel offered.

When we wandered back toward the horses, we caught Gwen and Sandy having a moment, kissing.

Olivia called over, "Ahem! Picked out your cabin site yet? I heard all of the lots are on sale, today, only!"

"Don't count us out. This is breathtaking, Olivia," Gwen answered.

"I know. I never took it for granted. Hey, let's get back. I want to put a call into Daddy's doctor's answering service."

There was a luxury SUV in the drive when we got there.

We thanked Miguel and the hands, and I waved-off Sandy as it looked like he might be going for his wallet to tip them. Their pride would have taken a hit, their feelings hurt. This was their home and hospitality carried no cost.

Ofelia greeted us and Tyler reached for me.

"Incredible," Sandy said.

"I never knew New Mexico had this kind of beauty, Ofelia," Gwen added. Ofelia nodded, graciously.

Ofelia looked at Olivia, "The doctor's in with him," and she led the way.

We walked in and saw a man with a stethoscope on Roberto's chest. He was rising and turning to us.

We all greeted Roberto who smiled and waved as the MD stepped aside.

"How was it? Beautiful, huh, my Olivia's Meadow," and we couldn't praise it enough for him.

"Dr. Walmeier?"

"You must be Olivia."

"Yes, and my husband, David, our dear friends Sandy Tuttle and Gwen McArdle."

"Pleased to meet all of you."

"Join us for coffee in the kitchen, Doc?" and he picked up the cue.

"Please. Usually, I'm a two-cup guy but I only got one this morning."

We arranged ourselves around the kitchen island.

"I know you're an RN, Olivia, and a fine one I hear."

"Yes, thank you."

"May I speak openly in front of your friends?"

"Certainly. Please."

"He's extremely anemic, and therefore the I.V.'s. I'm fighting like hell to bring down the leg swelling and it's mighty painful as you can expect. Decline in his bowel and urinary functions indicate rapid decline."

We braced ourselves on the way to the kitchen. This was worse than what I expected...maybe not Olivia, but me.

Olivia turned to me, Sandy and Gwen. She was in full nurse mode, as if explaining to the family of one of her own patients.

"Translated, all of that means he's nearing the end."

Dr. Walmeier interjected, "Olivia's right. I'm so sorry for you all. I'm going to keep him comfortable and think you should get an LPN in here, Olivia. I know an agency that can have one here, today."

"I agree. Please call them. He's my dad. I want a licensed practical nurse for him and all the pain meds you're willing to write for him, Dr. Walmeier."

"I'll make that call. Let me say goodbye to your dad and I'll let myself out."

We walked back in and gathered around.

"All right, all of you. It's not a secret that I'm going! I want happy faces, like the little yellow stickers! All of you! Now!" and he instantly injected cheer into a heavy moment bringing the smiles he needed to see at the time he needed to see them the most.

"I know you're leaving in a few hours. I'm in God's and your mother's hands. You're an hour away. So don't sweat it, none of you sweat it. *El jefe* has spoken!" He reached for David's hand and took it.

"David, while you were gone, Ofelia found that house plan and spread it on the worktable in my office. You can look at it or just roll it up to take with you. Either way. The builder of this house designed it and we think very highly of him. I strongly recommend you use him for whatever you and Olivia might decide."

"Thanks, Dad. I'll take a glance while Olivia's in the shower."

The house in the plan was genius, capitalizing on the view lines and a hundred percent consistent with Olivia and I discussed. It was her call and hers, alone. Olivia's home in Olivia's Meadow. It felt like it was pre-ordained.

Leaving that house with our bags was almost the hardest thing we ever experienced. The absolute hardest was watching Roberto hand Tyler back to Olivia, and then Olivia and her dad sobbing together uncontrollably, holding hands as Tyler rested on his mom's hip with an expression that was turning his little face into a portrait of foreboding. If I could only have escaped my own skin, done *anything* humanly possible to take-on Olivia's pain and Dad's, too....

I don't know that ten words were spoken in the sedan from the ranch to the Albuquerque airport.

We faced Sandy and Gwen from our seats in the boarding lounge. Olivia's hand rested on my thigh, Tyler straddling my other thigh holding onto my arm, shaking a rattle.

Olivia found words, "One hell of an engagement party, you two," and she burst out laughing, and we joined in. Inappropriate? No, survival, stepping out of the grief like one foot hitting the rug after lifting it out of the tub. She was getting herself steadied, grounded and centered.

Gwen said, "I tell ya what, Olivia, that meadow? Olivia's Meadow? I had goosebumps the whole time we were there because it looked exactly like the painting in your living room," and Sandy concurred.

"Yeah, that hit me, too. Nothing short of magnificent."

"I don't see how Olivia and I can do anything but make plans on how to transition our lives, there. There's every reason to go and the only reasons I can think of to stay are...well, they're selfish."

Sandy didn't react.

"I know, Sandy. This is uncomfortable for you, professionally. But my life, our lives, are right in front of you, and I think you'd make the same choices."

"David, the breath of fresh air in my life is the woman I asked to be my bride. I've been reevaluating what I want compared to what I need. Professionally, I'll handle it and not think twice. You have my complete blessing, friend," and he extended his hand, which I shook.

Olivia looked over, "You're in my thoughts, again, David. My head hasn't shut-up since we left." She looked at me. "I'm glad I have you to get me through all of this," and she gave me a kiss just as the boarding announcement began. Tyler was our enabler to board first and get settled on the 737's ride home.

We unbuckled before we were supposed to so we could pop-up and retrieve our stuff from the overhead bins. I had Tyler and Olivia put his bag and one of mine on my free shoulder. The passenger line crawled slowly toward the door and I began to long for our place, comfy, familiar surroundings to ease our tensions and pain.

"Jacuzzi after Tyler goes down, honey. I think we need the therapy."

Gwen overheard me, "I think that's what Sandy and I will do when we get to the house. Whatcha think, Sandy?" and he nodded in agreement.

As soon as we hit the concourse, our cellphones blew up. Without even a glance, Olivia shouted, "Not now, no!" and her premonition was correct.

Our phones had the same text. "Call home... Ofelia" We dumped everything into the seats of the boarding lounge we'd just entered, and Olivia dialed, saying she turn on the speaker.

Her mother answered, obviously fighting back the tears, "He's gone, Olivia..." and Olivia's hand with the phone dropped to her side. The phone fell onto the carpet, and she was in my arms, sobbing. Gwen was distraught, too, sobbing in Sandy's arms.

I managed to keep Tyler in my arms as I helped Olivia into a chair. I picked up her phone, handed it to her, and sat down beside her. Tyler crawled into her lap.

"I'm sorry, Mama, I dropped the phone."

"I'm here. It's hard, I know. He just closed his eyes and was gone."

"When?"

"I think, probably about 25 minutes or so ago. I was in no shape to call you...."

Olivia was physically wracked with the impact of the grief slamming into her at-will while trying to maintain enough composure to be coherent with her mom.

"Right now, honey, he's at Sanchez Funeral Home in Taos. They'll keep him there until you and me and David decide what we're going to do."

"We'll be there, Mama. David and I will get bereavement leave A.S.A.P. and get up to you, okay?"

"I love you, honey..." and Ofelia began to weep. "Tell Sandy and Gwen they can stay at the house if and when they come."

"I have you on speaker. They heard you, Mama."

"This is Sandy, Ofelia. Gwen and I are so, so sorry. We'll definitely come. I'll let Gwen and Olivia coordinate all that, okay?"

"Thank you, Sandy. Roberto...." and for the first time in a very long time, Olivia's mother slipped into Spanish.

"I love you, Mama. We need to get home from the airport because we called the instant we stepped off the plane when we got the message."

"Olivia, pray, please, for you and me, too."

"I will, Mama. Take care of yourself."

"Everyone is coming by from the ranch, Olivia. I'm okay. Everyone is looking out for me."

"Okay, good thing. Goodnight, Mama."

I was curious, "What did she say in Spanish, honey?"

"That my dad is among the angels and knows we love and miss him. That, as a family, the Lord will lead us through this."

Shooter's and Roberto's Reunion

Six hundred people from Roberto Santiago Macias'
past and present showed up to pay homage at his
funeral service, held at the main ranch complex in a
barn that had been cleared, scrubbed, sanitized and
made odor-free. The dining facility was used for overflow.

He was eulogized by Carl Simmons, Toro de Oro's
owner, and also by Rod Reynolds, the current President
of the Hall of Fame Cowboys Association and Museum.

Her father's wishes for a cowboy's sendoff were
carried out.

His brass-railed oak casket was slid onto a horse-
drawn wagon with a team of six gleaming quarter horses,
managed by a driver and assistant. Junior, Miguel's son,
insisted on driving the makeshift hearse without
objection from anyone. Following, was a black covered
carriage with Ofelia, David, Tyler and I, complete with
quilts for our comfort and warmth.

Anyone who wanted to ride a horse in the cortege
behind our coach could do so. There was an unspoken
request that no cars come up the hill but Ofelia and
Olivia knew some of the older folks may be too frail for a
horse or not have access to a buggy or wagon. Cars were
last in the procession up the East trail along the fence
line, where a grave had been dug about twenty feet from
Shooting Star's – *Shooter's* – resting place.

When Mr. Simmons asked ranch hands for four
volunteers to dig and prepare the grave, nearly 30 of
them volunteered, an outward sign of the love and
respect Bob earned from his men. It was Miguel Fuentes,
Roberto's right hand, whom Ofelia chose to address
those at the graveside gathering, first

*"We never felt our General Foreman was a rich,
numbers-only guy here to drive us like the stock we tend
to 24/7. Our jefe had our backs. He was one of us, a
caballero puro, one who made good, worked hard and*

looked out for us. He loved his life and family and our caballero ways. He was always firm but fair, a man of faith and conviction. We called him 'Berto' behind his back, a term of respect, actually. He inspired and earned fierce loyalty that kept us hands from going to other operations, seasonally or permanently. When our most difficult times and struggles hit, no matter how bad it got, he saddled up and was right there to take care of it the man's way, a caballero's way, with us by his side. We loved and will miss our jefe. Our hearts go out to Ofelia and Olivia, to Olivia's husband, David, and especially to Berto's grandson, Tyler, who became a beacon of joy until jefe's last breath. I can say that all of us gathered here are loved ones, in a way. My heart is broken. I'm sure yours are, too. His spirit will ride with us, always."

Miguel wiped the tears away with his sleeve as he replaced his dress hat on his head, accepted the reins of *Chongo* from one of the hands attending the bay stallion. He remounted his horse and put his hand over his heart. As he saw the priest approach the casket, Miguel removed his hat and lowered his head, his chin resting against his chest.

A Spaniard priest from Chimayo—Ofelia's idea— sprinkled the casket with Holy Water, muttered some words in Spanish and we all crossed ourselves. Eight of Roberto's men slowly lowered him to his rest, not far from his beloved mount, Shooter.

Ninety minutes later, the people were gone, the grave was covered with dirt on a hill of flowers and wreaths. We were overlooking the graves of Shooter and Olivia's dad to the higher side of the meadow off to our left.

Olivia didn't want to leave. She desperately needed a break from the grief and the energy it took to stand and thank the mourners who had taken the trouble to make the trek up the hill to the graveside service. We'd be here as long as Olivia wanted to stay. One of the cars would scramble up the hill to get us within seconds of getting my phone call. The post-funeral reception at the big ranch's main complex could handle itself without us for a while. The hacienda was filled with people and mountains of food.

Ofelia had asked if she could keep Tyler at her side. With our blessing, of course, her grandson was there to give her his strength and love. Ofelia was proud to introduce him to the mourners as Roberto's grandson.

I sat with my knees apart so Olivia could lean back into me as a backrest. My arms were crisscrossed over her chest. I swayed us gently from side to side, my senses filled with the smell of her hair and perfume, her soft skin. We were taking-in the meadow and by it, taken-in by the meadow that bore her name.

She reached out with her left hand and pulled a couple tiny winter twigs that she spun slowly in her fingers. She reached back and stroked my neck with her hand as we sat there snuggled up in the shifting breezes, as streams of tears came and went noiselessly.

"I was lucky, Olivia."

"Yeah, cowboy?"

"I was an orphan who got a mom and dad in his late 20s, parents who accepted and loved me unconditionally when they could easily have chosen to hate me for getting you pregnant. You wouldn't back down, fought for my chance to be around them so they could get to know me."

"Before you met them, David, when I would talk about you? I didn't exaggerate or embellish anything. It surprised them that I wasn't making you out to be larger than life, some bust-ass machismo media dude. I told them who you were, the real you. You were the guy a million girls might overlook as marrying material because they were blinded by myths, when, all along, I knew you were the oyster with the most precious pearl," she said, reaching up to touch one of the pearl earrings given her by Gwen.

"So, what now, Olivia?"

"I have an idea, a plan, David. Childcare and urgent care in the same building," and she pointed toward the hacienda.

"With the floorplan, I don't think it would be prohibitively expensive. I could get a nurse practitioner or MD to work with me on the medical side, and moms who need but can't afford childcare could be hired and, as a fringe bennie, bring their kids to work. Our kids would be close, accessible to both of us."

It was sensible and within our means, even if the ventures failed.

She continued, "We'll treat ranch hands, other locals and families, and have affordable childcare for lower income families as long as the single- or both parents work. I think we could do it."

"Sounds like you've been thinking about this for a while."

"I have. You're only hearing about it now because I wanted to keep trying to punch holes in the idea, why it wouldn't work. I can't see why it won't, David."

"It sounds like the end of Macias Ranch, Olivia. You're okay with that? Our house in the meadow overlooking two businesses in the hacienda?"

"Three, and she smiled a little sheepishly and looked at her feet before looking back up. "

"All of this is Rancho Macias-Callan, and we'll ranch on the greater expanse of the property. I want horses and a barn for them, David. I want the kids to ride. I want to be able to ride with them. I want to ride with you, get a horse you're comfortable on, and you might learn to love it. Could you see riding with me? And imagine rides with our children, honey."

That wasn't a loaded question or asking permission. The answer was easy.

"I'd love to learn to ride, honey. But I want to contribute, be relevant. I don't want to babysit for a living, and I'd be in the way in the urgent care clinic.

What's my place in the scenario? Better, what do you want me to do? What do you see me doing?"

"You are the Jefe, and even the big ranch's hands will regard you as that. Run our ranch or the hacienda facility or both or none. Work broadcasting in Taos, learn to shoe horses for all I care," and she turned to face me, "Or be a kept man. That old offer still stands."

I laughed.

"So does the old answer. Olivia, I believe in your vision. I'm all-in on our future. But first, I have a house to build."

I kissed my Olivia in the meadow bearing her name. My Olivia's Meadow.

Casita Ofelia and Three Kids Later

We built the home using the plans Roberto had given us and called the place Casita Ofelia ('Ofelia's Little House') because it's the one she originally wanted. At 2,910 square feet, it wasn't little by any stretch of the imagination. Ofelia was overjoyed to live in the house of her own dreams, and Olivia included and consulted her mom in the finish details.

After moved in, I found two Rhodesian Ridgeback puppies for the kids' Christmas presents. Robbie got one dog and Jamie and Amy got the other one. Robbie named his dog Boozer, because he was a little unsteady on his legs when he got excited. Robbie thought he looked like he was drunk, so 'Boozer' it was.

The twins' dog was named 'Snoozer' because she liked to sleep on her back and would often snore.

We neutered them as much for gaining bulk size as much as we did because they were brother and sister.

Early on, they became extremely protective of the kids and especially Olivia. At 82 and 91 pounds, respectively, Snoozer and Boozer could probably take down a lone wolf and keep a small pack of them at bay until the rifles arrived.

Typically, Olivia and I were dropping by the house to take breaks from our respective workdays. She'd come up from the clinic, and as the newly named Program Director in the Taos station where I worked (Thank you, Sandy and Norm!), I could come and go from the station as I pleased without any raised eyebrows. It didn't lesson my ranch responsibilities and our family routines weren't compromised.

It was pretty enough to be outside at one of the patio tables. Her hand was in mine. I noticed the three rubies in the gold rim of her engagement ring. I mused, "I wasn't all that surprised when Tyler started insisting that I call him 'Roberto,'" and she smiled.

"He wants to know every little thing about his *abuelo*. He's constantly asking me to show him video of him and Dad when he was a baby. He likes going through all of Dad's things from his rodeo days. He's demanding I call him 'Roberto,' and when he stomps his foot, I tell him, 'Go to your room, 'Robbie!,' You don't get to demand, cowpoke. I'm the mom, GOT IT?"

"When he does his demand thing with me, it almost *sounds* like your dad issuing some directive, you know? A little eerie."

"I think he's a chip off the old Macias block, for sure."

Something hit Olivia so funny that she lowered and set down her glass of tea, "Well, as the girls get older, I'm going continue to ride his ass to be nice to them and redden those little butt cheeks if he isn't as loving and respectful as his *abuelo* was to me as a little girl!"

"He'll be fine. The me in him will keep that in check," and I winked at her.

She smiled, "I'll redden *your* cheeks if that doesn't happen!"

"Ooh, is this a new side of you?"

"Ask me in bed, tonight."

We got into the 4x4 and headed down the hill to check-in on the twins, Amelia Lauren Renee and Jamie Janine Annelle, in the childcare center. Robbie—and I had to admit I was liking it as much as it seemed to fit him—Robbie was with his grandmother.

I commented on our big sign, bright at night: *Caballero Urgent Care Clinic & Children's Center.*

"Did you ever think this would be our future Olivia?"

"We worked out butts off to get here but I honestly don't know to answer that one, David... But since you used the 'f' word, 'future,' hand me my purse, please?"

She pulled out something I mistook for a drinking straw for Tyler and spun it around, holding it up to my eyes as her face transfixed into a broad smile.

"Here and now is just as good a time and place as any, David. I love you."

The home pregnancy test's indicator had a pink window that read "POSITIVE."

"I guess the one important discussion that somehow faded from my memory, Olivia?"

"I think we should plan a baby. I think I have one more in me. Let's try to have one more?"

"People plan for those things? Try?"

Eight months later, we welcomed Oliver William Somerset Callan into the world, with a birth weight of exactly ten pounds. Olivia, God bless her, gave me the sole honor to name him. I explained he was, first and foremost, named for her. His two middle names were from my favorite author, W. Somerset Maugham, whose first name was William. From the time he was born, we decided we'd call him 'Ollie' or 'Oliver.'

Boozer immediately adopted our newest son as his own charge. If Olivia or I picked up and carried Oliver anywhere, Boozer was right on our heels.

Seven-Year-Old Girls

Robbie practiced and practiced his rodeo skills. Almost 9, he was one of the most promising young cowboys in New Mexico's 4-H and Juniors rodeo events.

Miguel had meticulously evaluated the foals being born over at the big ranch and hand-selected Rob's horse for him. Rob chose his horse's registered name, "Berto's Shootin' the Breeze." Rob called him 'Breeze' and it was unanimous that his *abuelo* would have given him his blessing and been pleased.

He explained why he didn't call his horse, 'Shooter,' and it made Ofelia cry. Robbie said Shooter was the finest horse a cowboy could ever throw a leg over, but he wanted his horse, "Breeze," to be famous on his own. He was determined that Breeze would become a champion, one his grandfather could be proud of.

With their mom's urging and influence, the 7-year-olds, Amy and Jamie, took up barrel racing. It was Olivia's passion and she hated having to give it up for adult-type responsibilities working at two different ranches when she was young.

Amy rode a brown and white paint mustang whose face seemed like a knock-off from the main character in "Phantom of the Opera." She named him "Phantom," but Jamie constantly teased her, calling him, 'Funny Face.'

One day, he was tied at the house's hitching post and Amy walked around behind him just as the 22-pound barn cat, Raptor, screeched. Phantom kicked both back legs, hitting Amy squarely in the buttocks, sending her flying. To her everlasting regret, Robbie and her sister Jamie and I witnessed the whole thing. Amy hit the ground, rolling over through mud and fresh horseshit, screaming, "GOD <u>DAMMIT</u>, FUNNY FACE!"

Amy would be teased about Funny Face's horseshoe bruises on her buttocks (according to Olivia, who checked her for injuries) until she was ninety. Soft-spoken Amy had really let it fly and I'll deny whispering to myself that my little girl's cursing was adorable.

It was so funny I didn't have the heart to punish her for the expletive as I ran to help her up and make sure she was okay as her brother retrieved her hat, knocked the dust from it and handed it to her.

From that time on, her mount was 'Funny Face' and nothing but.

Jamie rode "Casper," a white mustang with large black spots and black socks. Casper could have been in the old, black and white Western movies because he looked hand-painted. Amy's 'Funny Face' was a terrific barrel racer, already, but Jamie's horse was lightning quick from a dead stop.

Olivia would let nothing get in our daughters' way of pursuing barrel racing to their hearts' content. There wouldn't be a single raised eyebrow if one or either of our girls quit. Olivia and I weren't forceful types of parents. We didn't compromise morals or family values; ours was a home for encouraging pursuit of one's direction to discover the self, within. Find your passion and put all you have in fulfilling the goals associated with it.

I learned to ride pretty darned good. The rides with Olivia and the kids were an experience hard to describe, surrounded by the natural beauty of one's own ranch, sharing campfires at sunset on a couple more trails we developed on our property. Again, Olivia had been right: there was nothing comparable to our family rides.

We shipped the kids off to a rodeo skill-building camp at Prescott, Arizona, for two weeks. Ofelia kept to herself in the 'mother-in-law-unit' we had included when we built our house.

There was a different air in the house just four or five days after the older kids left.

I noticed a post card on the kitchen counter. It showed a young girl hunkered down in the saddle in a tight turn, cutting a barrel as close as a horse can angle it without dumping the barrel. I flipped it over and the message was neatly printed, probably by Jamie, the more docile and quieter twin.

The rider in the photo was Amy, aboard one of the training academy's barrel horses. Their livestock was excellent in both rodeo skills and with younger riders trying to build competition skills.

"Mommy and Daddy,
This is so fun. Thank you.
Love,
Jamie   Amy
p.s. Can we bring Funny Face and Casper next time?"

I picked up my wine glass, "What a great deal that they thought to send a card. I guess we're raising them right, honey."

Olivia laughed, "For what it costs? I'm sure the card was a forced requirement by the camp staff, David," and I found it funny and considered it may just be true. "And I don't know if you noticed the boarding fees if the girls do have their own horses, there, David. Plus the trailering fees?"

I put my hands on my hips, "The next time they go, their horses are going, Olivia. Casper and Funny Face are A-quality livestock and are used to Jamie and Amy handling them. It's a safety thing. Their horses will go."

Olivia looked at me a long moment with a serious expression, and a smile began, "*Jefe* has spoken."

"Yes, *Jefe* <u>has</u>. Now, care to join me on the patio, gorgeous?"

"And?"

"And maybe I just might let you snuggle with me on the double lounger."

"And?"

"Come and find out," and I held the door open for her. The fragrances of lavender and the high country's wildflowers rose and was hanging on the humidity of a small summer shower we had, earlier. I flipped the cushions over on the lounger, lay down and Olivia was quick to follow.

I took her in my arms and looked into Olivia's eyes and knew humility and gratitude. I knew love. I knew who I was, where I was, and why.

I caressed Olivia's face and tousled her hair.

"I lost you, once. You found me twice, Olivia. If life is lost and found? Found is better."

"And?"

"And you get your pick of the indoor or outdoor Jacuzzi. I'm goin' in naked either way."

The Family Barn

The breeds in our barn varied but each was a horse known for strength and stamina.

For Olivia's 35th birthday gift, I consulted people in the know about American Saddlebreds. They recommended I consider a 2-year-old stallion out of the best stock in the United States. He was crazy expensive, but this was as good looking a horse as I'd ever seen. His registered name was Charlemagne of Ozarkana Saddlebreds. I bought him via electronic internet auction and had him trailered from Missouri.

We secreted him away in the barn. I got up early in the morning told the kids to tell their mother they wanted to take her for a trail ride and picnic for her birthday. There was no way she would turn that down.

Olivia worked in the kitchen preparing the picnic foodstuffs and Robbie volunteered to bring her horse up to the house. Olivia dragged all the food onto the porch, silently cursing the kids for disappearing and not helping. She wondered where Robbie was with her horse.

We were all on horseback singing "Happy Birthday" at the tops of our lungs approaching the house with Amy and Jamie in front, followed by Robbie and then me. I was on my horse, Claire, with Ollie harnessed to my chest so he could see. I held Charlemagne's reins and Olivia instantly knew he was her gift. Amy and Jamie made bows to put on the gleaming bay/black stallion's ears.

The kids dismounted and took the reins from me, walking the horse to their mom. "We love you, Mommy," was coming from their mouths as they hugged her.

"His name's Charlemagne, Mom," Robbie said, handing her the reins. My wife, the fountain of tears she could sometimes be, turned it on.

She looked to me, "Saddlebred, David?" she said, stroking the horse's neck, patting it and talking to him.

"Yep, from a top bloodline and he's able to breed."

She was in love, and I didn't know if she was cooing at the horse or me.

"Hop on and give him a go, Olivia! The kids and I are dying to see you ride him!" The kids cheered in agreement.

Olivia threw a leg over, patted the horse's neck once and gave him a small kick that jolted him into a lope. They were twenty yards from us when we saw her lean forward and heard "GIDDUP, <u>CHARLIE</u>!" and gave him a boot. The saddlebred instantly responded as if he were in the home stretch of the Kentucky Derby, sending up a dust cloud nearly obscuring them. At 150 yards or so, she put him into a sharp, skidding 180-degree turn and raced back toward us.

Now just forty yards away, she let him slow to a walk, and as they got close, Olivia was winded from the excitement and exhilaration, "My God, David, he's a rocket!"

"Robbie, take Ollie so you kids can go stand by your mom and I can get a picture," and they stood next to Olivia and posed for a photo I'd later have on my dresser, carry in my wallet, and put on my desk.

Christmas and a New Fur Baby

Early on, Olivia and I decided we would not give each other Christmas presents. We opted to gift each other on December 12th, our anniversary.

It was early morn and she got out of bed to go to the bathroom, I thought, but she left the master bedroom.

When she got back in bed, she coaxed me to lie on my back and she put a 'fur baby' on my chest, a year old or so cat she found that looked remarkably like Phoebe.

Of course, I named her Phoebe. And of course, when I needed time to sit and sort out my thoughts, I would sit on the stoop and feed Phoebe sardines from a can with my fingers. I never had to ask or tell the kids to leave me alone. They steered clear, throwing me the look that canned sardines are "gross" (Robbie), "yucky" (Amy), and from our resident snob, Jamie, "completely disgusting Daddy."

The first time Jamie informed me of that, she was sitting next to me while I was feeding Phoebe the sardines. As soon as she said the word "disgusting," I put half of a sardine between my lips and wiggled my head at her as I sucked it into my mouth like spaghetti and chewed it up. She ran off toward the barn screaming, "SO disgusting."

I hollered back, "You're still getting your bedtime kiss with these lips! Does this mean you're not bringing me any crackers?" My kitten answered the question. She looked at me and meowed. We shared the last two fish in the can and got on with our day.

For my birthday, Olivia had given me a horse known for its comfortable ride and 4-footed gait, renown for being sure-footed on trails. It was a dappled gray Pasofino mare. Olivia had reserved her, unborn, and gotten her as a foal. Her registered name was "Macias' Saint Claire" because St. Francis of Assisi was Olivia's favorite saint and Claire was significant in his life. The kids gave me a saddle from a local saddlery known for its

superb fit and materials. Together, Claire and her black
saddle contrasting her dappled coat were beauty to
behold.

Lay of the Land

The clinic and childcare were in the black, making money because the community attitude of 'taking care of our own' in business was extended to Olivia. The Macias name earned respect for she and her family. She was Macias and Macias was Abiquiu-Taos. Roberto's addition to 'The Golden Bull Ranch' (Abiquiu Toro de Oro, Inc.) and his success carried big, long-term influence.

The Golden Bull spanned 5,800 acres (9½ square mile) in the mesquite covered scrub brush hills of New Mexico, approximately 116 miles north of Albuquerque, just northwest of Taos. This ranch gained its world-class reputation for consistent breeding of top-rated bulls for professional rodeo and beef cattle production worldwide, with semen shipped to more than 71 countries a year, boasting a 99% insemination/ live birth success rate.

Much of the ranch's success was attributed to their early acquisition of Olivia's dad whose full name was Roberto Santiago Macias. He was recruited by the company in 1989 after his first five years of professional bull riding earned his place alongside all-time rodeo greats at the Hall of Fame Cowboys Association and Museum, inducted at just 22 years of age.

The Golden Bull's owner helped Roberto acquire the 600-acre Macias Family Ranch adjacent to The Golden Bull, separated only by a highway and a couple small roads, one, unpaved. It was more Abiquiu than Taos.

Roberto rightly reasoned he could breed quarter horses specifically for ranching. He called-in some favors from the rodeo industry and got leads on three breeding pairs and that got him started. He financed ranch hands' purchase of individual horses until the big ranch's owner partnered with Roberto to be the provider of the stock. Still, ranch hands could come to Roberto for a specific horse they liked and wanted.

A Dozen Years Since Scottsdale

Sandy Tuttle's career seemed to soar with Gwen in his life. He was bumped-up to Corporate Vice President of Operations, responsible for traveling to the company's stations to ensure strict adherence to corporate standards and policies. He could have jumped for joy when he learned he was to be Albuquerque-Santa Fe based.

Because of her family's established reputation and business volume, he wasn't so thrilled about breaking the news to Gwen, but she shocked him. She put the business up for sale and told him they would hold the house and lease it seasonally to the spring training baseball players. Her relationship with the league would make that a non-issue. The superstar players would jump at the chance to reside there.

Tomás and Elena were given the option to stay-on at the house, rent- and utility-free in their apartment and continue to draw salaries. They were allowed to freelance as they saw fit, and accepted the opportunity to stay.

Sandy's dream home was ultra-modern and featured an infinity pool that overlooked Albuquerque from its Eastern hills. Sunsets on that patio looked to be hand painted by God. Of course that put them just 120 miles from us and we could spend time with them.

Gwen wasn't accustomed to sitting around and didn't. She leased some high-end retail space and opened a small jewelry store featuring turquoise set in gold and other uniquely southwestern-themed pieces.

Gwen and Sandy surprised the world with a baby which Gwen carried full term and without incident.

She gave birth at the McArdle House with the help a midwife and Sandy at her side. Olivia was looking on, holding Gwen's other hand, exchanging teary smiles with Sandy.

The Tuttle's son was christened Devin Edward Tuttle, from the first names of his grandfathers, and just a year younger than our Amy and Jamie.

Robbie was the most promising young cowboy in both Junior Rodeo and 4-H Rodeo. He specialized in calf roping and was dominating among his peers all over the state of New Mexico. Olivia attributed his keen skill set to having watched her resume barrel racing once we got our ranch established.

He rode 'Breeze' masterfully.

Miguel's son, Junior Fuentes, hand-selected Robbie's horse and personally began training him on the big ranch during his time off. Robbie was just learning to ride on his own and had no clue the horse Miguel was training was for him.

Miguel was a frequent dinner guest and knew he never needed an invitation. He was a surrogate uncle whom the kids could relate-to and look up to. He'd put Ollie on his back and hoot and holler around the living room acting like a buckin' horse, sending Ollie into fits of laughter.

Where There's Smoke

In full bloom, wild lavender ride on the changing breezes giving a nice bouquet to the crisp air.

Summer's rain showers usually didn't last. They'd blow in on wispy clouds in the afternoons and it would just sprinkle or drizzle, but not for long. The raindrops were cold, stinging like needles when they hit your arms, face, and neck.

Amy and Jamie and their horses returned home from the summer's annual skill-building camp with top honors, as did Robbie. Ollie had been out of sorts when his brother and sisters left but quickly learned to soak up his siblings' generous helpings of attention from Ofelia, David, and me.

Boozer and Cruiser weren't themselves without the kids to frolic with and watch over and you never saw two happier dogs once the whole Callan family was back together.

Finishing dinner, David said, "After the table's cleared and your kitchen chores are done, I need you kids to get the barn picked up and anything that's loose that's lying around. A storm front's coming in around midnight and the weather guys tell me it's gonna be with us for a couple of days."

"We could use the moisture, David," I told him.

"Oh, I agree. It's been awfully dry."

"Where are you going, honey?"

"To get two cans of sardines. Phoebe and I need to talk."

"Two cans? That's a big talk."

"The occasion calls for each of us getting our own can. Wanna join us?"

"I dunno. Those are usually pretty serious talks."

"Lemme rephrase that, will you please join us?"

She did, and with a box of our favorite crackers. Phoebe sat between us, glancing at Olivia like I was being unfaithful or something. So I had to make it up to her by petting her more than usual. Olivia just sat with us, completely relaxed. It was the peace we sought and found in living here.

Pandemonium

It was 5:35 in the morning when Boozer went from
whimpering to low, gravelly barks, to loud baying
that awoke Oliver and the rest of the house. All of us
were up like a shot, knowing some kind of danger lurked.
Boozer was telling us something was wrong, terribly
wrong, and he was terribly right.

It smelled like smoke and I ran toward the door
praying to God our barn wasn't in flames. It wasn't our
barn. The foothills across the small road toward the big
ranch, East of our place, were sending a wall of sooty-
looking black smoke into the blue-black sky.

It was a wildfire due North of us and it looked like it
was coming this direction.

From the direction of the Poshuouinge Ruins,
straight North, wider smoke trails were moving and
changing shape and direction in the indigo sky backlit by
the billion nightly stars above us. The fire's glow was
intense, even at that distance.

Ash began falling, drifting down like the beginnings of
a light snow. Later, the ash would fall as hard as a bad
snowstorm. It was the advanced notice of the firestorm to
come and we had everything to do with little time to get it
done.

"I have a plan going in my head."

"Thanks, baby."

I called the station and told the overnight engineer to
break into the programming, announcing an area
wildfire. I told him to monitor the scanners and keep me
posted by text message. I made him repeat my
instructions and transfer me to the announcer: "Get and
keep getting the word out on the wildfire that's raging
North of my house. Engineering is monitoring the
scanners and will keep you updated. It could be life and
death, so I need you focused and on it," and nothing
more needed to be said.

Olivia was on the phone to the clinic and ordered that two of the playrooms be converted to treatment rooms. She directed that the landing lights and flashing beacons on the helipad be turned on and left on.

"David, would you notify Taos fire that our helipad is all lit up and we're ready to triage. We can take 21 patients to stabilize and hold until they instruct us how they want us to proceed further."

"I may have to text. But I'll keep trying, honey. But you better know we may need to evacuate."

"Got it."

"Olivia, I have the kids. I told them to stuff themselves because it's going to be a long and difficult day for all of us."

As soon as Olivia and I roared up to the clinic's front door, she said, "David, I have some energy bars—a whole new box—in my lower desk drawer. Would you grab four of them and two coffees, and we can have a romantic breakfast, cowboy?" and she winked at me. Cool under fire. Even literal fire.

Miraculously, I got through to Taos fire. They were grateful and passed the info to the Fire Manager. It wasn't until then I snagged the energy bars and caught up with Olivia.

We sat at the reception counter enjoying the moment and coffee, taking deep breaths to let it all sink in.

I texted Sandy and asked him to call me ASAP and he did.

"Sandy, I don't know if your guys are aware of it or not, but we've got a wildfire up here, a big burn and it's on the big ranch heading straight South toward us, from the looks of it."

"How can I help?"

"First, if it isn't already out on the air, could you get the word out and that will start Albuquerque resources mobilizing. I'm sure our local fire departments have already started reaching out."

"You got it."

"Next, it's going to be hard for us to know what's going on up at the fire line. We have scanners but can you find the fire manager's radio frequency and text it to me?"

"I'll get on it. I'm ordering our Q-MEG chopper into the air, like 9-1-1 now, for some live feed. I can send that link to your phone. If you want eyes-on for something, anything for you or your place, text me."

"Thanks, Sandy. Our clinic's helipad is lit-up like Christmas. Use it if you need it."

"I'll pass it on. Our chopper pilot just texted me. He's a combat chopper vet and already has rotors turning at Albuquerque. Do you need a drop, David? Ask Olivia. Do you need us to airlift anything to you, immediately?"

"I'll ask Olivia and let you know, Sandy. My dying wish may be to get my kids and Olivia out alive."

He didn't acknowledge that. He heard it, all right. It's hard to reply to the unthinkable.

"Our bird flies over 175 knots an hour so we'll be there in a blink, David."

"Thanks, Sandy."

I grabbed the clock radio at the end of the reception counter and tuned into the Albuquerque station that carried the most news and they were already reporting a major blaze had been spotted, guessing the area correctly as Poshuouinge Ruins.

Olivia dialed Ofelia and put her on speaker.

"Mom, get everyone around the kitchen table, asap, please, okay?

"They're here already, Olivia, eating everything in sight."

I took the phone out of Olivia's hand and got a look that didn't convey happy. She shrugged her shoulders at me in resignation.

Roberto's words roared up from within my memory, the ones he spoke as he left our house to return home without Ofelia: *You don't know your capability until you put on that hat, David. Life can be funny that way, son.*

467

*Sometimes it's a moment when life calls us to 'man-up'
and we do it without hesitating. Trust me, you'll be fine."*

The strength and resolve in my voice and attitude
was newfound and had to have come from Roberto's
influence on me.

"Okay, family, here's the deal. Your mom has turned
the clinic into an evacuation station. I've got a call into
your mom's E.R. doctor friend, Maddie, to see if I can get
her and her husband here to do triage. I don't want bad
injuries to overwhelm our capabilities. If she can't get
here, your mom knows a lot of great people who may
come to help. We're in for a crazy day."

"Ofelia? I'm going to have you do one thing and one
thing only, today. You are in total and complete charge of
Oliver. You are to let us know where you are every
minute of the day. Easy enough?"

"I've got this, David!" Ofelia responded.

"Make sure your phone is fully charged, Mom,
okay?"

"Yes, son."

"Then, Ofelia, I need you to go through the house
with the girls and point out everything that needs to be
loaded into my 4x4 and one Mercedes, irreplaceable stuff
only. Load up the family photographs, mementos,
documents, and records. Amy and Jamie? You are in
charge of finding boxes for all that stuff and making
absolutely sure you grab a bag of dog food, girls."

"Everyone clear so far?" and they all answered
positively.

"Robbie, you've got to be my outside guy, our eyes
and ears. First, I need you to take all the keys and make
sure the SUV and truck are gassed-up. Make yourself
available to help your grandmother with the loadout from
the house, okay, son?"

"Can do, Dad."

"Did I miss anything Olivia?"

"Just this," and she kissed me.

"Also, you didn't kiss our babies and tell them you loved them this morning."

"Kids? Tell her the truth, that I did, or no one gets allowance this week."

We heard the kids giggle, "Your mom doesn't see everything, does she!"

"I have to be serious for a minute. Listen. It's okay to be scared. We all are, your mom and me included, but we are going to be okay. Your grandfather always said is true: "Family gets through things and gets things through.""

"We'll run up and check on you! Love you!" and the kids said goodbye before our disconnect. I handed Olivia her phone.

"Nicely done, cowboy. I'm going to call Taos Medical's answering service and get all the oxygen tanks I can get our hands on and tell them to get their asses out here with it. I suspect smoke will be our biggest injury problem, initially."

"Honey, I'm texting Miguel to see if there's anything we can do to support them over there." Before I could move, my phone rang. Miguel.

"Miguel, let me put you on speaker."

"It's really bad up here, brother. The fire is coming down from our northeast and the beef cattle in the remote grazing areas are starting to panic. We're evacuating the breeding barns to get the prized bulls trailered out of here. To where, I don't know yet. We'll figure it out."

"I'd say bring them here, but that bastard of a fire seems to be aiming at us."

"Not there, *Jefe*. South, yes, but then I think East is the way. We'll see.

I've got some guys in serious danger up that way. The heavy smoke's too risky to go in for them or even get close because of the wind's direction changes. I told them on the walkies that the cattle will take care of themselves, and they need to get out. If they can try to steer the cattle away from the fire and away from heading down to the highway in the process, all the better."

"Olivia?"

"Yes, Miguel, I'm here."

"Olivia, we're using the "B" frequency of the walkies at the ranch. If you or David can monitor us with one of your walkies, we may be able to help each other. I can let you know if we have any injured coming your way."

"You got it, Miguel. I'm working on getting more medical folks here. David helped me convert a couple of the childcare rooms into treatment rooms. We're as ready as we can be."

"Hey, warn everybody on or near the road the cattle may stampede right into them. There's no way I can tell how many of them or when. OH JESUS, I gotta go and I mean now! I love you guys." And the call disconnected.

"I completely forgot about the walkie-talkies, David. They're in the tack room, big box. We have four and four chargers. They'll receive and send, even in the chargers. Can you please run-up and get 'em?"

Robbie had already decided he was going to do something to help Junior and he enlisted Amy as an accomplice. He could yell at Jamie. She'd stay put and not be a tattletale.

Once the girls had gathered things up, Jamie was made to swear not to say where her brother and sister had gone until 10 minutes after they left. Robbie and Amy were determined to help Miguel and Junior any way they could.

Robbie had Roberto's guts and determination. At his age, it wasn't hard for Robbie to know he and Amy might need every ounce of skill to steer stampeding cattle away from the road where the first responders and their equipment were probably staging. Hundreds of people could be hurt or killed if the cattle charged onto that road. At his age, Robbie didn't have the analytical skills to sense how wrong it could go for him and Amy. Their lives might be in jeopardy.

Olivia's phone rang, "Olivia, this is Maddie."

"Oh my God, Maddie!"

"It doesn't sound like you got word I'm coming. Albuquerque's Saint Ann's is going to load their chopper with supplies and pick Danny and I up at the Albuquerque airport. We're enroute to you. If there's anything else you need, tell me. I'm told our ETA is about 80 minutes."

It was unusual for Olivia to start weeping, "I'm keeping it together, but I can sure use support from you guys. Thank you, I love you, Maddie," she said, sniffling.

"I love you too, girlfriend. I'm not leaving you hanging on this one, not without doing my God-damnedest, anyway."

"The clinic's helipad is pictured on our website. It's lit up and has rotating beacons. You'll see it."

"Gotcha, kiddo. We're a-comin'!"

As first light was hitting, some vehicles began skidding into the parking lot near our doors with minor burn and smoke inhalation victims.

Olivia stepped back, letting the staff follow her instructions. There was no telling when the on-call Nurse Practitioner, Peter, could or would arrive. There was no sense trying to contact him. He had family, too. Her insight to peoples' character told her he'd be there as quickly as humanly possible if he could. Until then, she and the two assistants could manage.

Near Dead

Olivia happened to look up at one of the TV screens in the lobby. The news was showing live aerial shots. They were showing how the fire and smoke were being pushed Southward, down a hill. There were 400-500 rampaging cattle coming down the hill.

A couple hundred yards ahead of the cattle were two specks, moving downhill, too. The camera zoomed in and you could make out it was two mounted riders. The chopper neared as the camera kept adjusting its focus and zoom.

David heard Olivia scream and whirled to watch her collapse onto her knees, yelling, "No! No! No! My babies, NO!"

It was Funny Face, unmistakably so, next to Breeze. The kids were running for their lives, spurring each of their horses at a full gallop.

We watched as Breeze started to falter, throw his head from side-to-side, fighting Robbie's rein. Suddenly, Breeze's front legs collapsed and hurled Robbie's body into Amy just three feet to his right, knocking her out of the saddle and onto the ground that was moving fast under her. She hit hard and tumbled, coming to rest completely still.

Olivia's screams were like icepicks on the eardrums, watching her children about to be trampled on live television, now, nationwide.

Breeze suddenly lay still where he had fallen, probably dead. Funny Face's sense of survival continued taking him down that hill at a dead run.

Robbie appeared to crawl to Amy, who was on her back. He took her hand. They knew, everyone watching knew. It's wasn't only a fire that was coming. It was hundreds of wild-eyed, terrified cattle charging down the hill at them. A cattle stampede was about to kill two children on live television. My two children.

My phone buzzed. Text from Sandy: "Hold my beer."

Olivia's screams of, "No. Not my babies, God. No!" continued.

I screamed at her, "<u>OH MY GOD</u>! <u>OLIVIA</u>! <u>OLIVIA</u>! <u>LOOK</u>!"

The camera on the helicopter instantly zoomed back as wide as possible. In what can only be described as an emergency, battlefield-type circular descent, another helicopter's tight-cone of a turn was leveling out to put the aircraft's skids about twenty feet from the kids.

The pilot positioned the aircraft facing the oncoming herd, swaying back and forth, using his prop wash and the engine noise to detour them. It worked.

We saw someone hop out, and then another. The other was Sandy, who got Amy onto the airship and then got Robbie loaded.

It lifted off in a semicircle pointing at what seemed to be our direction.

My phone rang.

"Dad! We're okay!," and I couldn't help weeping, "Just a second, son, let me put you on speaker for your mom."

"We're okay, Dad," Amy said, and I knew she was injured.

"Amy's leg's messed up and my shoulder's messed up but we're okay," Olivia's sobs were articulated with relief, hope and joy, thanking God.

"It's Mommy! I'm waiting for you."

"David, I'm putting you on speaker for the pilot."

"Standby, Caballero Clinic. Unidentified chopper about 160 degrees on a one-eight-zero heading. I have visual on you. This is QMEG *chopper November Kilo X-Ray One Niner Five, copy?*"

"*QMEG aircraft, this is St. Ann's AirMed2. I have a doctor, nurse, and medical supplies, Priority One, inbound to Caballero Clinic pad.*"

"*Copy you St. Ann, this is QMEG. I have two injured aboard. Sir, recommend you offload the MD first so they can take my patients.*"

"`10-4, QMEG. St Ann has the pad for quick off-load. I'll circle out at heading two-seven zero for your ninety-degree inbound approach unless you advise otherwise."*

"Copy, St. Ann. Thank you, sir. QMEG following you in."*

"Copy that. We're allowed on-station another hour. Will set down on the other side of the complex to assist any additional evac."*

"10-4, St. Ann. QMEG out."*

The pilot gestured for Sandy to hold the cellphone closer.

"Caballero Clinic, we just set up an aerial ballet for you. That doc will be on the pad less than 30 seconds before your patients land. They' clear your pad in a hot minute for my touchdown,. copy?"*

I still couldn't stop the tears, "Sandy...."

"You can tell me when you see me, David. I'm a man on a mission," and somewhere within himself, he found a comforting and consoling laugh that instantly made Olivia and I feel better.

I ran out toward the pad, keeping a safe distance from the two choppers roaring in.

Maddie Hale and her trauma trained RN husband were standing next to the gurneys we had staged when the helicopter gently settled onto the pad. Maddie and her husband insisted on personally transferring the kids to gurneys.

Robbie was first off.

"Robbie, I'm Doctor Hale. I'm a pal of your mom's from Scottsdale. My husband's an emergency room RN. We're gonna take care of you, young man."

"Hey, there, son! You mom's watching from the doors. See?"

He nodded as I was leaning over to kiss his forehead.

Through his pain, Robbie managed a weak smile.

As Amy came off the bird, Maddie said, "Hi, Amy, I worked with your mom at Scottsdale. I'm a doctor there.

My husband and I are going to take care of you," and Amy just nodded slightly in acknowledgement.

"Hey, sweetie! Mom's at the door waiting for you, worried silly!"

She mumbled something unintelligible as I leaned to kiss her forehead before she was whisked away on the gurney.

I helped Sandy jump out of the helicopter as I heard Olivia squeal at being beside our injured kids.

"You saved my kids' lives, Sandy."

"You'd do the same. Robbie's shoulder's bad and I think Amy broke her leg or hip."

"Olivia's friend's an E.R. doc. She'll check them over from stem to stern, Sandy."

I couldn't help it. I threw my arms around my former boss and was weeping like a baby.

"You risked your life for them. You could have been killed, Sandy."

"Good fortune smiled on us, David. We've got to get back in the air."

"I understand."

"Yell if you need anything, here. There's talk that Abiquiu and Taos could be evacuated if this monster shapes-up the way it's looking."

"We'll be ready to go."

We shook hands and Sandy boarded the chopper. I yelled at the pilot, who lifted one of the ear cups of his headset away to hear me, "YOU'RE MY NEW HERO!" and he yelled "THANKS. I'VE GOT KIDS, TOO," and he gave me a thumbs-up as the door slid shut and the aircraft cleared our helipad.

Olivia let Maddie and her husband evaluate the kids. As she worked, Maddie said, "This is impressive, Olivia. Even a helipad."

"There's more," Olivia said, "we have imaging down the hall."

"You're kidding."

"Only urgent care I know that I know of that has it, Maddie. My tech made it in and is standing by."

Maddie looked at her husband, "If we ever move to New Mexico, honey—"

"Noted," he said, his eyes smiling above the surgical mask he wore.

"Okay, let's get some pictures of Amy's leg and a hip series, and a shoulder series for Robbie. While that's happening, can a girl get a cup of coffee around here, anywhere?"

"My office. This way," and Maddie and her husband followed as the gurneys rolled toward X-ray.

We were emotionally spent. Olivia looked like she aged twenty years. Then, Olivia smacked her own forehead.

"My GOD, honey, I've got to get those walkies from the tack room."

"God, I forgot, too. I'm on it. I'll make sure Ofelia and Jamie are okay and bring back whatever food I can scrounge up for all of us."

I turned to Maddie and her husband, "Thanks. Just...thanks," and Maddie waved me off like, 'No big deal.'

I pulled up in front of the tack room and opened the Mercedes' rear hatch. I walked right to the box where the radios were, got the heavy box into the SUV, and pulled up to our front door.

I made a beeline to Oliver and picked him up. He was happy to see me, "You taking care of your *abuela*, buddy? You better be! You're the man of the house, huh!" and I kissed him.

"Ofelia? Jamie?"

Ofelia met me, "Jamie's crying in her room. She thinks it's her fault Robbie and Amy got hurt."

I kissed my mother-in-law, "Thanks, let me get in there."

I knocked gently on the girls' door, "Jamie, it's Dad." No response, and when I entered, she was sobbing with the pillow over her head. I sat on her bed and took her in my arms.

She immediately hugged me, "I'm so sorry, Daddy. I didn't mean…"

"Shh, baby. They're gonna be okay. It wasn't your fault and you're not in trouble. In fact, I need you to help me, okay? Will you help your dad, here?"

Jamie looked at me with questioning eyes as she wiped her tears away from them and nodded.

"Will you help your abuela and I make some sandwiches or something for everyone at the clinic?"

"Daddy, she's been in the kitchen, cooking," and I hadn't noticed the smell of what seemed like Mexican food. Jamie followed me into the kitchen. I was stunned.

Ofelia had been making burritos. There must have been three dozen huge, foil-wrapped burritos sitting on the counter. Ofelia just looked at me, smiled and shrugged her shoulders. "It's what I do."

"I really did marry a young version of you, didn't I, Mom?"

"Not really. I'm a better cook than Olivia but only because I've been doing it so much longer. I've got beef, bean 'n cheese, and veggie burritos done. They're labeled…. Jamie?"

"Yes, Grandma?"

"Would you please go in the pantry and grab a couple big jars of that salsa I canned? And if there are big bags of chips, those, too." And Jamie opened the pantry just six steps from her, putting the salsa and three big bags of tortilla chips on the counter.

"What can I do, Ofelia?"

"Can we get the burritos into a cooler to try to keep them somewhat warm, David?"

"Jamie, take your brother, please," and I handed him off.

"On the way, Ofelia. It's clean and right inside the garage," and I was back in a minute with a 60-quart, high-end cooler that Ofelia and Jamie packed. It was big but not heavy, so Ofelia and I managed to get it out to the SUV.

"Mom, I'd feel better if you grab a few things and bring your SUV down to the clinic. Maybe grab a change of clothes for Olivia and the kids, please? If we get the word to evacuate, I need everyone present and accounted-for."

Amy had a broken ankle and a simple greenstick fracture of her leg. Maddie and her husband were shaping a plaster-backed splint with cling wrapping over the top to control swelling.

Robbie's shoulder injury was more serious. It would probably give him fits later in life. Olivia would ensure he'd have all the physical therapy he wanted and then some.

We all caught our breaths and grabbed a burrito. Olivia opened the soda machine so everyone could help themselves. I pulled a chair up between Robbie's and Amy's gurneys.

Amy was wolfing-down her burrito and had a can of orange soda. I was helping Robbie manage his burrito and soda. I felt a familiar hand on my back that began rubbing it softly.

"I haven't seen your dad feed you two since you were babies," and Olivia's grin lit up the room, answered by grins from the kids.

"It doesn't hurt as much as it did before, Mom. I'm doing better."

Olivia stroked his hair, "You're doing better because Dr. Hale and her husband are taking care of you, and, you are full of pain medicine, cowboy."

The day had worn on into early afternoon and the falling ash was constant. Patients continued to straggle in and were seen immediately.

"Your burritos saved us, Mom!"

"Roberto used to say, 'An army marches on its stomach,' or something like that, David."

"Let's head for the conference room, Mom. The break room's too small, already."

The walkie talkies were on Fire Control's main frequency, texted to me by Sandy. The other 2 walkies were on the big ranch's channel B. One of them squawked and I nearly dove to grab it.

"QMEG chopper to Caballero Clinic."

"Go for Caballero, this is David."

"We are ten mikes out, requesting landing clearance if your pad is clear."

"Do you have patients on board?"

"Negative. Human cargo and some cases of bottled water for you folks."

"10-4, QMEG. The pad is clear. Will advise if we see or hear any inbound traffic, copy?"

Less than ten minutes later, *"Caballero clinic, the pad is in view. Request landing, please."*

"This is Caballero, you are green-lighted to land, QMEG," and the chopper swooped in and gently settled on the pad just as I was walking out the receiving doors.

The first thing I saw was Gwen, bounding off of the helicopter coming for me at a dead run, "Oh my God, David, you are a sight for sore eyes!," and we squeezed each other tightly.

"I am? You're married to a hero that saved my kids' lives, Gwen," I told her as Sandy hopped down onto the pad and we embraced.

"She insisted coming, David. The promotions department had cases and cases of bottled water for our remotes so I figured you could use some. Ten cases, 20-ounce bottles."

"Ofelia's got a hot lunch laid-out in the conference room so chow-down. Homemade burritos."

"We're famished, thanks."

"Again, you're a Godsend." I turned back to Gwen, "My wife could sure use a hug from you right about now, Gwen."

"Aieeeeeee!!" we heard Olivia squeal gleefully as she ran toward Gwen from the receiving doors. They practically jumped into each other's arms and chatter-boxed their way back inside and into the conference room. We sat across from Sandy and Gwen as they ate. The pilot was happy to get some food, too, and was gulping down black coffee like it was just invented.

"Our son's at one of his friend's houses. I couldn't stay away, Olivia. I was worried sick."

"I love you, Gwen. But I don't want you here because there's talk we're going to have to run for it. Evacuate."

"I had to see you and we thought you could use the water."

"And we can use it, thanks. Let's get it off-loaded and get you out of here, okay? The ash is beginning to fall heavier and there may not be a chance for aircraft to get out."

"It's not the bum's rush. It's true, Sandy," I told him.

The pilot agreed, "They're right. Conditions are worsening. And reports I've heard don't look good for this area. Not good at all."

As soon as the water came off and they boarded, we waved and blew them kisses. Might it be the last time we ever saw them? I'm sure Olivia was thinking that, too.

Egress

I went to the desk as soon as we got back inside.

"Olivia, put me on the P.A. please," and she picked up the phone's handset, hit three keys and handed it to me.

"This is David. I want everyone in the conference room as soon as possible, please. No exceptions."

Olivia did a silent headcount: x-ray, two LPNs, Maddie and Mac, Ofelia and Oliver, Jamie, Amy and Robbie on the gurneys, and me made 12.

"Here's the evacuation plan. First, Maddie, are you staying or can we get you out with the St. Ann's bird right now?"

She looked to her husband, "We're all in with you and Olivia. Mac and I will get Amy and Robbie loaded, ASAP. Olivia and I kissed each of them as Maddie and Mac each got behind a gurney heading for the exit nearest the chopper. We heard it take off. Maddie and Mac returned huffing and puffing.

"Thank you and thank God because you solved a problem before it became one. Ofelia, you and Oliver and the dogs will be in your SUV. You're our lead vehicle because you know the terrain. Maddie, you'll be in my 4x4 pickup following Ofelia."

I pointed at Mac, Maddie's husband. "Mac, are you good to drive an SUV behind Maddie's?"

"Sure. Anything."

"What about ME, Daddy," Amy asked, feeling sad and overlooked.

"Honey, you have one of the *importantest* jobs of all," I said, changing my look over to Olivia.

"You and me and Mom and are going to ride out and bring the dogs with us.. You don't think Daddy would leave our horses behind, do you, punkin'?"

She shook her head, "Then what about the kitties?"

"Phoebe's going to ride inside Daddy's shirt, and Raptor, if we can find him, can go in a kennel cage in one of the SUVs. Ollie will ride with Mom in the canvas carrier, mmm-kay?”

Olivia looked stunned. “Ride out?”

“Trailers will be impossible to find. If the fire’s all over the roads, we’ll have to go cross-country.”

“Which way, David,” Ofelia asked.

“South. We follow the creek bed. Depending on the fire, we’ll turn Northwest and head for the lake. Or not.”

“Everybody, charge your cellphones, now. I want these radios in the chargers until the very last minute, okay?”

“Staff, you can go as soon as we get the evacuation order and sooner if your families need you, all right?”

Everyone was in general agreement.

“Any questions? Anyone? Any questions?”

I smiled over at Olivia, “We’ve got this.” I saw a potent mixture of love and pride when we locked eyes.

“Yes we do, *jefe*,” and her eyes were twinkling with love.

The radios crackled, “This is fire control. Evacuate Abiquiu and Taos. We don’t even have 5 percent containment and the wind is changing constantly, sparking new burns. Repeat, Evacuate Abiquiu and Taos.”

“Fire control to Caballero Clinic.”

“Go for Caballero, Chief.”

“You folks have done some fine work, but I need you gone from there.”

“We have a plan and are ready.”

“Great job. Do you need assistance?”

“Negative, Chief. We’ll be moving South along the creek bed inside of 20 minutes with your approval.”

“I like it, Caballero. Maintain radio contact and thank you folks for your assist, there. Fire Control, out.

Mack gave Jamie, Olivia and I a ride up to the barn.

Jamie would trail Oliver’s little Morgan horse.

“Olivia, how about if you take Funny Face and I’ll trail Casper. That sound okay?” I got two thumbs up.

Amy's horse seemed to be in good enough shape to go. Since the two girls had grown up riding together, their horses were acquainted with each other.

"Fine, honey."

"Let's get up to the house. I'm gonna grab some sardines to lure Phoebe out. Why don't you do a run-through in the house, medicine cabinets, any last-minute things you can think of. We can just put stuff in pillowcases and tie them together."

"Okay, baby," and she disappeared to the back of the house while I grabbed the remaining twelve cans of sardines for my Phoebe and me.

I sat on the porch and pulled the pop-top off the sardine can and heard her familiar, 'Meowwwww." Boozer and Cruiser were stretched out in front of me.

"There you are, Phoebe!," and I picked her up and held her in my arms. "I'm gonna get us out of here just as soon as you and I have our snack, deal?" and she meowed and rubbed her head against my arm.

"The house is clear, David," I heard Olivia say behind me.

"Leave the doors unlocked, honey. First responders may want to check the house for occupants."

"I'll do better than that. I'll make a quick sign and put "EVACUATED. NO ONE HOME.""

"That'll work, too."

We rode slowly away from the home we had built and into which we had brought three of our babies. The horses were in tow behind us. Olivia was riding beside me and we kept wordlessly reassuring each other with smiles. The air was fouled but we were doing fine.

The vehicles were in line at the clinic, exactly as I had directed.

Maddie walked over to Olivia, 'My God, what a gorgeous horse."

"A birthday present from my David."

"I need your keys to get the controlled drugs out of the lock-up, Olivia."

"My office, lower left drawer on a red fuzzy keyring. Good catch, Maddie."

Mack walked out with the radios and handed me one, and Olivia, another. He and Maddie would carry the other two.

Olivia keyed the mic, "Caballero Clinic to Fire Control."

"Go, Caballero."

"We're out in ten minutes. Do you want us to leave the oxygen tanks or empty them so a fire doesn't turn into an explosion?"

"Keep them intact, Caballero. We may need that O-two for my smoke eaters, and I can task someone to get it."

"10-4, all yours, Chief. We're heading South along the creek bed, now."

"God bless and Godspeed, Caballero crew. Fire Control, out."

Less than a half hour away from the clinic, a familiar voice came over my radio on the B frequency.

"David or Olivia, copy?"

"Go for David." It was Junior.

"Nothing more we can do here. We're out. You gone yet?"

"We're out, Junior. Our SUVs and horses are moving South along the creek bed."

"I'll head your way and join up."
"We may turn Northwest toward the lake, depending on the fire."

"Gotcha. It's still headed for your place, David."
"Yeah, we know," and Olivia looked at me with a somber an expression.

About 90 minutes later, we spotted a small dust cloud getting kicked-up and saw a single rider.

"That you, Junior?"

His radio crackled, "Yep. I see you."

"We're going to stop here for potty and some drinking water. No need to hurry. I have a burrito with your name on it."

"Don't make me cry. I'm so hungry my saddle horn was looking good."

"Spare it. We have chips and salsa here, and if you beg, I bet I can find a beer."

"I just begged."

As we got everyone stopped and everyone was getting out to stretch or pee or grab some water, Olivia said, "We don't have beer, David! Why did you do that to him!??"

"Jamie, honey, I need you to ask your grandmother for the dog food. Feed Boozer and Cruiser, and get them water. Mac will help you get some water from the ice chest. They're probably exhausted. Do it now, please. After they eat and drink, I want you to check them for ticks, okay? If you find any ticks, let your Daddy know, okay?"

"Alright, Daddy," she replied with a salute and a grin, something she got from her mother.

Ofelia reminded me, "There's plenty of Gwen's bottled water, too, David. I'll get some for Jamie."

I yelled over, "Mac! There's an 80-quart chest in the back of my truck. Finders keepers, and grab us all one."

Mac approached drinking an ice-cold beer, handed one to Olivia and me, to Ofelia and Maddie. He used the drain on the ice chest to fill the dogs' bowl.

"We have beer, honey," I said after my first pull, smirking at my beautiful wife.

As she popped the top, she shook her head and said, "Always full of surprises, David, you sneaky wonderful so-and-so!" and laughter broke the tension.

Mac said, "Looked like three cases and two different flavors to me, Olivia," and she grinned.

"Mr. Considerate is one of my pet names for him, Mac."

I teased, "I didn't do it for you, Olivia. It's for Ofelia. I know how she feels about a good cold beer every now and then," and I held up a can toward her, "Mom? Another beer!?"

She nodded and Mac handed her another one while she was loading up a plate for Junior.

When he rode up, Ofelia handed him the beer before he even dismounted. He tipped his hat and walked *Chongo* over to lash him on a small pine.

"There's a hundred-pound sack of horse pellets in the back of the pickup if you want me to feed Chongo while you eat. My guys gotta be hungry, too."

It was Ofelia, "I'll feed the horses, David. I fed you, now the horses eat." My mother-in-law never failed to step-up.

Junior sat right down in the dirt with us, piling food into his mouth as he did. "I think I ate yesterday. I'm sorry if I look like a pig."
Olivia leaned over and patted him on the shoulder, "I grew up feeding you hungry cowboys, helping Mom. Remember, Junior?"

"That was you? I remember Ofelia's helper was young and cute, but mouthy??? She was a pain in the backside," he razzed Olivia.

Olivia picked up a small stone and threw it at him.

"Hey! I'm eating!" protested Junior, jokingly.

She looked at Mac and Maddie, "Excuse me," and then she gave Junior the finger which wasn't lost on Jamie who saw it and giggled.

Without even looking at her, Olivia said, "If I see you give anybody the finger, young lady, you're grounded until you're 21."

As we gathered everything up, Junior produced a brush and curry comb and took care of all the horses just before we mounted up.

Almost three hours later, under a smoke marbled sky, we knew we were safe. We were well to the South and heading toward the reservoir.

Ofelia piped up, "Junior, get us a dug-in campfire going. I have beef we can cook on skewers," and magically, Ofelia and Junior made that happen. Again, the protein was a big lift and from Ofelia's mastery, out-of-this-world.

"Fire Control to Caballero Crew."

"Go for Caballero, Chief."

"The news isn't good. The fire turned East. We fought like hell but couldn't keep it from getting to your house." He paused to let the news sink in.

Our group was stunned silent. Olivia, holding Oliver, dropped her head. She wasn't the only one weeping. Maddie came over and consoled her. I rummaged around and found a can of sardines and walked about 20 feet away from everybody and plunked down with Phoebe in my lap.

"What don't I put you through, kitty. Two big ole dogs, a crazy feral cat, and kids being kids." We shared the sardines as I mourned the loss of our home and tried to imagine the 'what next' for my family and friends.

I heard the radio call, "It's gone, Mr. and Mrs. Callan. I'm sorry. We're working to save the clinic, now, and that's looking promising. So don't give up hope, copy?"

Junior grabbed the walkie because Olivia and I were in shock.

"Fire control, they heard you."

"We'll keep you posted on the clinic. Fire control, out."

We pressed on and were advised it was safe to take the road to the reservoir where dozens of support teams and vehicles were based. We were exhausted when we got there.

Maddie got Olivia into the hands of the ground ambulance crews, showing her I.D. and telling them she had privileges at St. Ann's, Albuquerque. She told them, "This woman's in shock and her kids have already been admitted to St. Ann's."

Some of it was a lie but it worked. I kissed Olivia and she was whisked off in the ambulance.

I checked in at the FEMA tent, told them our home
was gone. They had me sit and answer questions as a
young guy filled out some online forms.

"We can get you shelter in Albuquerque. Hotel rooms
for all of you."

"What do I do about our livestock?"

"An area rancher will take them. Tell me whatcha got
and I'll have trailers for them inside of 2 hours."

"I didn't know the Fed could move so fast."

"It's that fast because we *didn't* have anything to do
with it. Local relief groups put that together for you.
You'll have them to thank."

It was one of Albuquerque's nicer hotels. I texted
Olivia and told her where we were and that I'd shower
and get a cab to St. Ann's.

Because I fibbed to the hotel and told them we all
lived together, they gave us their premier suite and four
rooms, enough beds and foldouts for sixteen people.
Everyone got a bed.

I reached the Peds wing of St. Ann's, meeting up with
Mac, Maddie, and Olivia. The kids were fine and sleeping.
Sedated. Maddie, Mac, and I grabbed a cab out of there
and headed for the suite where I promised strong
cocktails all around.

Ashes, Ashes, Nobody Falls Down

The 'El Charma River Valley Fire,' as history recorded it, burnt down our house without destroying our hopes and dreams. A massive wind shift and the heroics of the firefighters saved the clinic and daycare center. Many of those firefighters had been to the clinic or taken advantage of the availability of affordable childcare. For them, it was a labor of love that paid off. They felt terrible fighting to save the house only to see it get consumed.

Our house plans were on file with the County Recorder and the building permit folks. We were insured to the hilt and had cash to get things rolling. With a couple minor floorplan improvements, we'd walk into the new house in under 100 days. For now, the rented house just out of Taos would work.

I called Olivia out of the clinic and led her to a ladder on the side of the clinic.

"Don't tell me we have roof damage, David."

I started up the ladder, got onto the roof and peered over the edge at her, "Nothing like that. C'mon, the view's nice up here," and I extended my hand to help her negotiate the last rung.

Olivia was on all fours and rotated to sit next to me.

"I'm grateful, Olivia. I've been coming up here to tell God I'm grateful." Olivia was still and pensive.

She looked over, "I took you out of your element. I took you away from the city, from a storied career and put you through the endless headaches of realizing my dreams while left yours in the dust."

Olivia sounded pissed, "And you can tell God that you're grateful."

"You didn't take me away from the city life, Olivia. I offered my heart, prayed you would take it and you did, willingly and lovingly. We couldn't know our destination. No one does because that's up to faith and hope and a lot of luck and effort thrown in. I was willing to make the journey without looking back. Without regret. If for only a short while, I had a dad who loved me, thanks to you. I had a dad who made me feel like a kid with a dad."

I spread out my arms as if to hug the Western sky.

"God and you have given me everything, Olivia. Everything. A big portion of the small talk your dad and I made...on the patio, getting the Christmas tree, Christmas shopping and running around together? It was about the inner workings of this ranch: How it ran profitably and his vision for its future. It never occurred to me he might have a purpose in explaining all that. He did it to prepare me. He was sick and trying to give me a primer while he could."

"Probably so, David."

"And then, as soon as we knew we were facing catastrophic consequences from the wildfire, it seemed as if he was guiding me, steering me toward the next right thing to do."

"I noticed. I'd never seen you so assertive. Like Daddy, you were calm but firm. Maybe firm's not the right word. Inner conviction and, in hindsight, every call you made was the right one. I wasn't sure what changed inside of you, but you were changed. I stepped back for you to lead."

"You saved a lot of our lives, David. I'll tell you a secret: I was coming apart inside, the pressures of being a mom, business owner, concerned for the safety of our volunteers and employees, losing the house or businesses or both. Your newfound strength let me regain mine and get my wits about me."

"Olivia, I soaked up every nuance, thought, and action during my painfully short time with Roberto. He gave me inspiration and a compass to follow, something an unadopted orphan may never have," and I could only put my knees up and rest my elbows on them, with my face cradled by my hands.

Olivia tugged my shirtsleeve, "You're my lifelong love and hero, cowboy," and a wide grin spread over both of us before she tenderly kissed me.

No sooner did our lips part than I noticed that Olivia looked like it was taking all of her strength to suppress a smile and maybe even a laugh.

I had to ask, "Okay what's going on between those ears of yours? I used to think that I knew but anymore I'm not so sure."

She looked at me grinning like the Cheshire cat and said, "I realized it's usually times like these that I tell you we're going to have a baby."

"And?"

"Ha! Gotcha."

"I would never have dreamt we would have a family of six, Olivia, and I couldn't be happier if you *were* to tell me we were pregnant again."

I shook my head, loving her all the more and said, "What on Earth am I going to do with you, Olivia!?"

She's sat up and slipped her arms around my neck, and kissed me gently. She locked her gaze onto mine, "Nothing. You're going to do nothing different, cowboy. We've gotten it right so far. We're not going to change what's continued to work for us."

I had my arms crossed and tucked up under her breasts. Olivia's head was against my collarbone and I whispered in her ear, "Can you believe we have everything we ever wanted?"

She thought a minute, "Come to think of it, you're right but.... Did we really ask for much? I mean, we never had money problems, and that's a situation few people ever experience. We set some goals and worked our butts off to achieve them. Our success never wrecked us, made us hate each other. Your love and presence kept me going, David."

"I agree, we had a head start financially, but other people have had that and bungled or pissed it away, frivolously, with nothing to show for it. We stayed grounded, centered."

Olivia let that sink in for a long moment, just pondering it.

"Yeah but you know what we *need?*

"Need? We don't need a thing, do we?"

She repositioned herself and moved my arms to her waist.

She slowly turned my hands over and placed my palms against her tummy, "We need names, cowboy. I guess I was testing your reaction a minute ago."

"Oh my God, Olivia, we *are* expecting?" And I started to laugh and couldn't stop. I yelled, "Woo Hoo!! We're getting a new ranch hand!!" I patted her lower abdomen and went into a full belly laugh.

"Ya done went and did it again."

"Woo Hoo! Five kids!!" I kissed her with all the intensity and love that was coating the moment. I moved my arms back up to her rib cage and pulled her more tightly into me.

She looked back at me over her shoulder, "Six is a good number, David."

She saw my 'dumb cow stare' and held up two fingers, ""David?"

"Yes, my love?"

"We are getting a *pair* of new ranch hands. Twins again, cowboy. This time we have a Carey and Mary in Mama's oven. Or Ronnie and Bonnie. Might be Dean and Eileen or Andy and Randi."

I know she heard me suck wind....

"I got my ultrasound in Taos so nobody at the clinic could ruin my surprise."

"And?"

"27 and 1/2 weeks from now, the boys get a baby brother and the girls get a little sister. But..."

That straightened me up, "But?"

"If it's okay with you I think I'm calling it quits after these two, David."

"I'm completely okay with that! I'm surprised we didn't stop after the twins. I love you and I love every hair on each of our kids' heads. Now, about those names....

"I obviously had time to think about it. I like Lynne and Quinn. Thoughts?"

"Love 'em. Done."

"I'll leave the four saints names up to you."

"And?"

"And the last one naked in the bed has to cook breakfast. Since I'm preggers, I get the ladder first."

Center Stage

In April, Sanderson Tuttle was called to center stage at the Broadcasters and Cable Operators National Association meeting in Las Vegas. He was named 'Broadcaster of the Year' and given a special citation for heroism for placing his life in danger to save two children on a remote hillside in New Mexico, while still generating critical news feed back to the station.

As a BACON-A member, I was allowed to attend. Our family was asked to stand. When we did, Sandy couldn't hide the tears.

Less than 2 weeks later, just before Mother's Day, the landline at the house rang. Robbie grabbed it and looked at me.

"Dad? They said it's the President of the United States?"

I sneered at him even though only a literal handful of people had this number.

"Hand me the phone, son.... Hello?"

"Mr. Callan, I'm calling for the President of the United States to invite you and your wife to the White House. The President would like you to participate in a presidential citation being given to Sanderson Tuttle."

"You're kidding, right?"

"My name is Mrs. Samantha Holland, the President's appointment secretary. I can give you my private line's extension and you are welcome to call The White House operator's line and ask for extension 46125."

"No, that's okay. You convinced me. You can understand my skepticism. Sandy saved my children's lives. He's deserving of that and more as far as I'm concerned. We'll be there."

"The President wanted me to tell you that he was watching live television as Mr. Tuttle saved your children's lives during the wildfire. He was touched, moved beyond belief. We will provide your airfare and two nights in a hotel with shuttle service by White House personnel."

"I'm...I don't quite know what to say except yes, we will be there. I'm sure my wife would want our children to be there, all six of them."

"It was the President's hope that you would bring them and he's included them in the transportation and accommodations. We have your address on file and we'll send you an information packet by certified mail. I have Mr. Tuttle on hold and would like to bring him into the call."

"By all means, please do so."

"Mr. Tuttle, Mr. Callan is on the line with us."

"Can you believe this, David?"

"Of course I can, Sandy. The whole country saw it on live television. You deserve every accolade possible for saving my kids' lives. And you know we RSVP'd yes for the trip to Washington so we will see you there."

"Gentleman, my duties require I end this call. Please watch for your respective certified mail packets and I look forward to meeting you and your families at the White House."

Onward

There's an 8x10 photograph on our mantle. It is Sandy and Gwen Tuttle and their son standing next to the President of the United States. On the other side of the president is Tim Bloom, the helicopter pilot who saved our kids. In the foreground, down on one knee, are Olivia and I. I am holding Quinn with Robbie and Oliver to my right. Olivia is holding Lynne with Amy and Jamie to her left.

The Presidential Medal for Civilian Heroism is dangling from the necks of Tim and Sandy. If one looks very closely, there's a wet tissue in Olivia's balled-up hand.

I held Olivia's hand and stoked her hair and forehead at her bedside when she went in to get her tubes tied. Trying to lighten the moment, I quipped, "After this, sweetheart, you'll be a sports model!" and I chuckled. She smiled warmly at me and our eyes connected.

"That first time we made love, David? When the door knock scared us that we had been caught? I'm sure it was the fear that you hadn't noticed. I was a virgin. I...I just never figured there was a reason to bring it up. You were my first and my forever from the very start, David."

My heart swelled and I leaned over and tenderly kissed her, "That will never change, cowgirl."

We built two, 1000 square-foot cabins about 200 yards from the house. Each is equipped with a stone fireplace, bunk beds and a queen-sized bed, fire pit and hitching posts for guests' horses. The deluxe appliances were chosen with Tomás and Elena in mind.

As soon as they were completed, we insisted Sandy and his family and Tomás and Elena visit at the same time to experience the cabins. They raved about them. Their word-of-mouth advertising demanded we get a computerized reservations system and website.

We're involving the kids by paying them to maintain the cabins when we rent them out to summer and ski vacationers, and niche vacation guests who want a dude-ranch experience.

The fruits of good fortune are in full bloom for us.

Every evening at supper, we hold hands to pray and remember to thank God for getting us through the fire. After the kids go to bed, Olivia and I retire to the porch, joined by Phoebe enjoying her sardines as Olivia pinches her nose and fans the air with her other hand.

"I don't know how you can do that, David."

"Like everything else in life, it's easier with you beside me, Olivia. Care to take a converted city boy to bed?"

"I was gonna rope you if you didn't come willingly."

"Scram, Phoebe. A *jefe's* work is never done."

\#

Acknowledgements

Linda Wells, Ed.D., Editing & Assistant Publisher – for her tireless commitment helping me to put the polish and shine on the story of Olivia and David, I'm forever grateful.

Brett Walton, Photographer – After searching hundreds upon hundreds of photos, Brett's shots in the Abiquiu-Taos area were stunning. The cover shot perfectly depicted my vision of Olivia's Meadow. It's beyond coincidence. He consented to my use of several of his photographs for which I'm ever grateful.

God – Your love and strength keep me going through harrowing times when I have dwindling time left in my journey. You propel me by grace.

The Callan Family – David and Olivia, Robbie, Jamie, Amy, Oliver, Lynne and Quinn, you captured my heart. I imagined you'd be an incredible family and you are, if only in my mind.

About the Author

I was a junior in high school when my literature teacher pulled me out of the classroom for a sidewalk chat. Mrs. Ruth Boyle said words to the effect, "I've been teaching high school literature for 20 years. The level at which you write is far beyond your age and surpasses anything I've read from any student. You may want to consider a career as a writer, Dwight. I mean it."

I didn't take it to heart in 'The Age of Aquarius,' the Viet Nam War era, hippies, 'Free Love,' and music. I excelled in music all through school. I focused on baseball, rock 'n roll, girls, and performing arts. (Did I say "girls?")

I loved manipulating the language in ways I hadn't read elsewhere. Creative writing was a guilty pleasure, seen by no one, and hidden in plain sight. In spiral notebooks. There were story ideas, poetry, lyrics to songs my teen band trashed, and commentary about my perceptions of events in the world and around me. Disclosure: Okay, there were love letters to girls I was too shy to even speak to. I could perform music, theatre, anything in front of a crowd, big or small. If a cute girl flirted with me? Grin. Smile. Run.

Thanks to an online group of 'flash fiction' writers I discovered in 2010, I dumped my creative energies into cranking out short stories, some 236 of them. The drawback? Working for two blue chip corporations that scanned social media for disgruntled employees bashing the workplace. I countered that with a *nom de plume*, a pen name, under which a few of my pieces were published in anthologies.

Retirement gave me the time and freedom to sift through those 236 stories to find the 'bones' I could develop into longer works. For example, the original "Cupcakes in Love in War" was a shorter version I wrote in 2011.

Olivia's Meadow sent me from a sound sleep to the keyboard in October, 2021. I didn't know or care about its length. I kept writing and writing what was developing in my mind. That's consistent with my notion: I'm a storyteller. There's a beginning, a middle, and an end. I write until the story ends. I never have a clue how long, how many pages it's going to take to finish my story. The 500-pound gorilla in the room is my 500-pound *Olivia's Meadow* novel.

I hold an Associate in Arts degree from Phoenix Community College, 'with high distinction,' in Mass Communications. My Bachelor of Arts Degree, 'Magna cum Laude,' is in Radio & Television from San Francisco State University, where I pursued broadcast journalism and writing.

I've worked on-air as a 'D.J.,' had a syndicated classical music show, written and delivered broadcast news, and advertising campaigns.

This, my real work, was worth the wait. It's now my job to make my writing worth your precious time. Tell your friends and please leave me some feedback.